The
Girls from
Greenway

ELIZABETH
WOODCRAFT

ZAFFRE

First published in Great Britain in 2019 by
ZAFFRE
80–81 Wimpole St, London W1G 9RE

A CIP catalogue record for this book is
available from the British Library.

ISBN: 978–1–78576–785–2

Also available as an ebook

1 3 5 7 9 10 8 6 4 2

Typeset by IDSUK (Data Connection) Ltd
Printed and bound in Great Britain by Clays Ltd, Elcograf S.p.A.

Zaffre is an imprint of Bonnier Books UK
www.bonnierbooks.co.uk

For my mother Peggy Perry (1924–2016)

CHAPTER 1

CHRISTMAS EVE WAS COLD. THERE WAS almost snow in the wind that blew down the narrow street. Roger had finally decided what he wanted – a jumper from Battini's. So, head down against the sleet, Angie made her way to the new boutique.

She had hoped it would be a girls' boutique. Chelmsford was no London, and if they wanted anything really up to date she and her best friend Carol had to trek over to Southend or Stratford. It was so hard to be someone who dreamed of becoming a fashion designer when the closest you could get to it was looking at the pictures in a magazine. So even when it turned out to be a men's boutique she was still interested.

It had been a horrible afternoon. She'd traipsed round a million shops trying to buy presents for people. She'd found the perfect earrings for her sister Doreen, but just as she was counting out her money on the counter a woman had pushed in front of her and snatched them up. Coming out of the shop Angie realised she'd lost half a crown somewhere, so she had no present for Doreen and even less money to spend on it. Money was always tight in their house and half a crown made the difference between sausages and a slice of toast for tea. And now she had to spend good money on something for Roger. And worse than what to buy for the Roger was the problem *of* Roger. He was nice, he had a good job, he was everything her mother wanted for her. She honestly liked him, she felt safe with him, but he wasn't exciting, wasn't glamorous. She knew he was crazy about her, but she . . . she wanted so much more.

Her head down, worrying about Roger and the money, she didn't see the drunk man before he bumped into her knocking her off balance. Clutching her shopping to stop it falling, she stepped straight into a puddle. She looked down at herself. She always took such care with her clothes, and now her shoes were ruined and her suede coat was soaking. She hoped it wasn't ruined; it was an early Christmas present to herself and she loved it.

But now she looked more like a damp rat than a sleek mod.

She was wet and miserable when she pushed open the door of the boutique. She'd been quite looking forward to seeing this Gene Battini; there were so many stories about him. In the Orpheus, the mods' coffee bar in London Road, someone had said his name wasn't Gene Battini at all, his name was really Gerald Battle but he'd changed it, trying to sound as Italian as Vespa and Lambretta scooters. All that talk of Rome and Milan was rubbish, they said, and in fact he came from north London – Enfield or somewhere. But the boys in Chelmsford were themselves all talk at times. Perhaps Gene Battini was the real thing. At least he was working in the right business.

But now she really didn't care. She just wanted to buy this jumper and get on with the rest of her shopping. The boutique was empty except for the clothes; racks of jackets and trousers and shelves of shirts. It smelt of the new wood that lined the walls, with the smell of new clothes added in. There was a small Christmas tree glittering on the counter in the corner.

A man came out from the back, shrugging into a sheepskin coat. He looked older, twenty-six maybe twenty-eight, too old to be working in a boutique. He was very tanned; maybe he was Italian. He smiled regretfully, and in a loud cockney accent he said, 'Sorry love, we've just closed.'

On top of the awful afternoon she'd had, now she wasn't even going to be able to buy Roger's Christmas present. She felt she was about to burst into tears.

'Hey!' The man's smile vanished. He looked worried. 'You OK? Want to sit down? Want a glass of water?'

'I want to buy a jumper.' She dashed away the tears with the back of her hand.

'I've got some funny ones,' he said, 'but they don't usually make people cry.'

'But you're closed.'

'Well yes, but you're here inside the shop and so am I. So in a funny kind of way you could say we're open. I know, how about a cup of tea?' He looked at his watch again. 'I've probably missed my train anyway. I've got a kettle out the back. And why don't you sit down?'

'Because there aren't any chairs!' she said angrily. She felt so stupid.

'I've got chairs too,' he said. 'And some malted milk biscuits.'

'You can keep the biscuits.' She didn't like malted milk biscuits. 'But yes, I'd like a cup of tea.'

'Keep your eye on the shop and I'll put the kettle on. Sugar?'

'One please,' she said. 'Can I take my shoes off?'

He looked surprised. 'You can take off anything you like, darling.'

'It's because they're wet,' she said, but she laughed. She slipped off her moccasins and began to feel better.

'By the way, I'm Gene,' he said.

'I'm Angie.'

'Pleased to meet you,' he said.

'Yes, you too.'

While he was in the back, clattering spoons and cups, she ran her hands over the sweaters on the rail. She knew the one Roger wanted. It was bottle-green with two thick, vertical navy and white stripes down one side. He'd said

Dave Clark had one similar, but not the same. She couldn't think how you could tell when the telly picture was in black and white.

Gene brought a tray through with two mugs of tea and a flowery plate of biscuits on it. He put the tray on the counter and then went back out, returning with two fold-up chairs. 'Your tea's the yellow one,' he said, unfolding the chairs.

'Mugs,' she said, sitting down. 'That's very trendy.'

'This is a boutique, darling. Trendy is its middle name.'

'How does that work?' she said. 'It's called Battini's. There's nothing to be in the middle of.'

'The full title is Battini's Trendy Boutique,' he said. 'We just couldn't get it all on the sign.' He switched on a small transistor radio and the Spencer Davis Group advised her, tinnily, to keep on running. 'So why the tears?' He held out the plate. She shook her head, but as he put the plate back on the tray, she realised they were chocolate diges-tives and suppressed a sob.

As if he had read her mind, he held the plate out again. 'Go on,' he said.

She took a biscuit. She loved chocolate digestive biscuits. They never had them at home. This was nice. It felt safe and cosy in the shop. There was a small electric fire behind the counter which was pumping out heat. She undid her coat.

'There you go,' he said. 'Make yourself at home. Nice outfit.'

She smiled. 'I'm a mod,' she said simply. She was wearing her suede coat of course, it was part of the mod uniform. It was maroon, straight and three-quarter length. Under it, she wore her brown and white dogtooth check skirt and her thin, loose, emerald-green sweater. Her dark brown hair was cut in a mod bob, shorter than the Cleopatra look a lot of girls went for, but with the same straight fringe. She was proud of her hair, although it didn't look its best at the moment. It was damp and windswept. She ran her fingers through it, and smoothed down her fringe.

'So, tell me,' Gene Battini said, 'what do you think of the shop?'

She wondered if he was serious or was just making conversation. She didn't care, she'd give him her opinion. She looked round. 'I think there are too many thick jumpers.'

He laughed. 'Is that a comment on my outfit?'

'Maybe,' she said. He was wearing a sweater with a horizontal stripe round the chest. Another just like it was hanging on the rails. She took a mouthful of the strong sweet tea, then looked over at the window display. 'I love those trousers.'

'What mine?'

'No! I mean, not necessarily.'

They both laughed.

'These days fashion is all about what people are wearing on *Ready Steady Go!*,' she said. It was the mods' programme on ITV on Friday evenings. 'You should watch it then put the things that are on there, in the window. If you've got what they want, people will come in and buy it, won't they? And it won't just be me and you in the shop.'

'Don't forget I'm technically closed.'

'That's stupid. Christmas Eve is when everyone does their shopping. Like me.'

'But that's why I closed the shop – I've got to do mine.'

She wondered briefly who he might be buying presents for.

'But to tell you the truth,' he said, stretching out his legs, 'I don't usually get home in time to watch the telly.'

'You should.'

He laughed. 'You don't mind telling people what to do, do you?'

'You asked!' she said.

'I did. And it's all very interesting. I'm glad you dropped in.'

'So am I.' She was feeling better. 'I like fashion,' she said.

'I can tell.'

'I could be your fashion adviser.'

'You could.'

She dipped her biscuit into her tea and skilfully lifted it to her mouth, tipping her head back to catch it before it melted. Gene Battini watched her.

'Now that's a nice jumper,' he said. She wondered if he was looking at her breasts. 'What's it made of?' He leaned forward and she trembled as his hand stretched out to touch the fabric. She didn't know if she was disappointed when he caught the hem, folded it over and rubbed it between his fingers. His fingers were brown, tanned. His index finger had a deeper stain of tobacco at the tip.

'Wool,' she said. He raised his eyebrows. 'Wool mixture,' she added quickly. 'I'm not sure what. I got it in Romford.'

'Romford,' he said. 'I go there a lot. To the dogs. Have you ever been to the dogs?'

'I feel like I go to the dogs most weeks,' she said.

He laughed again. He had a rasping, coughing sort of laugh. She liked it. She liked that she'd made him laugh. 'Well, you're here now. And I hope this is better than Romford dog track.'

She looked round the shop again. 'Not bad. Nice cup of tea.'

'So,' he said, 'who's the lucky man who's going to find a Battini jumper under the tree on Christmas morning? I'm hoping it's your dad but I'm afraid you're going to say it's a big burly boyfriend.'

'I don't know about the big and burly, but yes—' she coughed; she had a frog in her throat. 'It's for my boyfriend.'

'Just my luck,' he said. 'So, what's his name, this boyfriend of yours?'

'Roger.'

'What does Roger like in the way of jumpers?'

'Who knows?' she said. 'But I know the jumper he wants for Christmas.'

'So he's a bit of a mod, is he? Like you?'

Angie smiled. She pointed out Roger's chosen jumper and Gene Battini rose and took it off the hanger. He checked the label.

'He's medium,' she said.

'That's a bit unkind.'

'Shut up.' She laughed.

'I'll put it in a nice bag for you.' He wrapped it in tissue paper, then slid it into an expensive-looking carrier bag. Standing at the till he said, 'And because it's you I'll knock ten bob off the price. Four pounds nine and eleven – how's that?'

'That's very nice, thank you.' She stood up to go but she rather wanted to linger there in the warm, eating chocolate biscuits, surrounded by modern, sharp clothes and talking about style with this man with the exotic name.

He held out the bag. 'Happy Christmas,' he said.

'Happy Christmas.'

'Let me give you a Christmas kiss,' he said.

She made a face, then smiled and they leaned together and he kissed her on the lips.

'Next time we'll have a longer one,' he said.

'Next time!' she snorted.

'You know where I am,' he said. 'Ten 'til five every day, except Sunday and Wednesday afternoon.'

Now she really didn't want to leave but she still had her mum's present to buy. She was trembling as she walked away, past the Saracen's Head, past the *Essex Weekly News* office. She could still taste him faintly on her lips as she crossed over to the milk bar where her sister Doreen was waiting.

Doreen was upstairs on the first floor, gazing out of the large window. Two cooling cups of tea sat on the table in front of her. She looked at her watch. 'What time do you call this?'

Angie held up the expensive carrier bag and explained what had happened.

Doreen said, 'You what?'

'I kissed him.'

'What about Roger?'

'It was a Christmas kiss. Everyone kisses everyone at Christmas.'

'No they don't. How old did you say he was?'

'I dunno, twenty-five? Twenty-six?'

'Does it matter?'

'He's twenty-six? And he kissed you?'

'For God's sake. It's not like I'm pregnant.'

Doreen shook her head. 'What's he doing with a girl of your age? That's what? Six? Seven years difference?'

'He might be twenty-five or twenty-four. Or younger.'

'Then you must have led him on.'

'I didn't. He was nice.'

'Yeah, they always are. At the beginning.'

'Shut up,' Angie complained. 'I'm going to get Mum's present.' She stood up.

'What about your tea?' Doreen said.

'Not thirsty,' Angie called as she ran down the stairs, the bag from Battini's banging against her legs. She ran across the road and ducked into the bright, sparkling Christmas light of Bonds, the department store, where she bought her mum some soap and bath salts.

CHAPTER 2

ANGIE CAME IN FROM TOWN, SMILING. The afternoon had ended successfully. She'd forgotten about the row with Doreen. She had bought all her presents and on top of that there'd been the kiss from a new, exciting man in town.

She was surprised to see her dad was indoors, in the kitchen chatting to her mum while they got things ready for tea. This meant it would be a good evening. Mum was putting cups and the teapot on the tray and Dad was standing by the stove, heating the frying pan. On the draining board was a loaf of bread – always an uncut loaf on a Saturday – a packet of Stork margarine, and a box of six eggs. In the living room, beside the small Christmas tree with its array of coloured lights, the telly was on.

Angie and her family had lived in the Crescent for almost ten years now. They'd been some of the first residents on the new council estate. It was perfect in every way. The once-hourly number forty-five bus ran right through the estate, a dark-green, double decker which chugged in from the town, into a bus-driver's road of dreams, straight,

straight to the top, passing the redbrick houses, the neat gardens, the small parade of shops, and the other roads that turned off, including the Crescent.

The family had moved onto the estate in the mid-fifties, when Angie was in her last year at primary school and Doreen was on the verge of leaving school altogether. Angie could still remember how on their first day in the house, Mum had walked in and out of the rooms for a long time, wondering at the joy of the space, the cleanliness, the dryness. From the perfectly appointed kitchen they could walk into the hall, or alternatively go through the arch into the living room. The front room, which would be for best, had two doors, one from the hall, and one from the living room. There was a sturdy staircase up to the bathroom and three bedrooms. They had stood in the living room and looked out at the neat plot that was their back garden. There was a shed for tools and a lawn-mower next to the coal shed and the outside toilet. Two toilets for one family. Luxury, they had thought. As the years had gone by the newness had worn off, but Mrs Smith was still house-proud. She used the carpet sweeper every night and the windows were cleaned every week. When they had first moved in she had refused to have the sooty paraphernalia of Mr Smith's job as a chimney sweep in their lovely new house.

Angie had heard the argument. At one point her mum had said she wasn't prepared to have him there at all. But he came. And one day, after the rent man had been, Angie had caught sight of the rent book and saw that instead of the name Mrs Smith, or even Mr and Mrs Smith, her dad's was the only name on it.

At first it had seemed to Angie that there were arguments all the time, as there had been in the flat. Sometimes her dad would storm out of the house, banging the door, leaving Mrs Smith sobbing quietly in the kitchen. Sometimes the police came and stood in the hall and talked calmly and reasonably to him, and he replied equally calmly and they would go away, then the next day her mum would have bruises on her arms, and once she had a black eye. But that was years ago, and now he had calmed down, her mum said, and when he came home now he carried a ladder and a bucket. He had become a window cleaner. He said it was seasonal work and that was the only reason he never had much money.

But Doreen still said his earnings were poured down his throat or gambled away. She said it was the women in the family that kept things going, her wages, with her mum's and Angie's were what they lived on. But it was hard at home. Some weeks Angie would buy the Spam and the Pan Yan pickle on Saturday for her sandwiches for the week, but by Wednesday it would all be gone. Even if she hid everything in the biscuit tin or right at the back of the cupboard, behind the plates, her dad would come in after drinking all evening in the Railway Tavern or the White

Hart, fancying a snack, and he would find them. Her mum couldn't stop him. 'At least he comes home,' she'd say.

She didn't know when the Saturday evenings in front of the telly had started. It must have been about the time they moved onto the Greenway estate. Before that, in the flat on the other side of town, they'd only had the radio. Now, when everyone was in and her dad wasn't too drunk and her mum had been able to buy eggs, they all gathered in the living room to watch the football results. She and Doreen sat on the floor and her mum and dad sat in the armchairs. Mum looked happy and Dad didn't seem so angry with the world. On those nights they had tea on their laps; Dad made the toast, big thick slices and lots of marge with a fried egg on top, and Mum built up the fire so the room was really hot. Angie would bite into the toast, and she would see the imprint of her teeth in the margarine. Sometimes they had a cake for afters, cut thin, to make it last. Fruit cake was Angie's favourite, with its sweet sultanas and glacé cherries.

Angie wasn't interested in football. Nothing could bore her more. But this hour at tea-time on a Saturday had little to do with football. It was about numbers. During the season her dad held the pools coupon that he and Mum had completed in the week, and as they were eating, he checked the results on the TV against the copy of the coupon they'd filled in and handed to Reg, their pools collector. Once, a few years before, Dad had won ten pounds and they had all gone out to the pub after the results had finished and had a drink. She and Doreen had had lemonade and a packet of crisps, Mum had had port and lemon, and Dad had a glass of beer and a shot of whisky. 'Good will to all men,' he had said, as he threw the whisky down his throat. He had told jokes and made them all laugh and it was just like Christmas. Angie couldn't imagine what it would be like to win the jackpot.

Saturday evenings were always full of hope and happiness. Even when they didn't get the results they wanted, there was always next week to look forward to. And tonight it was Christmas Eve, which made everything even more special. She ran upstairs and quickly wrapped her recent purchases in the sparkling paper she had bought from the newsagent's.

When she came downstairs her dad was ticking off the results as they were announced in the sing-song voice of the announcer. 'No,' her dad was saying. 'No.' At the end he screwed up the coupon and threw it on the fire. 'No worries,' he said. 'I had a bet on with a bloke in the pub that I wouldn't win anything tonight. And I didn't, so he owes me a drink.'

'Was he drunk?' Doreen said. She looked at Angie and they laughed quietly.

'That's enough sauce,' he said. 'I'll just finish my cup of tea, and then I'm off out.'

Angie enjoyed this part of the evening too, when Dad heaved himself out of his chair, put on his cap and scarf and banged out of the kitchen. The atmosphere lightened. Mum pulled a bar of chocolate out of her bag and handed round a square each. Doreen slid into Dad's chair and Angie made a fresh pot of tea. With Dad out of the house it was time for *Juke Box Jury*. They guessed at which way the jury would vote. Angie usually got the jurors' verdicts right, even when she didn't agree with them.

As the programme ended Doreen asked, 'Angie, what time are you going out? Who's having the first bath?'

'Well, Roger's coming round at seven,' Angie said. 'So me first. That'll give you time to wrap up my Christmas present.'

'Ha ha,' Doreen said. 'For your information, it's already wrapped.'

'Ooh!'

'Roger's such a nice boy,' Mum said. 'I like him.'

'I know you do,' Angie said.

'You want to be careful and hang on to him,' Doreen said pointedly.

'Thanks for your advice.' Angie made a face. She knew Doreen was thinking about the kiss in the boutique. 'What happened to that bloke you were seeing? Dave, was it?' she said, changing the subject before Doreen said anything more.

'I finished with Dave months ago,' Doreen sighed. 'If you mean Barry, we've decided not to see each other anymore. His wife doesn't like it.' She laughed.

'Doreen!' Mum said.

'It was nothing serious,' Doreen said. 'He hardly even held my hand.'

'I bet,' said Angie.

'Anyway, Janice and I are going for a drink at the Angel. It's going to be a great night tonight – I don't think! Janice is having trouble with her boyfriend. Expect me home about half past eight.'

They all laughed.

Mrs Smith settled herself into her armchair and broke off another piece of chocolate. 'Well, hurry up and get going. My programme's coming on.'

'Oh God, it's Billy Cotton,' Angie said.

She and Doreen ran out of the room.

CHAPTER 3

THREE WEEKS LATER, DOREEN STILL COULDN'T stop thinking about Angie and the kiss from that old man in the
boutique. Christmas kiss? Yes, that was likely. Any excuse.
Doreen knew about men like him. And she knew from
the way Angie had talked about it that Angie had thought
it was the most exciting thing in the world. Doreen
wasn't a square, but this couldn't go on. She of all people
knew where it would lead. And it wasn't sweet love and
romance.

She'd been a bit younger than Angie when she and
Janice had dared each other to enter the Carnival Queen
contest. It had been a bit disappointing that Janice was
voted the actual Carnival Queen, but it was Doreen's
smile that had caught the eye of the photographer. On
Carnival Day they'd both worn white dresses with full
skirts, white shoes and white gloves. It was really sunny.
They waved at the crowds and a few boys wolf-whistled.
It had all been lovely.

She remembered it like it was yesterday. The bloke who took the photos of them in their Carnival dresses, had offered to take some pictures of her. They were nice pictures, all very decent. Just her wearing her tight pink Capri pants and her tight blue sweater. 'To show off your assets,' he'd said – dirty bugger – but he was a good sort, and he hadn't tried anything. She'd had to kiss him and go to the flicks with him, otherwise she'd have had to pay the full twenty-five quid, but that was OK.

Once she had the photos she just knew she had to do something with them. Add them to your portfolio, he'd said. Portfolio. Sometimes, she used to say the word 'portfolio' out loud because it sounded so professional and impressive. 'I have a portfolio.' She knew she should send them somewhere, to the telly. She could do that, go on telly. 'Good evening and welcome to tonight's edition of *Tonight*.' Her teeth were good enough and she had her smile.

The photographer had given her telephone numbers. They looked magical and strange. At the time she couldn't imagine standing in a phone box and dialling. But this was her chance, and so she had made the call and left the phone box with an address.

She was still at school then. That day she'd said she was ill. Then when Mum and Dad had gone out to work and Angie had left for school, she'd jumped out of bed, put on her make-up, more than she usually would, and went up to London. She would never forget that day.

It was a lovely day, really hot and sunny. The streets were so busy, everyone rushing around like mad. They all seemed to have somewhere to go. And so did she! It wasn't hard to find the address the lady on the phone, Mrs Treadwell, had given her. 'Just off Kings Road!' she'd said. It was a doorway between two shops. Doreen went up the stairs. Along a landing was a door with a sign saying 'Sylvester Raymond studios.' Doreen tapped on the door.

A woman's voice called, 'Come in!'

The room was small and seemed to be filled with chairs and cigarette smoke. Even though it was 10.30 in the morning the room was dark and the light was on. A middle-aged woman in a cardigan was sitting behind a battered table, smoking. 'Hello dear,' she said. Doreen recognised her voice as the woman on the phone. 'Have you come to have your photo taken?'

'I . . . I don't know. I've brought my photos.' She held out the folder.

'He won't need those,' Mrs Treadwell said. 'That will be two guineas please.'

Doreen frowned. 'What do you mean?'

'Two guineas.'

Doreen was still frowning.

'Mr Raymond is a very talented man. Two pounds two shillings is a small price to pay.' Mrs Treadwell looked expectantly at Doreen.

Doreen took two pound notes and some sixpences from her purse, and laid them on the table. She had less than half a crown left.

Mrs Treadwell scraped the money into her hand. 'Sit over there.' The phone began to ring and she answered it. 'Sylvester Raymond studios.'

There was another girl sitting on one of the hard chairs, reading a tattered magazine. Doreen smiled. The girl shook her head. 'Don't try and be friendly. Nobody wants to be friends.'

Doreen sat still, looking straight ahead, her stomach churning, wishing she could think of something cutting to say. She noticed that the girl didn't have a portfolio with her.

'I'll take you up to the studio,' Mrs Treadwell said. They climbed another floor. It didn't look like the studio Doreen had imagined, with lights and movement and people bringing the photographer a cup of coffee. It looked like a dirty empty room. There was no carpet or lino, just bare floorboards, and no curtains at the windows, just smears and a faint view of more dirty windows in grey buildings. At the far end of the room a man was fiddling with a camera.

Mrs Treadwell said, 'You can change in there.' She pointed to an open door.

Doreen could see a grey-green wall and part of a toilet seat. 'Change into what?'

'What have you got?'

'You don't have to change into anything,' the man said. He waved Mrs Treadwell out of the room. The door closed with a click. 'Just take your clothes off.'

'What do you mean?'

'Come on darling, we haven't got all day. Why don't I help you off with your coat?'

'Thanks,' she said.

He put the coat on a grubby sofa behind her. He was looking her up and down. He leaned forward. 'Just relax. You've got a nice figure. Let's have a little kiss first, to get you in the mood.' He put his arm round her shoulder and pulled her towards him.

'You what!' she said. She almost laughed. She'd read about this; she'd seen this in films. She knew what was going on. First he'd want to kiss her. Then he'd want to see her in the nude. And then what? In this horrible dirty room in London, on this filthy sofa? No! No!

She pushed him away. 'Stop it!' she said.

But he didn't. His grip on her shoulder tightened and his other arm was sliding on to her breast. He pressed his leg against hers so that she lost her footing. He was pushing her back towards the sofa. She was tripping and stumbling. She called out. Surely Mrs Treadwell would hear! The man's bear-like hand came over her mouth, squeezing her cheeks together. She could smell petrol and cigarettes and another sweet smell that she'd never smelt before. She kicked her legs and knocked over a chair with a clatter. Someone must have heard that! Nobody came and she slipped and slithered as he pushed her towards the sofa. She brought up an arm and punched him on the back but he just laughed. 'You're a bit feisty, aren't you?' he said. 'What do you girls fucking expect? Except a bit of fucking?' He laughed at his own joke and slid a finger into her mouth.

She bit down hard on to his finger. Again and again. She tasted blood in her mouth. Then he was swearing and pulling his hand away. She was spitting, getting the taste of him out of her mouth, breathing hard. He stared at his finger unbelieving. 'I'm a fucking photographer! I use my fucking hands!' he shouted and lunged at her. She slid to the side so that he crashed onto the sofa on to her coat and her precious portfolio. For half a second she looked at it, but then as he began stumbling to his feet she ran to the door. It wouldn't open. It was locked. At the top of the door she saw the Yale lock. She turned it and flew down the stairs.

Mrs Treadwell was calmly typing at her desk. The other girl had disappeared. Doreen stared at Mrs Treadwell, wanting a kind word, an understanding smile, but Mrs Treadwell simply shook her head and murmured, 'You young girls, you just waste his time.' Tears streaming down her face, Doreen ran out on to the landing, down the stairs and out into the street.

On the train on the way home Doreen was furious with herself. She was nearly sixteen. How could she have been taken in? That awful man, with his thinning hair and big belly. And she couldn't get the taste out of her mouth. Two guineas! That was almost all her savings. And that girl she'd sat next to in the waiting room, she obviously knew what was going on. Why didn't she say anything?

She stared at her reflection in the small mirror in her compact. God, she looked awful, tear stains on her cheeks. She smiled at herself, a fake smile but she saw the pretty Princess from the Carnival, her blonde bouffant hair, like Brigitte Bardot, her almond eyes and her full lips. She repaired her make-up, tidied her hair and lifted her chin.

London wasn't what she'd imagined. She blamed Frankie Vaughan. He had that song, 'Kisses Sweeter Than Wine.' She'd imagined Frankie Vaughan sitting in the secluded corner of an elegant bar, or in an expensive flat, sitting on a comfortable couch, wearing an expensive suit, with a bow tie, suavely kissing gorgeously dressed women. She'd seen herself, going to London, having some nice photos taken, and then she would find herself sitting with Frankie on velvet cushions. Instead she was sitting on the scratchy seat on the train, with no portfolio, no money, and no coat. But she was on her way back to Chelmsford, where she knew who was who and what was what. In Chelmsford she knew how to behave, who to avoid. In Chelmsford she knew who she was.

No point thinking about that now . . . In the end, Doreen supposed, that episode had taught her a lot. She picked up her bag, left the house and got into her car. She loved her car. It was second hand, a little Hillman. But it went, on the whole, and it was turquoise. She could change the tyres and, if necessary, she could deal with the starting motor and of course, she could put in petrol and check the oil. Having a car was great. It opened horizons and made her feel powerful. Her mum and dad weren't happy. They said it was a waste of money – well, Dad did. Mum didn't say much when Dad was around. And Angie liked it. She was a good little sister. She wanted Doreen to teach her to drive. They went up on the old airfield sometimes and Doreen let her have a go. Angie was wild – she wanted to go as fast possible, screeching the tyres, making sharp turns, skidding in the puddles slick with oil. In the passenger seat Doreen was terrified and slammed her foot onto an invisible brake, but Angie laughed out loud with the pleasure of it all. Then she would reverse fast with her arm over the back seat to get them back to where they'd started.

Oh Angie, she was so young. She didn't know anything. Doreen felt responsible for her. Wanted to protect her so she didn't have to go through the same stupid things she'd gone through. And she would protect her. In fact, she'd do it today. She'd take an early dinner hour and go to that boutique and have it out with this Gene fellow. She'd sort him out. It would be the last Christmas kiss he'd give Angie. She parked the car and headed into work.

Doreen strode along New Street to get to the shop before it closed. Not only was the man with the Italian name bringing London clothes to Chelmsford, he was bringing his London ways to Chelmsford, in particular to her little sister, Angie. So now he had to know there were consequences to his actions.

She was feeling good – she'd sold two quite expensive wedding dresses this morning, and a very interested bride-to-be had promised to return. She was feeling smart; today she was wearing her white coat with the belt tightly done up. And she was determined. She waved hello to Harry in the barber's, gave the belt on her coat an extra tug and went into the boutique.

Two or three boys were looking at shirts. A bloke came out from the back of the shop with several pairs of beige trousers over his arm. This had to be the famous Gene Battini.

Yeah, well, he didn't look too bad. In fact, she realised, he looked very nice. He was big and tall and tanned. When he saw her he raised his eyebrows and smiled. She'd taken care with her make-up today. She was wearing dark Pink Passion on her lips and just a slight upward flick of black eye-liner over her eyes.

He might look attractive but that was no excuse. She took a deep breath. 'Could I have a word, please? In private.' She indicated a door which she assumed was some sort of stock room.

'Be my guest,' he said, surprised, half smiling. He led her into the room. She looked at his shoulders as she followed him. They were broad and strong, a film star's shoulders. What was he doing in Chelmsford?

She noticed a kettle and a bottle of milk and a camp bed. She knew his game.

He leaned easily against a small sink. He crossed his ankles, he folded his arms. But he frowned slightly. He looked at her. 'Is there a problem? I haven't sold your boyfriend a tie that doesn't go with your coat, have I?'

'Shut up,' she said.

He half laughed. 'I haven't sold him a shirt that shrank in the wash?'

'You haven't sold anyone anything.'

'Well, that's a relief. Although, of course, it's not quite true. We're not doing too badly.'

'And just before Christmas you did very well indeed.'

'Well that's hardly surprising is it?' he said. 'I'd have been a rubbish salesman if I didn't make money at Christmas. In fact, the shop's doing very nicely. People in Chelmsford have been fantastic.' He smiled again. Nice teeth. Lovely eyes.

This was awful. He was being so friendly, so nice. He wasn't at all what she'd imagined. There had been no lewd comments. He wasn't that old, either, probably not much older than her. He seemed so professional. Instead of shouting at him, she found herself wanting to engage with him, one professional to another. She couldn't help herself. She agreed with him. 'I know. I had a good Christmas myself.'

'Aha! You're in retail.'

'I am.' She smiled.

'Well I'm pleased about that, but you should know that I'm probably losing a few sales standing here talking to you, pleasant though this is. So . . . ?'

But she was silent. The words she had prepared wouldn't come. They had sounded so perfect and appropriate as she stood in the staffroom, smoothing her hair back into its neat French pleat. But now they sounded gauche, infantile, silly.

He looked at her again, half smiling. 'You OK?'

And there he was, being considerate not taking advantage, looking attractive, a lock of dark hair falling over his eyes as he looked at her intently. Instead of outrage she felt her stomach fluttering. The stock room was neat and tidy, a pile of boxes obviously of shirts or something in one corner, and a rack of things with notes pinned on: 'sold', 'awaiting

collection', 'deposit paid', in another. He was obviously serious about his job. Even the camp bed was neatly made.

'Think about it,' he said. 'I've got to get back to the
shop.' He pushed himself away from the sink, to go back
out into the shop. He was brushing past her. The moment
was going. She had to do something. Now. She took hold of
his arm. The cotton of his shirt was soft under her fingers.

He turned and looked at her.

'Sorry,' she said. 'Sorry. I think I've got the . . . wrong
person.'

'No problem, darling. It was nice to meet you. Come
back any time.'

CHAPTER 4

ON FRIDAY NIGHTS ANGIE WAS ALWAYS anxious to finish tea quickly. Tonight Dad had his usual sausage and mash and the others had beans on toast. As a treat they finished with silver-paper covered marshmallows. Then Angie ran upstairs. She was getting ready, like every Friday, to go out with Carol.

But before that she had a date with the television. She needed to be in the living room in front of the TV, ready to watch her programme at half past six, the unmissable, the vital, the cool, *Ready Steady Go!*.

Her mum stayed in the kitchen, doing the washing up. Doreen was upstairs having a bath and even her dad sat quietly at the kitchen table with a cup of tea, reading the *Daily Mirror*. The living room was hers.

She threw herself onto one of the chairs, hunched forward, elbows resting on her knees, hands cupping her chin, as numbers flashed onto the screen and Manfred Mann sang '5-4-3-2-1', the start of the programme. The song faded away and the presenter, stylish girl-about-town Cathy

McGowan, appeared on the screen. This programme was Angie's Friday night piece of heaven. *RSG!* had everything a mod needed to see before heading out on a Friday night. The weekend really did start here. Every week there was the best new music, the Animals, the Beatles, The Who, and all the acts from America – the girl groups with tight shimmery dresses and crazy backcombed hair-styles, the men clicking their fingers and twirling round in smart suits and shiny pointed shoes. And there was fashion to follow. Angie studied Cathy McGowan's outfit and the clothes of the girls in the studio, the length of the skirts, the fall of the sweaters, the cut of their hair – the smooth bobs, like her own, or the short pixie cuts like Carol's. There was no back-combing in the audience. Mod girls didn't do back-combing. And she tried to remember the dance steps, each week a new cool dance, which she and Carol would rehearse, tripping down Sperry Drive to catch the bus.

As the closing credits faded from the screen and the adverts began, Angie went out into the hall to put on her maroon suede coat. She slipped into her navy slingbacks and picked up her basket. Her dad had already slunk out to the pub and now her mum moved into the living room to watch *Tonight* with Cliff Michelmore, waiting for *Comedy Playhouse* to start.

'Doreen!' Angie shouted up the stairs. 'Are you ready?'

Tonight Doreen was giving them a lift into town.

Doreen came down the stairs in a long pink Sloppy Joe jumper, tight tartan slacks and flat ballet shoes. She grabbed her white coat from the hook and said, 'Come on then.'

The two of them chorused 'Bye!' to their mum and stepped out of the house and into Doreen's car. Doreen had a date in town. Doreen always had a date in town.

Carol was waiting for them on the corner of Greenway Road.

By seven thirty Doreen had parked in the road by the bus station and gone off to meet someone called Richard outside the library, and Angie and Carol were strolling through the streets of the town. As they walked along Duke Street, the High Street, and round into London Road, they nodded to the other girls they knew, who were also walking through the town, arm-in-arm, their baskets in the crook of their elbows, window shopping, looking out for interesting people. Doreen said all mod girls looked alike in their straight skirts and their suede coats. But if you knew about mods, if you knew about style, you realised they were quite different from each other. The coats were worn in different lengths, some in suede and some in leather, and the colours were different, the mod colours of navy, maroon, bottle-green, grey.

Angie and Carol made their way to the far end of London Road, quiet at this time of night, and there in the middle of a stone block of non-descript shops and council buildings, was the Orpheus. It was important to go to the Orpheus. It was as important as watching *RSG!*. The cellar coffee bar in the centre of town was where mod life happened.

From the outside it was just a doorway, with no sign or distinguishing marks. You had to know where you were going to find the Orpheus. The give-away was the scooters parked in the road outside; Lambrettas with their flat panel sides, in blue, maroon and green and Vespas with their bubbles of chrome and white and purple.

Angie and Carol stepped up the two worn stone steps, through the open doorway, into the dingy narrow corridor that led to the dark, narrow staircase, that twisted down into the dim, shadowy depths.

Angie always enjoyed this moment, stepping into the half-light of the coffee bar, with its peach tinted mirrors and its walls marking out different areas. She felt at home here, relaxed, part of the group. Even better, tonight, their arrival was accompanied by the rich harmonies of the Four Tops singing 'Baby I Need Your Loving', a song full of longing and pain, her current favourite.

The Orpheus' jukebox was a small chrome and glass box on the wall opposite the stairs, beside a large mirror. Standing in front of the mirror, glancing at her reflection and idly flicking through the metal pages of the jukebox, was a girl whose hair swung in a proper Cathy McGowan,

Cleopatra bob. She had on a stylish white dress in Nottingham Lace. It looked good. But not as good as Angie's own new dress. She had made it herself. She caught sight of it in the mirror, peeping out from under her coat. She loved the look of it, royal blue with a high waist and a softly gathered skirt. She smiled to herself.

To the right Brenda stood behind the counter, looking tired and a little harassed in her dark overall, more like someone's mum than a person serving coffee in the coolest place in Chelmsford. She was trying to sort out a group of mods, boys from out of town in their khaki green parkas, who were laughing and pushing each other, contradicting themselves over their orders. They all had short hair and fresh faces and wore Hush Puppies, the suede lace-up shoes were another part of the mod uniform. 'All right!' Brenda raised her voice. 'So that's two Coke and lemons, two teas and a glass of milk. Are you sure now? Because that's what you're getting.'

At the far side of the room, leaning against the stools by one of the pillars that held up the ceiling, were two or three Chelmsford boys in work clothes, talking quietly. They'd come straight off the building sites in their dusty jeans and jumpers and heavy steel-capped boots, and would probably leave soon to go home and change into their sharp mod clothes. Through the arch on the other side of the mirror were the booths where the shadows were the deepest, and where Angie and Carol always sat.

They took it in turns to buy a drink. Tonight was Angie's night. As Carol turned away towards their booth Angie murmured, 'Look who's here.' Behind the out of town boys a man was leaning against the far end of the counter. He wore a dark mohair suit, with a sharp pale shirt and a thin tie. As the boys in the parkas jostled and jumped the man bent his head and lit a cigarette. Smoke drifted towards the ceiling.

'Who is he?' Carol said.

'It's Cliff Evans. He went to our school. He was in the same year as Doreen. Except when he wasn't.'

'What do you mean?'

'When he was in trouble. He had to go away.'

Carol stared. 'Perhaps that's why I don't recognise him.'

'His mum is Mrs Evans, my mum's friend.'

'Really?' Carol said. 'He doesn't look like her. He looks too . . . thin to be her son.'

'Perhaps he takes after his dad. My mum said he works in the big markets in London.'

'Doing what?'

'I don't know. With his record, probably beating people up and nicking the takings. But doing it in London! That's not bad.'

'Don't!' Carol said.

'Well, give me an Italian who sells clothes any day,' Angie said. They both laughed.

Carol went to their booth while Angie stood waiting for Brenda to complete the order for the out-of-town boys. From time to time Brenda looked over at her and smiled. Angie tapped her foot as Levi Stubbs, the rich syrupy throated lead singer of the Four Tops, told her that without the one you love, life was not worthwhile. She loved the crescendo at the middle of the song, begging her to come and fill his empty arms.

Brenda interrupted her thoughts. 'Two coffees?' Brenda knew their order.

Walking in time to the Four Tops, Angie carried the coffee across to the booth and found Carol still standing, talking to Roger.

She frowned. She didn't usually see Roger on Friday nights; he was at his Car Mechanical Engineering class. She had been looking forward to talking to Angie about the clothes on *RSG!*; a tailored suit that one girl had worn, and what shoes you would wear with that, whether you could make it yourself. Their conversations always led back to clothes. But tonight Angie had almost ached with yearning to be part of the world of *RSG!*, the style, the clothes, the design, and tonight she had really wanted to talk seriously to Carol about the possibilities of finding a job in fashion.

But here was Roger. He looked upset, there was a frown on his open friendly face and he wouldn't sit down.

'Roger's just had a bad day at work,' Carol said.

'Oh dear,' Angie said.

'I spent all day under a car fixing a new exhaust and then the bloke came and said we hadn't asked him if he wanted a new exhaust. But he'd said do anything it needs to pass the MOT, and it needed a new exhaust. And it had been bloody hard to do it. Excuse my French. And then there was a big barney. Anyway, I was filthy by the end of it and I was too late to get washed and go to my class.'

'That's a shame,' Angie said. 'Will it make a difference in the exam?'

'It better not,' Roger said.

'I'm going to see if they've got anything new on the jukebox,' Carol said.

Angie said, 'Roger will give you the money. Go on Roger, give her some money and then we can all sit down.' Roger gave Carol a sixpenny piece.

'What do you want?' Carol asked.

'Oh anything,' Angie said. 'Four Tops, anything. The Animals. Yeah, the Animals, "I'm Crying". That's how we're all feeling, isn't it?'

'Angie!' Roger said.

'Oh, all right, how about, "Baby Let Me Take You Home"?' She smiled at him. They sat down. It was nice to see him. It was always nice to see him. And that was the problem. Roger was just so very nice. He had never made her heart go pitter-pat, he had never made her catch her breath the way Gene Battini had. She couldn't stop thinking about that kiss.

'Little Piece of Leather' was playing and the high, falsetto voice of Donnie Elbert filled the room. 'You're my baby and I love you so,' Roger said, echoing the words, putting his arm round her.

'Oh Roger,' Angie said.

'I've seen a new scooter I want to buy,' he said. 'It's still a Lambretta of course, but it's going to be a 175.'

'Mmm, speedy,' Angie murmured.

'Might even get up to sixty on the bypass.'

'You reckon?'

'If you tune it right.'

'What colour panels?'

'Not that it makes any difference to the speed, but maroon as it happens.'

'That's great, it'll go with my coat,' Angie said.

They were laughing. Angie hadn't felt this relaxed in a long time.

The insistent bass guitar notes of 'Baby Let Me Take You Home' rolled round the room and Angie hummed the tune with Eric Burdon. 'You know what, I feel like dancing,' she said.

'There's a dance on at the YMCA tonight,' Roger said. 'Mark Shelley and the Deans, your favourites.'

'Oh, let's go!' Angie said. 'Perhaps Carol wants to come. There was a really good dance on *RSG!*. We could show it off.'

'Show me up, you mean.'

'Oh ha ha!' Angie looked over towards the jukebox. 'Who's Carol talking to? Oh my god. What's Doreen doing here? Oh no. Do you think she's seen us? Don't let her come over here. This is embarrassing. Look what she's wearing. Those trews!'

But Carol and Doreen were walking towards the booth.

'Don't say anything about going to the YMCA,' Angie hissed.

'Fancy seeing you here!' Doreen drawled.

'What happened to your hot date?' Angie said, as Carol sat down, looking apologetic, and Doreen pushed herself on to the bench beside her.

'We went for a drink and he was so boring that I went to the toilet and didn't go back.' Doreen looked round the room. 'I just came to see whether the place had changed since we used to come here.' Before the Orpheus became the mods' coffee bar, business men and beatniks had called it their own. She sniffed. 'I see Cliff Evans is hanging around. I'd hardly call him a mod.'

'He'd probably say the same about you,' Angie said. 'Why don't you go and talk to him?'

'Well, unless my eyes deceive me, I think that's him disappearing up the stairs,' Doreen said. 'That's a shame.

He could have bought me a drink.' She glanced round the room again. 'So what's happening?'

'Nothing,' Angie said.

Doreen shrugged. 'Well, I won't stop. I know you youngsters want to be on your own.' She stood up. 'Nice to see you Roger. Nice to see you looking after Angie.'

'Doreen!' Angie said.

'And now I'm going to find some real action.' Doreen laughed. 'See you later, alligators.'

'Thank God for that,' Angie murmured. She turned to Carol. 'Fancy going to the YMCA, Carol? Roger says Mark Shelley and the Deans are playing.

'Really?'

'If we go now, we won't miss anything,' Roger said. 'Drink up!'

'Let's just listen to my record,' Angie said. She smiled. She might have lost her chance to talk to Carol, but dancing to a group she loved would be a fair exchange.

CHAPTER 5

THIRD TIME LUCKY DOREEN HOPED, AS she walked into the Saracen's Head. The place was heaving. There were too many people for her to get to the bar. So she said quite quietly but firmly, 'Don't DO that!' as if someone had touched her inappropriately. Enough people turned around to see what was happening for her to push up against the polished mahogany of the bar and call out to Phil. 'A G&T please!'

'Hang on, Reen!' Phil said. As he passed by her with two glasses of Guinness he said, 'We're busy here tonight. You don't fancy coming behind the bar and helping out for half an hour?'

Doreen looked round the room. There was no one here she wanted to talk to. The evening was a wash-out, she might as well say yes.

She slid behind the bar and began serving. It was mayhem. Beer, rum and Coke, gin and bitter lemon, more beer. Now she remembered why she'd given up working in a bar. Some lads from the warehouse at Bolingbroke's wanted shandy. Hardly seemed worth coming out for. Everyone was holding up pound notes as if she would get to them quicker, waving them in the air, calling 'Doreen!' A couple of whiskies, more pints, Britvic Orange and a Cherry B. And then there was a five pound note, someone holding it lazily, between two fingers, with his elbow on the bar. 'A martini, please. A martini cocktail.' She must have looked a bit blank because he added, 'Like James Bond would have drunk.'

No one asked for that sort of thing in Chelmsford. She looked up into a pair of melting brown eyes and a dark golden face, with a straight nose and a lovely full well-defined mouth. There was a faint smell of some light, sharp aftershave. Gene looked even better tonight than she'd remembered. He was really very attractive. She felt a flash of guilt at the thought, but Angie hadn't mentioned Gene again and her worries about the kiss all seemed a little silly now.

'Remind me how James Bond likes his martini,' she said, as if she had ever known. Or cared.

The drink was a touch of this and a splash of that, he said, and then, 'shaken not stirred,' they said together, because she knew what he was talking about. She knew she was flirting, but there was no harm in that, surely. It was what barmaids did, wasn't it? 'A martini,' she said. 'That's a bit suave for Chelmsford.'

'Perhaps,' he said. 'I'm having a suave evening.'

She looked behind him to see who he was with. He laughed and shook his head. 'On my own.'

'That's interesting,' she said. 'When I try to be suave it's usually when I want to impress someone.'

'Well, am I impressing you?' he said.

She let her eyes roll over him slowly. She enjoyed this kind of conversation. He was wearing an expensive sheep-skin coat, open to show a white polo neck underneath. It was a fine-knit polo neck. You never got that much style in the Saracen's. She looked back at his face. He smiled. 'What's the verdict?'

'It's a good look. Of course, I haven't seen your lower half.'

'Haven't you?' he said. 'Would you like to?'

'I'll just get the vodka,' she said. She couldn't get drawn into that sort of conversation when she was behind the bar.

'You're lucky,' she said, as she pushed the glass towards him, 'tonight we have ice.'

'I would say, "Have one for yourself",' he said, 'but I wouldn't like to think of you drinking alone.'

She looked at him. 'Oh I shan't be drinking alone,' she said. 'Take this G&T to that table over there and I'll be with you in a jiffy. I think I've done enough behind the bar for one night.'

He glanced across to the table, then back at Doreen. He smiled knowingly. Oh, she liked that kind of confidence, that self-assurance. He picked up her G&T and took his own drink at the same time. 'See you in a minute.' He moved through the crowd like Moses parting the waves. The sheepskin coat sat really well on his shoulders, and the tan of the sheepskin accentuated the dark shine of his hair, she noticed with her professional eye. She had to open a new box of crisps and she was called down to the far end of the bar. 'I'll stay another five minutes,' she said to Phil as she passed him. 'Then you're on your own.'

'Thanks, Reen,' he said. 'Take a quid out of the till and get yourself a drink.'

She pulled two or three more pints and half pints, a rum and black for a little mod who didn't look old enough to be out on his own, let alone drink, and a Coke and lemon and a pineapple juice for two girls who didn't look old enough for anything, made herself a G&T, took a pound note from the till and slid out into the room. The rush was over, the early evening crowd had gone home for their tea, and the high-livers who started their evening at half past eight weren't out yet.

She was afraid he would have gone, found some other girl to chat to, flirt with, kiss even, but he was still there, waiting, leaning back on the seat, watching her as she walked over to him.

She sat down next to him and picked up her drink.

'I'm afraid the ice in your G&T has melted,' he said.

'In Chelmsford that's nothing new. Cheers, anyway.'

She looked at him over the rim of her glass. He was watching her. 'What are you looking at?' she asked.

'I was just wondering . . .'

'Oh yes?' She wanted to know what he would say, 'Wondering what?'

'How a lovely girl like you comes to be sitting in a bar in Chelmsford with me.'

She raised her eyebrows. 'Well, that's easy. I live here and you work here. And,' she added daringly, 'we're the two most attractive people in the place.'

'How right you are,' he said, smiling.

He took the complement for himself and accepted the truth of what she said. How mature, how unlike the boyish retorts that such a comment would usually receive in this town. She realised that what she would like now would be to kiss him.

As if he had had the same thought at exactly the same moment, he slid his arm along the back of the seat and bent his head down towards her. He kissed her on the lips.

A bell rang. Phil, the barman, called, 'Last orders, gentlemen please. And ladies!'

'Do you want to go somewhere else?' he said, his arm still loosely round her shoulders.

'I would love to, but . . .' she said.

'You already have somewhere to go?'

'Not particularly.' She wasn't sure why she was being so coy. Perhaps it was all about Angie. After what she'd said to her about that Christmas kiss, she could hardly go home with the bloke herself. Or perhaps it was that she didn't want this just to be a quick fumble out in the car park. Perhaps she wanted more than a one-night stand with this man. 'I've got my car,' she said. 'Do you need a lift anywhere?'

'No, it's just a short walk to my humble abode.'

An image of the bed in the back room of the boutique flashed through her mind. Yes, she was better off going home. It could only end in tears. But she wouldn't mind another kiss. She could still feel his mouth on hers, the confident way he'd held her. She wound her arms round his neck and pulled him to her. She pressed her lips against his. He opened his mouth. She slipped her tongue inside. *I could get used to this*, she thought.

She stood up and said, 'Thank you for a lovely evening.'

'We must do it again sometime,' he said.

'Maybe,' she said.

'I'm usually in here or the Fleece on a Saturday night, before I get the train. Might see you then?'

'If you're lucky.'

CHAPTER 6

ANGIE SAT AT HER TABLE AT English Electric. She'd spent most of the day fitting tiny pieces of copper wire into the ceramic shapes that would become valves. The job wasn't bad, but she was definite this was not going to be her future. She had hopes for something bigger and better. She had had so many dreams at school. A lot of them she'd given up on – she couldn't see herself as the inventor she'd dreamed of when she was seven, but she had some dreams she would never let go.

When she was at primary school she had dreamed of going to college, being a teacher, perhaps a doctor or a scientist, travelling round the world. Anything seemed possible. Then her mum and dad said she couldn't take the eleven plus exam and she knew she must change her dream to something less academic, less fantastic.

There was no sense in wanting things to be different. You had the parents you had. They'd said she wasn't brainy enough to take the eleven plus, and anyway what did she want with a fancy education and exams? She was only going to get married and have children. She didn't need exams for that, and, her dad had added that what she really needed was to get herself a job and pay back some of the money it had cost to bring her up. There had been a terrible row. Angie had shed tears of frustration and rage that they thought she couldn't do it, that they thought she didn't deserve the chance. Especially since Doreen had sat the exam and Carol was going to take it. She didn't care that Doreen had failed it, and then so had Carol, at least they'd been given the chance. So Angie and Carol had gone to the local secondary modern together. It was nice to have your best friend with you, but Angie still felt cheated.

But it was at secondary school that she had found her real dream. Miss Darling, the old, strict needlework teacher had introduced Angie to the delight of sewing; to French seams, to lazy daisy stitch. She taught Angie how to read a pattern and turn a piece of material into a beautiful garment. It was like magic and Angie was a good magician. She was so good that Miss Darling had said at one point that she personally knew people in the fashion houses of London and even Paris, where *haute couture* dresses were designed and made for wealthy customers. Miss Darling had worked there. That was a shock – Miss Darling had worked in France! In fact, she said, if her health hadn't let her down, she'd be working in those famous design houses still. Miss Darling said couturiers would be very pleased to offer a job to someone as nimble-fingered as Angie. Angie could work on designs made in the thickest, richest materials – silks, brocade, shantung – sewing on pearls and diamonds, pinning on handmade lace. The pay would at first be low, very low, but in five or ten years' time she would be able to move up, as she had, to cutting and maybe even more. Angie had started to have dreams.

Angie still felt sick with rage, remembering her dad's response. He'd laughed in her face. 'Five years before you start earning a decent wage? Who does this old bat think you are? Making dresses for posh nobs, dresses you'll never be able to wear. Come off it! My mother would have had a fit if I'd said I wanted to work in some measly workshop on tuppence a week. Angie, that's not what we do. Get back to reality!'

There'd been nothing she could do when her parents said she couldn't take the eleven plus, but this time she wasn't prepared to give up. Yet as she approached her fifteenth birthday, the pressure at home began to mount. She had to have a job. Her dad said it. Her mum said it. Even Doreen said it. She had to earn her keep. And not just her own keep. She had to help keep the household together. Still she had argued she'd like to stay on at school and maybe take some exams, or maybe go to the local tech college. It would pay off, she'd said. It would mean she'd get a better job in the long run. Her mum's answer had been immediate. 'Oh no you don't! We can't afford it. Especially not now. You're lucky you can stay on till you're fifteen. I had to leave school at fourteen. The rent's due every week and it doesn't pay itself. The electric doesn't come for free. The gas doesn't come through the pipes for nothing. You say you want a new carpet in your room? We CAN'T afford it!'

Angie had made the mistake of shouting, 'Why don't you say that to Dad? Where do his earnings go? That's when he bothers to go to work. He drinks it all away! So now I've got to go to work to pay for Dad. Isn't it a dad's job to pay for his family? Or at least pay for himself.'

Her mum had slapped her face and then burst into tears.

So when the time came to leave school, Angie had taken the job at English Electric. It was good money but to Angie it felt like a step backwards. She'd been a Saturday girl in the fabric department in Bonds. She'd loved it. They'd let her buy the materials cheap, cut-offs of velvet, snips of satin, pieces of crêpe. She'd smuggled them into her bedroom, concealing them at the bottom of her basket. She didn't want anyone seeing them, there'd only be a row. But working in the fabric department couldn't lead anywhere. Not in Bonds. If you were lucky you might be allowed to order the fabrics, like Miss Sharpe who had been there all her life. There was nowhere else to go. And it certainly didn't pay enough.

English Electric was where her mum worked. True, she had ended up in the department where she needed to be good with her hands instead of the shop where the general bits of valves were made. In the workshop you had to wear a white coat as you bent over the delicate components, the thin pieces of copper, the small pieces of ceramic. She appreciated the logic and the purpose of the work and even the beauty of it. The construction of the valves was quite an art – twisting the wire, joining it to the ceramic, getting it into the right place, at the right angle, to look neat and perfect – but it wasn't the job of her dreams. At first there were only two of them in the team, Angie and Graham, her boss. Then a year later the junior, Mandy, started and Angie shared the skills she now had. She and Mandy laughed together a lot, sitting at their benches, leaning over the valves, carefully wielding their screwdrivers and pliers, talking about the Peter Cook and Dudley Moore programme and *Top of the Pops*, and Graham didn't mind as long as they got the work done. Sometimes they all went out at dinner-time, in the hot weather, and sat by the river. Sometimes, when there was food in the fridge at home, she brought sandwiches that she'd made.

She had been at English Electric for over three years, and she was well on her way to achieving the first few items on her list of ambitions that she had written before she left school:

1. *Have a job*
2. *Get engaged*
3. *Save up for a house*
4. *Get married*
5. *Have children*

She knew this list made sense. It was sensible. And she had already achieved number one – she had her job at English Electric. As for number two on the list, she had Roger, which might lead to an engagement. He had asked her, about two weeks after they met, if she would marry him. She had thought about what it would mean, choosing a ring, wearing the pretty diamond on her left hand, watching it flash as she made a point, casually waving her hand in front of the girls at work, being one of those girls who aroused envy in the others, moving into a small house in Chelmsford, having children . . . No, she didn't want that. Not yet. She wasn't sure if she wanted it at all. But she had started saving, a few bob a week. She told her mum it was for her bottom drawer, a wedding maybe or maybe for the house on her list. But what she was really saving for were the things on her secret list. The dream she wouldn't give up on!

1. *Learn everything there is to know about fashion*
2. *Work in the fashion industry*
3. *Design fashion*
4. *Fashion fashion fashion*

Angie had done some research, found the names and addresses of fashion houses and designers, as well as fashion colleges. There were places in Soho and Kings Road. And there was always Oxford Street. That's where she would like to go.

She bought *Honey* magazine, and pored over the pages. *Honey* was for young, modern girls. She recognised herself in the springy, smiling models. She studied the shapes and the lines of the dresses and skirts; she thought about the fabrics and how easy or difficult it would be to create something similar. Sometimes, if she was lucky at the dentist or if it was busy in the newsagent's and Mr Johnson wasn't watching, she got the chance to flick through the more expensive magazines, sometimes *Vogue* or *Harper's Bazaar*, drinking in the sumptuous textiles and the elegant draping of glittering evening dresses, frowning at the classic tight shapes of the suits worn by the serious long-legged models.

And she was determined to be practical. She signed up for an evening class, at the technical high school on the far side of the estate, dipping in to her savings to buy the fabrics and tools she needed. Miss Darling had suggested it. Angie had told her mum it was shorthand and typing and she bought herself a notepad and an official looking pencil. She did squiggles in the book, in case anyone came looking, but they didn't. The course, every Thursday evening, was in fact fashion design. Those evenings were the best part of the week for her. She studied patterns, how to create on paper the shapes of the dresses she and Carol, and Mandy at work, and even Doreen, wanted to wear, cutting the flimsy paper, pinning it carefully following the weft and weave of the material, learning how the fabric moved, how to create different effects. For those three wonderful hours she used the language of creation, lining, ruching, draping; peplums and bodices, gathers and pleats. It was a marvellous world of strange words and special skills.

At first, she didn't say a word about the class to anyone, not even to Carol. The family she knew would be outraged, although Doreen would probably just laugh. Roger wouldn't understand, he would probably look sad and be worried that she was going to leave him. And he'd probably blurt it out to his mum or worse to her own mum. As for Carol, Angie was afraid that her friend would think she had ideas above her station as her dad would say, and she wasn't sure she was ready for anyone to criticise her work.

But last week she had completed a dress that even the tutor, Miss Brown, had been impressed by. Miss Brown had stood by Angie's side and had stopped the class so that everyone turned to look at Angie and the dress, displayed on her tailor's dummy. She had drawn the attention of the class to the fit of the sleeves, the position of the darts, and the way Angie had used two different fabrics, to create a modern but classic look.

This wonderful experience was what she had wanted to talk to Carol about on Friday, in the Orpheus, but instead they had spent the night dancing and laughing to the rock 'n' roll classics that Mark Shelley and his group had played. It had been great. But tonight Carol was coming round, and Angie was going to tell her all about it.

Carol had brought some magazines for Angie to look through. It was their arrangement. Carol bought *Woman's Own*, which was weekly; Angie bought *Honey*, which was monthly. Now Carol flicked through a copy of *Honey* that Angie had put by her pillow. She knew better than to take it home, since Angie used it for inspiration.

Now that she was here, Angie was suddenly shy. What if Carol did think it was a stupid idea to want to work in fashion? What if she didn't like the dress?

'Oh, I like this one.' Carol held up the magazine and pointed at a model wearing a small beret and a dress with long sleeves and a curvy hem.

'Really?' Angie said. She was thinking she could have made one ten times better than that. And Miss Brown thought she could too. 'What about this?' She went to the wardrobe and drew out the dress that she had smuggled home from her class. It was in two shades of blue, in a geometric pattern, with a round neck and short sleeves. In one panel was a hidden pocket.

'That's fab!' Carol breathed. 'Where did you get it?'

'I made it,' Angie said. 'Do you really like it?'

Carol stood up. 'Ange, it's gorgeous. Those colours are lovely. Did you really make it?'

Angie held it up against herself and twirled round. 'Yes, I did. I've been going to a class, at the Tech.'

'As well as the shorthand and typing?'

'I'm not doing shorthand and typing. I'm doing fashion.'

'You sly dog!' Carol laughed. 'So when are you going to work in Carnaby Street?'

'As soon as I can.'

'Really?'

'I don't know. I've been applying for every fashion job I see, and I'm building myself up to go to London to see what's up there. You never know . . .' Angie laid the dress gently on the bed. They both stared at it. 'But you know what my mum and dad are like.'

'So that's why you're supposed to be doing shorthand and typing?'

'Yes. They think I'll earn even more if I'm a secretary.'

'Oh, Ange, you can't be a secretary,' Carol said. 'Fashion needs you. You've got to keep at it.'

'I could make you a dress if you like,' Angie said.

'Like this? Could you? I can't believe you've been doing this and not telling me. I thought you were going to be taking a letter in some swanky office in Marconi's.'

'But actually, I'll be crawling round on my hands and knees, sticking pins in models. I didn't dare tell you in case you thought I was stupid.'

'Oh Angie! I just think it's great. You're so lucky to be able to do this'

'Well, now I've got that off my chest, let's put a record on.'

While Carol carefully put The Chiffons' LP on to the turntable and the words of 'He's So Fine' filled the room, Angie went to the wardrobe and pulled out a carrier bag. She took out some pieces of bottle-green velvet. 'I've got to finish this for the class,' she said. 'Don't worry I can talk and tack at the same time.' She put a pot of pins between them and pulled the material onto her knee.

'How long have you been doing this class?' Carol said.

'About a year.'

'Have you been doing this all this time?' She indicated the carrier bag and the fabric and the pins.

'Yeah.'

They were silent, listening to the record, occasionally singing along.

Casually, but with pins in her mouth, Angie said, 'You know that Italian in the boutique.'

'The one who's not really Italian.'

'Do you think he is actually married?'

'Angie. You're not still thinking about that kiss, are you? That was weeks ago! Everyone kisses everyone at Christmas. He probably would have kissed me if I'd gone in there.'

Angie was silent.

Carol looked at her. 'Oh, all right. I'm sure he wouldn't,' she said. 'I'm sure he thought you were the most amazing person he'd seen ever since the boutique opened.'

'Really?' Angie said hopefully.

'I don't know. But what about Roger?'

'Oh Roger.' Angie sighed. 'I don't think Roger's even heard of Italy. And sometimes I wonder if he's even a mod at all. I mean, that thing he gave me for Christmas!'

'The umbrella? I thought that's what you'd asked for.'

'Yeah, but I wanted a maroon one. A *maroon* one. And what did I get? What did I get, Carol?'

'You got a red one, Ange. A bright red one.'

They both laughed.

'How can he not know that red is not a fashionable colour, and that I don't like it? I've only told him a couple of hundred times. Sometimes I think he doesn't listen to a word I say. But how can he expect me to carry that around with me? For a start it clashes with my suede, which he'd know if he even looked at me for five seconds.'

'Perhaps he thought you'd like it, since you're so artistic.'

'Oh, you mean like modern art. Colour clash!' Angie spread her hands theatrically, the material lying on her knee. Her face fell and she picked up the cloth once more. 'Yeah, perhaps he did. Or perhaps he forgot till the last moment and went into Bonds and it was the only umbrella left in the department.'

'He tries,' Carol said.

'I know he does,' Angie said. 'I just wish he'd succeed. That's the difference between him and the Italian.'

'Do you think he's succeeded? I mean, he's come to Chelmsford, hasn't he? Some people might say that's a bit of a . . .'

'An experiment. A wild and crazy experiment,' Angie said. 'At least he's got out of his home town.'

'Perhaps he's escaping.'

'What from?'

'I don't know. You tell me.'

'I'd have to talk to him to find out, wouldn't I? I'd have to go back there, wouldn't I?'

'That's not really what I meant,' Carol said.

'Ha. Well either way I'm off to my "shorthand" class.'

'Yes, of course. We wouldn't want you to miss that.'

The girls walked down the stairs laughing. As they walked into the kitchen there was a knock on the door. 'That'll be Reg,' Mrs Smith said. 'Oh I feel lucky this week.' Reg from the flats always came on a Thursday to collect the pools coupon.

Mrs Smith snatched her bag from the table and opened the door. 'Hello Reg, come in. I'll just find my purse. Have you got time for a cup of tea?'

Reg stepped on to the doormat. He was a small man in a beige mac and a flat cap. 'Thanks but no thanks Mrs S. I got a load more to get to yet and I don't want to be late.'

'Don't want to miss *Top of the Pops*, I suppose,' Angie said.

'No, I'm hoping I'll miss it,' Reg said with a straight face. 'But I'm taking the wife out for a drink at the Clock House.'

'With all your ill-gotten gains?'

'Now then, Angie. I don't know what we'd do without Reg sending in the coupons.' Mrs Smith rummaged in her large cream purse. She pulled out half a crown. 'A drink at the Clock House will be very nice. And my coupon is . . .' She walked across to the sideboard and looked behind the teapot. '. . . here.' She handed over the money and the completed coupon and he gave her a blank coupon to fill in for the next week.

'When I win the pools I'm off to the sun,' he said, as he always did, followed by his customary, 'Fingers crossed!'

'It's all pointing one way,' Mrs Smith said, as she closed the door.

Having said goodbye to Carol, Angie headed off to her class. She liked to imagine that doing the evening class was almost as good as having passed the eleven plus.

Every Thursday she scraped together her pieces of cloth and sometimes a dress she had half-finished and pictures she had taken from a magazine. She shoved them into a plastic bag along with the notepad and pencils, then walked along Pierce Avenue, past the parade and turned into Patching Hall Lane. Other people were walking that way, some girls she was sure were doing typing, giggling and laughing, and boys doing carpentry lugging bags with pieces of wood that might be shelves or stools or coat hooks sticking out. A lot of people looked tired as if they'd already used up their daily ration of energy at their day job. She was pretty tired herself, but her step always lightened as she got to the steps up into the grounds of the school.

In the class she sat in her usual seat, near the front, to the side.

She had created the pattern for the new dress she was making and the teacher was impressed. She was always one of the first to finish the tasks set by the teacher. Often she would help other girls who were slower or who were having trouble threading the cotton on to the machine.

In the break in the school dining hall she bought a cup of tea and chatted to the other girls in the class. There were two she liked particularly, Maureen and Cath. They always brought in interesting pictures from magazines. She'd known Cath before, because she worked in the fabric department of Bonds. She knew all about cloth and materials. Maureen worked in a wool shop on the parade. They all shared a similar interest in the new fashions that were appearing in the newspapers and on *Ready Steady Go!*. They discussed trends and colours and dancing and music.

She loved this class.

CHAPTER 7

DOREEN LOVED HER JOB IN BOLINGBROKE'S. She knew exactly what she was doing when she smiled at the nervous and excited brides-to-be creeping in, anxious and hopeful. She instilled them with confidence and courage. She knew how to find something in everyone, because everyone had something – 'The net falls perfectly over your soft shoulders,' 'He will love the way your curves are there; a promise for him,' 'You have the loveliest back I've ever seen!' but she didn't take any nonsense. She knew how to be firm, still with a bit of a twinkle, because there were always appeals from a future bride for a lower cut or a shorter skirt or from a mother for a cheaper version, or easier terms. Mrs Preston said she was the most successful assistant she had ever had. And over Christmas she had excelled herself.

So today, Friday, two months after Christmas, a good period of time for the accounts to come through, and before the shop closed for the day, Doreen asked for a raise. And she got it. She tripped lightly down the stairs from the Accounts Office. Just in time to buy a new set of underwear in Ladies Lingerie.

She went home elated, hugging the bag with the new purchases, and with the promise of an extra £2 a week. She would surprise the family, give them a treat, suggest an outing. A trip to the Odeon, maybe, her mum loved the pictures. Or they could go out for a meal. To the Chinese restaurant in Baddow Road – no, her mum and Angie would never cope, she'd suggest the County Hotel. She would pay. 'I'll pay!' she would say.

She opened the backdoor and stepped into the kitchen. Her smile drooped.

Dad was trying to change the plug on the Hoover, swearing under his breath. From the expression on his face and the clumsy way he was holding the screwdriver she could tell he'd been drinking. Mum was silently peeling potatoes. Angie was at the table, flicking over the pages of the *Daily Mirror*. Nobody spoke. Nobody dared.

For once, she thought, couldn't they just, for once, be a normal family? Smile when a person comes in, say, 'Hello. You look pleased with yourself, have you had a good day?' Or just 'Put your feet up. Have a cup of tea.' It was as if they were all strangers, living in some sort of rough boarding house. It was too bad. Well, from now on, she thought, as she had often thought before, she would look after herself. Oh, maybe she'd keep an eye out for Angie, but Mum and Dad, no. Well, perhaps Mum.

'I'm going out,' she said, flinging onto the table the bag of sweets she had bought at the kiosk in the bus station.

'You've just got in,' Angie said, without looking up, reaching for the sweets.

'I've come home to change.' There was no way she was going to take them out for dinner, miserable sods. She would go for a drive. Perhaps she'd ring Janice. They could have a drink, somewhere. Or maybe she could see if Gene was in the Saracen's. That had been a good evening.

She went upstairs and threw off her work clothes, the pink cardigan and the straight blue skirt, and put on the new underwear. You never knew, she might get lucky. She admired herself in the mirror. Yes, these were nice things. They had class. She opened the wardrobe. The green dress? The red? No! She slid a sheath of blue taffeta over her head.

She went downstairs, her black handbag under her arm. The Hoover lay beside the kitchen table, its cord slithering across the floor, still without a plug. Her dad had disappeared. Angie was studying a picture of two girls in short dresses and white stockings, posing in front of a bus. Her mum was still at the sink.

She took in the scene. It was so sad. She relented. Perhaps she wouldn't go out for a drive. Janice might not be in and Gene probably wasn't in the Saracen's. 'Who wants a treat? Who wants to go out for tea?'

'Who's asking?' Angie said

'I am.'

Her mum turned round. 'But I'm not dressed.'

'You are!'

'But not nicely!' She slid her hands across her pink overall.

'I don't care. Do you want to go or not?' Doreen looked at her watch. 'We'll go in the car. Go on Ange. You can borrow my black jumper if you like.'

'I don't think so!'

'It's nice. It was very expensive. You should learn to appreciate good clothes.'

Angie raised her eyebrows.

Doreen looked at Angie unwrapping a chocolate caramel. 'On second thoughts, don't wear it, you might spill your dinner down it. Don't eat that, you'll spoil your tea.'

Angie grinned and wrapped the sweet back up. 'OK. I don't know what to wear though.'

'Well, are we going out or what?' Mum said.

'Ask Angie. She doesn't know what to wear.' Doreen picked up the lead of the Hoover and the discarded screwdriver.

'What about Dad?' Angie said.

'Yeah, what about Dad?'

'He's gone out,' her mum said.

Doreen snorted. 'His loss. Now go and get ready! Be quick.'

'Come on Mum. The Queen has spoken. Perhaps I'll wear my Fred Perry.'

Doreen slid the red, green and black wires into their places and screwed them in tight.

The restaurant was busy, but Doreen smiled at the man in the black suit and bow tie who welcomed them at the door, and he smiled back longingly. Two small tables were pushed together in a corner by a large Swiss Cheese plant, the table-cloths and cutlery were rearranged and they were seated.

'This is nice,' her mum said. 'I've always wondered what it looked like inside.'

'Oh my god,' Angie said.

'What?' Doreen twisted in her seat and followed Angie's gaze. 'Oh my goodness!' She turned her back.

'What?' Mum was holding her serviette uncertainly.

'Nothing.' Angie and Doreen spoke together.

Doreen looked at Angie.

'It's that Gene Battini! From the boutique,' Angie whispered.

'Oh Angie,' Doreen said. She felt a jolt of guilt.

'Don't you remember? I told you.'

'Yes, I know. And remember what I said?'

'What?' Mum said.

'Nothing!' they chorused.

'Do you think he's seen us?'

'I don't know and I don't care,' Doreen said.

'Who's that he's with?'

'How do I know?'

'It's rude to stare, Angie,' Mum said.

'God, I bet that's his wife.'

'I bet it's not!' Doreen stared at the table, straightening her knife and fork. This was so unfair. Gene looking relaxed in a tweed jacket and tie, chatting easily with his companion, their heads together. She'd felt they might start something special when they met again, and now here they were both in the same room, but she was with Angie and he was with another woman.

'It must be his wife. Mick Flynn in the Orpheus said he was married. And he said she wears glasses. I don't know anyone who wears glasses.' Angie was peering across the room.

'Your Uncle Sid wears glasses,' Mrs Smith said.

'I mean people we know,' Angie said. 'Oh, what *does* she look like? Those glasses! And that hair! It's like Carol's mum's. Oh my god, she's got a clip in it.'

Doreen threw a quick glance over her shoulder. Gene's wife, if that's who she was, had glasses that flew up at the ends yes, but the cardigan over her shoulders was a pretty plum colour, and it matched her lipstick. She could see the attraction. Five years ago, maybe. 'Stop staring and look at the menu.'

'What's he eating?' Angie said. 'I'm going to have the same as him.'

'I can't see and I'm not turning round again,' Doreen said. 'Oh Angie! what are you doing?'

Angie was waving, a small, embarrassed wave. 'He smiled,' she said. 'Oh, I think they're on their afters. Do you think he'll come and say hello?'

'He'd better not,' Doreen said. That would be just too awful.

The waiter came. His white jacket already had one or two small gravy stains. 'Have you decided?'

'We're all going to have steak,' Doreen said. 'And all well done, thank you.'

'They're leaving!' Angie said. 'You'd have thought he'd come and say hello.'

'Why would he do that?' Doreen said. 'You hardly know him. Or –' a terrible thought struck her '– or do you?'

'No,' Angie said sadly. 'I've only spoken to him that once.'

Doreen gave a sigh of relief and sat back in her chair. She'd been right, Angie's Christmas kiss was nothing.

'I have no idea what you're talking about,' Mum said. 'Does it come with potatoes?'

Doreen had asked if she could take home her dessert – pineapple upside-down cake. The bag started to leak pineapple juice and cream onto her mum's skirt as they drove along Broomfield Road.

'Don't worry, Mum, a bit of Surf will bring that out,' Angie said, sitting forward in her seat at the back of the car.

'Or you could eat it,' Doreen suggested.

Her mum giggled. She'd had a small bottle of Mackeson's with her meal. 'I should have worn my apron,' she said.

'That would have looked very nice in the County Hotel,' Doreen said.

'They might have mistaken you for the staff,' Angie said.

'If you were a member of staff, we could have brought home the whole cake!' Doreen said, as they got out of the car. She walked round the car, locking the doors.

'That's an idea, Mum, you could get yourself a little night job at the restaurant,' Angie said. 'You could really bring home the bacon!'

They walked into the kitchen laughing. Their dad was leaning against the sideboard, holding a bottle of beer. On the sideboard were three empty beer bottles. His face had the red and purple hue that they all recognised.

Mum turned to Doreen and Angie. 'Go to bed,' she said. 'Now.'

Doreen ignored her. 'Sorry we're a bit late, Dad. That was my fault. Something went wrong in the car.'

Angie snorted.

Dad pulled himself up to his full height. He was almost six feet tall. As he opened his mouth to speak a wave of beer breath made them all recoil.

'I've been waiting in here for an hour,' he said. His eyes didn't seem to focus.

'Where were you before that?' Doreen asked.

'Hush,' her mum said.

'We waited for you,' Angie said. 'You could have come out with us and had your tea with us.'

'You went out. You didn't care where I was.'

'I think we knew,' Doreen murmured.

'I come back, the place is like the bloody *Mary Celeste*. It's freezing. I've had no tea. Where was my wife? She was out gallivanting! Look at you.' He spoke directly to Mrs Smith. 'I can see you've had a drink.'

'You're a fine one to talk!' Doreen said.

'You shut up,' he said without looking at Doreen. He stepped towards his wife.

'Leave her alone,' Doreen said. 'It was my idea.'

'Your idea! Since when do you have ideas? Fucking stupid bitch. The two of you.' He turned his face towards Angie. 'What did I do to deserve two such stupid daughters?'

'Ohhh, don't start that, Dad,' Doreen said, coolly, angrily. She took Angie's arm. 'Angie, go to bed. I'll sort this out. Go on. Go on!'

Angie turned to her mum, who gave her a pleading look.

'Go on,' Doreen said.

Angie stepped out into the hall.

'We've had a nice evening out,' Doreen said, 'and we thought you were having one too. Don't spoil it now.'

'Shut up!' He swung his right arm towards Mrs Smith, but Doreen stepped forward and the blow hit her on the head.

'Dad!' Doreen said. 'Stop it!'

He raised his left arm and slapped Mrs Smith hard on the cheek. She staggered back.

'Dad!' Doreen said. 'If you don't stop, I'm going to ring the police. I've done it before and I'll do it again.'

He slapped his wife once more.

Angie peeped into the kitchen. 'Shall I go to the phone box?'

Her dad roared, 'If you go out this kitchen, you don't come back!'

'Angie, just go to bed,' Doreen said.

'But Mum's crying. I can go.'

'Angie, love, just go upstairs,' Doreen said softly. 'I'll sort it out, don't worry. I'll come and talk to you in a bit.'

A tear rolled down Angie's cheek.

A pang of fury rose in Doreen's chest. She smiled at Angie. 'Go on, lovely. I'll see you in a minute.'

Angie retreated back into the hall, and closed the door.

'Dad!' Doreen shouted. 'I'm going to put the kettle on and make a cup of tea. If you like I'll make some toast. You can also have this bit of cake, if you like.' She took the bag from her mum and held it out to him.

He dashed it to the floor. 'Cake! Fucking cake! What do you think I am?'

Keeping her eyes on him, Doreen bent down and picked up the cake. 'I'm going to make a cup of tea,' she said slowly. 'We all need a cup of tea.'

She walked in front of her mother, over to the stove. She took the kettle and began to fill it at the tap. She turned to see her dad punch her mother in the eye. 'Just stop it!' Doreen shouted. She threw the kettle at him. It hit him above the eyebrow, knocking him off balance. Water poured over him as he fell to the floor. He lay still.

'Oh God,' Mrs Smith breathed. 'He hasn't done this for months, years. I thought we'd got over it.'

'Mum, he still drinks like a fish.' Doreen picked up the kettle. 'It was only a matter of time.' She stepped over to her mum and peered at her face. 'You'd better go upstairs and put a cold flannel on that eye. Don't worry. I'll check he's OK. He can sleep here, but you'd better sleep in my room, just in case. I'll bring you up a cup of tea.'

'You're a good girl, Doreen,' her mum said. 'Don't worry about me. I'll sleep in my own bed. He'll have forgotten about this in the morning.'

'Oh Mum,' Doreen said.

There was a snore from the floor. Her dad was asleep. Doreen knelt and pushed him onto his side.

'Oh, he's never sick,' her mum said.

'It would be just my luck that tonight he would be,' Doreen said.

Mrs Smith went into the hall and came back with her husband's winter coat. 'Put that over him.' She went into the living room and came out with a cushion.

Doreen covered her father with the coat, put the cushion under his head, and switched off the light. She and her mum walked out of the kitchen and upstairs.

Her mum disappeared into the bathroom.

Carefully Doreen opened the door to Angie's room. 'Are you asleep?' she whispered.

'No. You can put the light on.'

Doreen switched on the light. Angie was sitting up in bed, her knees drawn up under her chin.

Doreen sat on the bed. 'It's all right,' she said. 'He's fast asleep downstairs.'

'Is it going to start again? He hasn't been like this for ages.'

'I think it's because we were out and then we came in laughing. He doesn't know how to enjoy himself anymore and he doesn't like anybody else doing it.'

'But what about Mum?'

'She's all right.' Doreen sighed. 'She's just brushing her teeth. Or putting them in a glass.' They both laughed. 'We had a nice time though, didn't we?'

'It was lovely,' Angie said. 'And fancy seeing that Gene bloke.'

'Yes, fancy that.'

Doreen switched off the light and went into her room.

CHAPTER 8

DOREEN WAS JUST GOING FOR AN ordinary Saturday night out. The memory of Dad lashing out at Mum the night before was still in her mind, and for Mum's sake she needed to be anywhere but at home, in case she said something she'd regret later. She might see some of the girls from work, she thought. She might bump into that Gene fellow. Maybe not. But she dressed carefully, a tight emerald green dress that fitted every curve of her body, and stopped just on her knees. She had some green shoes too that matched, pointed, high heeled, that showed off her slim ankles. She put on a coral necklace and chose a lipstick that went with it perfectly. She smiled at herself in the mirror.

She went downstairs as Angie was putting on her coat in the hall. 'Where are you off to?' Doreen asked.

'I could say the same to you,' Angie said. 'All dolled up like that.'

'It's Saturday night,' Doreen said. 'Everyone should look good on Saturday night.'

'I'll tell Roger that,' Angie said. 'He might stop wearing that parka, get himself a decent leather.'

'Yes, you do that.' Doreen reached for her coat.

'We're going to the pictures in Maldon,' Angie said. 'On the back of the scooter. Don't tell Mum. Do you think I'll be warm enough?'

'Take my scarf,' Doreen said.

Roger was in the kitchen chatting to Mrs Smith.

'Evening,' Doreen said as she and Angie walked in.

'Evening,' Roger said. He looked at Angie. 'Ready?' he asked, and they left the house.

Doreen picked her car keys up from the table. 'I'm off now. Will you be OK?'

'Yes, yes,' her mum said. 'Don't worry. He's gone out. Anyway, he's been as nice as pie today. He even made a cup of tea this afternoon.'

'Pretending nothing's happened. As usual,' Doreen said.

'You know what he's like. He'll be fine now.'

'Till the next time.'

'We'll cross that bridge when we come to it. You just go out and have a nice evening.'

'If you're sure.'

'I am. Off you go.'

Shaking her head, Doreen walked out to her car.

She couldn't decide if she should go to the Saracen's or the Golden Fleece. 'God, I'm turning into my father,' she murmured to herself. 'I could write a book. *My Life in Pubs.*' She decided she'd go to the car park of the Fleece, and if there was a space she'd park and pop in there, see who was about, see if there was anyone worth talking to, maybe have a drink. And if there was no one around she'd stroll over to the Saracen's and look in there. Just like a normal Saturday night.

But she knew what she was really hoping was that Gene would be there. She wanted to see him again. He was the most exciting thing that had happened in Chelmsford for a long time. She walked round to the front of the pub and walked into the saloon. And he was there, standing at the bar, chatting to a group of young mods, all eager to talk to the owner of the boutique. She felt herself relax. He looked good, in his sheepskin coat, grinning at some joke one of the boys had made. He was on his own with them, she could see. There was no one with him. He was hers for the taking.

She smiled and walked up behind him. She tapped him on the shoulder. He looked round, saw her, recognised her, then turned to face her. 'Hello,' he said, drawing the word out. 'Fancy seeing you here.'

'Likewise,' she said.

'What are you having?'

She frowned. 'I don't know. What are you drinking?'

He looked at the malt brown drink in his glass and whispered, 'Guinness. Unless you really like it, don't have one.'

She laughed. 'I'll have a G&T.' She undid the belt of her coat.

He signalled to the barman, who came straight away. 'Two G&Ts,' he said. 'With ice.'

'You'll be lucky,' Doreen said. But the drinks came clinking with ice, the glasses frosting up.

'I am lucky,' he said. 'Lucky to get a decent drink, and lucky to see you.' He looked her up and down. 'And lucky that you're wearing such a fantastic dress.' He guided her through the room to a small table in the corner and they sat down. 'So, what's a nice girl like you doing in a place like this?'

'I live here. More to the point – what's a nice guy like you doing here?' She wasn't afraid to call him a nice guy. Men liked it, if you said it the right way, confidently, but with a certain irony. Well, some men did, the men she liked did. She looked at Gene to see what his reaction was.

He gave her a big beaming smile. 'What this nice guy is doing is talking to a nice girl like you.' He picked up his glass. 'Cheers.'

The glasses made a light clear ringing sound as they touched. It augured well for the evening, she thought. She sighed and stretched her legs. 'Well, I'm glad I came out this evening.'

'So am I,' he said. 'You're not working behind the bar tonight?'

'No, no. I work in Bolingbroke's, bridal gowns.'

'I thought you worked in the Saracen's Head. I saw you there.'

'Good memory you've got. I used to work there. I help out sometimes. I served you a – what was it? – dry martini? Shaken not stirred?'

He laughed. 'So you swapped the demon drink for demon brides.'

'Something like that,' she said.

'I can imagine you'd be good at that.'

'It's all in the personality,' she said.

'Absolutely,' he said. 'Personality sells. You've got it. And so have I!'

There was a song called 'Personality' that was always played on *Two-Way Family Favourites* and she began to hum it. He joined in softly.

'God, we're like two old codgers in the Public Bar,' she said.

'That's all right, as long as you don't get up and start swirling your skirt in the air.'

'In this dress?' she said. 'Not possible.'

'I like you,' he said. 'You know what's what. There's not many people in Chelmsford I'd say that to.'

She purred with pleasure. She moved an inch closer to him. She could smell his sharp cologne.

'They've got a restaurant upstairs,' he said. 'Fancy a bite to eat?'

'Yes, why not?' she said. The egg on toast was hours ago. She could manage a bowl of soup.

He looked at his watch. 'Yes, I've got time before the last train.'

They went out into the foyer and up the stairs. He put his arm round her waist. She leaned into him. The room was bright and filled with young married couples, presumably having an evening out while the grandparents looked after the kiddies, Doreen thought.

As Gene handed his sheepskin to the waiter, the waiter said, 'Shall I take your wife's coat?'

Gene and Doreen looked at each other and raised their eyebrows.

He ordered a steak and she chose an omelette. She pushed it round her plate as he demolished the steak in great mouthfuls.

'Have a chip,' he said, as he wiped his mouth with the serviette and pushed back his chair to take out a cigarette.

She shook her head. 'But I'll have a cig,' she said.

'And coffee?'

'And coffee.' This was very nice, she thought. Being with a bloke with money, confidence and nothing to prove.

When he'd finished his coffee, he looked over at the spiky gold fifties clock on the wall. 'Now I really have got to go,' he said. 'Walk me up to the station?'

'I'll drive you, if you like,' she said. 'I've got my car.' She imagined sitting in the car with him, perhaps having a cigarette together in the dark, perhaps kissing.

'A gal who drives. Now that I do like,' he said. 'But it's not far enough for that.'

'All right, walk me to my car then,' she said.

'You're on.'

He gestured to the waiter to bring the bill and he paid from a roll of notes he drew from his trouser pocket. As they walked out to the car park, she felt sharp and alive. Happier than she'd felt for a long time. 'This is my car.'

'A Hillman. Nice reliable motor,' he said. 'But I had you down as more of a sporty type, something nippier.'

'In my dreams,' she said.

Suddenly he was very close to her and his arms were round her. His face was close to hers. Her heart began beating fast. She parted her lips and they were kissing. Yes, this was just what she had wanted.

Then he stepped back, still with his arms round her. 'All right gorgeous girl, I'd better get going.' He kissed her lightly on the lips. 'You and I should have a proper date, you know.'

'I'll think about it,' she said, though inside she knew that was exactly what she wanted.

'I'll see you soon, I hope.'

'So do I,' she said, because she knew she could say that to him, show him that she liked him, and he wouldn't think she was desperate and run a mile. They understood each other. It was casual, but it was something they both enjoyed.

She drove home singing 'Personality' to herself.

CHAPTER 9

A WEEK AFTER THE NIGHT WHEN her dad had hit her mum Angie dreamed about Gene Battini. She couldn't remember it all when she woke up, but he'd been there, in their kitchen. He'd smiled at her. Said he liked her dress. He put his arm round her.

As she sat up in bed she felt as if she knew him. She smiled. As she brushed her teeth the feeling stayed with her. She went down to breakfast, and her dad was there, sitting at the kitchen table, reading the paper, smoking a roll-up, and she still smiled.

'The kettle's just boiled,' Dad said. Then unusually he added, 'Do you want a cup of tea?' He stood up and went to the stove.

'No thanks,' Angie said carefully. She looked at his back as he stood at the sink. Even a week on she was torn between fear and rage that her dad could behave so badly to her mum. Making her a cup of tea wasn't going to make up for that. 'I'm going into town,' she said. It was Saturday morning.

On the bus Angie decided to get off at the cathedral and walk through the churchyard. She would go and say hello to Harry. He was family. It was natural. Then she might just pop her head into the boutique, say hello to Gene. Why not? Where was the harm?

Harry was giving a man a shave as she walked in. 'Watcha, cuz,' Harry said. 'This is my cousin, Angie,' he explained, bending over the other man who was swathed in a white gown and with a beard of shaving foam. 'The sharpest mod in the whole of Chelmsford.' He slid his razor up the man's cheek.

The man in the chair glanced over at her. 'Hello beautiful! I'll be with you in a minute.'

She recognised his voice. It was Gene Battini, the man himself. Colour rose to her cheeks. He'd spoken as if he thought she'd come to see him. What a nerve! How would she have known he'd be in here? But she said nothing. She sat in one of the waiting chairs and watched as her cousin smoothly scraped off the shaving cream, from the other cheek, his chin, under his nose, gradually revealing the smooth features of a Londoner running a boutique in Chelmsford. Harry wiped Gene's face with a flannel and then Rose, Harry's timid assistant, came across to offer a range of aftershave. Angie was surprised that Gene Battini didn't choose Old Spice but went for something lavender.

'Do you like lavender?' He spoke into the mirror at Angie.

She shrugged. 'Yeah.'

'Good.'

'Do you want a cup of coffee?' Rose asked Angie.

'Well . . .' she hesitated.

'If you're asking me,' Gene Battini said, 'I haven't got time. I've got to open the shop.'

'Isn't it open yet?' she asked. She looked at her watch. 'It's gone ten.'

'No one comes in at this time.'

'I was going to,' she said. 'You've lost a sale.' She felt confident talking to him. The dream was still with her.

'Why, what were you going to buy?'

'I've changed my mind now.'

'Tell you what, come into the boutique with me now and we can have a cup of tea in there and let's see if I can persuade you to buy whatever it was you were thinking of.'

Her cheeks were hot again. She looked at Harry.

'That's OK,' he said. 'You go on. I think we've got a customer. Rose, can you sort out this sink, please?' The bell over the door tinkled and a man and a little boy walked into the shop. 'See you later, alligator,' Harry said.

'In a while,' Angie replied.

'Crocodile,' Gene said.

Gene and Angie stepped into the street. Gene carefully positioned himself on the outside of the narrow pavement as they walked the three yards to the boutique.

He bent to unlock the door. 'After you.' She stepped into the shop. It smelt of new clothes and quietness. 'So, missy,' he said. 'Have you come back for the longer kiss?'

He'd remembered!

'Ah, you're blushing! So that is what you're here for,' he said.

'I thought we were having a cup of tea,' she said.

'You know that's not what you came for.'

She looked at him. 'If I'm truthful . . .' she said.

'Of course.'

'. . . after we saw you in the County Hotel . . .'

'Oh yes.'

'Well . . . I had a dream about you. So I just came to see you again. Not for the kissing.'

'Well, dreaming about me's a good start. I'm pleased you're here.'

'So, let's have that cup of tea,' Angie said.

'And then we'll see where that gets us.' He grinned and disappeared into the back of the shop.

She thought about him as she ran her hands over the rails of clothes. She liked how he spoke to her. If she'd told anyone in the Orpheus that she'd dreamed about them there'd have been a whole song and dance, embarrassment, shouting to their mates. But Gene had just accepted it and said he was pleased.

He brought through the fold-up chairs they'd sat on before, then the tea. He handed her a mug. She looked at it appreciatively. 'You're good at making tea, I'll give you that. Nice and strong.'

'That's me all over,' he said. 'What's your name again? What did Harry call you? Anne? Anna?'

'Angie.'

'Hmm, Angie, Angela. Nice name for a nice girl.'

'Yeah,' she said. 'Don't forget, we're just having a cup of tea.'

They sat in silence, looking past the display dummies in the window, to the street outside. There were few passers-by at this time of the morning.

'Why—?'

'Where—?' They began speaking together. 'After you,' he said.

'I was just going to ask you why you came to Chelmsford.'

'I was looking for a girl like you,' he said.

'We're still drinking our tea,' she said. 'Hold your horses.'

'My horses are champing at the bit,' he said. 'I was going to ask you where you work.'

'English Electric,' she said. 'For the moment.'

'Oh, are you looking for a new job?'

'All the time.' She was surprised at herself. Only Carol knew about her attempts. 'It's hard, you fill in the application, send it in with a stamped addressed envelope and then you never hear back. It's expensive.'

'You could come and work here. I could do with a bright sharp assistant.'

'Oh, ha ha. You couldn't afford me.'

'Couldn't I? That's a shame.'

'And it's not just about the money. I think I'd be hopeless at it, if I'm honest.'

'I like a girl who's honest. Restores my faith in human nature.' He stood up and took the mug from her hand and put it on the counter. 'Makes up for the rest of us.' Then he pulled her to her feet. 'I like you,' he said. 'I like you a lot. I wonder why that is.'

'Probably because I've already got a boyfriend so I'm not going to chase after you.' He was still holding her hand.

'No. I liked you that day when you came in, before Christmas, wasn't it? And you were a bit upset, and you told me you didn't like malted milk biscuits.'

'I don't,' she said.

'But you made me laugh. And of course, that glorious head of hair and those grey eyes of yours. Irresistible. I like grey eyes.' He drew her to him and leaned down to her face. She could smell the tart lavender aftershave. 'What's that Roger got that I haven't?'

'Well, he hasn't got a wife for one thing.'

'Oh Cynthia. She and I are through.'

'Given the glasses she wears I'm not surprised,' Angie said. 'That was her you were with that night, wasn't it? In the County Hotel?'

'Yes, it was my lovely soon-to-be-ex-wife. She occasionally deigns to bring down some stock from the London shop.'

'So you're not divorced, then?'

'No, but as good as.'

'Have you got any children?'

'No. Cynthia didn't want them, and I'm not bothered.'

'I want children.'

'Do you? We could make some now if you like. I've got a little camp bed out the back.' He turned.

'Ha ha. Just stay here,' she said slowly. 'Stop joking. I've got to think.'

'What are you thinking about?'

'You.'

'Oh yeah?'

'Yeah.'

'So, what are you thinking?'

'Whether I should kiss you now.'

'I think you should.'

'Shut up! I've got to think. I'm not like you. I don't kiss just anyone. There is Roger, after all.'

'Oh Roger. Well I don't want to kiss *him*.'

'No.'

'Don't take too long,' he said. 'There's work to be done. But I should say I've been wanting to kiss you since you walked into the barber's this morning. You've got a lovely mouth, you know.'

'All right,' she said. She leaned into his face and kissed him. He put his arms round her waist and she wound her arms about his neck. This was lovely. After a few seconds he opened his mouth and she let her tongue creep in. His tongue met hers. She felt she was melting. Roger had never kissed her like this. Oh, Roger.

The bell on the door tinkled and they jumped apart.

'Good morning, young man,' Gene said, rubbing his hands together. 'What can I help you with today?'

The fresh-faced mod boy who Angie didn't recognise looked at the floor and then said, 'I want one of those Fred Perrys you said were coming in.'

'I said they were coming in and in they have come. Now what colour would you like?'

Angie sat back down and picked up her mug of tea. She watched Gene talking to the mod boy, discussing colours and size, making the boy relax and feel important. She could almost see his chest swell as he looked Gene in the eye, and talked about the number of buttons and the way the collar sat. She was impressed by how cool Gene was being, as if they hadn't just had such a wonderful moment. She ran her tongue over her bottom lip. She was glad she had come back. She had wanted to for a long time. She didn't know how it would affect her relationship with Roger. Her stomach twisted a little. She would think about that later.

Gene was behind the counter, taking the money, making small talk. The mod said something and Gene laughed. 'Bye,' the boy said.

'Bye,' Gene and Angie said together.

'I'll see you tonight then?' he said to Angie.

'Tonight? I can't tonight.'

'How about next Saturday then. I'm usually in the Golden Fleece about eight. Will you be there?'

'Yeah,' she said, as casually as she could. 'We're usually in there about then. We'll be there.'

On the bus on the way home she thought about him, this morning, and now next week! Maybe next month. She imagined him leaving his wife for her. She decided she wouldn't tell Carol about the arrangement because Carol might not want to come out and Angie needed moral support. For one thing, he might not turn up. And she wouldn't tell Roger, there was no need, because next Saturday night Roger was out of town.

CHAPTER 10

It had been a hard day at work. Graham was away ill and Angie realised how much she depended on him. She'd had to cover his work too, and one or two little mishaps had occurred, some valve components had been sent back to be done again and Mandy had got upset. On the way home, waiting for the bus, a car had driven through an enormous puddle and soaked her shoes and the bottom of her skirt and had splashed her suede. She longed to be indoors, take off her wet shoes and stockings and sit down in front of the telly with a good programme.

When she walked through the back door into the kitchen, unusually her mum and dad were both at home. The kitchen table was covered with bits of paper, brochures and photographs. Mrs Smith was standing, looking at them thoughtfully. Her dad was leaning against the draining board, studying the racing pages in the newspaper. Neither of them looked up when Angie walked in.

Angie went through and hung her coat in the hall and took off her shoes. Back in the kitchen all was silent.

She stood beside her dad and washed her hands at the sink.

'Put the kettle on for us,' her mum said. 'I'm dying for a cup of tea.'

'Dad's standing here. Why can't he do it?'

'Don't start,' Mum said. Dad moved to the other side of the room with his newspaper and leaned against the sideboard.

As the water splashed into the bottom of the kettle, over her shoulder Angie said, 'So how was your day out in London?' She looked at the paper on the table. 'What's all that?' She saw the words 'Australia', and 'Ten Pounds'.

Mum began to scrape the pages together. 'Nothing. Nothing.'

'Doesn't look like nothing,' Angie said.

From the living room, Doreen called, 'Tell her!'

Mum sighed. 'Oh, you might as well know. We . . . we went to Australia House. We thought we'd just go and have a look.'

'A look at what?'

'You know.'

'No, what?'

Doreen shouted from the living room. 'They want to move to Australia.'

'What? What do you mean?'

Doreen walked into the kitchen. She was wearing a flowery cotton housecoat and she had rollers in her hair covered with a blue nylon mob-cap. She looked like a milk-maid with black eyeliner. 'They want to go to Australia.'

'Why?' Angie said. She looked at Doreen.

'To get away from their past?' Doreen laughed as she examined her stockings. 'I might get some stockings without seams for a change. What do you think?'

'Why do you want to go to Australia?' Angie asked again.

Doreen looked up. 'You're coming too.'

'Me? No, I'm not. Why would I want to go to Australia?'

'You're the one who's always moaning about not doing anything or going anywhere. Well, here's your chance.'

'That's not what I meant.' Angie looked at Doreen to make her shut-up.

'It's a whole new start,' her mum said. 'It's warm, they have houses, they'll get us a job. Your dad won't have to clean windows anymore. They want people like us.'

'People like us?' Angie said. 'What does that mean?'

Before her mum could answer, Doreen said. 'They want people with style and ideas. People who want to go places. Like me. And you, if you could be bothered. Anyway, there'll be nothing left for you here. We'll all be gone. You've got to come.'

'Hush,' her mum said. 'Angie's got Roger. I can see that might be a worry for her.'

'It's not just Roger,' Angie said. 'It's . . . everything. My job, my future, all my . . .'

'All your what?' Doreen said.

My dreams, Angie thought, but she was silent. She looked over at her mum. 'Are you serious?'

'Very serious,' Dad said. 'Look.' He lowered the newspaper. 'I even went and had my hair cut before we went up there.'

'That's only because Harry gives you a special rate,' Angie said.

'A haircut's a haircut. Not that your friends would know that. Long haired idiots.' Dad lifted the paper again and continued reading.

'It's . . . it's because we want a change,' Mum said. 'A fresh start. There are so many opportunities. Things would be different there . . . For me. For your dad . . . For all of us.'

'Well, good for you. Have a nice life. I'm not going.'

'Of course, you're coming,' Dad said from behind the paper.

'If we're not here, where will you live?' Mum said.

'I don't know.'

'There you are.'

'Give me a chance. You've just sprung this on me. I could . . . I could live with Carol.'

'They haven't got room for you.'

'I could share Carol's room. Or I'll get a place of my own. Or Carol and me could get a place together. I don't know, do I? I'll stay at the YWCA. Anyway, I'm not going.' Angrily she heaped tea into the teapot.

'If we go, you go,' her dad said, not looking up.

'That's a nice attitude,' Angie said.

'Come and have a look at these.' Mrs Smith spread the brochures out on the table again.

'In a minute!' Irritated, Angie lifted the kettle from the stove, poured the boiling water into the teapot and covered it with the green and red knitted cosy.

Her dad stood up straight. 'Nearly time for my programme. Bring my tea in.' He walked through to the living room and switched on the television. Angie thought: *just like him* – declare they're moving to Australia and then walk away.

Mrs Smith on the other hand carried on. 'You remember Ivy Beckton, who I went to school with.'

'I've never heard of her,' Angie said.

'Yes, you have,' Doreen said. 'She came round once with a cake she'd made. When Dad . . .'

'Doreen!' Mrs Smith hissed.

'When Dad wasn't here.'

'Oh, her. She was nice,' Angie said.

'Yes, well. She's gone out there. And she loves it. She says that when we go we can live with them for a bit.'

'Really?' Doreen said. 'They must be mad. How many kids has she got?'

'She's got two kids. They're out there too, but they don't live at home. They work. One of them's a nurse, I think. That's a nice job.'

'I don't want to be a nurse,' Angie said.

'They live in Melbourne. She put a picture of their house in her Christmas card. It's lovely. I'm sure I showed you. But even if we couldn't stay with her, they give you a place to stay in when you first get there, anyway.'

'Yeah, but they're not that nice,' Doreen said. 'A woman at work, her sister went and it was like a camp.'

'Another reason not to go,' Angie said.

'I think they're hostels. But that's what I'm saying. We wouldn't have to stay there. It'll be so nice to see Ivy again. She was such a good friend. And they have a really nice life. Barbecues on the beach at Christmas.'

'That is not natural,' Angie said.

As the TV set warmed up the sound of a serious voice came through into the kitchen: 'Australia – a young country for you and your children.'

'There, listen! The advert!' Mrs Smith said.

'It's just an advert,' Doreen said.

'But it's an advert for Australia!'

'Oh Mum!'

Mrs Smith pushed Angie and Doreen into the small living room. 'Shh, watch. Look at that! Look how hot it is. Ice cream all year round.'

'Mum!'

'And that, there. Sandy beaches, lovely waves.'

'But Mum . . .'

The advert ended. Mrs Smith looked from Doreen to Angie. 'Say what you like, but we've just been and got all those leaflets and now the advert's come on telly, the very same day. Don't you think that means something?'

'Oh Mum!' Doreen and Angie chorused together.

'What? I thought you wanted to go.' Mrs Smith looked at Doreen.

Doreen shrugged. 'Maybe.'

'Do you really?' Angie turned to her sister.

'Why not? It would make a change. See some different people. Get a tan. Wear a bikini.'

'Yeah, I expect that's what they want. More people to wear bikinis on their beaches. I thought you were supposed to have a skill.'

'We've got skills. Your dad's got skills.'

'I've got skills,' Mr Smith muttered

'Such as?' called Doreen.

'Don't be so bloody cheeky. Now get out and let me watch the television in peace.' It was a programme about the war.

'I wouldn't mind,' Doreen murmured, 'but he wasn't even in the war.'

Mrs Smith hustled Angie and Doreen back into the kitchen. She began pouring the tea. 'He did his part up at the airbase,' she whispered. 'He's done a lot of things you don't know about.'

'Things we don't know about? Like what? Changing his pub?'

'Hush! He was an engineer. And then there's me. I've got my thing.'

'What thing?' Doreen asked.

'The glassblowing.'

'You?' Angie was astounded.

'I did it just after I left school,' Mrs Smith said proudly. 'I was the only girl at Crompton's who did it. When they had visitors, they used to bring them round to see me.'

'Why did you stop? What happened?'

'Your father.'

'Tell them I was an engineer!' her dad called from the living room. 'I did seven years' apprenticeship.'

'When? He's never been an engineer in my lifetime.' Doreen said. 'Bloody hell. How come there are all these things about my family that I never knew? And now you say he's changed pubs!'

'You were small. He worked at Crompton's. That's where we met.'

'I knew that,' Doreen said. 'I just thought he was a cleaner. When did he stop working there?'

'You would have been about seven or eight. He lost his job.'

'Why?'

'There was some trouble.'

'What kind of trouble?'

Mrs Smith said nothing but gave them a look that said, 'You can guess.' She held up her fists in a fighting stance. Aloud she said, 'He was young. Anyway, he's got the qualifications they want.'

'So why was he a chimney sweep and why is he cleaning windows if he's got all these skills?'

Mrs Smith made another 'you can guess' expression.

'What are you saying now?' Mr Smith called.

'Nothing,' Mrs Smith called back. 'We could have a whole new start there,' she whispered. 'It would be good for all of us. We've all got skills. Angie, you've got your valve work and Doreen, well, you can sell stuff, I suppose.'

'I do book-keeping too,' Doreen said, 'when Mrs Preston's not there.'

'There you are! We're set.'

'Where's the tea?' Mr Smith shouted.

'A really good new start would be us going and leaving him here, Mum,' Doreen said.

Mrs Smith laughed. 'Yes, that would be something, wouldn't it?'

'But I suppose it's his engineering skills they really want,' Angie said.

'Probably.'

'So, why don't you just send Dad and you can stay here with me?' Angie said.

'No.' Mrs Smith shook her head. 'That wouldn't be fair.' She took a cup of tea through the arch into the living room.

Doreen and Angie stood in silence. Angie's mind was churning. *How could they go to Australia? Their family was a mess. Surely no one would want them. One thing was definite. She wouldn't go. She had too much to do here.* She looked at her watch. She definitely had something to do now. 'What's the time? I'm going to be late.'

'And where are you off to?' Doreen said.

'I've got my class,' Angie said, 'And not that it's any of your beeswax, after that I'm seeing Roger.' She ran into the hall to fetch her coat and her bag. It all seemed a bit irrelevant, tonight, the class, her relationship with Roger, the worry over Gene, after this bombshell from her mum and dad. Her family wanted to move to Australia. She could hardly take it in.

'You seeing Roger?' Mrs Smith said, coming back into the kitchen. 'Ask him if he wants to come to Australia with us. Then he can make an honest woman of you and I'll get some grandchildren.'

'Not likely!' Angie said. 'I'm still young. Speak to Doreen, she's the oldest.'

'Thanks, but no thanks,' said Doreen. 'I'd have to find someone first, someone who fulfilled my strict requirements. And that is why I'm spending tonight in.' She was spreading jam onto a slice of bread. 'It comes to something when all I have to look forward to is ogling Dr Kildare on the telly. Is there any hot water? I want to have a bath first, in case a miracle happens and he steps out of the TV screen and into our living room. I want to be prepared.'

'Is it Thursday? Oh my god, my coupon.'

'Oh Mum,' Doreen said. 'Why do you do it? You never win. It's a waste of money.'

'If Viv Nicholson can win the pools, so can I. And then, you'll see. I shall spend, spend, spend!' She looked at Doreen, wiping jam from the draining board. 'The jam jars!' she went into the pantry and came out with four empty jam jars. 'Drop these round to Mrs Evans for me.'

'What, me?' Doreen said. 'What about Angie?'

'I'm going out. You just said you were staying in.'

'Yeah, staying in. Not going out in the cold and dark, tramping up and down the streets. Why don't you take them with you? The bus doesn't go for ten minutes.'

'No time,' Angie said and was gone.

Angie walked down the stairs of the Orpheus with her sewing class materials in her basket, tucked under a head scarf. Roger sat at a table with a glass of hot blackcurrant. Angie smiled when she saw him. She always smiled when she saw Roger. He had a reassuring face, not handsome exactly, but he had a friendly smile and calm blue eyes.

It was a face that would see you through any difficulties. He had taken off his parka and he was wearing a new pale grey Ben Sherman shirt. He plucked at the sleeve as she sat down opposite him. 'What do you think?'

'Nice,' she said. She took a breath. 'My mum and dad want to go to Australia.'

'Australia. That's a long way to go for a holiday.'

'No, to live, forever.'

'Australia,' he repeated slowly. His face had gone pale. 'Are you going too?'

'I don't know.'

'Do you want to go?'

'Not really.'

'What is there out there for you?'

'I don't know. Nothing, probably.'

'Do you want me to come?'

'Why? Do you want to live in Australia?'

'It would make a change. I'm a mechanic. Well, I've nearly finished my course. And they need mechanics.'

'How do you know?'

'My mum and dad were talking about it last year.'

'You never said!'

'We'd only just started going out. I didn't want to jinx it by saying I was leaving. But if you're going anyway, we could go together. You could really make something of all your fashion ideas. I'd mend a few cars. We could have a sheep-farm and you could knit all the jumpers they need in Australia. Do you want a drink?'

'Yeah, a glass of milk please.'

As he stood at the counter, she watched him. Did she want to go to Australia with Roger? Did she want to go to Australia? Of course, they probably did need fashion out there but here in England was where fashion was really happening, all the markets in London – Petticoat Lane, there was one in Soho, other places. People were making clothes, thinking up styles and shapes. The Beatles were wearing all kinds of weird jackets, with odd necklines and fake pockets. And she'd just discovered some fabric by a company called Rose & Hubble, with intense flowers in deep colours. She was thinking of a blouse with interesting sleeves that she could use it for. She was sure they wouldn't have Rose & Hubble in Australia. They probably didn't even have Liberty's. Knitting jumpers for sheep farmers wouldn't be much better than working for English Electric.

But it wasn't just about fashion. What about the Orpheus? She loved drinking coffee, wearing her suede, discussing *RSG!* and music with Carol, listening to the jukebox. She needed to be close to Liverpool and all the groups that came from there, and Newcastle and Manchester. She needed to be close to America and Tamla Motown, to Soul and R&B. And then, if she went to Australia, she would never see Gene again . . .

She couldn't go to Australia, she was sure. She needed to be here.

When Roger came back, she said, 'No. I'm not going to Australia.'

'Oh.' Roger sat down heavily. 'I just put this on the jukebox for us.' It was 'Road Runner' by Junior Walker and the All Stars. 'That could be us, travelling across the world.'

Mrs Smith pulled a plastic bag out of a drawer. 'I don't know when Mrs Evans finds the time to make jam, not with all those children, but I said I'd give her some of our empties. I've washed these out for her.'

'Well, I hope she's going to give you a couple of jars for your trouble. Let's hope it's not gooseberry,' Doreen said.

'Would you run them round for us? It won't take long,' Mrs Smith said.

'What about my programme?'

'You don't care about the news. It'll only take you a couple of minutes. I've got to do my coupon before Reg comes.'

'Oh, for God's sake. Does she need them tonight?'

'I saw her in the shop yesterday and said I'd drop them round today. She's probably got the fruit on the boil already.'

'Oh, all right.' Doreen sighed. 'You're lucky I haven't got a better social life, or I wouldn't be able to do this sort of thing.'

'I think you have a very good social life,' her mum said. 'Better than mine anyway. And it's only five doors up the road. You don't even have to take the car.'

The Evans family was well known on the Greenway Estate, because of the children. There were at least six, some of them foster children, living in the house in the Crescent. Mrs Evans was a cleaner at the schools round the Lane. She often popped into the Smith's kitchen, 'for a bit of peace and quiet,' she always said, but Doreen thought it was more to do with keeping an eye on Mrs Smith. Mrs Evans knew all about Mr Smith and his pastimes.

It was cold and dark outside. Doreen wrapped a scarf round her face and walked the few yards along the road. The jam jars clattered together in the bag. *Was this what her life had become?* she thought. *Staying in and running errands for her mum?*

She was about to press the Evans' doorbell when the front door opened. A wall of light, heat and sound hit her; a baby crying, toddlers screaming, a woman shouting and the urgent opening music of *Compact* shrilling from the telly. The person who had opened the door and now stood in the doorway, silhouetted in the light from the hall, was Cliff. *Cliff Evans*, thought Doreen. *I don't see him for a hundred years and then I see him twice in two weeks*. Today he wasn't wearing the smart suit he'd been wearing in the Orpheus, now he was in jeans and a white

T-shirt, and his dark hair, quite short at the back was a riot of curls at the front, glistening with some sort of grease, just like at school. He'd always wanted to be a Teddy Boy, she remembered.

He was holding a leather jacket in his hand as if he had just unhooked it from the wall. He frowned. 'I can't talk to you now. I've got places to go.'

Doreen looked round. There was no one else there. 'Well I don't really want to talk to you,' she said. 'I'm just delivering jam jars.' She held out the bag.

'Jam jars?' He gazed at her blankly. 'Jam jars?'

'Yes, real honest to goodness jam jars. You know, for jam. They're not for you.' He was reaching out for the bag. 'They're for your mum. Unless you've got a taste for cooking.'

He peered at her. 'Bloody hell, Doreen Smith!' He laughed. 'Sorry. I thought you were from the Conservatives, about the election. Doreen Smith. I haven't seen you for ages!'

She snorted. 'Well, I saw you in the Orpheus the other day.'

'Really? Yeah, that was a waste of time. People don't turn up when they're meant to. Well, well. Doreen Smith.' he said. 'You should have come and said hello.' He was grinning at her.

'What shall I do with these?' she said.

'Oh yeah. Put them there.' He pointed to a table by the door. 'Ma!' he shouted. 'Sadly,' he said, 'I've got to go. See you later.' He bent down and kissed her on the cheek as if they knew each other well, as if they'd been together for years. She remembered him from school. He always had the chat, and the charm, and more cheek than was good for him.

She blinked and touched her face, then turned and watched him walk down the path, shrugging into his leather jacket, adjusting the collar. He had taken a few steps when he turned, as if he realised what he'd done. He smiled. She smiled back. He raised his eyebrows as if to say, 'What about that?' Then he ran off down the road. She shook her head. What was it with these men? First Gene and now Cliff.

'I thought I heard voices.' Mrs Evans bustled down the hall. Doreen couldn't imagine how she could have heard voices above the noise in the house. 'Doreen! Hello! How are you love?'

'I've brought you the jam jars Mum promised you.'

'Oh lovely. Has he gone?' She peered past Doreen and they both watched as Cliff turned the corner. 'He owes me ten quid.' She looked back at Doreen. 'How is your mum?'

'She's fine. She's just filling in her pools coupon before Reg comes.'

'Good idea, you never know your luck. Come in for a minute?'

A small child with a drooping nappy came down the hall and draped himself round Mrs Evans' left leg. 'What's for tea, nanny?' he said.

'You've had your tea,' she said. She looked at Doreen. 'He's had his tea, he's just trying it on.'

Doreen laughed. 'Better luck next time,' she said to the boy. 'I won't stop, thanks. I said I'd only be out a minute or two. Dr Kildare might drop by and I wouldn't want to miss him.'

'Oh, well, I've been waiting for Leslie Howard for quite some time,' Mrs Evans said. 'He never comes. Another day.' She looked down at the little boy. 'Come on you, you can have a biscuit.' The child hopped with pleasure and grinned at Doreen. 'The lady's going, say bye bye, Curtis.'

'Bye bye, see ya,' Curtis said.

CHAPTER 11

THE ATMOSPHERE IN THE HOUSE HAD changed and it wasn't just that it was Saturday evening. Mum and Dad were happy and easy with each other as if the thought of a new life in Australia had wiped out all the bad memories of the past. Dad hadn't said a rough word since the incident. But then he was always sorry afterwards. They were all sitting in the living room watching the telly. The fire was bright and everyone was in a good mood. Mum was quietly sure she'd succeed in getting Angie to come to Australia with them, and Angie was just as sure she wasn't going.

Dad had fried the eggs without a word and put a thick layer of marge on the toast. Doreen made jokes about the names of the football teams, and Mr Smith didn't tell her to shut up. And Mrs Smith was smiling because everyone else was happy. The bruise on her eye was hardly visible.

Mr Smith had the pools coupon on his lap. There had been some big matches today and the football commentators had been talking very excitedly.

The Grandstand announcer was still ploughing through the list of results as Angie collected the plates and went out into the kitchen. She slid them into the sink to soak, while she put on the kettle for a second cup of tea for her mum and dad. Then, quickly she scrubbed the egg yolk from the plates and put them to drain on the draining board. 'The kettle's boiled,' she called to Doreen, and ran upstairs to the bathroom for a bath.

She came downstairs, buttoning her cardigan, ready to go out and lifted her suede from the hooks in the hall. Her mum and dad were in the kitchen staring at the pools coupon. The television was on in the living room and faint twanging guitar notes announced the start of *Juke Box Jury*. Doreen was leaning against the sink eating a last piece of toast.

'Why aren't you watching the telly?' Angie asked Doreen.

Doreen stood up straight and brushed crumbs from her chest. She lifted her eyebrows and nodded towards Mum and Dad.

'It can't be,' her mum said.

'It is,' her dad said.

'You must have worked it out wrong.'

'No, I didn't. I know football.'

Doreen slid her plate into the sink. 'Are you sure?'

'Five draws! Five draws! I'm telling you, this is all correct. Grandstand doesn't lie. We've won a lot of money.'

'Well, if you've managed to predict that, you can bet your bottom dollar half the country has too, so you'll get about £10.' Doreen looked at herself in the mirror of the door of the broom cupboard.

'I wouldn't mind if I did get £10, but this is going to be a whole lot more.'

'You hope. Anyway, I can't stand round here dreaming the impossible dream, I'm going out.'

'Where are you going?' Angie asked. 'I thought you could give me a lift into town.'

'No, I can't.'

'Why not?'

'Because I'm not taking the car out. I'm going to the Clock House with Janice.'

'Shut up girls, this is important. Looks like we've won big!'

'Yeah, yeah.' Doreen walked out of the kitchen. She stopped at the door. 'Just so you know, when the men come to take your photo with the big cheque and they ask you what you're going to spend the money on, I want a new car, a new bedroom suite, I want a light over my bed, and I want some new slippers.'

'Oh, can we choose?' Angie said. 'I'd like a new record player and all the records Tamla Motown ever made . . . and a new suede. And one for Carol too.'

'Be serious,' Mrs Smith said.

'All right. I'd like the Encyclopaedia Britannica – is that serious enough?' Angie said. 'And all the other stuff I said.' She laughed.

'It is serious.'

'First thing I'm going to do is get myself some new gnashers,' her dad said. He shifted his teeth in his mouth. 'Apart from that, my life won't change at all. Ha ha ha.'

'He's not drunk,' Mrs Smith whispered. 'I think he's right. Well, I know the first thing I'm going to do next week. I'm going to try that new hairdressers on the Parade.'

Angie looked at the two of them, her mum and her dad. Her dad's eyes were shining in a way she hadn't seen before. A natural shine, not the dull glow of alcohol. Perhaps it was true. Perhaps he had won. 'Do you mean enough for Doreen to buy a car with?' she asked.

'Two cars. Three. And a house.'

'Really? Really? Can I tell Carol?'

'Don't tell anyone till it's all signed and sealed,' her dad said. 'And not even then. I put X in the box for no publicity. I don't want every beggar in the world asking for money.' But he grinned.

Angie ran upstairs. She looked into Doreen's room. 'He means it!' she said, breathlessly. 'He thinks he's won.'

'God help us.' Doreen was sitting in front of the mirror, carefully applying cream to her face. 'He thinks *he's* won,' she repeated, 'but it's Mum that fills in the coupon and Mum that pays Reg.' She turned to Angie. 'But if it's true this could be the best thing that's ever happened to our family.'

'Mum's already going mad, she's talking about having a new perm next week.'

'A new perm! You see,' Doreen said, 'it's going to turn our whole world upside down.' They laughed.

'Perhaps this will stop them thinking about Australia,' Angie said thoughtfully. 'If they've got money, they can have a new start here.'

Doreen turned back to the mirror. 'Maybe,' she said, dabbing more cream on to her forehead.

At seven o'clock Angie and Carol caught the forty-five bus into town as usual. Angie had so much she wanted to say to Carol about the pools win but she didn't dare. She felt it might almost disappear into nothingness if she said a word. She couldn't even go back to talking about Australia for fear she'd mention the new development – the money could change everything. And she didn't want to talk about Gene, just yet. They chatted about work, Angie's problems with Graham being off, and Carol's boredom with her filing job at the Britvic factory on the edge of town. 'We should go and work in London,' Angie said.

'Good idea!' Carol said. It was a conversation they often had.

They got off the bus at the bus station and wandered, arm-in-arm, into the Golden Fleece. They ordered two

Britvic oranges. Angie said, 'We should get a discount since you work there. Like they do in Marks and Spencer's.' She kept looking at her watch.

Carol said, 'You're not expecting Roger to turn up, are you?'

'I hope not!' Angie said. Roger was away playing football, staying overnight at his auntie's house in Somerset.

By half past eight Gene hadn't appeared and she and Carol were on their second glass of orange. They'd said hello to Blond Don and his sister. Sailor had come by and had a chat. But Gene wasn't here. Angie felt bitterly disappointed. She had so enjoyed that kiss, she wanted more of it, more of him. He'd been so confident in the way he'd put his arms round her, the lovely things he'd said. 'Shall we go somewhere else?' she said sadly.

'OK.' Carol stood up and began buttoning her mac.

Then the door opened and he walked in.

He hadn't seen them and he stood in the middle of the bar, casually, not looking round, not seeming to worry about meeting someone, someone he'd said he'd see at eight o'clock. The boy who had bought the Fred Perry went up to him and Gene slapped him on the back as if they were old mates. He said he'd buy everyone a drink. Then he'd looked round and made a face as he realised how many people there were and how much it was going to cost him. The gold rings on his fingers glinted as he took out a roll of notes. He was rich. Being rich didn't count for anything with her. Although it might be nice not to have to worry about having enough for a drink *and* the bus fare home. Then she remembered, her dad had probably won a lot of money. She'd never have to worry about the bus fare home again. She couldn't quite believe it. And now Gene was here. This was fantastic.

Carol whispered, 'Do you think we're included in this round of drinks?'

'We'd bloody better be,' Angie said. 'Take your coat off.' She sat up straight.

Carol looked at her.

'What?' Angie said. 'What?' She couldn't stop smiling.

'What's happened?'

'Nothing. Well, something. He kissed me again!'

'Really? When?'

'Last week!'

'You never said. You're not safe to be let out on your own.'

'I know!'

'So, what now?'

'Let's wait and see.'

An hour later they were still sitting in the Fleece, Angie with a rum and black, Gene with his second G&T and Carol now with a pineapple juice. 'You can't have the same thing every time,' Gene had said. 'Look at you, you'll turn orange.'

Angie was vaguely aware that she should say, 'You can talk!' or something similar. But she only smiled. She wondered if she was drunk.

'I'm going home now,' Carol said, at half past nine.

'OK,' Angie said.

Carol looked from Angie to Gene. She shook her head slightly.

'Bye,' Angie said.

Carol put on her suede jacket and Angie watched her make her way through the crowd in the pub.

Five minutes later, Gene said, 'I'm sorry, honey bun, but I've got to go too. I need to get back to London, and I don't want to rely on the last train. Come on, let's walk up to the station. We'll get you a taxi.'

'OK,' she said. It was enough. She knew she had had too much to drink.

The next week Dad gave them all money. He put the notes down on the kitchen table – twenty pound for Angie, twenty pound for Doreen and twenty-five for her mum. He sat back in his chair, grinning with satisfaction. 'Don't spend it all at once.'

'So when do we get these new bank accounts?' Doreen asked. He had said on the Monday after the big win that he had decided to open a bank account for each of them and divide the money up between them all.

'Hold your horses, greedy guts,' Dad said now.

'Because I've already arranged an overdraft on my own account, and it isn't cheap.'

'Those who ask, don't get.' Dad leaned forward as if to take back the notes. 'The money hasn't come through yet.'

Doreen snatched up her twenty pounds. 'Well, thanks for this, anyway.' She crushed the note in her hand.

It was Saturday morning. Doreen was going into work late. She and Angie went into the hall. They were going into town together.

'Let's get the early bus,' Angie said. 'I want to be there when the shops open.'

'Good idea,' Doreen said. 'Knowing Dad these are fake twenty quid notes and if you don't spend them soon, the rozzers will come and take them all away. I'm just going to fritter this, I might buy a new bag. I'm going to spend a lot of money. And you should too. Do you know what you want?'

Angie put on her suede. 'Yes, yes I do.'

Angie went into Bonds and headed for the haberdashery department. Ever since she had worked here as a Saturday girl, it had been her favourite place. There was a hint of magic about the calm quiet area, as the rolls of rich materials and the brilliant embroidery silks waited to unlock the stories of the clothes they would help create. She enjoyed the tranquillity of the women standing at the books of patterns, turning the heavy pages with a soft crackle, pausing now and then, tilting their heads to imagine the dress or the jacket made up in their material, seeing what it would look like on them, and the quiet conversations with the assistants who advised and suggested. She'd been one of them. She felt at home here.

Today it was even better. Today, as she walked into haberdashery she felt lighter, almost breathless, she felt rich. She smiled at Cath from her dressmaking class who was advising someone about the difficulty of a pattern.

Angie had made another list:

Dressmaking equipment
Scissors – large, small and pinking
Packets of needles
Pins
A pretty thimble
Tailor's chalk
Maybe a new box for all the new equipment

The money was going to buy all the things she needed for her dreams to come true. She wandered round the department in a daze, her fingers trailing over the racks of 'notions'. Cottons, silks, bias binding, interfacing, Vilene, tacking cotton. She stopped in front of the rolls of fabric. She would buy three yards of some lovely cloth and lining silk to match, not with any plan in mind, but just because she could, and because it was a wild and extravagant thing to do. She moved over to the sewing machines, and she lingered.

Doreen had known all along what she wanted. The day after they'd won the pools, she'd discovered the Hillman had a flat tyre. It was a sign. Of course, the flat tyre itself was no problem. She could change a flat tyre, no trouble. She did it in five minutes. But she'd been thinking for a while that she needed something newer, something snappier, something that would look good parked outside their house. She'd had her eye on something in the motor showroom on the corner of Duke Street and Market Road for a while. She thought it was funny that Gene had said he'd imagined her having a sports car. How right he was.

She got off the bus at the railway station. She tightened the belt on her white coat and walked into the showroom. She wove her way through the cars on display, looking at each car and smiling at the thought that they were all, all, within her reach. There was a small office in the corner of the room where a man and a younger man were drinking something that looked like tea. The cups had roses on. She smiled expectantly. The men looked over to her and said something to each other. Then the younger man stood up and came out of the office towards her. He looked all of sixteen. She could see fair, soft hair on his chin. They had sent out the boy. She was going to be spoken to by the *boy*.

He grinned. 'Good morning madam. Are you waiting for your husband?'

'No, I'm here on my own behalf.'

'Oh! Well – eh – we have some very nice ladies' cars.'

'Do you? Well I'm not a very nice lady,' Doreen said.

He went on, 'We have them in colours that all the ladies go for. And as it's for yourself, can I suggest an automatic car – that's a car where you don't need to use the gears. Many ladies do say they find them easier to manage.'

'Really?' Doreen shook her head. 'Can I speak to your father?'

The boy looked back at the office. 'He's not my father. He's my uncle.'

'I'd like to speak to him.'

'He can only sell you the same cars I can, dear.'

'Did you just call me "dear"?' Doreen said. 'Now you may be right and he can only sell the same cars as you can, but here's the thing, if I've got to take attitude from someone in order to buy a car, I'd rather take it from someone my own size. Go on, go and get him.'

'Well, madam,' he said, as if he hadn't heard. 'I can show you some of our newest models.'

'Look, you little twerp,' she said. 'I've got money burning a hole in my bag that I want to spend on a car. I don't have to buy it here. I can buy it down the road. Will your uncle be happy with that, do you think?'

Reluctantly the boy turned and walked to the office. There was a short exchange of words and then the older man left the office and came, smiling, towards her.

'Sorry about that,' he said, tilting his head towards the boy in the office. 'It's his Saturday job. I thought he could do with a little practice.'

'Yeah, well, I didn't want him practising on me. Now then, I want a sports car.'

The man's face lit up. 'Walk this way, madam.'

On Monday, home from work Angie was hanging up her coat in the hall. 'What's that?' she said. There was a table by the front door that hadn't been there before.

'It's a telephone table,' her mum called. She was in the kitchen, peeling potatoes.

'Oh, ha ha,' Angie said.

'Doreen just brought it home.'

'Why?'

'Don't ask me. You know what she's like.'

'We're not – we're not getting a phone, are we?'

'That's what she said.'

'That's fantastic!' Angie said. No more having to queue for the phone in Sperry Drive. No more having to go to people's houses to deliver messages, now she could just ring them up. She could ring Carol and chat to her. Carol had had a phone for years. Carol could ring her and chat. They would be like normal people. She could drop it into conversation. 'Oh yes, you can ring me. Our number is . . .'

'What's our number?' she said.

'I have no idea,' Mrs Smith called.

Doreen was coming downstairs 'How come we're getting a phone?' Angie said.

'Every family should have a phone,' Doreen said. She ran her hand lovingly over the small, low teak table. 'This is G Plan. See it's even got a seat to sit on.' She sat down, then immediately stood up, following Angie into the kitchen. 'I need a phone to keep in touch with my friends.'

'I can ring you when you move to Australia,' Angie joked.

'Well, you could,' Mrs Smith said, 'but if you come with us, you won't need to.'

'But I'm not coming.'

'Well, don't count on getting phone calls from us, because they cost a fortune.'

'I thought we had a fortune. I thought we had so much money we could do what we wanted, so I can pay the rent on this place after you go, and I can keep the phone too.'

'Ringing up people abroad would be the best way to spend it fast. Anyway, that's what paper and envelopes are for – so you can write letters.'

The next day Angie lugged a large heavy box up the stairs.

'Well!' Doreen said, coming out of her bedroom. 'What have we here? Your face is all red.'

'You said I should buy something big. I've bought a sewing machine.'

'I didn't mean buy something so . . . so boring. I meant something special and exciting, like a ball gown.'

'This is special and exciting for me,' Angie said, leaning against the bannister. 'Our sewing machine is always on the blink. I know it was Nan's and I know she loved it, but that was 1923. We're living in the '60s now. Let me put the box down. It's really heavy.' She walked into her bedroom and carefully eased the box onto the floor beside the dressing table. 'This one is perfect. It's top of the range. The tutor in my class said it was the best money could buy. It does everything.'

Doreen followed her in. 'How does a shorthand tutor know what's top of the range in a sewing machine?'

Angie rolled her eyes to the ceiling. 'Because she's not a shorthand tutor . . . I might as well tell you, before you say something you shouldn't. She's a tutor in fashion design. I've been doing a course.'

'In fashion? You kept that secret.' Doreen sat on the bed.

'Because Mum and Dad kicked off when I said what I wanted to do. But I suppose now that money's no object, I can tell you. I want to be a fashion designer.'

'Thank God. I thought you were going to say you wanted to be a model.'

'My tutor says I'm good. And with this sewing machine I shall be even better.'

'Can it make a silk purse out of a sow's ear?' Doreen said.

'Probably.' Angie knelt on the floor and began to open the box. 'It does zig-zag, overstitch, button-holes. It's fantastic. It even does eyelets. Eyelets!' she said proudly.

'I don't understand a word you're saying,' Doreen said. 'But you don't need a sewing machine. We've got money now. You don't need to make clothes or eyelets or whatever. You should be out buying up all the fashionable clothes in town.'

'But it's not just about having all the fab clothes, I want to make them. I want to design them.'

'Design them?' Doreen repeated.

'Oh, Reen, it's something I've wanted to do for ages. And the money's giving me the chance.'

'I'll tell you what,' Doreen said, 'if you can make them, we could wear them.' She laughed. 'We could walk round town in them, and then you'll be discovered.'

'Do you mean that?' Angie looked at her sister.

'Why not?'

Angie laughed. 'Well, I've already spent the money Dad gave us.'

'What on?'

'All the things I bought in the haberdashery department in Bonds – I told you. I got loads of things, some lovely scissors.'

Doreen rolled her eyes. 'And how have you paid for the sewing machine?

'I used my savings. Well, for the deposit. The rest is on the never-never.'

'You shouldn't have had to use your savings, Angie,' Doreen said. 'That's awful. Where's all the money they won? These bank accounts are taking forever. Dad's says it's the pools people's fault. Sometimes I think he hasn't won at all.'

'Oh, don't say that,' Angie said. 'That sewing machine cost the earth.'

'But don't you want anything silly? Luxurious?'

'I've seen a really lovely suede I'd like. It's full length with a leather collar.'

'Well buy it.'

'I can't afford it!'

'Get it on HP. Then pay it off when the money comes in. Or get an overdraft, like me. Or I could lend you some.'

Angie pulled pieces of cardboard from the box. 'Oh, it looks lovely,' she said. 'Help me.' Doreen held the box while Angie pulled out the sewing machine. 'Oh, look at that!' She ran her hand over the smooth body of the machine. 'They don't seem to be talking about Australia so much since they won the money. Do you think they've changed their minds?'

'I don't know.' Doreen stood in the doorway. 'Mum's the one who wants to go. I don't think Dad's that bothered. He thinks he can live off the money for ever. He doesn't need a new start.'

'Do you want to go?'

'I don't know. I'll tell you when the new car arrives.'

'Is it the blue one you wanted?'

'Yes. God, it's going to be lovely.'

A week later, when Angie came home from work there, sitting on a doily on the table in the hall was the phone. It was black and shiny, with a little tray underneath for notes. Its silver dial of finger-holes twinkled in the setting sun. A twisted brown fabric-covered flex snaked from the back of the phone over to a small box on the wall by the windowsill. Beside the phone sat a large thin book entitled *The Chelmsford Telephone Directory*.

Angie gazed at the phone. In the middle of the dial was the number – Chelmsford 5135. Their number. They had a phone.

It began to ring.

'But no one knows our number,' Angie said.

The phone continued to ring.

'Phone's ringing!' Angie shouted.

Her mum came out of the kitchen. 'Well, answer it.'

Angie snatched up the phone. The mere action felt wonderful.

'Hello. Err, Chelmsford 5135, hello.'

There was a rattly clatter of coins as the caller in a phone box somewhere pressed button A.

'Hello!' It was Doreen's voice. 'What do you think of the phone then?'

'It's great. I can hear you!'

'That's handy. That means it works.'

'Where are you? Why are you ringing up?'

'I'm in the phone box on Sperry Drive. I just wanted to say hello. Now you can ring up all your friends.'

'I know! As long as they're not in Australia.'

'Of course. And don't forget to pay for the calls you make. Or it's not fair.'

There was a click, then silence.

They had a phone. She had a sewing machine. Angie's eyes shone. She was so pleased they were rich.

CHAPTER 12

DOREEN WAS LOOKING AT THE HOSIERY stall, in the middle aisle of the market. Friday was market day. The place was heaving, people from the villages around Chelmsford who had come in for the morning to do their shopping and pick up some bargains, children hanging around the toy stalls, women from the estate who'd come on the same bus she had, to buy cheaper vegetables.

She needed some new nylons. Both pairs of her work stockings had ladders and she had stopped them as far as she could with clear nail varnish, but she had a crisp ten pound note in her purse, so there was no need to keep dabbing.

She was picking over the crackling plastic packets of stockings, marvelling at the long-legged, lean models on the front, wondering whether anyone really looked like that, when she saw Cliff Evans. He was standing in front of a flower stall, in deep discussion with the stall holder. She looked back at the stockings, but despite herself kept glancing over at Cliff. His dark hair was brushed back off his face and as he stood talking she could see his dark eyes and his interesting mouth. He looked good, if a little menacing, in his long black leather coat. And then he looked straight at her. He smiled. He walked towards her. He took the packet of stockings from her hand. 'She'll take these please,' he said, 'two pairs,' and he handed the stall holder a ten shilling note.

'Well, if you really want to,' Doreen said. 'It's your money.'

'I'm feeling generous this morning,' he said, dropping the stockings into Doreen's bag. 'Wanna cup of coffee?'

The stockings she had come for, she had now acquired. She'd thought she might investigate the shoes in Saxone's or Lilley & Skinners, she still had the ten pound note after all, but she had no real plans. She looked at her watch. 'OK,' she said. As they walked out of the market, into Tindal Street, Cliff pointed to the pubs they passed, describing the standard of beer in each one, from bad to worse. She laughed. She wasn't sure if that was because he was being amusing or because she couldn't believe she was walking down the road with Cliff Evans.

In the Milk Bar she went upstairs while Cliff ordered two coffees. She could hear him flirting with the woman behind the espresso machine – making her laugh too. She was sitting by the window, looking out over the High Street when he came up, balancing the drinks and a

Chelsea bun on a plate. He sat down with a sigh of satisfaction and took out a packet of cigarettes.

'Do you always smoke Embassy?' she said.

'I usually smoke Bensons. I only smoke these when I'm running a bit low.'

'Then you shouldn't have paid for my stockings. Or the coffee for that matter.'

'Oh well that's me. Last of the big spenders.'

As Cliff lit a cigarette, Doreen stirred her coffee, then put a spoonful of froth in her mouth. 'What was that all about? In the market. You and that woman.'

'Joan? Oh, she's all right. I had to sort out something about the flowers.'

Doreen frowned.

'You know where I work don't you?'

She shook her head.

'I'm an undertaker.'

'Really?'

'In a manner of speaking.' He heaped sugar into his coffee. 'I do a lot of lifting. And I help out when things get rowdy.'

'Do people get rowdy at funerals?'

'You'd be surprised.'

'Yes, I probably would.' She took a mouthful of coffee. 'Are we going to eat this bun?'

'It's for you.'

'I can't eat it all.'

'Cut it in half and I'll have some.' He slid out of his chair and across the room to a jar of cutlery and brought back a knife. He presented it to her.

As she sawed through the bun she pondered how domestic this seemed, so ordinary.

'Did my mum ever give you any of that jam she made?' He leaned back in his chair, smoking.

'I don't know,' Doreen said. 'I'm not a great jam eater. I like marmalade.'

'Marmalade!' he said. 'Thick peel or thin?'

'Any way it comes,' she said. 'My mum only eats shredless.'

'It's not marmalade then, is it?'

'That's what I say!' They laughed.

Suddenly he put his cup down, slopping coffee into the saucer. 'Now there's a man I do need to see,' he said. 'He owes me big time.' He pushed back his chair and stood up, thrusting a piece of the bun into his mouth. 'If I'm not back in five minutes, doll, go without me.' He leaned down as if to kiss her again, in that easy, nonchalant way he had kissed her when she was delivering the jam jars. But he stopped and grinned. 'Another day,' he said and wove his way through the tables and ran down the stairs.

She watched through the window as he ran across the road and put his hand on the shoulder of a man in a grey gabardine mac. The man turned – he was old, forty at least, and he was going bald. He wore glasses. As he recognised Cliff a smile came across his face. They shook hands and Cliff briefly held his arm. They stood on the corner, moving in close to the wall as shoppers and pushchairs and other men in grey coats and trilbies walked past. The man in the mac put his right hand into the inside of his coat and drew out a slim envelope. He handed it to Cliff. Cliff opened the envelope and glanced inside as if he wasn't that interested in the contents. He slid the envelope into the inside pocket of his own coat. The two men talked, they laughed. The other man looked at his watch and Cliff squinted up at the window of the Milk Bar. Doreen looked away quickly. She didn't want him to know she had been watching all the time. He might get the wrong idea. He might think she fancied him.

When she looked back down both men had disappeared. She waited to see if Cliff would come back upstairs but he didn't. She sat for a little while longer. Drank her coffee. Took a sip of his, just to see what it tasted like with all that sugar. And to drink from his cup. She cradled the cup in her hands. It was time for her to get back to work.

In the middle of the zebra crossing there was Cliff coming towards her. He began to walk backwards, so they reached the corner together. He held up a packet of Benson and Hedges. 'See, we're really in the money now. Where do you want to go, girl? To see the pyramids in Egypt, or a beach in Tahiti? How about a lion hunt in Africa?'

'I'm going to work,' she said primly. 'Some of us have proper jobs you know.' But she stood there. 'What did that bloke give you?'

'So you're interested in me, all of a sudden.'

'I'm interested in what goes on in Chelmsford, doing business in the street, brown envelopes, handshakes, dirty dealings.'

'You've got a vivid imagination.'

'Have I? I don't know how your mum puts up with you.'

'She loves me really. Look, I'll walk you to work,' he said.

'Don't put yourself out.' She laughed.

'Why, where do you work?'

'Here,' she said. 'Bolingbroke's.' They walked the few feet to the anonymous grey door that was the staff entrance.

'You work here? I never knew that.'

'Clearly you don't know everything.'

'I think I knew you worked in a shop. But Bolingbroke's? Swanky.'

'I'm glad you noticed,' she said. She put her hand on the door handle. 'Well, thanks for the coffee. And the stockings. Really you didn't have to.'

'Look, Doreen. Do you wanna go out?' he said.

'Why?'

He laughed. 'I dunno. Have a laugh. Chat. Talk about old times.'

'Really? I didn't enjoy school and from what I remember you didn't enjoy it that much either. I don't know anything about you now.'

He frowned. 'What do you want to know? I work in an undertaker's. Apart from lugging coffins out of hearses and onto my shoulders plus a bit of crowd control, there's not much to tell.'

'So why aren't you at work now? What were you doing in the market this morning?'

'I was waiting for you.'

'Oh, ha ha. You were having that big discussion.'

'I was sorting out flowers.'

'So what happened to them, the flowers? And that bloke in the street? What was that all about? What do you really do?'

'I don't know what you're thinking, but it's wrong. Where do florists make most of their money? Funerals. We sort out deals so people can afford it, she gets the business and we get a cut. And that bloke Chris, he's just a mate. I put a bet on the gee-gees with him. And for once I won. There you are – the story of my life. So how about it?'

'Well, now I know everything about you, what would we talk about?'

'This and that. I dunno. The weather? God, you don't make it easy, do you?'

'In my head I keep seeing you in your school uniform.'

'Didn't I look cool?'

'Not really.'

'Well, if you went out with me, you'd get used to seeing me like this!' He spun round in front of her and the ends of his leather coat flew out, like a magician doing a trick.

'Now you're making me dizzy.'

'That's something.'

'I've got to get back to work.'

He looked at her and shook his head. 'Sure?'

'I am.' She looked at her watch. 'I'm almost late.'

'You're really sure?'

'Why? What's the hurry?'

'You've got to get back to work. And hey, we're not getting any younger.'

'So do you think we should run off together now?'

'If you like.'

'I don't think so.'

He gazed at her with a small smile. Then he said, 'OK, you win. I'll see you around.' He leaned towards her as if to kiss her, and she flinched. He laughed. 'Don't worry, doll. I don't kiss on a first date.' He paused. 'Well, not usually.' He looked at her and raised an eyebrow. 'But that's our secret, isn't it?' He turned and walked towards the High Street. Then he stopped. He looked back. 'And I'm not talking about the night with the jam jars.'

A woman walking past looked at him and he laughed. 'Don't worry, madam, we don't use the jam jars in public.'

The woman turned her head sharply as if she had suddenly smelled something bad, and Cliff and Doreen both laughed.

Then, 'Our secret? *Our* secret?' she called, but he was gone. 'What do you mean?' she murmured to herself as she pulled open the door and walked up the stone staircase to the staffroom. She didn't know what he meant, idiot. But as she hung up her coat and tidied her hair, she realised she'd enjoyed the last couple of hours. She'd got two pairs of stockings, and she still had the ten pound note. Cliff Evans. Who'd have thought? She shook her head. She was quite happy with the easy relationship she had with Gene. She didn't need Cliff to complicate matters.

CHAPTER 13

'What do you think?' Angie twirled round in her bedroom. She was wearing a new dress that she had made herself. She'd spent hours on it, sitting downstairs in the front room, long after everyone had gone to bed, using her new smooth, silent sewing machine.

Carol inspected the dress. It was moss green, with long sleeves. It was quite formal, with a small collar and two rows of buttons, military-style, down the front. 'It looks very nice.'

'I couldn't have done it without the new sewing machine. This material is quite thick. But do you think Gene will like it?'

'I'm sure he will.'

'He should, the time it took me. It's lined as well!' She turned up the hem. 'It's not all that mod, but it's smart, and anyway he doesn't really know what's in for girls. But these shoes – they should be black.'

'They look black. I only know they're navy because I know,' Carol said. 'You look fab.'

'Oh, but he's going to see me eating.'

'So?'

'He'll see me holding my knife and fork and cutting things up and chewing. Perhaps I should have something to eat before I go out, then I won't have to eat at all.'

'That's mad. You're going out for a meal. Anyway, you eat like a normal person.'

'Do I? But he'll be watching.'

'He'll be eating too. Honestly, Angie, if you're worrying about anything you should be worrying because he's married.'

Angie stopped looking at the hem of her skirt. 'Don't you like him then?'

'I don't know him. He seemed very nice when we had that drink. But you know, I was going crazy on pineapple juice, so I don't remember much.' They laughed.

'Well, I don't care that he's married. He doesn't care, so why should I? Plus, he's practically divorced.'

'What if she comes down and wallops you?'

'I'd like to see her try. Anyway, Gene says that's not her style. The only person she'll have a go at is him. And she probably won't do that.'

'Do you really not care?'

'I don't know. Not at the moment.'

'And what about Roger?'

'Oh don't. It's not as if we're married. We're not even engaged.'

'Only because you won't say yes.'

'Well there you are. What does he expect?'

'Oh Angie.' Carol shook her head. 'Well, that dress does look fab. You'll knock him for six.'

'I hope so.' She looked at herself in the mirror again.

Angie had been waiting for this for days, all her life she felt. Since that night in the Golden Fleece Angie had daringly rung him, and one day she had dashed into the boutique in her dinner hour and spent five minutes there, leaning on the counter, talking to him. This would be their second official date. They would meet in the Saracen's Head and have a drink and then he said they would go to a restaurant. A restaurant. She shivered at the thought. Looking at a menu, making a choice, not worrying about the cost – even if she had to pay herself. Apart from the times Doreen took them out as a family, she'd never been to a restaurant before, not even on a date. She didn't count going out for a Wimpy with Roger.

Gene was already in the Saracen's. The saloon was full of people in groups, laughing, shouting. There was the early evening smell of perfume and spirits. Gene was leaning against the bar, alone, a glass of beer in front of him. He was studying the beer. He was wearing his sheepskin coat and she could see underneath a light grey sweater she had admired in the shop. That pleased her. She wove her way through the crowd and he looked up as she approached. He smiled that wonderful smile. It reassured her. It was going to be all right.

'Do you want a drink?' he said.

'No, let's get going,' she said.

He swallowed some of his beer and pushed the glass away. 'Right. Let's go.'

They walked through the High Street. This was Roger's night class night so she felt free. 'Can I link arms with you?' she said.

'Cynthia's not going to jump out from behind a bollard,' he said. 'Go on.'

Holding his arm, feeling the soft suede of the sheepskin, she felt proud to be with the most exciting man in Chelmsford. They walked over the river, past the Regent. There was a short queue. She hesitated, looking at the film title.

'You don't want to go to the pictures, do you?' he said.

It was *The Greatest Story Ever Told*. 'I don't think so,' she said.

'Good,' he said. 'I've been looking forward to talking to you.'

'Really?'

'Yes.' He took hold of the hand tucked through his arm and stroked it. 'I like that dress by the way.'

Angie's heart soared, he'd noticed and he liked it. But now they were turning into Baddow Road and walking towards the Long Bar. Angie shrank against Gene. A mod so close to a rockers' hang out!

'What's the problem?' Gene asked.

She shook her head and whispered, 'They're rockers. I'm a mod. Let's cross the road.'

'They've got some nice bikes there,' Gene said mildly, looking at the array of machines parked outside. 'All right, all right, we'll cross the road. But you're with me. You don't look like a mod, you look like a young stylish woman out for the evening with her stylish companion.'

'I am wearing a suede coat,' she murmured. 'That makes me stick out rather.'

He drew her close to him.

They crossed the road and turned into the Chinese restaurant. The place was quite dark and completely empty. She was pleased about that. What if she was expected to use chopsticks? This meal would be humiliating enough without half of Chelmsford there to see.

As if he had read her mind Gene murmured, 'Don't look so worried. You won't have to use chopsticks. Unless you want to.'

They were seated at a table in the corner, under the glow of a small wall lamp with a pink shade. Angie looked round at the paintings on the wall. Each one featured thin and wispy birds with Chinese writing. It was all so strange.

'Cheer up,' he whispered. 'We're here to have a good time. Look – you've got a knife and fork!'

She smiled, but when the waiter handed them each a menu she looked at in dismay. There was only one thing she recognised, Chow Mein, because she'd had Vesta Chow Mein at Carol's once. She hadn't really liked it.

She looked up at him. 'I don't know what any of this is.'

'Shall I order a selection?' he said. 'Then you can just taste things and eat what you want and don't eat the rest.'

He called the waiter and pointed to a hundred things on the menu it seemed. He ordered a bottle of white wine. But when the wine came she discovered that she didn't like it.

A stream of dishes appeared on the table and there was a lovely smell. There was chicken and beef and mushrooms and rice and something with peas and carrots. She was hungry, she realised, and she hoped it would taste nice. She tried some chicken. It was soft and tender in her mouth. She took a little more. She added some rice and a couple of peas. Yes. It was very, very nice. Now she had to be careful not to eat too quickly. She was so hungry, but she would look like a pig.

Gene was drinking the wine. She looked at her glass, still there, still mocking her for her lack of sophistication. She picked it up and took a sip. If she had a mouthful of food it didn't taste too awful. If you thought of it like vinegar on fish and chips it wasn't really that bad at all.

She looked over at him and smiled. He smiled back. He picked up his glass. 'Cheers,' he said. They clinked glasses. 'Enjoying yourself?' he said. She nodded. 'Next time we'll go up West. I know a nice place near Leicester Square.' He winked at her. 'You'll like it.'

Her stomach clenched. He was talking about another date. In London. 'Don't forget I'm at work till half past five, six sometimes. And I have to get up at seven.'

'Or we could go to the dog track in Romford. You like Romford, don't you?'

'Still too far.'

'Some other time. How is work, anyway?' he said.

She raised her eyebrows. 'All right.'

'What exactly is it you do?'

She looked at her plate. There was so much more to eat.

'If you have a pause it makes the food last longer,' he said.

She balanced her fork at the edge of her plate. She took a sip of wine and she talked. She talked about her job, about the delicate pieces of wire and ceramic that seemed so simple but were vital to so much equipment. She talked about music, dancing at the Corn Exchange, the local group she liked, Mark Shelley and the Deans for their rock and roll excitement, the Four Tops for the pain and longing in their songs. She drank more wine and she found herself talking about clothes, her course, the lovely new sewing machine, her dreams of working in fashion. 'My dad just won a bit on the pools,' she said casually. She even talked about her own designs. He seemed interested. He asked her about them, about fabrics and cut. He said he would like to see them. He was impressed she'd made her dress for this evening. She revelled in his praise.

He reached out and touched the collar. 'This is really good tailoring,' he said. 'Shame you don't make men's clothes. I'd sell them in the shop.'

She laughed. She was having the best time of her life.

Dishes were appearing like magic. 'You dip the meat into the sauce,' he said.

She did so. 'It's like toffee apples,' she said.

He laughed. 'You're funny.'

'Funny ha ha, or funny peculiar?' she said.

'Funny sweet. I like you.'

'That's helpful,' Angie said, 'otherwise this would be a bit strange.'

'And I hope you like me.'

'I don't think you need ask me that,' she said. 'It's written all over my face, isn't it?'

'I don't know. You're a bit of a dark horse.'

'Am I?' She was pleased. 'So are you,' she said.

'Me? No. I'm an open book.'

'All right. How old are you, actually?'

'Actually, I'm twenty-six.'

She didn't know if she believed him.

'And how old are you?'

'Not old enough to get married.' You had to be twenty-one to get married, unless your parents gave their permission.

'What would your mum say? If we wanted to get married.'

Angie's eyes widened. 'What . . . ?' She coughed. 'She'd say what she always says – ask your dad. And he'd say no. It doesn't matter what it is.'

'I can wait a couple of years,' he said. 'I'm a very patient man. Shall we get some more wine?'

The bottle was empty. They had drunk it all!

'I don't mind,' she said. 'I'm probably drunk already.'

'Want some banana fritters?'

'I don't really like bananas.'

'Try some.'

The bananas would take ten minutes, the waiter told them.

A fresh bottle of wine came sooner. Gene poured wine into her glass.

'Did you really change your name?' Angie said.

'Yes, but that was ages ago.' He took out a packet of cigarettes and offered it to her. She shook her head. He lit a cigarette and inhaled. 'A mate of mine started it, because I wore good clothes. He said I looked Italian.'

'Honestly?' she said, although she didn't really know what an Italian might look like. 'Does anyone call you Gerald?'

'Gerry,' he said. He pulled the ash-tray towards him. 'Some people call me Gerry. My family, my dear old mum, my nan. A couple of aunties.'

She liked the idea that he had family, a grandmother, aunties. It made him seem safer. It answered Doreen's concerns.

'What does Cynthia call you?'

'That depends what mood she's in.' He tapped his cigarette on the side of the ash-tray. 'Usually Gerald or Fuck-face, excuse the language.'

'Does she really? That would be horrible. I'd hate it if anyone called me Gerald.'

'Ha ha, yes,' he said. 'It isn't very nice. That's why we're getting a divorce. The only problem ...' He stubbed out his cigarette, crushing it into the glass of the ash-tray.

'Here we go,' Angie said. 'The only problem is you love her really.'

'No, I wasn't going to say that at all.' He took another cigarette from the packet and lit it. 'No, the problem is she's a partner in the Boutique. Well, boutiques. We've got another one in Enfield. It's probably going to be more dif-ficult to end that situation than to end the marriage. That's what my brief says, anyway.'

So he had a lawyer. He had talked about divorce. Perhaps he was free.

'Why did you marry her, if you don't love her?'

'I did love her once.' He tapped his cigarette against the ash tray. 'I'm not a monster. Love changes. It can go either way. It can get better or it can get worse. And here we are.'

The waiter arrived with the banana fritters.

She picked up her spoon and cut through the batter. She lifted the fritter to her mouth.

'Don't eat them yet!' he shouted.

The banana seared her lips.

'They'll be too hot . . .'

She laid her spoon down. 'Before we go any further,' Angie said seriously, 'knowing my mum and dad, and there is always Roger, perhaps we shouldn't tell anyone about our . . .' She waved her hand between them.

'Relationship?'

He thought they were having a relationship! 'Well, yes. Perhaps we shouldn't talk about our . . . relationship.' In fact it was Doreen she was most worried about, what Doreen thought about his age and his marriage, and who he might really be. 'I'll obviously tell Carol, because she's my best friend and I tell her everything. But otherwise . . .'

'Mum's the word,' he said.

She felt confident now. 'When did you decide that your marriage had gone the wrong way?'

'On the honeymoon.' He laughed.

'You didn't.'

'No.' He blew a plume of smoke in the air. 'We got on well for a couple of years. We both liked clothes. We were very modern. We were modernists. Did I tell you I used to have a scooter? Then I was a naughty boy and she didn't like that.'

'What do you mean, "naughty boy"?'

'There was a girl in the shop. It was stupid.'

'You were stupid, you mean.'

He looked at her. 'Yes, I was. Anyway, Cynthia gave me an ultimatum and I pulled my socks up.'

'The socks you sell in the shop?'

He laughed. 'Exactly, I pulled up the socks and the sweaters and the shirts, and we made it work for quite a while. Then it was her turn.'

'What does that mean?'

'She had a thing with one of the reps.' He shook his head. 'They had a dirty weekend in Margate. Why am I telling you all this?'

'Because I asked you and because you said we were having a relationship.'

'Oh my god, did I?'

'Shut up! Yes, you did.'

'You're right, I did. I would like a relationship with you. Very much. I like your style. Let's drink to that!' They raised their glasses. 'I think the banana should have cooled down now.'

She tasted it. 'It's nice,' she said. She ate it quickly and ran her finger round the plate and licked off the sauce.

He called the waiter and took out his roll of notes. She couldn't stop looking as he peeled off two ten pound notes. She thought what she could have bought with that. She shook herself. She didn't have to think like that anymore.

'Come on,' he said. He shepherded her out of the restaurant. 'We'll get a cab.' The word 'cab' made her shiver with pleasure. Everyone else in Chelmsford said 'taxi'.

They walked through the town, arm-in-arm. She saw one or two people from the Orpheus, Don and Mick Flynn, no one who really knew Roger. Not that she cared, at this point. It couldn't last with Roger. He was a boy. Tonight she was with a man, a real man, a solid man who had strong hands and who, she knew had lived a life, though she also knew she had drunk a lot of wine.

He came in the taxi with her, but she asked the driver to stop at the end of the Crescent. Gene put his arm round her and pulled her to him. He kissed her softly. 'Mmm, you taste nice,' he said.

'That will be the bananas,' she whispered. She touched his sweater. 'You feel nice,' she said.

'We'll do this again, won't we?' he murmured.

'Yes,' she said, sensing the wine again. 'Yes, we will.'

'OK. Next week we'll do something special, like I said. Come into the shop and we'll sort it out. You're really something, you know?'

'Am I?' she said.

'Yes. And you'd better go now, or I'll do something that I'll regret. And so will the driver.'

'He'd probably enjoy it,' she said.

'Cheeky.'

She got out of the car and waited while the taxi did a cumbersome turn and disappeared into Sperry Drive. She was still smiling from the conversation and the meal and the wine.

She crept into the kitchen. Doreen was at the table painting her fingernails. She looked up. 'Well, I was going to ask if you'd had a nice evening, but given you look like the cat that got the cream, I already know. So, where've you been?'

'Oh, oh, nowhere.'

'With Roger?'

'No. A . . . a group of us. We went to the Chinese restaurant in Baddow Road.'

'Good food?'

'I had banana fritters.'

'I've never had those.'

'They were delicious. But I think I'm a bit drunk.'

'Well, don't let Dad see you. As long as you had a good time.'

'I did! What did you do?'

'Nothing. I watched some boring telly and Mum and I had a cup of tea. The highlight was when I threw out that chair in my bedroom, and Mum and I threw out the armchairs and that tatty old rug in the front room. We don't need them now, we're going to get some new ones. We were looking in the catalogue. And now I'm painting my nails. A fantastic evening.' She held out her hands. 'What do you think of this shade? Should I do my toenails too?'

'Yes,' Angie said. 'It looks very nice.'

'Oh, why is my life so boring?' Doreen said. 'All this money isn't doing me any good.'

'You're getting your car.'

'Yes. Yes. And it's going to be fab. I'm picking it up next week, they say.'

'Can I drive it?'

'Angie! You can buy your own now.'

CHAPTER 14

DOREEN WAS EXCITED. THE SHOWROOM HAD rung and said the car would be ready for collection at ten on Tuesday. Finally the day was here. She had taken time off work, specially.

She had sold the Hillman for thirty pounds to a girl who worked in the make-up department. The girl and her dad had picked up the car the week before. She had finalised all the insurance issues in her dinner hour, using the thirty pounds to pay the extra premium for the new car.

She was ready.

She dressed carefully. She selected her black Sloppy Joe and her pink capri pants, and neat lace-up shoes. She wanted to look like an elegant and sophisticated woman when she opened the door and sat in the driver's seat.

When she came down to the kitchen, her mum and dad were there, getting ready to go to London. Today was the day of the interview for the ten pound passage to Australia, to find out if they were eligible. Doreen had said she and

Angie would go on another day. She was buying time for Angie, and maybe for herself she realised.

Her mum stood in front of the mirror on the door of the broom cupboard, fretting with her hair. The perm hadn't achieved the effect she had hoped for.

'Mum, it was never going to make you look twenty-six again,' Doreen said. 'You look great. Just the sort of person Australia wants.'

'I think my haircut makes me look twenty-five,' her dad said. 'But then, I've stuck to the people I know, not tried fancy new establishments.' He pulled his knitted waistcoat straight and put on the jacket of his new suit. It was tweed. He looked almost like a country gentleman.

Doreen checked her watch. She was cutting it fine if she wanted to catch the forty-five bus. She pulled on her coat and, wishing them both the best of luck, left the house. She walked briskly around the Crescent and turned into Warwick Avenue. As she was reaching the top of the rise she could see the bus trundling down Greenway Road. She began to run up the incline. This was hopeless. And she was getting a stitch. She waved her hand as she limped across the road. The bus stopped. It wouldn't wait, she was sure, she was going to miss it. She would be late. But for goodness' sake, she told herself, they're not going to sell the car to anyone else. She slowed down, bending over, feeling her side.

But the bus was still waiting at the stop, the engine knocking its calm, regular rhythm. She couldn't think why it didn't go.

Then she saw Cliff Evans hanging half on, half off the bus, his black leather coat flapping in the wind. Cliff Evans. What was he up to? She really didn't want to get mixed up with him. But he was keeping the bus from moving. As she got closer she could hear the conductor shouting, 'Get inside! No standing on the platform!'

As she climbed on to the bus Cliff grinned at her. 'I thought you were trying to miss it, for a moment.'

'If I'd known it was you holding it here, I would have.' They grinned at each other. She liked this kind of chat. She hardly even knew him, but straight away they were teasing each other. Perhaps it was something to do with the fact they lived five doors apart. They knew each other.

'Too late now. You're on.'

The conductor shouted again, 'No standing on the platform!'

'Coming up top?'

'Yes. Not with you!' she added, looking at his expression.

He loped up the stairs. She followed him and as she reached the top, he pulled her sleeve and she toppled onto the seat beside him at the back of the bus. 'I saved you a place,' he said.

'Thanks.'

He put one foot up on the seat in front. His shoes were long and pointed. 'Where are you going, looking so snazzy?' he said.

It was the coat, the whiteness of it always made an impact. 'Somewhere where snazziness is the order of the day.' She glanced at his dark outfit, the leather coat, the dark suit, the grey button-down shirt. 'Where are you off to, in that smart tie?'

He looked down at the thin strip of black leather. 'I've got some business to do.' He took out a packet of cigarettes. 'Work. A place where wearing a tie is always the order of the day.'

'Really?' she said.

'You should drop by sometime. We could be snazzy together. Come with me now, I've got to arrange some flowers. You could get lucky.'

'No, thanks, I've got places to go. And no thanks, I don't smoke Embassy. One to the Railway Station, please,' she said to the conductor and smiled.

Cliff struck a match and lit a cigarette. 'Let me guess, you're taking the train to hit the flesh pots of Braintree. Yeah, the cathedral please.' He took his ticket. 'I know, hot rod driving in Hatfield Peverel.'

'In this outfit?' She opened her coat slightly. 'Well, clever clogs, you're almost right. If you must know, I'm about to buy a new car.'

'Good for you. Well, you're wearing the right clothes.' He paused. 'That's a nice sweater.'

'Oh this,' she said carelessly.

'I like a girl in mohair.'

'Well, I hope she likes you. It's my stop. Gotta go.' She stood up, tying her belt round her waist.

'Well . . .' He yawned, trying to look cool, she thought. 'Have a nice time looking snazzy in your new car.'

She smiled. 'I will.' The bus was slowing down. She slid her handbag over her arm.

'Perhaps you'll give me a ride sometime.'

She looked at him, up the stairwell. 'Perhaps I will.'

She watched the bus sail down Duke Street. He was a funny bloke. But he was a lot more attractive than he had been at school. He had a sort of twinkle in his eye, and a cool way of looking at you, that was really nice. *You go for ages without any love-life at all*, she thought, *and then two blokes turn up at the same time*. If it hadn't been for Gene she might have had serious thoughts about Cliff. But Gene came first. She was satisfied with him. He was so different, so intriguing.

The car was parked outside the showroom and it made her heart sing – a pale blue Triumph Spitfire, a convertible, a soft top. The bonnet gleamed in the watery sunshine. The salesman came out of his office to greet her. There were two more forms that needed her signature, she wrote a large cheque and then the car was hers.

She slid into the low seat and for a moment sat in the parked car and enjoyed the smell of the new leather seats, the feel of the steering wheel, and the quiet beneath the soft roof. She put the key into the ignition and turned on the engine. The car purred into life and she put it in gear and drove away. Half way along Victoria Road she stopped and put down the roof. She wrapped a scarf round her head and then set off again. She made for the A12 and drove up to Hatfield Peverel. The car was neat and speedy and the steering was a dream.

She drove back the same way, through Springfield, past the prison, and turned right into town. She could show the car to Harry. She pulled up outside the barber's. She jumped out of the car and peered through the shop window. It looked busy. Harry was cutting someone's hair. Three people were sitting waiting in chairs. Rose, Harry's assistant, was handing out cups of something. Doreen waved and walked along the street.

'Hello!' Gene said as Doreen stepped into the boutique. 'I was just thinking about you.'

'Oh really? Well, I was thinking about you.'

'Oh yeah?'

'And your comments on the kind of car I should drive.'

He frowned. She could tell he didn't remember. 'God, you're hopeless,' she said. 'You said you thought I should drive a sports car.'

'Did I? Well I think you should.'

'Well now I do. It's parked just down the road.' He moved over to the door and she pointed out the car.

'Very nice,' he said. 'You'll have to take me for a spin. In the meantime, the kettle's on. Want a cuppa?'

'Oh, all right,' she sighed, but she was pleased. 'Have you got any biscuits?'

'Biscuits, blimey! All I said was "Do you want a cup of tea?"'

'Come on,' she said. 'We both know a cup of tea is pointless without biscuits.'

He looked at her. 'I suppose we do. Trouble is, I've run out.'

'Well, that's hopeless,' she said.

'I'll nip out to get some,' he said. 'You'd better stay here and keep an eye on the shop.'

'What do I do if someone comes in?'

'Sell them something.'

'All right, but make sure the biscuits have got chocolate on. Get some Penguins or something.'

'You don't want much, do you!' he said, but he was grinning.

'Ooh, you don't know the half of what I want,' she said. She wasn't sure she did either, but they both laughed.

He was only gone five minutes. 'Sorry, they didn't have any chocolate. Why are you smiling?'

'I sold two shirts and a belt.'

'Bloody hell,' he said. 'How did you do that?'

'Well, I smiled and said they'd look good and the lad bought them.'

'Bloody hell,' he repeated. 'You don't want a job, do you?'

'Why? What are you offering?'

'I dunno. Nine quid a week?'

'And commission?'

'Blimey. You don't mess about, do you?'

She shook her head. She didn't need a job, she liked working in Bolingbroke's. Now they had the money she didn't need a job at all. But it didn't hurt to show him how a real professional did the job. Two mods came in and she walked over to them. 'Hello boys. What you after today? We've got some new trousers in that people seem to like. I just sold a pair actually.' She took the trousers off the rail. They were stylish, iridescent with a narrow cuff. 'See, they tell me these are very big in London, but I think they're going to look better in Chelmsford! What size are you? These should be all right.' The boys looked at the trousers, looked at each other, then one of them sagely nodded his head. 'Yeah, I'll take them.'

'Bring them back if they don't fit, mind, and we'll replace them. Gene, can you do the business?'

When the boys had paid and left, he laughed. 'No honestly, do you want a job?'

'Thanks, but no thanks. I'm quite satisfied where I am,' she said.

'That's right – bridal wear. You know, my wife used to sell wedding dresses. You certainly earn your money there.'

'Yeah, people think it's like shooting fish in a barrel – they're getting married, and you've got the dresses – but it's not that easy. Still, I like it. Where does your wife work now?'

'Well, let's be clear, she's almost not my wife now, we're getting a divorce.'

'Oh yeah?'

'Yeah. But it's fair to say she runs the other boutique we've got. It's just business.'

'Business,' she said slowly. 'Well, I'd better be off.'

'What about that cup of tea?'

'Another day, I just came to see how you're getting on.'

'All the better for seeing you,' he said.

'And I notice you bought malted milk. I could never work somewhere with malted milk biscuits.'

'Someone else said that to me recently,' he said.

'There you are. Listen to the people.' She looked round the shop. 'You've got some nice stuff here, Gene.'

'Call me Gerry,' he said. 'Special people call me Gerry.'

She laughed. 'But I think you should display it better.'

'Really?'

'Yeah. Move that rail under the spotlight there. And that spotlight in the corner isn't shining on anything. And get some more shelves for the sweaters, what are they? Cashmere? Show them off!'

'You sure you don't want the job?'

'No thanks. But I'll keep it in mind.' She left the shop and walked back to her car. He was big, he was friendly, he had a nice smile. But why was he calling himself Gene when his name was Gerry? Idiot.

CHAPTER 15

FOR MONTHS ANGIE HAD BEEN APPLYING for jobs, trying to find something that would pay her enough to leave English Electric and allow her to work in the fashion industry. So far she hadn't received a single offer of an interview, but she persevered, hovering in Johnsons, the newsagents, to scan the newspaper ads, occasionally dropping into the Employment Agency in Duke Street, sending off her letters of application with their stamped addressed envelopes for a reply. Now of course, she didn't have to worry about the level of wages, but still the right job eluded her grasp.

As she walked towards the bus stop Angie saw a figure she recognised. It was Miss Darling her old needlework teacher. Memories of those wonderful classes and all Miss Darling's encouragement came back and Angie smiled with delight, then cringed inside with embarrassment that she was going to have to confess she was working at English Electric.

Miss Darling smiled broadly, 'Angela! How nice to see you! What are you doing these days?'

Angie mumbled the words 'I'm at English Electric' and a fleeting look of disappointment passed across Miss Darling's face. 'But I'm still doing an evening class in fashion design,' Angie added almost desperately.

'Oh, I am pleased,' Miss Darling said. 'I always enjoyed teaching, but I have to say some of my happiest memories are of standing in one of the ateliers, watching one of my creations come to life. I always thought you were someone who could do that too.'

Angie's face coloured with pleasure. 'I do look for jobs in fashion,' she said, 'I just can't find one that I really want, or that really wants me.'

Miss Darling patted her hand and said, 'Don't be discouraged. The job for you is out there somewhere. In fact, only the other day I saw something that might be just the thing. Why don't I send it over to you?'

'Oh, Miss Darling, thank you. That would be fantastic.'

The next day a smooth, square envelope covered in large flowery writing was waiting for Angie at home. It was a letter from Miss Darling. It contained a small advertisement for a job in London at a College of Art. It was a technician's job 'but it might be interesting,' Miss Darling wrote. 'The college has a fashion department attached.'

Angie smiled. She couldn't imagine anyone in an art college would want her as a technician but she wrote an application and enclosed the SAE they asked for. She posted the letter with the others on the way to work, getting off the bus a stop early to catch the first post. The detour only made her a couple of minutes late.

Three days later she got to work, hung her suede on the hook, put on her white coat and sat at her bench. She was bending over a small ceramic shape, manoeuvring pieces of copper wire with a tiny pair of pliers, when Graham came and stood behind her.

'Go away,' she said. 'You're in my light.'

'I've got something to say.'

The tone of his voice made her stop. She put down the pliers and turned round in her seat.

'Look, I don't want to lose you,' he began.

Angie's eyes widened. 'Why? Have you got to? Are you giving me the sack?' Her heart was racing.

'No, of course I'm not giving you the sack. You're the best worker we've got. The best we've ever had, probably. That's why I don't want to lose you. But there's a job going, over in Section F. It's management. It's a job I think you could do. And personnel think you could do it too.'

'I don't know what you mean,' she said.

'You should go for it. There will be some paperwork. You'd be in charge of a small team. It will be like keeping an eye on four versions of Mandy. But it would mean we wouldn't see you. It's in another building.'

Angie looked at him. She looked at Mandy noting down with a pencil the measurements of the ceramic she was working on, the tip of her tongue visible as she concentrated.

'It would be more money, obviously,' Graham said.

'Obviously,' Angie said.

'You don't have to make up your mind till next week.' Graham had his hands in the pockets of his white overall. He looked so serious. She felt sad, a scraping inside her stomach. This was the time for a real decision. This was the offer of a big job, with real responsibility. If she took this it would take her down a different path, away from her dream. But it would mean more money, more respect. It was serious. But it wasn't fashion.

When she came in from work the letter was there, lying on the seat of the telephone table. She looked at the envelope. She recognised her own handwriting. A reply to one of her job applications. Which one was it this time? It didn't really matter. It would be negative. She knew what it would say:

Dear Miss Smith
Thank you for your application to work with us.
Unfortunately,
  a) you are too young
  b) you are too old
  c) you don't have the right qualifications

d) you have the wrong qualifications

*e) you are too late, you would have been perfect,
    but the job's gone*

She opened the letter. Even though it wasn't personal, it was always a bit depressing, always another person saying, 'You haven't got a chance of a job in fashion.'

It was a small piece of off-white paper. She glanced at the heading. Hornsey. She didn't even know where Hornsey was. She read the letter.

'Oh my god, oh my god!' she said. 'Oh my god.' It was the offer of an interview. Her heart soared. Someone had liked what she had to say. She tried to remember what she could about this place. It was an art school but with a fashion department. Fashion.

Angie passed the whole long weekend in a state of high emotion, one minute thrilled at the thought of the London interview, the next filled with anxiety about the English Electric promotion.

She hadn't said anything to the family about the English Electric offer. She knew what they would say. Her mum would be pleased it was management. If her dad was drunk he wouldn't even know what she was talking about, otherwise he'd probably say, 'Ideas above your station.' Doreen would say, 'You should do it. You should be earning more.'

She hadn't even mentioned the job interview in Hornsey. There was no point. Everyone would be so negative. 'London! Work in London! Who do you think you are! You call that a wage!?' her dad would say. 'Just because I've won this money, doesn't mean you can't still do an honest day's work for an honest day's pay. That's how I brought you up, pools win or no pools win.' The decisions and choices bubbled inside her. She didn't know what to do. She liked the idea of turning down a managerial job for the sake of fashion, but she knew there were consequences, not least how upset her mum would be. Perhaps she could take the English Electric job and then leave if she was offered the London job. No, her mum would be appalled. Did she have a hope of getting a proper job in fashion? This was just an interview, and even if she got the job it was just to be a technician. She'd be organising rooms, sorting out supplies, ensuring things worked. But it was the nearest she'd got, and it was London, at a fashion school. She'd be moving in the right circles, working in the right place.

But now it was Bank Holiday Monday and tonight she wasn't going to think about it. Tonight she was going out with Gene. Although first she had to prepare the tea for her mum and dad. She wiped up the plates on the draining board, before she started on the potatoes. She was humming, planning her outfit for the evening. She was going to dazzle Gene by wearing something she had made.

Gene had said he liked the green dress, but she wondered about going a little brighter, her royal blue top with the fitted sleeves, maybe, or the red dress she had made for Doreen. The red dress would make him look. A small smile played on her lips. He was coming back from London early. Just for her. She might try asking him about the job offer. She wondered what he would say. Would he say, no, don't take the factory job? Would he say, take a job in London and I'll close the boutique and we'll leave Chelmsford behind us? Would he say, marry me? Would that defeat the whole object?

There was a knock on the back door. She started. Who could it be?

It was Roger. Angie stared at him, 'What are you doing here?'

He looked at her with a long face. Angie's eyes widened. His olive-green parka, his pride and joy, was torn. And where there were usually small stains, badges of pride from his work as a mechanic, now there were large dark patches all over, that looked like oil or even blood.

'What's happened to you?' she said.

He stepped into the kitchen, looking anxiously round the room. 'Is anyone here?'

'No, my mum's gone to Great Baddow to see my auntie. And Doreen's out in the car somewhere.'

'Where's your dad?'

'Who knows? He's not here anyway.'

'Can I have something to eat?' Roger said.

'Well . . . yes.' He could have a quick slice of toast.

'I haven't eaten for two days.'

'You were meant to be in Clacton having a good time.' She went to the sink and filled the kettle.

'I was in Clacton. Well, once we got there. The scooter conked out just outside Colchester, in Elmstead Market or somewhere. A nut came off the fly-wheel. I had to push it to a garage. Then after I'd paid for that I lost my wallet with my last three quid in it. I dunno where it went. It must have come out of my pocket when we were heading off again.'

'Oh Roger!' Angie squeezed her eyes shut with frustration.

'So we couldn't afford anywhere to stay – Ron forgot to bring any money, bloody Ron, and Dave's mum had taken his pay-packet. So we couldn't afford the camp site Dave had said we were going to, and we had to sleep in a field. And it took us about an hour to get the tent up. It was Ron's dad's from the war. And the tent had a hole in, and it rained. Then we had to get up and out of there at the crack of dawn in case the farmer came, because we didn't have the money to pay him.' He slumped into a chair. 'So we went down on the beach, just looking around, having a laugh, no rockers or anything, it was all great, and then the bloody farmer turns up in his wellingtons – on the beach! – belly-aching about how much we owe him and he grabs me – the others ran off of course – and then he beats me up. And there was this big patch of oil on the sand and he threw me into it.' He looked astonished as if he still couldn't believe it. 'And I'm starving.'

Angie was doing rapid calculations. She could catch a later bus. She'd be a bit late, but he'd wait, surely. There was a tin of beans in the pantry that was supposed to be for tea tomorrow, but she would think about that later. And a couple of slices of bread wouldn't be too bad. She just wouldn't have any sandwiches to take to work in the morning. She shook her head. This pools win didn't seem to be making much difference in the kitchen. Her mum still didn't have enough money to keep the pantry stocked. 'There's no need to waste money on food,' her dad said, regularly, 'just because I've won the pools. We didn't starve before, you don't need more housekeeping.'

'Take your coat off,' Angie said.

'I'm cold,' he said.

'You can't sit there in that. It's soaking wet. And filthy. I'll get you a jumper.' She ran upstairs. In her mum and dad's room she opened the drawers of the dressing table. There was nothing useful. Her dad only had one cardigan and it wasn't here. He must be wearing it. In her room was her meagre collection of thin Marks and Spencer's cardigans. They weren't warm enough or big enough. She went into Doreen's room. And there was her big Sloppy Joe, it was black mohair, soft and warm.

Downstairs Roger was sitting at the kitchen table. He had taken off his parka which lay in a heap on the floor beside him. He was wearing his Christmas jumper, the one she'd bought from the Boutique. There were stains on that too.

He followed her gaze. 'Yeah, this got a lot of muck on it as well. Sorry about that. But you never liked it, did you?'

'That's not the point!' she said stiffly. 'Here.' She thrust Doreen's sweater at him.

'I can't wear this, it's a girl's jumper.'

'I know that, and you know that, but no one else is here and no one else will know. Put it on. It'll keep you warm.'

Reluctantly he pulled it over his head. 'How do I look?' he said, attempting a joke.

'You look very cuddly,' she said, surprising herself. She put her arms round him. 'Phew, you stink.'

'It was a pig farm.'

'Oh God.'

Roger laid his head on the table and closed his eyes. Angie got the clothes horse from under the stairs in the hall, propped it round the boiler and draped the parka across it.

She clattered through the cutlery drawer and eventually found the tin opener. She looked at the tin of beans. Should she really do it? He looked so sorry for himself. A wave of tenderness came over her. Oh Roger. He was such a nice chap. He was so kind, and thoughtful. He tried so hard. He wanted to give her the world. And she enjoyed seeing him. He even made her laugh sometimes, with his silly jokes. That's why she was reluctant to end it. She knew it was also because he was safe. He would never be like her dad. Roger was dependable, he'd never let her down. But he also drove her mad, he was so . . . so boring sometimes. The last thing you could say about him was that he was exciting. He was the complete opposite of Gene. Would she really leave him for Gene? Oh, she wasn't sure. She had so many decisions to make. Her head was spinning. She looked over at Roger, slumped over the table. Of course she would feed him, she would take care of him. And then she would send him on his way. She banged the old metal opener into the lid of the tin and sawed her way round it. She eased up the jagged edges and emptied the contents into a saucepan. She found the matches, and lit the hob and the grill. It was all taking so much time. With two slices of Wonderloaf on the tray under the grill and the saucepan of beans on the hob, she put two spoonfuls of tea into the pot, then reached for a plate and two cups from the cupboard.

She put a cup of tea in front of him.

'Thanks,' he murmured. He was half asleep.

'You're too warm now, aren't you?' she said.

'I'm just nice,' he said and grinned.

'Wash your hands,' she said.

As he stood at the sink, she put marge on the toast and piled the beans on top. She handed him a towel and pushed him by the fluffy shoulder back into his chair. She put the plate and a knife and fork in front of him then sat down opposite him, with her own cup of tea, and watched as he cut into the bread. He put a mouthful of beans and toast into his mouth. Then another. He was silent as he chewed. Then he said, 'This is like caviar.'

'When have you ever had caviar?'

'Never. But this is the best meal I've ever had.' He took a mouthful of tea. 'Honestly, I was starving. All day yesterday, we couldn't even afford a bag of chips. This is fantastic.' He put another heap of beans onto his fork. 'I love you, Angie.'

'Do you?' she said. *Oh Roger,* she thought, *not now.*

'Do you mind if I . . . ?' He held up his finger.

'Oh, go on,' she said.

He wiped his finger round the plate, then sucked off the sauce. 'Ahh.' He sat back in his chair.

Angie looked at her watch. 'You can't stay,' she said, an ache of guilt in her stomach. 'I've got a lot to do. I've got to finish peeling these potatoes before I go out.'

'You're going out tonight?'

'With Carol,' she said quickly. 'I've made the arrangement. You're not meant to be here. You're meant to be in Clacton.'

'But it was raining!'

'I'm not a weather forecaster. I didn't know what the weather in Clacton was going to be like.'

'Carol won't care if you're late, will she?'

'She'll be hanging round the bus stop. It's not fair.' He looked so miserable. 'You can drink your tea while I peel the potatoes.'

'I could peel them, if you like,' he offered. 'My mum says I'm the best at peeling potatoes.'

She sighed. 'Yeah, I bet you are.'

'I'm good at scraping carrots too,' he went on.

She peeled the potatoes before they spoke again. He was stifling a yawn.

'You're tired,' she said. 'You should go home. You need a good night's sleep.'

'I don't mind if I do,' he said in a silly Goons' voice. He stood up.

'Here.' She hauled the parka off the clothes-horse. 'It's almost dry.'

'God, it's filthy,' he said. He was putting it on.

'Excuse me, I need the jumper back.'

He took off his parka and pulled off the jumper. As she took it from him she gasped. There was a sheen on the front that looked horribly like an oil stain, and it reeked of something like manure. She looked up at Roger. 'This is Reen's,' she whispered. 'She's going to kill me.'

CHAPTER 16

GENE WAS SITTING IN THE SALOON bar of the Golden Fleece. It was quiet tonight, the end of the Easter weekend. None of the rowdy out of town kids, or the local mod boys were here. This was good. They must all be at home asleep in bed ready to get up for the next day of their apprenticeships in Marconi's or Hoffmann's or English Electric. Then they'd be ready with oozing pay packets to spend in the boutique next Saturday. He'd done his homework before he decided to take a chance on the lease of the new shop. Chelmsford was a successful town with a lot of youngsters who wanted to wear the latest fashions. And it was far enough away from London that he wouldn't be bothered by any of the complications with Cynthia.

He should have stayed in London tonight, sorted out some new deliveries, but Angie had said she'd meet him. He liked Angie. He liked her a lot. She was smart and funny and pretty and she had a great body – not that he'd ever seen it naked. Not yet. But she made being in Chelmsford a real pleasure.

He took a mouthful of beer. He didn't know why he'd bought it. He'd have preferred a gin and tonic, but he'd learned that in Chelmsford that marked you out as an in-comer, an outsider, a stranger, and he wanted to be accepted as a Londoner with style, but also one of them. He wiped his mouth with the back of his hand. He looked at his watch. Angie had said she'd be here at eight, eight thirty at the latest. It was already nine o'clock. She wasn't coming, obviously. He needn't have come down after all. He thought about the narrow camp bed in the back room of the shop. It would be an uncomfortable night. He wondered if he should get a room. The Saracen's Head had rooms. The County Hotel, possibly. On the other hand, he could get the last train home. And then almost immediately he'd have to catch an early train to get back here. Would be cheaper than a hotel though. He took another mouthful of beer.

The door of the bar opened and he looked up. It was an angel in high heels and a belted white coat. Well, well, he really was a lucky guy. He might not see Angie tonight, but Doreen was here, and she was just as good. She was sharper, pushier than Angie, but that wasn't bad, kept him on his toes. She was another one of his favourite reasons for being in Chelmsford. Doreen was gazing around the bar as if she was looking for someone she was supposed to be meeting, but he knew that look. It was the look of someone who needed a person to talk to.

He lifted his hand and smiled as if he was the person she was here to meet. Her brief smile of relief showed him he was right.

He stood up as she approached. She looked gorgeous. She looked like Cynthia had looked in the early days before he had got used to her; smiling, soft, willing. 'What will you have?'

'I dunno. A Bacardi and Coke.'

'Coming right up. Sit down.'

She sank down onto the bench seat and unbelted her coat. As he brought back her drink, and a whisky for himself, he took in her tight purple V-necked sweater that showed the beginning of her breasts and the tight blue skirt which had ridden up, showing her thighs.

He sat down. 'So, what's a lovely girl like you doing in a pub like this?'

She smiled, 'Hoping to meet a man like you.'

'Well, you're in luck,' he said, 'because I'm here and I'm celebrating.'

'Oh really?' She laughed. 'What are we celebrating?'

'The fact we're here!' he announced. 'Cheers,' he said, and they clinked glasses.

Doreen was pleased she'd decided to come in here. It was a whim really. She'd spent the afternoon with Janice and then they'd gone for a drink, but Janice's dreadful boyfriend had turned up in the Saracen's, just as they were about to order another round. Doreen had said goodnight but she hadn't wanted to go straight home. That was too depressing on a Saturday.

She picked up her glass and enjoyed the sweet burning taste as she swallowed a mouthful of her drink.

'You hungry?'

'Maybe – not really. I had a packet of crisps in the Saracens.'

'I tell you what, since we're celebrating, why don't we do it properly, with champagne? I've got a bottle in the shop.' He looked at her expectantly.

'I don't think they let you bring your own drinks into a pub.'

'No, the champagne doesn't come to us. We go to the champagne.'

'Champagne,' she said slowly. 'We're going to drink champagne in your shop. At ten o'clock at night.'

'It's the perfect time.'

'In your shop.'

'Yes.'

'Where I know you have a room with a bed.'

'Come on, I hardly know you. I'm just offering you a glass of champagne.'

'Really?'

'What do you take me for?'

'You don't want to know.' Words slithered through her brain – married, smooth, fast and loose. Handsome, sophisticated, exciting.

'It's just a glass of champagne.'

'I think champagne's overrated. It's a bit like cider really, isn't it?'

'If that's what you think of it, you've been drinking the wrong sort of champagne.'

'Maybe.' She looked at him.

'But you drink it?'

'Yeah, why not?'

'Come on then, put on that fabulous coat, and let's go and see what real champagne tastes like.'

She shivered with anticipation and picked up her coat. They walked out of the pub together. *Thank goodness I warned Angie off*, she thought. *I know he's a rogue. I know what he's up to. She's too young.*

He put his hand on her back to guide her across the road into the murky grounds of the cathedral.

'Ooh, it's a bit spooky at this time of night,' she said. He put his arm round her.

New Street was empty on a Saturday night. The shop was in darkness. He unlocked the door and pushed it open and she walked in. He followed, locking the door again behind them and switching on one light that beamed over a rail of jackets. Her suggestion, she noticed.

'Just a minute,' he said. He went into the back room and she heard the sound of a fridge door opening and bottles or glass jars clinking inside. She didn't know what was going to happen, but she was looking forward to it, as if a good film with two great romantic stars was about to start.

He walked back into the room, a bottle of champagne and two slender champagne flutes in his hands.

'I like the glasses,' she said. 'Very posh. Where did they come from?'

'I brought them down specially,' he said. He put the glasses on the counter and unpeeled the foil from the bottle. 'Look away now.' There was a loud pop and quickly he poured small amounts of champagne into the glasses.

'Isn't it meant to fizz everywhere?' she said.

'That's for people with more money than sense. I don't know who you've been drinking with, but that's an unnecessary waste of good champagne,' he said. 'Cheers.' He raised his glass.

'Cheers.' She sipped her drink. 'Mmm, not bad.'

'This is good champagne.'

They sipped their drinks and Doreen looked round the shop. 'Is that a record player?' she said.

'Yeah.' It was sitting on a chair beside the counter. 'What would you like to hear? I've just bought a Dave Brubeck LP.' He moved over to the record player. He put down his glass and opened the lid. 'I've been playing it all week in the shop. I can't get enough.' He put the needle on the record and the soft drumbeat and then the gentle piano notes which opened 'Take 5' filled the shop. 'Let's dance,' he said.

'This is a shop.'

'We're having champagne. Nothing is out of bounds.'

She put her bag on the floor and placed her glass on the counter next to his. There was a small box there. It had the name Walkers on the lid, Walkers were the local jewellers. 'What's this?' Doreen said.

'Oh nothing.'

She opened the box. It was a charm bracelet.

'Fancy,' she said. 'What's it doing here?'

'It was my wife's, I gave it to her years ago. All those charms, meant a lot at the time. She's just given it back to me. That's when you know things are really over.' He looked at her as she played the charms through her fingers. 'You can have it if you want it.'

'No thanks,' she said. 'Not my style.'

He held out his arms and she moved into his embrace. They rocked silently to the music. She could smell his after-shave, a sort of lavender, and a faint hint of fresh sweat.

'We should be jiving to this,' she murmured.

'Not tonight.' When the track ended, he didn't move. 'And, now, I think, a celebratory kiss.'

'You and your kissing.'

'It's a celebration!'

'No, it's not! We just met in the pub, that's all.'

'Oh, go on. We're here, we're alone, we're dancing. Just one little kiss.'

'How many times? It's not a celebration.' She was laughing. His arms were still around her. She stretched up and pecked him on the mouth. 'There you are!'

'No, I want a proper kiss.'

'Oh, all right,' she sighed.

She put her hands up to his face and pulled him to her. It would be a kiss on her terms. She put her lips to his. The kiss was soft and tender. She closed her eyes. When they drew apart, their arms were still round each other.

'How was that?' she whispered.

'Oh, that was nice,' he said. He bent his head to her again.

'One kiss!' she said. 'We agreed.'

'Just one more.'

'Bloody hell,' she said. But her heart was pounding.

They kissed again, this time it was a hard, urgent, exciting kiss. He pressed her against the counter and leaned his weight on her.

'Oh God!' he breathed. He looked at her. 'You know what I'm going to say.'

'Oh God.'

'I want you.'

'Do you?'

'Yes. And I know you want me. You do want me, don't you?'

There was no point denying it. She nodded.

'Come on.'

She looked over her shoulder as he led her into the back room.

Angie toiled up Sperry Drive. Every step seemed an impossible struggle. She thought her heart would break. She pulled open the heavy door of the telephone box and dialled Carol's number. She answered on the second ring.

'Can I come round?' Angie whispered.

'Yeah,' Carol said, sounding uncertain. 'Where are you?'

'In Sperry Drive.'

'Where's . . . your friend?'

'Oh don't, don't.'

'Ange, are you all right?' Angie was crying. 'Oh my god. What's happened? Yes, come round!'

Angie tapped on the door and Carol immediately threw it open.

'Don't say anything.' Angie stepped into the kitchen. 'I know I look a mess.' Her smudged make-up and pink eyes were in stark contrast to her glamorous red dress.

'What's happened?' Carol asked. 'Do you want a cup of cocoa?'

Angie smiled weakly and shook her head.

'Let's go up to my room,' Carol said.

Angie sank onto the bed.

Carol sat beside her. 'So what's happened?'

'Gene.'

'What?' Carol searched Angie's face. 'He hasn't finished with you, has he?'

'I don't know. Has he?'

'What? What do you mean?'

'It was all Roger's fault. It's always Roger!' Angie threw her hands in the air. 'He came round.'

'Round yours? I thought tonight was Gene's night.'

'It was! I didn't know Roger was coming. I had to make him beans on toast. So I was late to meet Gene. And I got off the bus at the cathedral and I was just about to cross the road to the Golden Fleece. And then . . .'

'What?'

'Then I saw him,' she whispered.

Carol frowned. 'Where? Is he all right?'

'Oh, he's fine. He was walking by the cathedral.'

'What was he doing there?'

'He was with someone.'

'Are we talking male or female someone?'

'Female.'

'Are you sure? It's really dark there at night. Perhaps it wasn't him.'

'It was him. No one else in Chelmsford has a coat like his.'

'Perhaps he was just going to church and she just happened at that moment to be going too.'

Angie looked at Carol mournfully.

'Perhaps it was a business associate.'

'He shouldn't be doing business on Easter Monday. He was supposed to be seeing me. Oh, but I was late!' She thrust her fist into her mouth.

'But you know Gene, he's not what you'd call a normal business man. He probably does business on Christmas Day.'

'It was nothing to do with business. Unless you do business with your arm round someone in high heels.'

'Who was it?'

Angie shook her head. 'It was too dark to see. I mean I just caught a glimpse. It was an impression really.'

'Perhaps it was a trick of the light.'

Angie's chin sank onto her chest.

'How do you know he had his arm round her?'

'He did. I thought about running after them but Mick Flynn came up and wanted to have a conversation about Clacton. He asked me if Roger got back all right, because he'd heard there had been some trouble.'

'Perhaps you had a narrow escape. If Mick knew you were in the Fleece with Gene, word might have got back to Roger.'

'I suppose so,' Angie said.

'Perhaps it was Cynthia.'

'Why would she be in Chelmsford on Bank Holiday Monday?' Angie paused. 'Maybe it was her,' she said hopefully. 'I could hardly see her. It was really shadowy down there.'

'I bet it was Cynthia,' Carol said.

'Yeah. But even so, he shouldn't have had his arm round her. They're meant to be getting a divorce.'

'Anyway, I bet it's nothing,' Carol said. 'Cheer up! Go and see him tomorrow.'

'Oh, I don't want to have it out with him. If it was something he shouldn't have done, he'll only lie, won't he? Or else he'll pack me up, which I don't want him to.' She threw herself back on the bed. Then she sat up straight. 'Of course, the reason I was late was Roger. My boyfriend. I'd just kissed him goodbye.'

'Mm,' murmured Carol.

'So really, I suppose, I'd been with another man. So I suppose there's not really any difference between us is there?'

Carol nodded silently.

'I mean, Gene's married to Cynthia. And I'm almost engaged to Roger.'

'Are you?' Carol asked.

'I'm just saying,' Angie said. 'Gene was with another woman, I'd been with another man. Can I really complain?'

'You're right,' Carol said.

'But then again, I pushed Roger out of the door. Gene didn't look as if he was going to push anyone out of anywhere.' She stood up.

'So what are you going to do?' Carol said.

'I don't know. I'm going to sleep on it.'

The next morning, at the top of Sperry Drive Angie ducked into the phone box again. It was ironic that now they had a phone at home she was using the phone box so often, but she couldn't afford to let Mum and Dad hear this.

'Graham? It's Angie. I can't come in today. I've been up all night . . . and now I've got a real gut ache. I must have eaten something off over the weekend. I'm going back to bed now.'

She walked to the bottom of the road and joined the bus queue.

Carol was there. She looked at her watch. Angie had to be in work before Carol.

'You're cutting it fine,' Carol said. 'What are you doing here?'

'I'm not well.'

Carol looked at her.

'I'm going to see Gene.'

'Oh, Angie. I thought we'd decided it was Cynthia.'

'I don't know what to think. I'm going to have it out with him. I've told Graham I'm ill.'

'Be careful,' Carol said. 'Just because your dad's won all this money, you can't muck them about.'

'I'll probably go in later. I'll say I've had a miracle recovery. Or that we've run out of toilet paper.'

The bus came and they ran up the stairs. It was good to see Carol on a weekday morning. It gave her courage.

The boutique wasn't open. She pushed open the door of Harry's shop. Harry was cutting the hair of a someone who looked like a business man. Rose, the assistant, stood at the back, folding towels.

'Hello, cuz,' Harry said. 'Don't often see you in here on a Tuesday morning.' He looked at her face. 'You need a cup of tea. Rose. Where's she gone? Rose, can you put the kettle on?' He looked in the mirror at his client. 'Cup of tea, Arthur? Tell Rose that's four cups, will you Ange?'

Angie went into the small kitchen where Rose was filling the kettle. Angie looked at herself in the small mirror hanging crookedly over the sink. Mirrors everywhere, telling the same story. No wonder Harry had said she needed tea. She looked so pale, with dark rings under her eyes, and her hair wasn't lying flat at all. As they waited for the kettle to boil, Rose gave her a timid smile. Angie almost burst into tears. She realised she didn't want to believe that Gene had been with Cynthia. If it was Cynthia and he put his arm round her that must mean he still cared for her. Whereas, if it was just a strange woman, it might be no more than a one-night stand.

The kettle was boiling. They made the tea.

Angie's hands were shaking as she handed a cup to Arthur. She sat down on one of the waiting chairs, her hands wrapped round her cup as if she needed to warm her frozen fingers.

At a quarter past ten she said goodbye to Harry and walked to the boutique. The door was open. She walked in.

Gene was bent over the till, sorting through a pile of notes. 'Morning,' he said cheerfully, without looking up.

Angie was silent.

Lazily Gene lifted his head. 'Angie! Darling! What a lovely surprise.'

He'd never called her darling before. It sounded so loving and tender.

He slid the pile of notes back into the till and came round the counter. 'What a treat to see you on a miserable Tuesday morning. Where did you get to last night? I waited for you.'

You didn't wait that long, she thought. 'I was late,' she murmured.

'Are you OK? And shouldn't you be at work? You don't look too hot. Tell you what – why don't I lock up for an hour, it's always quiet just after bank holiday, and we can go and have a coffee somewhere. We'll make up for last night.'

'What is there to make up for?'

'We missed each other, didn't we! I missed you. I came back to Chelmsford early, specially to see you. Come on. Let's walk down to the Saracen's. I'm sure they do morning coffee.' He pulled the door of the back room closed. 'Tell me all about your weekend.' He looked at her again.

'You know I really did miss you last night.' He stroked her hair, then pushed her gently out of the front door and locked it behind them. He drew her arm through his and they walked towards the town.

In the quiet pub she sat down. He brought over two watery cups of coffee. 'Good job I'm not really Italian,' he said, moving between the tables to sit beside her. 'I'd have to complain to someone about their espresso machine. Or their Maxwell House jar. Anyway, here.' He reached inside his coat and pulled out a small box. 'I got you a present.'

'You didn't. What for?'

'I did! Because I like you, sweetheart. Ooh, that tough face! Go on, open it.'

Slowly she opened the small square box. It was a silver charm bracelet.

'See?' he said, as she pulled the bracelet out of the box. 'It's got a little scooter and a pork-pie hat because you're a mod and a horseshoe for good luck. Oh, and this is a heart, because, well, I care about you.'

A heart! She swallowed the sweetness of it. 'And what's that?'

'That? Oh, that's a silly Christmas tree because . . . it was Christmas when we met. And as we go on, we can get more charms to mark special days. You'll be weighed down with them all! I was going to give it to you last night, but you didn't turn up.'

She found herself near to tears again. This couldn't be happening. This was the loveliest thing she'd ever received. She must have been wrong about last night. At least she hadn't said anything!

'Do you like it?' he said.

'I love it. I love it.' She swallowed a sob. 'I love it.'

CHAPTER 17

THERE WAS SO MUCH GOING ON. There was Gene, there was Roger, there was the offer of the management job. And there was the interview. It was all so crazy, she almost forgot that she'd taken Doreen's jumper to the dry cleaner's and she needed to collect it. Roger and the oil from his scooter had completely ruined it and Angie hadn't been able to do anything about it herself. There was a message attached to the sleeve when she picked it up:

Jumper has been badly washed. Wool – apparently mohair – has become matted and tight. Several stains noticed, particularly around the neck and the cuffs. An attempt has apparently been made to remove stains with various substances.

The lady in the shop said it was quite unusual for a note like that to be written, but seeing Angie's face she had said the shop wouldn't charge her.

As she left the shop Angie peeped under the cellophane. 'Oh. Oh.' It was awful, though given all the choices she had to make, it was the least of her worries.

She had to make a decision about the English Electric job by the end of the week. Should she take it? Should she become a respected part of the English Electric family? Should she put herself in line for even more promotions? But if she did, was she doomed to stay at the company for ever? Would any of her dreams ever come true? And what should she do about Roger? Should she leave him for Gene?

Usually if she had problems like these, she would discuss them with Doreen. Doreen always had sensible things to say. But Doreen would disapprove of Gene. Perhaps she could talk to her about the job and just not mention Roger or Gene. Yes, that's what she'd do.

She took a deep breath and went to find Doreen. She was in her bedroom trying to coax her hair into a new style of flick-ups.

Angie stood in the doorway. 'Reen, can I ask you something?'

Doreen spoke to Angie's reflection in the dressing table mirror. 'Actually, I'd like to ask you something.'

'What do you mean?'

'My sweater.'

'Oh. Oh?' Angie tried to keep the same expression on her face.

'It was in my drawer and now it's not there. And I know Mum and Dad haven't got it.'

'Have you asked them?'

Doreen was fiddling with a flick-up, rolling hair round her finger. 'Strangely, no.'

'Well,' Angie said, 'this isn't about clothes. It's about my job.' There was almost a sob in her voice.

Doreen turned away from the mirror and gazed at Angie. 'You look dreadful.'

'I've messed everything up,' Angie said.

'Have you? What? How?'

Angie took a breath, then shook her head.

'What?' Doreen repeated, half laughing. 'Come on, what's happened?'

Angie couldn't stand it anymore. She had to tell her, 'It – it was Roger. He, he came round.'

'Oh God, what's he done now?' Doreen put her arm round Angie's shoulders.

Doreen was being so friendly and nice. That would stop as soon as Angie said the word 'sweater.' She couldn't tell her. Doreen was looking at her, smiling in a warm, concerned way. She had to say something. 'Oh, I don't know what to do about him. Should I pack him up or what?'

'Pack him up? Why would you do that?'

'I don't know. He's . . . he's . . . ?'

'He's a nice boy. You're lucky to have him.'

'Well, you've changed your tune. You said he was boring.'

'Boring is not always bad. Someone like you needs someone dependable.'

They fell silent. Doreen lifted a lock of Angie's hair. 'You're so lucky to have this thick hair. Are you really worried about Roger?'

'Why, what else would I be worried about?' Angie felt her cheeks colour. 'Well, if you must know . . .' She took a deep breath. 'There's Gene.'

'Gene – what? That bloke in the boutique? You're not still interested in him, are you?'

'Well, as it happens, I am.'

'Oh God! But he's . . . he's so wrong for you.' Doreen coughed. 'He's married, he's older than you.'

'So? I think he loves me.'

'Why on earth would you think that?'

'He gave me this.' Angie pulled the bracelet from her pocket. 'Look.'

Doreen gazed at the box, then took a deep breath and opened it.

'Isn't it lovely?' Angie said, as Doreen lifted the bracelet from the box and laid it in the palm of her hand.

'Ohh,' Doreen breathed. She seemed transfixed by the bracelet. 'He gave you this? When? When did he give you this?'

'He gave it to me yesterday.'

'Really? Why?'

'I don't know. Because it was our two-month anniversary, I don't know.'

'You've been seeing him for two months!'

'Look, at all these charms. There's a horseshoe.'

'Really? You've been seeing him for two months? And now he's given you *this*?' Doreen was breathing heavily as she flipped through the charms. Without looking away from the bracelet she said, 'I thought you only had horse-shoes at weddings.'

'Perhaps that's what he's thinking! Because look, here, it's a heart. A heart!' Angie pointed at the heart that Doreen was staring at.

'Yes, I can see it's a bloody heart,' she snapped. 'But why did he give it to you? What did he say?'

'What do you mean? He didn't say anything. It speaks for itself doesn't it?'

'And he gave you that yesterday?'

'Yesterday morning. He was going to give it to me the other night, but I was late. I stood him up.'

'Did you?' Doreen looked at the bracelet. It slithered from her fingers to the floor.

'Careful!' Angie said, retrieving it from the rug. Tenderly she put the bracelet back in the box.

'Why didn't you tell me you were seeing him?' Doreen sounded almost breathless.

'After what you said about him?'

'Look Ange,' Doreen said. 'I don't think he's good for you. What do you know about him? I mean, he's still got a wife, and if . . . if he's cheating on Cynthia with you, for all you know he's got other women too.'

'He probably has. In fact, I know he has.'

'Do you?'

'I saw him with someone else.'

'Did you? When?'

'The other night, Monday. I was meant to be seeing him, but I was late.'

'Angie!'

'And I was late because I was cheating on him!' Angie sounded almost triumphant. 'I've got another bloke too. I'll never be able to wear the bracelet in case Roger asks where I got it. Gene and I are two of a kind!' she said proudly. 'I know he's a bit . . . wild, but then so am I.'

'Really?'

'And when he kisses me it just feels lovely.'

Doreen drew her head back. 'You – you haven't gone all the way, have you?'

Angie looked at her sadly.

'Oh no, you haven't! Please tell me you haven't.'

'I haven't, I haven't,' Angie said. 'He said he respects me too much.'

'Oh respect! That's a good one.'

'Sometimes I wish he'd go a bit further.'

'No, you don't.'

Angie smiled. 'Really, he's the reason I'm thinking of ending it with Roger.'

'Oh God!' Doreen said sharply.

'What? What?' Angie said. 'Don't you want me to be happy?'

'Yes, I do. That's why ... oh God.' Doreen seemed to shake herself. 'Look, why don't we go out for a drive? Stop somewhere for a drink? There's no rush to make a decision is there? Perhaps you should wait. Come on, I'll buy you a whisky. I certainly need one,' she murmured.

'Whisky! I don't like whisky! And look at the state of me!' Angie craned her neck to look into her dressing table mirror. 'I look terrible.'

'No, you don't. Just put on a bit of lipstick. You can borrow that new one of mine. Mystic Cherry. It will probably suit you more than me.'

'I don't know if I feel like it.'

'Go on. You can tell me all about Roger. You probably need to talk about it. We'll sort something out.'

This was just what Angie had wanted. Doreen's opinion – she was always so sensible.

Doreen stood up and went to the wardrobe. She began rifling through her clothes.

'Actually,' Angie said, 'there's something else I want to talk about. It's about a job. They've offered me a promotion at work.'

'A promotion! Well, you kept that quiet. What kind of promotion?' Doreen turned from her wardrobe. There was a strange look on her face. She almost looked as if she was about to cry.

Angie repeated, 'Yes, a promotion. Graham said they're looking for a manager in Section F – it's a similar job to the one I've got, but more money and – well – it's management. The job's mine if I want it. Me, a manager. Can you imagine?'

'Little Angie, all grown up and managing!' Doreen gave a small laugh. 'Well, good for you, gal. That's great.'

'Except that now I've got an interview for a job in London.'

'Oh my god! You're a dark horse. What's this one for? Company Director?'

'No, it's fashion. Well, not fashion exactly. It's a technician in a fashion school. It pays a lot less, but this could be my chance to get into the fashion world. You really might have to start wearing my dresses round town.'

'Oh Angie. What a time to have to make such a decision. I mean, you should seriously think about the management job.'

'Yes, but . . .'

'But fashion is what you've always dreamed of, I know. What do you know about this London job? Will it really take you to the places you want to go?' She looked into Angie's face. 'You want to do it, don't you?'

'I do. I haven't got the job yet – it's just the interview. Miss Darling from school told me about it.'

'Well, it's a tough old world out there,' Doreen began. Angie's face fell. 'But look. Miss Darling must think there's a chance. She always liked you, didn't she? And didn't she do some really high up job in one of the fashion houses, Cardin or somewhere? I never understood how she ended up in Chelmsford.'

'I think she had a stroke or something. I think she nearly died and she was told she had to take life easy.'

'But Chelmsford?'

'Someone said she had old friends who lived in Chelmsford and so she moved here, to Broomfield. One of those new houses near Mill Hill Lane. And then she got a job at the school. She was only part-time. But she was married and she was the first person who I ever knew who was married who still called herself Miss.'

'And what does her husband think of that?'

'Didn't he die?'

'Don't ask me. Anyway, with all that behind her, she must know what she's talking about. Go for it, Ange, you've got to go for it, you really have. Never mind Roger and – and Gene.' She picked up her handbag. 'Oh my god. Everything's happening so fast. Come on, let's go for that drink. Because we've got Australia to talk about too and this bloody interview we've got to go for.'

'I'm not going! Are you really going to go?'

'I don't know. More and more I think I shouldn't stay here. Let's talk about it in the pub.'

'But what if we see someone when I look such a state?'

'We shan't. We'll be in the middle of the back of beyond. Anyway, sod them. Because,' Doreen pulled Angie off the bed and pushed her towards the bathroom, 'with my lipstick and a bit of blusher, you'll look like the Queen of Sheba.'

Angie loved it when Doreen was kind and funny, like this. She went into the bathroom.

'You can wear my black jumper, if you like,' Doreen called from the bedroom. 'If I can find it.'

'No, it's all right.' Angie came back into the room, holding the little pot of rosy blusher. 'I'll wear my Fred Perry. It's . . . it's too hot for a jumper. Or a coat. You know you should get yourself a new coat.'

'Why?'

'Well, that girl I told you he was with when I was late – she's got one like yours. I saw it.'

'Did you? Oh God. Well, I'm throwing it out then.'

'It wasn't as nice as yours. It was longer, I think, and a bit worn out.'

'I'd still better put it in the dustbin. Right, where shall we go?'

Doreen was being so nice. Angie had to tell her. 'Reen, oh Reen. I've got something you definitely should put in the dustbin.'

'What do you mean?'

Angie went into her bedroom and groped under the bed. She pulled out the sweater.

She went out onto the landing where Doreen was leaning against the banister, jingling her car keys. 'What's this?' Doreen said, half laughing. She looked at Angie's face. She blinked. 'Is this what I think it is? Why is it in a dry-cleaning bag?'

Angie handed it to her. Doreen put her hand under the cellophane. She looked at Angie again. She drew the sweater out of the bag. 'Oh, Angie, Angie.'

'I'm sorry, I'm sorry. I wasn't going to tell you, but you're being so nice. I'm sorry.' She began to cry. 'It was all my fault. I gave it to Roger to wear because he was so cold and wet, and then it got oil on.' She sobbed.

'Oh Angie. Come here. It's just a jumper.' Doreen put her arm round Angie. She took a deep breath. 'Just a . . . jumper. How stupid we both are.'

'Why?' Angie's voice was muffled. 'What have you done? You can't have done anything as stupid as me.'

'Oh nothing. Everything. Come on, let's go for that drink and you can tell me all about these jobs you're being offered.'

'Reen! You're crying. I really am sorry.'

'I know you are, lovely. Don't worry.'

CHAPTER 18

THE NEXT DAY, IN HER LUNCH break, Doreen slid along New Street, past the bank, past the post office and the police station. How could this have happened? How could she have let it happen? Why hadn't she known that Angie was falling in love with Gene? Why had she, Doreen, let him kiss her and make love to her? Just when everything should have been going so well, all the money they had now, all the lovely things that were within their reach. Gene was going to break Angie's heart. And she would be responsible. She would speak to him, she would tell him that it wasn't on. But her own heart might break a little too. She cared for him. It was true. He wasn't just a one-night stand for her. She liked him, she liked talking to him, she liked his style, the way he was in the world, confident, loud, generous.

She pushed open the door of the boutique so hard the bell rattled for what felt like a very long time. The shop was empty except for Gene who was standing behind the counter, pinning price tags onto the slacks in a pile in front of him. She pressed her back against the door and stared at him.

He looked at her with a surprised expression. 'Hello! Fancy seeing you here.'

'What are you doing messing about with my sister?'

'Your sister? Can you be more specific!'

'Oh my god. How many women have you got on the go?'

'Calm down. I don't know what you're talking about.'

'My sister. Giving her bracelets! Raising her hopes.'

Gene's eyes widened and the colour drained from his face. 'Is Angie your sister? How was I to know she was your sister?'

'We have the same surname!'

'Smith? Is your surname Smith? Well, I'm not sure I would have guessed even if I'd known.'

'Oh Gene. How could you do it? How could you be going out with her and sleeping with me? Why didn't you mention it on Monday?'

'Because I didn't know she was your sister. And it wasn't really the moment.' Gene grinned.

'I thought you were free!'

'I was free for you.'

'But hasn't she ever mentioned me? Little minx.'

'Well, she said she had a sister Reen, which I assumed was short for Irene. Your name's Doreen, unless I'm very much mistaken.' He moved away from the counter.

'For God's sake! I think she's falling in love with you!'

'Is she?' He stopped. 'Well, love's a wonderful thing.'

'Not when the other person's married and you're sleeping with her sister!'

'She knows what she's doing. We've talked about it. We talked about Monday.'

'Really? You've told her you're seeing other people?'

'She suspects, but she doesn't care. She knows what the game is.'

'It's not a game for her. You gave her that bloody charm bracelet. She thinks you're in love with her!'

'Are you sure? Hasn't she still got Reliable Roger in tow?'

'But, but – you're older! You know what you're doing. She doesn't.'

'Really? Are we talking about the same girl? Angie wasn't born yesterday. She knows her way around.'

'What's that supposed to mean?'

'She's a bright kid—'

'Exactly. She is a kid. And you definitely aren't.'

'Oh, thanks for that. Look, if it's any consolation, Angie and I have not gone nearly as far as you and I have.' He looked at her, smiling.

'Oh, shut up,' she said.

'And it's not for want of trying.'

'Oh God!' Doreen exploded. 'You're taking advantage of her!'

'Not trying on my part! She's the one. She's forever on about it.'

'Oh yeah?'

'She wants me to be her first. She likes the fact I'm old. Older. She wants me to show her how to do it. I'm the one saying, "Let's take it slowly."'

'Really? You weren't that restrained with me!'

'Doreen, come on. You and I have been around. We know what we want. We take it. But are you sure you didn't have an idea?'

'If I'd had any idea, Monday night would not have happened. I can assure you of that.'

'But Angie likes to talk. She's told me about her sister. Reen says this, Reen says that. She really respects your judgment. I'm surprised she hasn't talked about me.'

'You mean you're upset she hasn't talked about you! Well, sorry, buster, she hasn't. Not till yesterday. Of course, she told me about you kissing her that first day, just before Christmas, when she was in there buying a jumper for Roger. But I pretty much warned her off and after that she kept it secret.'

'Why?'

'Why?' she repeated, incredulous. 'You're married, you're older, you're from London.'

He laughed. 'I can't help the London part. Or my age. What did you say when she told you yesterday?'

'There wasn't much I could say, was there? Not after Monday night.'

'Monday night was good, wasn't it?'

'That's got nothing to do with it.'

'You sure? Because maybe she's not the one who's got the problem. Maybe someone in this room is a bit jealous.' He came towards her. 'Has anyone ever told you you're gorgeous when you're angry? Your eyes flash and your red hair almost catches fire.'

'What!' she said. He took hold of her arms and drew her to him. Then he was kissing her, his tongue tangled with hers. She moved against him. He ran his hands down her back and over the swell of her buttocks and pulled her hard towards him.

She sprang away.

'Christ!' he said. 'Just doing that reminds me what a good time we had. You know, Doreen, when you and me are together, whether it's just a kiss or something else, there's a reaction. A strong reaction. And you can't deny it.'

She was breathing heavily. He was right. For God's sake, he was right. How could this be happening? 'That's hardly the point. What would Angie say? Or Cynthia for that matter?'

'Well, Cynthia wouldn't care and Angie's not going to know, is she? I mean, you're not going to tell her, are you?'

'I don't know. I should. She has a right to know.'

'A right to have her happiness destroyed? A right to lose all her trust in you? She's having a nice time with me, and I'm having a nice time with her. Why spoil everything? Look, I like your sister very much. I respect her. But here's the thing – I fancy the pants off you. And I don't want either of you to get hurt.'

'And how are you going to manage that, Mr Fancy Pants? Who's it going to be? Me or Angie?'

'I think there are more than two options. There's certainly a third option. And that is, I don't finish with anyone and you and I keep our mouths shut as tight as they can be. Except when we're kissing.'

She stared at him. 'Are you seriously saying that you would quite happily go out with both of us? Is that what you're saying?'

The bell over the door tinkled and a young mod in a parka came in, his eyes roving round the shop. 'Afternoon,' Gene said, easily. 'Thanks for that, Doreen. Ring me later, will you? It's my birthday next week, we'll do something nice. Anything you were looking for especially, mate?'

Doreen stood gazing at him for a moment. She was trying to understand what he had said. Surely he couldn't mean that he was prepared to keep both of them hanging on. She slipped out of the shop. Her mind was whirling. She didn't know what to think. There was a real pain in her chest. Tears came to her eyes. She remembered everything about that night, his hands on her body, the lovely things he had said to her, his appreciation, the feel of him inside her. How could he? How could he?

CHAPTER 19

ANGIE AND CAROL WERE SITTING ON Carol's bed, listening to 'Comin' Home, Baby' by Mel Torme. Angie had brought the record over with her and now Carol had taken off the arm of the record player so the record played over and over.

'Gene says I should listen to more jazz,' Angie explained.

'You don't like jazz. And why are you listening to Gene after what happened the other night?'

'Oh that. I think I got that wrong. I was in a state because I was so late. He really missed me that night. And look, he gave me this bracelet.' She held out her wrist. 'Isn't it gorgeous? I almost think he might be in love with me!'

'Oh, Angie, it's beautiful.'

'I know. Anyway, this record is sort of jazz, he said, and I like this. It's a soft start.'

'Why should you listen to more jazz?'

'He says all I do, now I've got this money, is buy Motown and Stax and stuff, and I should include some jazz.'

'But why?'

'Because it's his thing and he wants us to have shared interests.'

'That's what he says. But really, jazz?'

'He says I haven't had a proper education.'

'That's not your fault.'

'He doesn't mean it like that. He means a musical education.'

'Oh, what, and he's going to give you one?'

'Perhaps. But I don't care. I like learning things from him.'

The record began again. After the opening chords of the soft insistent piano and the beat of the drumsticks on the snare drum, they joined in with the backing singers, 'Doo doo doo.'

'Funny name, Mel Torme,' Carol said. 'I wonder what Mel's short for.'

Angie shrugged, 'Melvin?'

'CaraMel?'

'EnaMel?'

'Doo doo doo,' they both sang.

'So how shall we feel when we're coming home from London?'

Carol's eyes widened. 'London? When? Are we going to London?'

'Yes, we are! I've got that job interview.'

'So, what about English Electric?'

'I've told them I don't want the job.'

'You haven't.'

'Oh yes I have. I'm pleased. It's a relief. I talked to Doreen about it and she thinks I've made the right decision. Sometimes it's good having a sister. So the plan is to stay on in Graham's section till I sort out a London job. Because even if I don't get this job, I'll apply for another one. I can take my time now, with all this money. So, first stop, Hornsey.'

'But it's your interview,' Carol said. 'Where do I come in?'

'You said you wanted to work in London too! You can have a look round, see what's up there. I'll go to my interview, you'll go to a few employment agencies. And then we can meet up after and have a good time.'

'I never thought it would happen.' Carol sat back on the bed, grinning. 'London,' she whispered. 'But what about work?'

'Take the day off. Say you're not well. That's what I do.'

'That's because you don't care if they sack you. Oh, I don't know.' Carol frowned. 'What does Roger think about all this?'

'Oh Roger. He doesn't want me to leave Chelmsford. He thinks London is a den of iniquity. But he's pleased I've got the interview. It's the first one I've been offered and I've been trying for months. I know it's a technician's job. But I was thinking—' Angie paused. 'Because they do fashion courses there as well, I might have to help in the fashion department too. Then I might get talking to people and say I'm interested.' Her eyes shone. 'And then, who knows? Well, it's a start, anyway.'

'And it's what you've always wanted.'

'I know.'

'I think it's fantastic!' Carol said. 'I mean, I hate you for getting a job in London . . .'

'Haven't got it yet.'

'. . . but it is fantastic.'

'All right, don't go mad. They might take one look at me and say, "Oh from Chelmsford. We're not taking girls from Chelmsford. They're far too mod."'

'How can you be too mod? That's what fashion's all about. You'll be right up their street.'

'Do you reckon? But it's the Art department.'

'You look arty.'

Angie smiled. 'Well, what shall I wear to the interview?'

'Anything. You always look so – so cool. Look at you! That cardigan. And that skirt. And that's just your every-day clothes.'

'Too ordinary.'

'All right. Well, definitely your suede. To show them you know what's what.'

'Do you think I should? Perhaps I should buy some-thing fabulous and new. No expense spared, now we've got this money. I mean, it's come in the nick of time. The pay that the college is offering is pretty low. I couldn't do the job – even if they offered it to me – without the pools money. It seems you need to be rich just to get started in fashion. Once I've paid my fares and everything there'd be hardly anything left. Oh, wouldn't it be great if I got the job?' She hugged herself.

'It would! So why don't you buy something new and fab, just to make sure?'

'Well, for a start my dad's keeping the money very close to his chest. Oh, I forgot – he bought us all a new pair of stockings. They're the wrong size and they've got seams, but it was something. Doreen took hers back. She said she needed the 5s and 11d they cost. She's mad. But she's right. These bank accounts Dad's setting up are taking a bloody long time to come. And till I get the cheque book, I've got to rely on my own wardrobe.'

'How about a big Sloppy Joe jumper? A black one maybe.' They laughed.

'Don't,' Angie said. 'But she wasn't angry at all. It was strange. Perhaps she's getting calmer in her old age. But maybe I should buy a Sloppy Joe. That style is a bit beat-niky, isn't it? A lot of art students are beatniks, aren't they?'

'Probably. Or you could just wear your Marks cardigan done up to the neck. That's sort of arty.'

'I'll see what the weather's like.'

'Doo doo doo,' they both sang, looking at each other, laughing.

'Right, so now we've got a plan,' Angie said.

'Have we?'

'Yes! Next week, you sort it out at Britvic's, get the day off. We go to London. I go for my interview. You go to an employment bureau, and then, and then . . .'

'Our lives change forever.'

They laughed. 'Doo doo doo.'

'But what have I got to offer?' Carol said.

'Anything. You're good at organising. Sorting out offices.'

'You mean filing. I can do that anywhere.'

'Which means you can do it in London.' Angie's eyes roamed round the small room. 'Or what about that?' She looked at the guitar leaning against the wall. 'Don't say you haven't thought about it.'

Carol looked over at her guitar. She had been learning to play since Christmas.

'You could take it into some agency somewhere and play them a song. It'll be like a Tommy Steele film. And they'll say – "Thank goodness you're here, we need someone to step in tonight to play at the London Palladium. Dusty Springfield couldn't make it." And so you'll go and there'll be thousands of people and Brian Epstein will be in the audience and he'll come backstage afterwards and say, "I want to be your manager. Please say you'll come and join our happy family."'

'And I shall say, "Thank you, I will." I just need to add a few Beatles' songs to my repertoire.' Carol laughed.

'Go on, play us something,' Angie said. She took the stylus off the record.

The room was silent, then Carol, looking carefully at the fingers of her left hand, strummed the chords of 'All I Have To Do Is Dream.' Angie joined in and they harmonised as the Everly Brothers.

'Gee whizz, we're good!' Angie said. 'Brian Epstein is bound to pick you up. You can start, two weeks tomorrow.'

There was a knock at the door. 'Hello Angie.'

'Hello Mrs Hart.'

'Lovely as the two of you sound Carol, and you do, your brother Richard has to go to bed now. So, no more playing tonight.'

'OK, Mrs Hart. But did you really think we were good?'

Carol's mum put her head on one side. 'Not bad.' She stepped back and closed the door.

'So,' Angie whispered. 'We go to London next Thursday to seek our fortune.'

'Yes!' Carol said.

'OK. And I'll ask Gene to meet us up there, take us somewhere nice in the evening.'

'Oh.' Carol's face fell. 'Oh well, if Gene's coming, I'll come home when we've finished all the job stuff and you and Gene can go out and have a good time.'

'Don't be silly,' Angie said. 'It'll be good. He'll pay. Actually, that's a thought, I might ask him to lend me some money to buy a new outfit.'

'Really?'

'Yeah. He's so generous. He's already lent me money to buy a table for my room, so I can put the sewing machine on it.'

'A table? Couldn't you have got it on the never-never from Woodhouse?' It was a furniture shop on the High Street.

'I was going to but I was worried my mum would find out. She's ordered a new settee and a new bed from there. So Gene said he would lend it to me because, anyway, it will be cheaper and I'll pay him back when I get my cheque book. Doreen bought us each a book. She says I've got to write it all down, all the money I've spent and what people have lent me, so I know how much I've got to pay back. That pound you lent me to get my hair cut, and the money Doreen's lent me. There's a bit from Graham at work too. But Gene's lent me the most. He's always flashing the cash.'

'Are you sure?'

'Yes! He doesn't care. Anyway, he's definitely paying on Thursday. He owes me a date in London. He's been promising to take me to the West End for long enough.'

'So what, will he come up to London with us? I thought it would be the two of us. Like it used to be.'

'It will! Because he's got to work in the shop, hasn't he? We'll meet up in the evening. Oh, but just to warn you, Doreen's coming. And my mum and dad. Don't say anything about why we're going. I'm telling them we're going shopping. We shan't even see them. They're all going to Australia House. They're getting some more information or something, and Doreen's got her interview.'

'I thought you said Doreen didn't want to go.'

'She hasn't made up her mind. We talked about it the other night. Mum's been on at both of us. She really wants us to go with them, but I'm just not going. But Doreen, I don't know. She's started saying that perhaps she will go to Australia with them, after all. To get away from here. I don't know what's going on with her. Ohh, you know what that means?' She looked at Carol as she put the Mel Torme record back in its paper sleeve. 'If they all go.'

'What?'

'That means not just jobs, but you and me should probably look for a flat in London, too.'

They laughed softly and crept downstairs.

At home Mrs Smith and Doreen were in the living room, watching *Armchair Theatre* on television. Her mum was saying, 'Who's he again?'

'He's the one who left the parcel, but didn't go home.'

'Oh. Really?'

Angie came in and sat down. 'Where's Dad?'

Without taking her eyes off the screen her mum said, 'He's gone to the pub.'

'I thought the money would stop all that.'

'I don't know why you thought that, now he's got loads more money to spend. The only difference is, he wears a good suit when he goes out,' Doreen said.

'How come Dad's spending all this money and we're still scraping by?'

Mum turned from the screen. 'He says there's a good business deal on offer. He says he's worried if he gives us all the money straight away, we'll behave as if we've got money to burn.'

'So Dad's going to invest it for us!' Doreen said. 'At this rate there won't be any money for any of us to burn.'

'Shush,' her mum said. 'I'm losing the plot here.'

Angie gazed at the screen but she wasn't watching. She was thinking. *London. A new job. A chance.* 'Mum,' she said.

'Shh, this is the crucial moment.'

All three sat silently until her mum and Doreen exclaimed together, 'Oh, no!' And then the credits rolled.

'Well, I never saw that coming,' her mum said.

'I think they got the wrong man!' Doreen said.

'Mum,' Angie started again.

'Yes,' her mum said absently. She was peeling an orange.

'Next week, when you go to London, I might come too.'

'So we will all go to Australia, after all,' Mum said. 'Lovely. I'll write to Ivy and tell her to expect four of us. Oh, that will be nice,'

'Are you definitely going then?' Angie asked Doreen.

'I'm still thinking about it,' Doreen said. They both looked across at their mum.

'Well, I'm not,' Angie said. 'I'm just going to London for the day.'

'No need to decide yet,' Mum said. 'So what are you going to do up in London?'

'Oh, nothing,' Angie said. 'Carol and I just fancied a day out shopping, looking around.'

CHAPTER 20

ANGIE WAS LOOKING FORWARD TO THE day. She wanted to walk round Piccadilly Circus, across Leicester Square, through Soho, imagine what it might be like to do that every day, to be part of that world, to talk casually about fashion and art and how to cut cloth on the bias so it fell just right. She didn't expect to get the job. She couldn't believe that she'd be better than all the other people who applied for it. She was afraid she wanted it too badly. She couldn't imagine getting it. But she did want to smell the possibilities, imagine herself in the place.

'What do you think?' Angie said to Carol when she got to the bus stop. She undid her coat to reveal a navy shift dress, with a high collar. It had a red diagonal stripe across the body. 'It's got long sleeves, and red cuffs.' She pulled back the sleeves of her suede.

'It's fab!' Carol said. 'You look very arty. Did you make it?'

'I designed it and made it. Do you think it's all right?'

'I think you look great,' Carol said. 'They'll be falling over themselves to give you a job.'

'And if they don't . . .'

'Well, it's their loss. But what's that?'

Angie was holding a battered briefcase. 'It's my stuff,' she said. 'In case they want to look at it.'

'What's in it?'

'Oh, some of my designs from my night class and some . . . some sketches and pieces of fabric. I mean, Miss Darling must have suggested this job for a reason. She knows I want to get into fashion. She said it would be the perfect thing for me. So I'm going to show them what I've really got to offer.'

'They're going to love you!' Carol said.

At the railway station they queued to buy their tickets, then climbed the steps to the platform, Angie holding her briefcase close to her as if it might disappear if it wasn't wrapped in her arms.

At the far end of the platform stood Mr and Mrs Smith and Doreen. 'I thought you said we wouldn't see them!' Carol said.

'They must have missed their train. I planned it so that we wouldn't see them at all. I don't want to talk to them any more than you do.'

'Are you sure you don't want to go with them? Have an interview? Book your ticket?' Carol said.

'No, I don't. Who wants to go to Australia? You'd be tripping over koala bears and convicts and everyone would be singing "Waltzing Matilda". I don't think they've even heard of mods. Who'd want to go?'

'Your mum and dad, obviously. Perhaps that's why they missed the train. They've decided to kidnap you and get you on a boat today.'

'Oh, ha ha. I'd like to see them try.'

'Should we go and talk to them?' Carol said.

'Don't worry,' Angie said, 'Doreen's on her way over.'

Doreen walked up to them, smiling. She was wearing a new beige mac, with a tightly fastened belt. She looked very thin. The heels of her shoes were high. 'I don't know how she can even walk in those shoes,' Angie murmured, 'let alone go all the way to London in them.'

'Let's hope she's got a pair of plimsolls in her bag,' Carol said.

Doreen came up to them in a wave of sweet perfume. 'Don't worry,' she said. 'I'm not going to sit with you, I just needed a break from Mum and Dad. It's all talk talk talk about Australia, what I should say, what I shouldn't say in this interview.'

'Are you nervous?' Angie said.

'Not really. I don't care whether I get through or not,' Doreen said. 'Although with all this money we've won I reckon they'll just say, "Here are your tickets. Get on the next boat." Anyway, I'm wearing my highest shoes. If there's any nonsense I'll just stab a few people. God they're killing me.' She rubbed the back of her legs. You going for a job interview too, Carol?' Doreen batted her heavy black, Dusty Springfield eyelids at her.

Carol didn't reply.

'Yeah, she is!' Angie said. 'She's going for a job in the music business.'

Carol turned to Angie, her eyes wide. 'I haven't got anything organised. I'm just going to see what's up there,' she said stiffly.

'Well, be careful. There are a lot of creeps in London. It's what I say to Angie. Fashion is one of the hardest businesses to break into, followed closely by the music business. Everyone wants to be a pop-star, and it's just not possible.'

'Shut up Doreen,' Angie said. 'We might get lucky. If you must know we shall be in the middle of the music business tonight.'

'Really,' Doreen sighed.

'We're going to Ronnie Scott's Jazz Club.'

'Are we?' Carol said.

'I told you we'd go somewhere nice.'

'Jazz?' Carol said.

'Jazz?' Doreen said. 'You know what happens in jazz clubs and it's not just music. I know what I'm talking about, believe me.'

'We'll be all right,' Carol said. 'We're going with Gene from the boutique.'

'Oh, are you?' Doreen said. 'He should know better.' She turned on her heel and stalked back up the platform.

Angie looked at Carol. 'Don't listen to her. She's full of good advice for everyone else but she doesn't know what she's talking about. She doesn't know anything about music, let alone the music business. She bought a Perry Como record recently. That's what happens when you have money to burn.' They laughed. 'Too late to worry about it now, anyway. We've got our tickets and we're going to London. This could be the start of a new life.'

They found an empty carriage and Angie sat by the window, holding her briefcase tenderly on her lap.

As the train left the station, Carol said, 'Can I have a look at your sketches?'

'I thought you'd never ask.' Carefully Angie unbuckled the cracked leather straps. 'I don't want to be stupid but are your hands clean?' she said.

Carol rubbed her hands on her hanky. 'Yes.'

Angie handed over a pile of sketches. Carefully Carol looked through them. There were pencil sketches of tall thin women wearing simple shift dresses. In two sketches the woman looked like Doreen. 'That's the dress she's wearing today,' Angie said.

Further in the pile were more intricate drawings, different shapes and lengths with swatches of material attached to them. Then Carol said, in a surprised tone. 'That's me.'

There were some drawings of her – one wearing her mac, another of her in an interesting skirt. 'When did you do these?' she asked.

'Ages ago,' Angie said. 'I did them at home. I didn't stand outside your house trying to catch your best side. What do you think?'

Carol looked up from the pictures. 'I think they're fantastic. I love the dress with the black stripe down the side, and that one with the sleeves. That's like the one you're wearing, isn't it? God, Ange, I really didn't know you could draw like this. Honestly, they really are fab. When you go in for that interview, before you say anything you should just open the briefcase and say "Look at these. Now give me a job."' Carol handed the pictures back to Angie.

'That might be a bit strange, as it's a technician job, not a design job,' Angie said. 'But I want them to know I'm on their wavelength. And that I'll be more than just a technician. I'll be a technician with style!'

'Oh they'll definitely give you the job,' Carol said.

Angie crunched up the gravel driveway of a large Victorian looking house. She pushed open the heavy wooden door and stepped into a spacious entrance hall. There was the smell of paint and charcoal and in the sunlight that came in through the skylight over the door, motes of dust dashed through the air. It was terrifying but also alluring. On her left was a door labelled 'Secretary' and the sound of rapid, expert typing. She poked her head nervously round the door.

'I'm . . .' Her voice was a whisper. She coughed. 'I'm here for an interview.'

A young woman with whispy brown hair wearing a neat orange cardigan, looked up from her typewriter. 'Oh yes.' She looked at a list beside her machine. 'What's your name?'

'Angie – Angela Smith.'

'Yes. You're a bit early, but that's perfect. The last person didn't turn up. I'll tell them you're here then I'll take you up.' She stretched over her machine to a large telephone affair and picked up the receiver. She dialled a number and murmured something. Angie heard her name.

The woman ushered her back into the hallway and led her upstairs. Angie was conscious of the briefcase banging against her legs. She wondered if it was a mistake.

In a large room, panelled with dull brown wood and hung with pictures of red cheeked men in stiff white collars and black jackets, and waistcoats straining over their large stomachs, sat a man and a woman, behind a large wooden table. The man invited her to sit down in a chair opposite them and then introduced himself and the woman, but Angie immediately forgot their names.

The man looked down at a pile of notes. He picked up a letter. Angie recognised the flowery handwriting of Miss Darling. He read it silently then passed it to the woman.

She scanned it quickly then put it down in front of her and folded her hands on it.

Angie sat on the edge of her chair, ready to give answers to any questions they might ask. But for now it was just silence and the rustle of paper. This seemed to take about three hours but Angie realised it was probably only a few minutes. She tried to relax.

'Well Angela. Can you tell us a little about yourself and why you want this job?'

Angie took a deep breath. She'd prepared for this question but now she wasn't sure what to say. 'I love design,' she blurted. They looked at her, nodding in what she hoped was a kindly way. 'I mean, I know this job is fairly straight-forward, or I imagine it is, sorting out the rooms and the studios and making sure the students have what they need. I know I can do that. I could probably do it standing on my head, although that's probably not what you're after.' The woman smiled slightly. 'But . . .' She stopped. Already she loved the atmosphere of this place, the smell of it, the trees outside the windows, the old men in their shiny waistcoats. She wanted to come here so much. Did she dare to say what was in her heart? Would she sound stupid? She didn't care. She lifted her head. 'But, because I love design and fashion, and I think I'm quite good at it, what I really want is to work in an atmosphere where everybody loves it. Where I might have conversations with people about the way things look, how the light catches them, what is behind it all.'

There was silence. Had she messed it up? Had she ruined her chances but talking arty rubbish, that was nothing to do with the job? Had she given herself away?

'Well.' The man leaned forward and put his elbows on the desk. 'That's a very . . .' What was he going to say? 'That's a very refreshing thing to hear,' he said. 'You know you come very highly recommended by Miss Darling, who was at one time a student in this college. She tells me you do in fact do some designing of your own.'

Angie took a breath. 'Yes, I do,' she said. She bent down to the briefcase beside her. 'I've brought a few things with me. To show you. If you're interested.'

'I think we're very interested,' said the woman.

Angie opened the briefcase and spread the sheets of paper on the desk. Seeing her own designs, designs she was proud of, that were hers, gave her confidence and made her feel comfortable. Even if they didn't give her a job, they had to like her designs because she knew they were good.

At five past four Angie appeared, smiling. 'Sorry I'm late,' she said cheerfully to Carol. She held out her arms, the briefcase dangling from her hand.

'So,' Carol said, 'how did it go?'

'Oh, I liked it there. It's this huge old house, in the middle of this enormous garden. And I think they liked me. They talked to me for hours. And they looked at my sketches and they liked them. And they bought me a sandwich at dinner-time. And when I was leaving one of them winked at me. So, fingers crossed. They said they'd let me know soon. That's good, isn't it?'

'Yeah! That sounds great.'

'I know. It was fab. Oh, I would really love this job. But what about you, what did you do?' Angie asked.

'I walked around. I looked at the adverts outside an employment bureau in . . . somewhere, Crompton Street, Old Compton Street. And then a bloke came up and asked me if I wanted business.'

'Oh my god, he didn't think you were . . .?'

'Yes, he did.'

'He didn't!'

'Yes, because then a woman came along with a really tight skirt and took him upstairs.'

'Lucky escape! Good job Doreen wasn't there, she'd have carried you back to Chelmsford straight away. She hates that kind of thing.'

'Well, I wasn't mad keen on it, myself. I found a couple more employment agencies but they had nothing and then I went to the pictures.'

'On your own? Where?'

'Yes! It was in Oxford Street. The poster looked good. It was called *Suzanne's Career* – I thought I might get some tips. And it was just about to start. But it turned out it wasn't that sort of career, and it was French! It had, what are they called? Subtitles. You had to read as well as watch. I was so tired when I came out, I had to go and have a cup of tea. So there wasn't time to go looking for Brian Epstein.'

'Next time,' Angie said. 'There's bound to be a next time. We'll be coming back because I'm bound to *not* get this job.'

'Oh, I bet you do,' Carol said. 'It sounds like you made a good impression.'

'Oh, I hope so.' Angie looked at her watch. 'We're meeting Gene in an hour. He said he wants to take us to his favourite café before going to the jazz club. What are we going to do till then?'

'I might go home,' Carol said.

'No, don't,' Angie said. 'Let's go for a walk. Let's pretend we live in London, and we're just strolling round our streets, and we'll just casually end up at this café of Gene's in Frith Street.'

As they walked along Frith Street they could see scooters parked in the road, like the scooters that were always outside the Orpheus in Chelmsford. 'I wish we were going there,' Angie said.

And then they saw Gene, standing outside the café with the scooters. He was rubbing his hands in the chill of the twilight. 'I thought you'd stood me up,' he'd said, putting his arm round Angie and kissing her on the cheek.

'No chance,' Angie said. 'We came the long way round, down Charing Cross Road.' *It's almost like living here already*, she thought. *It all seems so natural – talking about the streets and the underground. As if it's my town.*

'Welcome to the Bar Italia,' Gene said. 'The hippest café in town.'

The café smelt of warm milky coffee, like the Milk Bar in Chelmsford, but somehow sharper. It was smaller, and the lights were softer, peachy. Angie and Carol sat at a small table in the back while Gene went to the counter to order their coffee. He came back with a tray of cups, each one piled high with froth, and three pieces of some strange but delicious looking cake, which seemed to be nothing but cream.

'It's cheesecake,' Gene said, knowledgeably, as if he was Italian. Perhaps he was a little bit Italian, Angie thought. The waiters in the café knew him, they'd shaken hands over the counter, one who was standing at the espresso machine had even said, '*Ciao* Geno' to him, and then he knew all about the cheesecake.

She liked this Bar Italia. It was stylish, just as Gene had said. There were mods but also people who looked like art students, certainly people who were interested in fashion, boys in sharp suits and Ben Sherman shirts, girls in dark straight dresses, a few in suede coats, all drinking coffee, talking and laughing. Angie thought she could happily spend the evening here. She could spend her whole life here. Oh London! She hoped, she really hoped she got the job.

As she pressed her fingers on to the last crumbs of the buttery lemon cake, Gene said it was time to go. It was just across the road. Over the door was the name, 'Ronnie Scott's Jazz Club.'

The place was dark but Angie could make out small round tables, and a bar and a small stage. 'It's not very big, is it?' she whispered.

'This is Ronnie's new place,' Gene said. 'It's not as good as the old one. That really had a jazz feel. This one, hmm, not sure.'

Gene was calling Ronnie Scott 'Ronnie', as if he knew him. Did he really know the owner of the club? Sometimes she wondered what his life was really like. All these things he'd done and people he knew.

Gene went over to the bar. Angie tugged Carol's arm to follow him. Before he'd ordered their drinks he turned to a tall thin man in dark clothes, leaning against the bar, smoking.

'Si, you old devil!' Gene said, slapping the man on the back. 'Angie, this is my old mate, Si Green. He's the one we've come to see. You'll never hear a smoother bass.'

Angie smiled and said hello.

'Si, I've been wanting to hear you for ages,' Gene said. 'Better make it good.'

The man smiled. 'Glad you could come.'

'Angie was desperate to hear you.'

Angie grinned. This was the first time she'd heard of him, but if it made people happy she'd agree with it. She held out her hand. She was in London, people shook hands here.

'Oh, get you, all stiff and formal,' Carol murmured.

As she shook his hand Angie felt the hard tips of Si's fingers, and the weathered texture of his palm. She looked at him. His face was open and his smile friendly. 'Bass?' she asked.

'Yes.' He gestured behind him. A large double bass lay on its side on the stage.

'Oh, double bass,' she said and laughed. 'I thought it was going to be . . .'

'Yes, unfortunately not a guitar. That would be much easier to carry around.'

'Yes.'

She smiled. He looked cool, in his dark grey shirt and his black jeans and his dark desert boots. If this was jazz it wasn't bad.

There was a shout. He twisted his head. 'Got to go. I hope you all enjoy the show.'

'Catch you later,' Gene said.

Si raised his hand and disappeared through a door at the side.

They were sitting at a table to the right of the stage, but near enough that they could see the keys on the piano and all the elements of the drum kit.

In a small leaflet on the table was a description of tonight's show, 'The Doug Bourne Trio play Ronnie Scott's for the first time!' Beside it was a tiny picture of three men, and one of them was Si, looking tall and slightly uncomfortable beside his upright double bass.

A man came on to the stage. 'Ronnie!' Gene murmured to Angie, out of the side of his mouth.

'Ronnie,' Angie whispered to Carol.

He was introducing the group. He made a joke about digging Doug, and the trio not being as Green as Si was cabbage-looking. There was a loud laugh from someone at the back of the room and a spattering of applause. 'Please yourselves,' the man said. 'A first for the club, a first for many of you, and not the last I'm sure – the Doug Bourne Trio!' He walked off the stage backwards, clapping.

The trio came onto the stage, Si was shaking his head. The three men murmured to each other as the drummer shuffled onto his seat behind his drums, Si leaned down to pick up his double bass and the third man sat at the piano on the far side of the stage. He ran his hand over the keys.

'Glad we've got the best seat in the house, so we can be sure we hear the drums,' Angie muttered into Carol's ear.

They both snorted.

Listening to jazz was, at times, like the year at school when she had tried to learn French. The teacher would mouth a string of incomprehensible words and then suddenly, with relief Angie would recognise the word *café* or *restaurant*. She would smile and congratulate herself. But by then the teacher was off again with another string of words until she heard *boutique* and she could smile again.

The men would play a series of notes, there would be a crash of drums and a thomp thomp thomp on the bass and then the pianist would play a chord and she would recognise it and maybe another and she could relax, and sway to the rhythm of a tune she knew, but then off they went again, playing strange notes with no recognisable melody.

There was a piano solo, complicated rhythms and positioning of hands, crossing back and forth, and Si and the drummer, watched, relaxed as the pianist bent over the keys.

She kept her eyes on Si, watching his left hand manoeuvring over the frets up by his shoulder and those hardened fingers of his right hand plucking and tugging at the strings to make a rhythm, a sound, almost a tune.

And then they stood up and bowed. It was over. She could relax. The trio left the stage, saying something to each other, laughing a little, as they walked through the door. The applause went on, someone whistled, people stamped their feet. They came back on. She couldn't believe it. She'd thought they could go home now. This was hard. She'd never understand jazz.

But the pianist's fingers ran across the keys and a tune she knew floated through the room. 'My Funny Valentine'. She knew it, she knew the words, she almost cried with relief.

And then it was really over. There was clapping and cheering from the audience. People stood up and whooped. The trio on the stage bowed. The lights lifted and Angie yawned.

'Drink?' Gene said.

'I don't know,' Angie said. 'Is there much more?' She turned to Carol and murmured, 'I'm half asleep.'

'There's another combo in the second half,' Gene said. 'But Si's set's over and it was him we came to see. We don't have to stay. But I told Si we'd see him in the interval.' Gene stood up. 'Let's have a drink with him.'

'All right,' Angie said. She yawned behind her fingers. 'I'll have a rum and Coke.'

'So will I,' said Carol.

'I think being in London has gone to your heads,' Gene said.

'Did you like that?' Carol asked Angie, as Gene walked to the bar.

Angie screwed her face up. 'If this is the sort of jazz they play all the time, well, I'd rather have Acker Bilk.'

'That's a bit drastic,' Carol said. 'I thought you wanted to learn to like jazz so you and Gene could share something.'

'Well, I don't mind him asking me to listen to Dave Brubeck or Mel Torme. I like Mel Torme.' They both sang, 'Doo doo doo,' softly. 'But honestly, that stuff tonight. I thought I was going to die. I could feel my ears dropping off.'

They laughed.

Angie tapped her briefcase. 'But I've got to get this job. I've got to be in London. I want to live like this every day. I'll get this job, or another one just like it, then I'll swan around with arty people, eat cheesecake in that café and then in the evening go to clubs, not like this one, I'm not a complete idiot. But just stroll over to the Flamingo, or the Marquee. They're round here somewhere, I know. When the money arrives in that new bank account, we'll come back and have a really good day in London. And I'll pay you back the money I owe you.'

'It's only a quid,' Carol said.

'But we'll buy you a new suede as a sort of interest. And then I'll buy a car and then . . .'

'And then we'll be sooo modern!'

'May I join you?'

It was Si. He sat down between Angie and Carol. 'Well, what did you think?' He looked from one to the other.

Angie looked at him. 'If I'm honest . . .'

'Yes?'

'I don't know much about jazz, so I don't know what to say, really. I don't understand what you're doing. I mean, you play fantastically. How do you get so much sound out of a double bass? It must be awfully hard on your hands.'

'You get used to it,' Si said. 'Sometimes jazz just doesn't speak to people.'

'I don't think it speaks my language,' Carol said.

'Or perhaps you just have to let it roll over you, like waves in the sea.'

'Not much fun if you can't swim,' Angie said. There was a pause. 'How do you know Gene?' she asked.

'I met him years ago,' Si said. 'When I was at school, I got a Saturday job in his shop in Kings Road when it was all very straight and three-piece suits. Gene was good to me. I worked on commission and he let me serve the customers who he knew would pay a decent amount for their clobber. And when he found out I played, he introduced me to one or two people in the music business, people he'd met through the shop, and he basically got me going.'

'So he really is a nice guy,' Angie said.

'Yes.'

'What's taking him so long, getting the drinks?' Angie twisted in her seat. 'Oh, he's talking to someone. Oh. Oh.' She stood up and the briefcase slid to the floor.

'What?' said Carol. She craned her neck to see.

'Anything wrong?' Si said. He turned round.

'No,' Angie said. 'It's, it's my sister.'

'Doreen?' Carol said. 'What's she doing here?'

'What a good question,' Angie said.

Doreen and Gene were walking towards them. Gene was holding a tray of drinks. He was frowning. 'There's someone to see you.'

Angie looked up. 'What are you doing here?'

Before she could answer, Gene said, 'I understand your sister likes jazz. Sit there, Doreen was it?'

'It was, and it still is,' Doreen said. She sat in Gene's seat, while he dragged a chair across from a nearby table.

'You haven't brought Mum and Dad, have you?' Angie peered past Doreen towards the bar.

'No, they're safely tucked up on the train home. I wanted to make sure my little sister wasn't getting into any trouble.'

'No fear of that,' Gene said. He placed the chair beside Doreen.

'And I just thought I'd come and listen to a little jazz. As you know, I like jazz.' Doreen took her mac off.

'Did you catch the set?' Si asked Doreen.

'I just caught the last couple of numbers,' Doreen said. 'Nice sound. You're the bass player, aren't you? A real hep cat!'

'Thanks. Yes, Si Green. Pleased to meet you.'

'Doreen Smith. But call me Reen.' She stood up and they shook hands across the table. 'Carol,' Doreen said, 'why don't you and I swap seats so I can talk to Si?'

'Did you just call him a hep cat?' Angie murmured to Doreen as she and Carol shuffled past each other.

'We're all hep cats here,' Doreen said, looking round. 'Aren't we?'

Si laughed. Doreen whispered something in his ear, and he laughed again. They clinked glasses.

Gene was looking at Doreen.

Angie took his arm and nuzzled her face on his shoulder. 'I'm sorry,' she whispered. 'I didn't know she was coming.'

'It had to happen at some time,' he said, taking a mouthful of his drink.

'What do you mean?' Angie said.

He patted her arm. 'Oh, nothing. No harm done. It's good to meet your sister, out in the open. At last.'

'And I think Si's pleased,' Angie said. 'They're getting on like a house on fire.' Doreen was running her fingers over the palm of Si's hand. 'Oh Gene.' Angie leaned against him and sighed. 'It's been a lovely day.'

Carol drained her glass. She looked at her watch. 'I should go.'

'We should all go,' Angie said. 'Mum and Dad really will think we're in trouble.'

'I doubt that,' Doreen said, 'knowing our parents.'

'I told you, you can all stay at my flat,' Gene said.

'Even me?' Doreen said.

'Even you,' Gene said.

'How about Si, too?' Doreen said.

'Let's not go mad,' Gene said.

'And what about your darling wife?' Angie said.

'She's not there. She's never there. I did tell you that.'
Angie smiled.

'Come on,' Doreen said. 'I've got to get these girls
home. Nice to meet you, Si. I hope our paths cross again.'

'So do I,' Si said. He took her hand and kissed it.

'And nice to meet you too, Doreen,' said Gene, rising to
his feet. He kissed each of them on the cheek, ending with
Doreen. He crushed a note into her hand. 'Get yourselves a
cab to Liverpool Street. And look after yourself. All of you.
Goodnight!' He turned away and walked over to the bar.

They hailed a taxi and climbed into the back. Carol
closed her eyes and her breathing became slow and regular.

'Could this day get any better?' Angie said. 'We're riding
in a black taxi cab. I'm glad you came, Doreen. Now you
can see how nice Gene is. He's generous and thoughtful.'

'Oh yes, very generous when there's something in it for
him,' Doreen said.

'Why did he give you the money and not me?' Angie
drooped onto Doreen's shoulder.

'Probably because you two have obviously had too
much to drink.' But Angie was asleep. 'Oh Angie,' Doreen
whispered.

CHAPTER 21

ANGIE AND DOREEN WERE SITTING AT the kitchen table, Angie was pouring cornflakes into a bowl. Doreen said, 'What time did we get in last night? I feel like I've had about five minutes sleep.'

'It was gone midnight,' Angie said. 'I'm going to ring work and tell them I'm coming in late.'

'I told Bolingbroke's I was having the morning off today. We'll both get the sack soon, if we're not careful,' Doreen said. 'And look, Dad's left us this!' She turned over the notes their dad had left on the table. 'I might go into town and spend it.'

'Things just keep getting better,' Angie said. 'I'll give some to Carol. I can't keep borrowing money off her.'

'Well, buy something for yourself as well,' Doreen said. 'Isn't it nice when you get a note in your hand like this? Makes you feel rich.'

'And we are rich!' Angie said. 'Oh, why don't they just buy a new house in that development in Springfield, forget about Australia, and we can all stay here and be happy.'

'Don't start,' Doreen said. 'We've all had the interviews now.'

'I forgot! How did yours go?'

'Oh, they said I passed. We've all passed, though I can't think how. I assume Dad didn't smell of drink, or else he just held his breath and let Mum do the talking.'

Angie reached for the milk bottle, 'So are you going to see that Si again? You looked very friendly last night.'

'Oh no, last night. I was just trying to make . . . make you jealous. Make you all jealous.'

'I don't think Gene was jealous!' Angie laughed. 'I mean he likes Si, but he had his hands full.'

'Yes,' Doreen said. 'I could see that.'

'And I don't think Carol could have cared less.' She pulled the sugar bowl towards her. 'And I had Gene so I was occupied. So no one was jealous of anyone.'

'Of course not. I meant, make you jealous that I understood jazz.' Doreen drew a cigarette from a packet on the table. She lit it and inhaled deeply. There was a feeling in the pit of her stomach, a grinding that made her want to bend over and wail. Why had she gone to the Club last night? What did she think she was doing? She'd thought at first she was making sure Angie was safe but she'd ended up trying to make Gene jealous. Why had she done that? She felt so stupid.

'Well, Gene—' Angie began.

'What's happening with you and Gene?' Doreen interrupted. 'Are you really keen on him? I mean really?'

'Yes. Why?'

'Oh, I don't know. I don't want to go on, but I think you should keep your wits about you.' Oh, this was so difficult. She wanted to warn her, but how could she do that without telling her everything, and that she couldn't do. It would break her heart.

'Reen, stop worrying about me. I'm a big girl.'

The phone rang. Neither of them moved. Angie sprinkled sugar on her cornflakes. The phone continued to ring. Angie said, 'It won't be Gene, and I don't care if it's Roger.'

Doreen said. 'It won't be for me. And if it is, they shouldn't be ringing me this early anyway.'

'What if it's Si?' Angie said, giving the name three syllables.

'I doubt it,' Doreen said, but a smiled flitted across her face.

Angie wandered into the hall, still holding a spoon. She picked up the receiver. A strange voice said, 'Can I speak to Angela Smith?'

'Yes,' Angie said. 'This is Angela, Angie.'

'Angela, this is Alison Fairfield, from the Hornsey College of Art.'

'Oh!' Angie's stomach flipped. The woman from the interview. She sat down on the seat attached to the table. 'Hello.'

'I'm ringing to let you know that we loved your interview yesterday and I must say, although it wasn't part of the job description, I really enjoyed looking at your designs. Most impressive. As I said yesterday, sadly it's not part of the job you applied for.'

Angie closed her eyes and took a deep breath, bracing herself for the rejection she knew was coming. She wondered if she would ever be able to find work in the industry that she yearned to be involved with.

Alison Fairfield was still speaking. 'But we would like to offer you the job you applied for.'

'Sorry,' Angie said. 'Could you repeat that?'

'The job is yours if you want it.' She paused. Angie was breathless. 'Now I don't know if it was mentioned to you, but all members of staff can sit in on lectures if it's appropriate and if it doesn't interfere with their own work schedule. We run some sessions in the evening that you could possibly attend. I'm only sorry that the pay isn't higher. So, will you accept our offer?'

I've got it, Angie thought. *I've got the job. And because we've got some money I can say yes.* 'Yes,' she said into the phone. 'Yes please. I mean, thank you. I didn't expect . . . This is fantastic.' She couldn't think straight. 'Thank you.'

'Do I take that as a yes?'

'Yes.'

'I'm very pleased. We'll be sending out some documents for you to fill in and then we can confirm a start date.'

'That's fantastic. Thank you.'

'My pleasure. We look forward to seeing you.'

Angie put the receiver down quietly and stood up. Then she sat down on the stairs. She put her head in her hands and she began to cry. She had never been so happy. This is where her life would begin.

Doreen walked into the hall. 'All right, big bum, can you move please? I need to go to the bathroom. Oh my god what's wrong? What's happened?'

'Nothing, it's wonderful.' Angie lifted her face and laughed. 'I've got the best job I could ever have and on top of that, they liked my designs.'

'Oh Angie, that's fantastic. This is your life. This is where it starts.'

Angie stood up. 'I'm going to ring work, I'm going to ring them now and hand in my notice. Hornsey want me to start as soon as possible.'

'Don't be daft,' Doreen said. 'There won't be anyone in the personnel department at this time in the morning. You'd better get dressed and go to work and sort it out properly then. But finish your cornflakes first.'

'Oh, I'm too excited to eat cornflakes.'

'Well, don't forget to pick up your ten pounds, or Dad'll have it back off you.'

'I'll take Graham and Mandy out for dinner. As a celebration. They'll love that.' She sat down again. 'Oh but I'll be leaving them. I'll be saying goodbye . . .

Perhaps I shouldn't do it. And then I'll have to tell Mum . . .'

'Oh yes, you should do it,' Doreen said. 'You've wanted to do this all your life.'

Angie looked up at her. 'Have I?'

'Yes! Don't you remember all those dresses you used to make for your dolls when you were small? And how we all had to do sewing lessons when we played schools?'

'You kept sewing the same bit of cloth. You covered it in in lazy daisy stitch.'

'Is that what it was? But you still made it into an apron for me. You were meant to do this, you've got to do this.'

'Really?'

'Yes. And don't worry about English Electric. You'll see them again. That Graham won't let you disappear into the sunset, you mark my words. And I'll speak to Mum for you. She'll understand.'

CHAPTER 22

Well, money hadn't made much difference to their lives, Doreen thought. She still had to work for a living. She had to keep paying for the overdraft.

She was tired and fed up. Another Wednesday afternoon and nothing to do. Wednesday was early closing in Chelmsford. Of course, it was nice to have the afternoon off, but what for? Everyone else was at work. Sometimes she went to the pictures with the girls from Womenswear. Sometimes she went to the library and sat in there for a bit. Or she'd go for a drive.

Sometimes on a Wednesday she went and said hello to Harry in his barber's shop. He closed early on a Wednesday too, but later than they did in Bolingbroke's. They'd go and have a cup of tea, after he'd finished for the day. But she didn't want to run the risk of bumping into Gene. She hadn't seen him since the night in Ronnie Scott's. She felt she'd rather shown herself up. She shouldn't have gone. She'd been stupid.

She decided to go for a walk. It was ironic, now that she had a fantastic car, that she had started to enjoy walking. You could think when you walked, you didn't have to keep stopping for traffic lights, and you didn't have to worry about old men drivers, wearing hats, who didn't understand the words 'mirror, signal, manoeuvre.'

It was a sunny day and she was wearing her new shift dress. The dress was simple, but modern and sharp. Angie had picked out the material. They'd met in town one Saturday, in Doreen's lunch break, and bought it together. It was cotton with a contemporary design of uneven blue and green lines with a slightly blurred edge. Angie had noticed it, had known the colours Doreen liked. Doreen had loved it immediately. Angie had designed it, she'd even made the pattern, cut it out and run it up on the new sewing machine. Two straight lines, a couple of darts and a zip. Angie was so careful with that sewing machine. And finally, Doreen had stood on a kitchen chair while Angie pinned up the hem. They'd laughed all the time, Angie had nearly swallowed a pin, and Mum kept coming into the kitchen to watch and make comments, about what was fashionable in her day and how she'd had a dress with those sleeves but she'd never wear anything like that now. Mum had been cheerful, and bubbly, so happy about the money, and Angie and Doreen had shared looks, smiling. It had been a lovely time. If she didn't think about Gene.

She walked past the Avenues, past Christy's, the High School and the Grammar School. It was a bit chilly when you got out of the sun and she wished she'd worn a cardigan, though that would have spoiled the line of the dress. When she got to the bus station she was tired. Her sandals were making her feet ache. She walked past Snows – oh they were all so young in there, drinking coffee in their school uniforms, pushing and laughing loudly. She walked past the Co-op butcher's and decided to go into the Cumf. It was a small café, no fancy espresso machine, just offering a nice cup of tea and occasionally a bun, oozing with butter and the sweetness of sultanas. That's what she'd have. A cup of tea and a bun, like a little old lady. She thought about it and laughed. Sometimes she felt about a hundred years old. But a nice bun with juicy sultanas was good to have, so why not? However much money you had, the simple things were sometimes the best.

She ordered at the counter and carried her cup and saucer and the plate with the bun to a table by the window. She looked over at the bridge and the railway line. She wondered if she should get on a train and go somewhere by herself, walk round Witham or Colchester. But now it was half past three. Far too late to go anywhere. She stirred her tea and gazed out of the window, watching the big green double-deckers lumbering in and out of the bus station. Yes, she'd just get the bus home when she'd finished her bun, back to the delights of the Greenway Estate.

'Watcha!'

She turned and looked up at a figure, outlined by the sun. She frowned prettily.

'We meet again. Hang on, I'll get myself a drink.'

She looked at him as he stood at the counter.

'Oh God,' she said. It was Cliff.

She should go. But she didn't.

He came over to her table, with a cup of tea. 'Mind if I . . .?'

'It's a free country,' she said.

He sat down. 'How's the new car? Did it match your swanky black sweater?'

'Don't talk to me about my swanky black sweater.'

'All right, if you say so.'

'I mean, it doesn't exist anymore.'

His eyes widened. 'Why? You seemed very proud of it.'

'Well, I was. If you must know my little sister's boyfriend wrapped it round his scooter or something and now it's no bigger than a dishcloth and twice as tight.' It was good to be able to complain to someone. At home the feeling of guilt stopped a lot of the conversations she wanted to have. 'Now I've got the car, but not the sweater,' she laughed.

'Well that's a real shame.' Cliff took a packet of Benson and Hedges out of his pocket and offered her one. She shook her head. 'Benson and Hedges!' he said, encouragingly.

'No thanks, not with my tea.'

'Mind if I . . .?'

'Be my guest.'

He put a cigarette in his mouth and took a small book of matches from another pocket. She watched him as he lit the cigarette and inhaled. He leaned across to another table and picked up an ash-tray. 'Not at work?'

'It's Wednesday,' she said. 'We close early on Wednesdays.'

'Whereas, in my business, we never close. People die all the time. This afternoon, by coincidence, I am not required by the dead.'

'Or the living,' she said lazily.

'OK,' he said. He pushed his chair back. She thought she'd gone too far, that he was going to move, but he was simply giving himself room to put one leg across the other, his pointed black shoe resting against one knee. He seemed quite contented. He held his cigarette in one hand and drank his tea with the other.

Doreen took another sip from her cup.

'You know what you look like, sitting there?' he said.

'The *Mona Lisa*?'

'Prettier. But you look so serious, drinking that tea. You look as if it's a job for you.'

'Oh well, yeah,' she said. 'I do this part time. Tea-tasting.'

'Then shouldn't you be writing stuff down?' he asked.

'No. I keep it all up here.' She tapped her temple. 'Then when I get back to head office, it goes into a big book we call . . . the teapot.'

'Do you want to know what I think?'

'Not really.'

'I think you should take other people's points of view into consideration.'

'Oh yeah?'

'Yeah. I've got a lot to say about tea.'

'Is that a fact?' She didn't know if he was being serious.

He picked up his cup and took a mouthful of tea. 'I take sugar.'

'Good for you.'

'Looking at your spoon I can see you don't. You haven't used it. So your tea will taste very different.'

She laughed. Then she watched as he picked up her own cup from the saucer and took a mouthful.

'Hey, watch it,' she said. 'I don't know where you've been.'

'Oh, it's not like we haven't shared saliva before.'

'What do you mean?' She began flicking through her mental diary. He couldn't know she'd drunk from his coffee cup in Wainwrights, surely. How could she explain that? 'Is this what you were talking about the other day? Because we certainly didn't share saliva when I came round with the jam jars. You just got a mouthful of Max Factor face powder.'

He laughed. 'Oh yeah. Not bad. No, I don't mean then. It was when we were at school.'

'All I remember of you at school was you and all your mates laughing at the girls when we went off to do our shorthand and typing class, and trying to nick our pencils. Give me a cigarette.'

He passed her a cigarette and lit it for her. He shook out the match. 'I was only messing about because we had technical drawing and I hated that lesson. But what about the dog thing? Don't you remember how that ended?'

'What dog thing?'

'You must remember, it was one morning, we were all on the bus on the way to school. I think you were wearing your school mac.'

She shook her head. 'I was always wearing that horrible mac.'

Their hands touched as they tapped ash from their cigarettes into the ash-tray.

'You were on the bus,' he said, 'and someone got on with a big dog.'

'Oh God.' She shuddered. A memory was returning. She took a deep drag on her cigarette.

'And the dog bounced up the stairs all on its own and came up to your seat and started nosing around. And you were shrink-shrink-shrinking up against the window. The bloke who owned it came up the stairs and just sat down at the back and left the dog to it. He didn't give a monkey's that you were scared. Though he could have seen that. Then the dog jumped up on the seat beside you. Bloody great big thing, it was an Alsatian.'

She held her breath. She could feel the enormous dog beside her, its saliva spraying on to her mac as it barked. She had been so scared.

'You didn't even dare turn round to see who the bloody dog belonged to. You just kept looking out of the window, like you could see something really interesting on the Main Road. And the dog started barking. I think you had your eyes tight shut, sitting there really straight and still. But tears were rolling down your cheeks.'

And then someone shouted 'Bastard!' she remembered, and suddenly the dog disappeared, dragged off the seat, and then the owner was tumbling down the stairs. 'And the bus stopped and they fell off the bus,' she murmured. 'It was raining. And some people clapped.'

'Yeah, well it wasn't me doing the clapping. I was the one who chucked him down the stairs.'

'That was you?'

'God, you don't remember, do you? I came up to see if you were all right and you threw your arms round me and kissed me.'

'Did I? Are you sure?' Another memory was coming back. Someone holding her tight, stroking her hair.

'You just looked up and kissed me.'

'I was obviously grateful. But if it helps, thanks again.'

'That's OK. The kiss was enough.'

She thought about it. 'And then, didn't you get off the bus? Without saying a word.'

'I'd just kicked a bloke down the stairs, I was a bit worried I was going to get done over by his mates, or the old Bill. Anyway, I had to get off at the next stop. I needed some fags for school.'

'You and cigarettes! But you never said anything after that. Are you sure it was you? I thought it was the Lone Ranger. I told Janice about it, and she said, "Well who was it?" and I didn't know.'

What Janice had actually said was, 'Well, who was it? He sounds gorgeous.'

'You could have mentioned it later.'

'I wasn't there.'

'Where were you?'

'I had one or two run-ins with the law.'

'Oh yes.' Another memory was coming back. 'Oh yes!' Police cars at the school gates, everyone rushing to the windows, someone in handcuffs, laughing, being led away.

'I was a bit too easy with my fists in those days. I'm a changed man now.'

She sighed. 'I should bloody well hope so. There's too many men who let their fists do the talking.'

'I'm sorry about that,' he said.

They lived so close, he had to know what she was talking about. There'd been police cars outside their house often enough.

'I only did it to save people,' he said. 'Well, a couple of times when boys at school wound me up. You're not the only one who's got family issues.'

She frowned. 'Your mum seems so nice.'

'If you mean my old woman in the Crescent, yeah, she is nice. But she's not my real mum.'

'Yes, I did hear something like that, something about the war?'

'Yeah. You know she fosters kids. Well, I was the first one. My real mum was a friend of hers who'd been knocked up by some bloke in France.'

'You're French!' That was a turn-up for the books.

'Maybe. Some soldier. I might be a Yank. Probably a Tommy.'

'What was your real mother doing in France?'

'Driving an ambulance.'

'God! What does she do now?'

'Heroin, I think. I don't see much of her.'

'Oh Cliff, I'm sorry.'

'Don't be. My mum is the one who lives in the Crescent. The other one – well, she doesn't know me, and I don't know her.'

'Oh.' Doreen took another mouthful of tea. 'After that I think I need a bit of sugar in this.' She took a spoonful of sugar from the bowl on the table and stirred it into her cup.

'Much better,' he said.

She took a sip. 'I'm not sure about that. But . . . thanks. For the dog thing.'

'All in a day's work.'

She laughed. 'What happened to him?'

'Who?'

'The man with the dog.'

'Oh, he was all right. He had his arm in plaster for a bit. Belly aching all over town about it, apparently.'

'He broke his arm because of me?'

'He broke his arm because of me,' Cliff corrected. 'Don't worry about it. It was years ago.'

'That wasn't why you went away?'

'No, no. That was some other arse. Who might have been my dad.'

She gazed at him. He had a smooth complexion, just the hint of a shadow on his cheeks, he had dark eyes, and that bit of hair that flopped over his forehead. And he could do chit-chat. She liked that. 'All right,' she said, 'you're forgiven.'

'What for?'

'Stealing that kiss, not for drinking my tea.'

'I stole nothing. You kissed me! Wanna do it again?'

She laughed. 'What!'

'Not now!' he said. 'Tonight. Why don't we go out tonight?' He raised an eyebrow.

She looked at him. He wasn't Cliff Evans, tie askew, mucking around outside the secretarial class, he wasn't Mrs Evans no-good son spending his life in jail, he was a man who had a job, who could chat, who could make jokes, who was quite good looking.

'All right,' she said.

'You see, I knew you wanted to.'

'Just for a drink. Nothing fancy.'

'OK.'

She watched him as he left the coffee bar. She liked the way he walked. His hands in his pockets, slightly hunched, nodding to an acquaintance. But for God's sake. He'd thrown someone down the stairs of a bus.

Doreen adjusted the scarf round her neck. It was her favourite, green and orange flowers on silky material. She touched her throat, briefly, thoughtfully. She picked up her handbag from the top of the new washing machine in the corner. 'I'm going out,' she said, gaily.

It was a warm evening and she felt light walking out to the car. She was looking forward to the evening with Cliff. She would forget all about Gene. Perhaps Cliff would suggest they sit outside in the setting sun. Perhaps they would sit in a dark corner with their drinks. She would choose rum and blackcurrant, it was so sweet and thick. She could almost taste it on her tongue. She licked her lips. She felt the lipstick. It was a new one – Pretty Pink. She tossed her head. It was Gene's loss.

She'd said 'Let's meet in the pub.' That's what she wanted, not him coming round to pick her up, she wanted it to be all very casual, no big arrangements, no wide eyes and knowing smiles from her mum. This was just fun, this was just a pleasant evening. She was being carefree like a young woman should be. Gene wasn't the only fish in the sea. She wasn't playing the field exactly, but just having a nice time. She remembered again how Cliff's arms had felt around her after the dog had slobbered all over her. But yes, it was she who had initiated the kiss, in relief, in gratitude, with those arms holding her so easily, for just long enough. Was it really him? Perhaps if he kissed her this evening she would remember. His lips looked soft. She wouldn't mind.

She looked at her watch as she got into the car. She'd be about ten minutes late. That was all right. Make him wait. It was the man's job to wait.

She drove along the Main Road, past Day's garage and the Methodist Church. She remembered coming this way to secondary school. She looked down at her knees. She liked the way her skirt rode up just a little when she drove. She liked her knees. She liked driving. Oh, she loved this car. She parked in the pub car park and walked into the saloon bar.

He wasn't there. He wasn't there. She stared into the dark corners of the pub. Had he stood her up? Bloody cheek. Well, sod that, she'd have a drink anyway.

'Rum and black please.'

'That's a big drink for a little girl.' He was there behind her, standing close to her, speaking over her shoulder. 'Not tea-tasting tonight?'

She turned, giddy with relief, almost into his arms. 'That's my day job. My evening work is a bit stronger. Where were you? I was looking for you.'

'Where were you? I was out in the garden.' He drained beer from a glass and pushed the glass towards the barman. 'Could you fill that up for us?'

'Do you want to go in the garden?' she said, watching him take a ten-shilling note from his pocket to pay the barman.

He slid the change into his pocket. 'It's a bit cold.' He was wearing the black suit. His dark hair was smoothed down and glinted with some sort of oil.

He looks great, she thought, *like the cat's pyjamas*. 'Why didn't you look like this at school?' she said.

'There's a limit to how good you can make a green and yellow tie and grey trousers actually look,' he said. 'Whereas you in that that grey pleated skirt you wore, with your white shirt. You always had a cool way of dressing.'

'Huh!' she said, but she was pleased.

He picked up the drinks and they walked to a secluded table.

She sat down and slipped off her mac. She took a mouthful of her drink. Its sweetness coated her tongue and ran down her throat. She smiled. She was going to enjoy this evening.

Later, after a couple more drinks, when the sun had gone down and the night was dark, they went into the car park and he pulled her to him and kissed her.

She pulled back a little and laughed. 'Was that really you who kissed me on the bus?'

'Yeah, but as I said before, you kissed me.' He ran his thumb over her lips. 'The next day at school you didn't say a word to me.'

She opened her mouth and bit the tip of his thumb. 'I didn't know it was you.'

'Well, you know now.' He kissed her again.

'Let's get in the car,' she said. 'That blue one, over there.' She pointed proudly.

'Looks comfy,' he said.

She unlocked the door. 'Shall we?' she said. She slid into the driver's seat then leaned across to open the passenger door. He got in and put his arm round her neck and kissed her. His hand slid down to her skirt, to her knees. It hovered there, and she could feel the warmth of his palm. Then his hand rose up, under the tight material of her skirt, over the top of her stocking, onto the bare flesh of her thigh. She sighed with pleasure. 'This is a nice surprise.'

He laughed softly. 'I've been waiting long enough.'

'You should have said.' They both laughed. She liked him.

The door of the pub opened and a man and woman came out and walked towards them.

'Oh God,' Doreen groaned. 'We should have put the roof up.'

Cliff moved as if to get out of the car.

'We can't do it now!' Doreen said. 'That would be a bit unstylish. And anyway, perhaps it's for the best.' She straightened her skirt.

He laughed and sat back in the seat. He took out a packet of cigarettes. 'If we're forgetting the sex, we might as well go straight for the cigarettes.' He held the packet out to her.

'Thank you,' she said. She took one.

The match glowed in the darkness as he lit both their cigarettes.

He breathed out a plume of smoke and looked up at the sky. 'Nice evening.'

She tilted her head and looked at the stars. 'Yes, it's so dark here, you can see so many stars.' There was a pale crescent moon. 'A new moon,' she said, quietly.

'Yes,' he said, 'but what I meant was, it's been a nice evening.'

She looked at him. 'Really? I mean, it's been nice for me too. I'm sorry about, you know, all this.' She pointed at the folded roof.

'I'm kind of glad we didn't do anything, you know,' he said. 'Not that glad, obviously, but I'd like our first time to be somewhere nicer than the car park of the Angel.'

'You old romantic, you,' she said, but she liked that he'd said it. She stubbed out her cigarette in the small ash-tray in the car-door. 'Shall we call it a night?'

'Yeah, let's do that.' He flicked his cigarette out of the window.

'I'll give you a lift home.'

He smiled. 'That's a first.'

She switched on the ignition and drove out onto the Main Road.

As she parked outside his house he turned and said, 'I was thinking of going to the flicks tomorrow night, if you're interested.'

She looked at him seriously. She did like him, but she shook her head. It was too risky. The whole thing with Gene had cut deeper than she'd realised. She'd been thinking of Gene when she kissed Cliff. That was no good for either of them. She had to sort out her feelings about Gene – and men in general – before she could even contemplate starting anything new. 'I don't think so.'

He sighed. 'I expect you'll be washing your hair.'

'Something like that.'

'All right. See you around.'

'Yeah. Look, no hard feelings? OK?'

'Oh Reen.' He turned and kissed her quickly on the cheek. 'I did have a good time tonight.'

'Yeah, me too.'

''Night.'

''Night. Have a nice life,' she said.

He jumped out of the car and walked up the path to his front door.

'Bugger, bugger, bugger,' Doreen said. She put the car into gear and drove down the road.

She drew up outside the house and turned off the engine. She reached in her bag for a cigarette and lit it, then she sat for a moment, looking out into the night, enjoying the stillness. The street was empty, a few lights on here and there, no one walking, no cars passing. She leaned back and let out a long sigh. She was pleased they hadn't done it, she told herself. No point tempting fate too often.

Everything was such a mess. Perhaps she should go to Australia. Her mum was still determined that they should go, even with all the money they'd won. She could go with them, make a place for herself. *People must get married in Australia*, she thought, *they must need to buy wedding dresses.* There'd surely be enough money to set up a little shop of her own. That would be good. Or she could start again. Have a different life. Get on telly over there. Maybe even change her name. She could call herself Debbie or Sandy, or Penny, perhaps. Put Gene behind her once and for all.

CHAPTER 23

ANGIE HAD BEEN AT THE ART school a week and she still couldn't believe her luck. She felt her whole life had changed. She didn't care that she had to get up at six, grab a bowl of cereal and eat it leaning against the sink, then fly out of the back door to catch the bus to town to catch the train to Liverpool Street. It was all part of the joy of working in London – even the tube journey and then the bus ride she had discovered she could take to get to the college. Mum had been happy for her, even though she'd hoped Angie would go to Australia with them in the end. And her dad had, grudgingly given her ten pounds to buy a season ticket.

She had handed in her notice at English Electric, and asked the personnel officer if she could leave straight away. Together they had weighed up the effect of the lost wages against the joy of taking the train to London on Monday morning to start her new job and she had decided she would lose the wages. She had taken Graham and Mandy to the pub for a sandwich and a Britvic orange and she had said goodbye. Graham had made her promise that she would keep in touch.

Her new job was interesting, although she knew that it would become routine, tidying studios, sorting out equipment, checking for breakages, noting what supplies were needed, paper, charcoal, graphite, pastels. Everyone had been friendly. Some of the lecturers had spoken to her, asked her if she was new, if she liked the job, thanked her for her help. And then there were the students. She liked being in the corridor as the sessions began and ended, as they left the rooms and studios. She would lean against a wall as they passed, talking about art, discussing colours and textures and shapes. Some were beatniks, in long sloppy sweaters and messy hair; some girls were almost rockers with white stiletto shoes and backcombed hair, and the boys they hung out with used Brylcreem; some looked as if they'd come from Poshville, in tweed jackets and shirts and ties, and the girls in suits with round collars that buttoned up to the neck. Several of the men smoked pipes and had beards, some wore old-fashioned round rimmed glasses. There wasn't a single mod to be seen. Angie felt proud to wear her twinsets and long straight skirts and her flat moccasins.

But her real joy was the lectures and sessions that she was permitted to sit in on. There were lectures about colour, about shape, about fabric. Every day she managed to attend at least one class, sometimes two.

One day a woman, stopped her in the corridor. 'Angela! How are you getting on?'

Angie looked at the woman. She was young with short wavy brown hair, and she wore a straight shift dress in grey, with a black cardigan buttoned at the neck. She remembered her from the interview. It was Alison Fairfield

'Oh, Miss Fairfield. Thank you. I really love it. Everyone's being so nice.'

'Good. As I think I said, we enjoyed your interview, and your designs. There was a very nice dress that I really appreciated.'

'The one with the strange sleeves, you said. Yes, I remember now.' They laughed.

'Have you managed to get to one of my classes?'

Angie shook her head. 'Not yet.'

'Please, do, if you think they'll be interesting. And they fit in with your work schedule. I'd like to know a bit more about your ideas. It's unusual to have a technician who can turn a seam!'

'Is it?'

'Oh yes. And you know Barbara Darling. Who, I think I can tell you now, said you'd be a delight to have in the college and, indeed, in lectures. I've known Barbara a long time.'

How strange to think of Miss Darling having a first name.

'Well, welcome to Hornsey.'

'Thank you.'

Angie hurried back to the technician's station. She scanned the timetable she kept in her bag. There was a 'Use of fabric' class led by Miss Fairfield this afternoon. She was determined to go to it.

Angie sat at the back and listened. She enjoyed the class. There was talk of shape and fall and flow and cut. She took notes, made some sketches. Towards the end of the class Miss Fairfield, walked round the room, commenting on students' work. She glanced at Angie's sketch pad, then stopped and asked to see some of her earlier work. She called it work! Miss Fairfield held up the pad, to show one of Angie's designs, telling the students this was an excellent example of what could be achieved with a single line, and how the set of a sleeve could alter the look of the whole outfit.

That evening Angie had to work late. She had been to another class, this time on pattern making, and then had spent two hours tidying rooms, noting what and how much paper and other stationery had been used, setting out easels and seats in the studios for the next day's class, tidying the area where life models would change, checking that the small electric fires behind their screens actually worked, changing a couple of fuses. It was almost nine o'clock when she left the building and walked to the bus stop.

She was exhausted. She had a long journey ahead. But she couldn't stop smiling at the delight of the job. She was going to have to give up her evening class at home, which would be a wrench, but it would be worth it. She couldn't wait for tomorrow and what new things she'd learn, what ideas they would spark.

She hadn't thought about Gene or even Roger for days.

On Friday evening Angie came in from work, laden with some new fabric she had bought in London. It had cost a fortune, *but*, she told herself, *a fortune is what we've got*. She bounded up the stairs and peered into Doreen's room.

She frowned. 'What are you doing there? Are you all right?'

'I've just got a bit of a headache. What have you been up to?'

'Buying some gorgeous material. I couldn't borrow that dress you're wearing, could I?' Angie said.

Doreen glanced down, she was wearing a rust coloured dress Angie had made. 'So who's it for tonight?'

'Roger,' Angie said. 'I want to be charming but serious.'

'I'd have thought you'd got past that with Roger. He's a very safe bet, isn't he? The last time I saw him he was looking at you as if you were the most delicate piece of porcelain in the world and he couldn't believe his luck that he'd got you.'

'Oh, he looks at everyone like that,' Angie said.

'No, he doesn't. If I was a gambling kind of person, I'd bet good money on him popping the question any day now.' Doreen sat up and swivelled her legs onto the floor.

'If Mum had anything to do with it, he'd be walking me up the aisle tomorrow,' Angie said. 'And that's what I'm afraid of. Sooooo, I've made up my mind. I'm going to chuck him. Tonight.'

Doreen's head snapped up. 'Why? Why would you do that?'

'You know why.'

'Gene, you mean? For goodness' sake.'

'Look, this new job is taking almost all my time. I haven't been out in the evening since I started. I haven't got time for two blokes. And when my head is not full of fashion and dresses, I think about Gene – there's no room for Roger. I've got to make a decision.'

'Well, maybe, but do you think the one you're making is the best one? I mean, do you know who Gene is? Even his name's made up. Is he really the man you think he is?'

Angie gazed at Doreen, then said, 'I don't care. I love him. Who knows anyone properly? What I know of him is all good, and gets better all the time. His mate Si, before you arrived, he had a whole new story about Gene that was really good, how he'd supported him and helped him get a bit of money. Like he's done for me.'

'What?'

'Well, he knows I'll pay him back when Dad's sorted out all the bank accounts.'

'Oh Angie.'

'Anyway, what do you care?'

'I care about you. And I care about your future. And I even care a little bit about Roger.'

'So does this mean you're not going to lend me that dress?'

'No.' Doreen sighed and stood up, pulling the dress off. 'Here.' She handed the dress to Angie. 'Pass me my house-coat,' she said.

At precisely 6.30 Roger arrived. He knocked on the back door. Mrs Smith answered and greeted him warmly. 'Roger! Very nice to see you.'

'And you, Mrs Smith.'

'Come in.'

'No time to come in.' Angie appeared behind Mrs Smith. 'We're off out.'

'The film doesn't start for an hour,' Roger said.

'I want to be at the front of the queue.'

'Always wants to be queen,' Mrs Smith said.

'Well, she's my queen.' Roger smiled.

'She's lucky to have you,' Mrs Smith said.

'Bye Mum.' Angie pushed Roger off the step.

They walked down the front path. 'You look very nice,' Roger said.

'Thank you.' He really was good, she thought. So kind, so considerate. He really tried to make her happy. *But that's the difference*, she told herself, *Gene doesn't have to try*. He made her happy just by existing in the world.

The scooter was parked behind Doreen's new car. 'Great car,' Roger said. 'I wouldn't mind having a car like that one day. We could go down to Clacton—' He saw her expression. 'Sorry, not Clacton, Southend, on a sunny day. Wouldn't that be great?'

Of course it would, she wanted to say, *but we're not going to be together when that day comes.*

'What?' he said. 'What's up?'

'Roger, I . . . I've got to say this.'

'What?' His face had gone pale. He knew what she was going to say.

'We can't . . . I . . . we've got to end it.'

'What do you mean?' He sounded breathless. His eyes raked her face in disbelief.

'Oh Roger. You're so good. It's nothing to do with you, it's me. But we've got to stop going out.' There she'd said it. She felt sick.

'Is it because of the money? Because you want someone who's as rich as you, now?'

'No!'

'Is it because of Australia? Because you'll have to leave me behind? I told you, I'll come to Australia too.'

'I'm not going to Australia.'

'What is it? Is it someone else?'

'No,' she said. Deep down she had always known, even before she met Gene, that it couldn't last with Roger. And she wanted to save him the hurt of it. 'I suppose it's because I feel trapped. I feel tied down. My mum keeps talking about us getting married.'

'Does she? Well, we could.' He sounded so hopeful.

'No, what I mean is, the thought of getting married makes me feel even more tied down.'

'We don't have to get married.'

'I know, but – but I know you would like to. It seems unfair to stop you. You should find someone who does want to get married.'

'Angie! I don't just want to get married to anybody. If it's going to be anyone, it's going to be you. And if you don't want to, well, then I'll just have to live with that.'

'But I can't live with you living with something. I want us to feel the same.'

'We can't feel the same. We're different people. Otherwise . . . you might as well . . . look at yourself in the mirror every morning and have a relationship with yourself.'

He'd never said anything so pointed. She admired him for that.

'Look,' he said, 'now I know how you feel, why don't we try and sort out how we are together? So you don't feel tied down and I get to see you. So we have a nice time.'

'Oh Roger. You're making this so hard.' She ran her fingers over the handlebar of the Lambretta.

'How about we leave it for a month, then we meet up and see how we both feel then? Who knows,' he said, trying a joke, 'I might have met someone else and be married with a kid on the way.'

'Well, good luck!' she said, feeling a spurt of jealousy for the new person he'd meet who'd be happy to settle down with him and have a family.

'Come on, what do you say? A month. I'm going to miss you.'

'I'm probably going to miss you too but that's not the point.'

'Sometimes I don't understand you, Angie.' He looked away. 'And that's why I like you.'

He sounded so sad, she couldn't bear it. 'All right. A month. Let's meet up in a month.'

'So, you don't want to go to the pictures now?'

'No, I don't.'

'OK.' He turned, without his usual kiss, and she felt cold and empty.

CHAPTER 24

ON SATURDAY MORNING ANGIE SAT AT home in bed, in her winceyette pyjamas, feeling free. It would be hard having a weekend without Roger, but she'd said goodbye for a reason, and now she could stop agonising about whether she should be with Roger or not and get on with her life. She could do what she wanted, make the choices she wanted, be who she wanted.

She was sketching a new design, a floor-length dress, with a bias-cut skirt, with long tight sleeves and a scoop neck dotted with a few pearls. It was a wedding dress. It was an idea she'd had when she had sat in on the Professional Finishing Techniques class at the college, making an element of the sleeve correspond to something on the neckline, through different sorts of embroidery.

As she sketched, she hummed a Beatles tune. At first, she couldn't name it, and then she realised it was 'If I Needed Someone'. 'Ah but I don't,' she whispered to herself.

There was a tap on her bedroom door. 'Angie.' Her mum's voice came softly. 'Are you awake?' Gently the door opened and her mum, still in her housecoat and with a head full of curlers, peeped into the room.

'Yes. Why, what time is it?' By force of habit, Angie began pulling together the sheets of drawing paper that were strewn across the bed, hiding them from public gaze. But now it was different, they had money and she could do what she wanted, it didn't matter who knew it. She looked at her mother's face. 'What's wrong?' She shuffled the sketches into a heap beside her and picked up her new watch. 'It's seven o'clock!'

'Did you hear anything?' Mrs Smith said.

'What? Your face! What's happened?'

Without answering, Mrs Smith called, 'Doreen! Can you come in here?'

There was the sound of the bathroom door opening. 'What? Where are you?'

'In here.'

Doreen came into Angie's room, in a nightdress with a towel wrapped round her head. She unwound the towel and began to dry her hair.

'Why is everyone up so early on a Saturday?' Angie said.

'I have to go to work on a Saturday,' Doreen said. 'Unlike some people.'

'You have Wednesday afternoons off.'

'Girls. Stop,' Mrs Smith said. 'This is serious. I need your attention.' She sank down onto Angie's bed. She began to cry.

'What? What?' Angie stretched her arm out to her mother.

Doreen sat down beside her on the edge of the bed. 'Mum? What's happened?' She studied her face. 'What's he done?' Mrs Smith was silent. 'He hasn't hit you?'

'No, no, nothing like that.'

'You're not ill, are you?'

Mrs Smith shook her head. She pulled a hanky from her sleeve and blew her nose. 'But it is your dad.'

'What's happened to him? Is he all right? Where is he?'

'He's not here.'

'Is he in hospital?' Angie said. She began to rise from the bed.

Mrs Smith shook her head.

'So what is it this time?' Doreen sighed. 'As if we couldn't guess. Drunk himself into a stupor and spent the night in a ditch in Boreham.'

'No. Well, I don't think so. He's gone.'

'What do you mean?' Angie said. She sank back into the blankets.

'When I woke up this morning he wasn't there. I went downstairs in case he'd gone down in the night and fallen asleep on the settee. He wasn't there.'

'Perhaps he's staying at a friend's,' Angie said.

'Well, perhaps. But . . .' She gulped. 'All his things have gone from the wardrobe.'

'What do you mean? Why? None of his things are worth taking, are they?'

'Oh, Doreen. He left this note on the draining board.' She drew a scrap of paper from the pocket of her housecoat.

'Are you sure?' Angie said.

'Draining board!' Doreen said. 'Doesn't he know you have to leave notes on a dry surface if they're going to be read?'

'He doesn't know what a draining board is for,' said Angie.

Doreen pulled the note from her mother's fingers. '"Sorry",' she read aloud. She turned over the piece of paper. There was nothing more. 'Sorry? Sorry? Is that it? Sorry for what?'

'For what he's done.'

'How far back are we going?' Doreen said.

'Don't be stupid. Give me that.' Mrs Smith snatched the note from Doreen's fingers. She stared at it as if hidden in those letters was the full story, their life together, the better, the worse, the sickness and the health. 'He's gone. And so are all of his things. Oh, I should never have asked about the money.'

'I thought he seemed happier recently,' Angie said. 'He made a joke last week, and another one the week before. I thought he was excited about Australia.'

'He was excited about the money,' Mum said.

'But before that. I thought he was looking forward to it all.'

'No, I pushed him too far about Australia. That's why he's gone.'

'Well, good riddance to bad rubbish, I say,' Doreen said.

'But that's not the worst part. I think – I think he's probably taken all the money.' Mrs Smith sobbed.

'He's what?!' Doreen bounced up from the bed. 'He's bloody what?!'

'What makes you think he's taken all the money?' Angie stroked her mum's arm.

'Well, you know, he set up a special bank account. The pools people paid it in there. They wanted to give him advice about what to do with it, but he said he didn't need it because it was all arranged. He was opening bank accounts for all of us.'

'Yes?' said Doreen, a guttural sound from the back of her throat.

'Well, last night I asked him about it, because you know, I've spent a little bit.' She touched her hair. 'And I know you both have.' Angie and Doreen looked at each other.

'I got a bloody great overdraft on the basis of it!' Doreen said.

'Well, half of that overdraft is mine,' Angie whispered. She thought about the new suede coat, the sewing machine, the yards of wonderful silk and taffeta she had bought, the haircuts she had had.

'So I said to him that we were all waiting. It was during the adverts. He'd come in when the news was on, and he sat down and it was all fine and dandy. He'd had a good evening. He said he'd seen a couple of mates he hadn't seen in a while. They'd bought him a drink. I thought it was the right time to mention it. And he flew into a rage. Just like that. Jumped up in the air. Shouting that we were all ungrateful, that he was a hard-working man doing his best. No one gave him respect, he said. Respect! Where did he get that from? I was just pleased you girls didn't hear. I haven't seen him like that for a long time.'

Again, Angie scoured her mum's face for bruises, but saw only red eyes.

'And this morning,' Mrs Smith raised her hands hopelessly, 'he's not here.'

'No, no, it can't be . . . Perhaps the note just means sorry for the row,' Angie said.

'Don't be daft, he means sorry about the money,' Doreen said. 'Mum, tell me, please tell me that your name is on the main bank account!'

Mrs Smith shook her head.

'Oh Mum.' Angie and Doreen looked at each other.

'He's always looked after the money.'

'Oh Mum,' Doreen groaned. 'That means he owns it all. All of it. No bank accounts for us, no measly five pound, ten pound handouts when he feels like it. Nothing. Nothing! It's all gone. He's gone.'

'We don't know that. Perhaps it's not forever,' Angie said. 'Perhaps he'll be back soon.'

'Get you, Miss Sunshine,' Doreen said. 'Perhaps he's had a personality change, and grown another three inches and got his own teeth back.'

'He took all his clothes,' Mrs Smith said, her voice wavering. 'His warm winter clothes and his trousers as well as stuff that he wears in the summer – that shirt with the flamingos on.'

'Perhaps he's just gone on holiday,' Angie said. 'We don't know, do we?'

'He's not coming back.' Mrs Smith was still holding the note, in her hand, with her hanky.

Doreen took the note from her. 'Don't get it all creased up. We should keep this as evidence,' she said.

'Evidence of what?' Angie said.

'For when we are accused of murdering him and we have to plead justification.' She flicked the note with her fingers. '"Sorry"! I'll make him sorry.'

'Did you hear anything in the night?' Mrs Smith said to Angie.

'No. Well, apart from Doreen coming in, and you going to the toilet. And then him. I thought he was going to the toilet.'

'Don't you ever sleep?' Doreen asked.

'Oh God,' Angie said, 'his suitcases. It's nothing to do with your conversation last night, Mum. He's been planning this.'

'What do you mean?'

'I went into the shed to get a screwdriver to put a plug on my new sewing machine, and there were two suitcases tucked away on the bottom shelf. I looked in one and there was a big woolly sweater I'd never seen before and some fancy slacks.'

'Why didn't you say something?' wailed Mrs Smith.

'I just assumed it was to do with Australia. I thought you'd both been out buying jazzy clothes for the trip.'

'He obviously has.' Doreen hissed, 'Ohhh, what's the betting that's where he's gone?'

'No,' her mum said. 'I don't think so. He wouldn't do that. He doesn't want to go to Australia.' She looked at Doreen, 'Don't make that face. All right, maybe he has. Maybe,' she said hopefully, 'maybe he's gone to get it ready for us. To make it nice.'

'And maybe he's flown Pig Airlines. When has Dad ever done anything like that?' Doreen said.

Mrs Smith's head hung lower and she sobbed again. Angie put her arm round her. 'It's not all bad, Mum.'

'Isn't it?'

'We've got each other. We've got our health and strength.'

'Speak for yourself,' Doreen said. 'I think I might have a heart attack.'

Angie frowned at her. 'We won't have the smell of beer all through the house. He won't be sick in the bathroom anymore.'

'But all that money!' her mum said. 'I was going to get you both such lovely things. It was going to make such a difference.'

'Well it already has,' said Doreen. 'I've pretty much spent my share. I was working on the basis he was a decent human being and when he said he'd give us all something that that's what he was going to do. Share it out equally, so we could all buy a car and maybe even a house each. And so like a fool, I arranged the overdraft with the bank. And then I bought the car. Oh, the car!' She sank down on the bed. 'My lovely beautiful car. Whatever am I going to do?'

'How much have you spent?' asked her mum.

'Let's just say it goes into four figures, and then some.'

'Oh, love,' her mum whispered.

Angie put her hand over her mouth. 'Oh no. Oh no! This is terrible.'

'We know!' Doreen said.

'But really terrible for me. My new job. I can't do it. I can't afford it. The wages are almost nothing, and with my fares and everything, I'm paying them to employ me. If the money's gone I can't afford it. I'll have to leave,' Angie whispered. Tears trembled in her eyes.

'Oh Angie,' Doreen said.

'And then we'll have to send everything back.' Angie looked over at the smart, shiny case beside her dressing table, the case that held her sewing machine – the magic of stitches and all the clothes she was going to create, the gowns, the dresses, the jackets, the boleros. She scrambled out of bed. 'I'm going to get dressed.'

They gathered in the kitchen. Mrs Smith had swapped her housecoat for an overall. She had taken out her curlers but she hadn't brushed her hair and she had tight roller-shaped curls all over her head. In silence, she put the kettle on the stove. Doreen put slices of bread under the grill. Angie clattered in the cutlery drawer for knives and took plates down from the cupboard. She put the marge and marmalade on the table.

They sat down and looked at each other.

'So,' said Doreen. 'What are we going to do? I'm the eldest, so I have to ask the questions. Mum's in no state. She went through three hankies while the kettle was boiling.'

'Haven't we got to find out if it's true or not?'

'How? He's not here,' Doreen said.

'Perhaps he's had a heart attack,' Mum said. 'Perhaps we should ring the hospital and see if he's there.'

'Or the police station to see if he's there.' Doreen began spreading toast with margarine.

'He left a note,' Mum said.

'That is so dramatic, it must be true.'

'Well, it might be true he's gone, but it might not be true he's taken the money,' Angie said.

Doreen snorted. 'He's said sorry. That's what he's apologising for.'

Mum's voice wavered. 'Shouldn't we check?'

'The banks are closed,' Doreen said.

'Would the pools people know? Reg might know. He might be able to stop it.' As each new idea came to her, Mum's eyes lit up for a moment.

'I don't think so.' Doreen put more toast on their plates. 'Dad was determined to do it his way, with no one knowing our business. We didn't even know our business! So I doubt Reg would. And I don't think Reg has got that kind of power, anyway.' She looked at her mum's red eyes, and Angie's tear-streaked face. 'I think we should wait till Monday. Then we'll really know what we're dealing with.' She leaned across the table and picked up a packet of Benson and Hedges. She walked across to the stove and leaned over a burner to light her cigarette. She inhaled deeply. 'Back to Embassy after this.' She sat down again. 'I'm going to have to get rid of the car, obviously.'

'Will they take it back at the garage?'

'They'd better. Or I'll put an advert in the paper. One careful lady owner. It's as good as new.'

'But you love that car,' Mrs Smith said.

'Well, if what's happened is what we think has happened, I'm in deep financial doo-doos. I'll just return the car to the manufacturers. It's got less than a thousand miles on the clock.'

'And I'm going to send back my sewing machine,' Angie said.

'No, you're not,' said Doreen. 'That's just mad. You will do nothing with that sewing machine until we see how bad it really is.'

'But it was expensive and I owe . . . I owe Gene all the money.'

'Who's Gene?' Mum said.

'The bloke from the boutique,' Doreen said. 'She goes out with him.'

'What happened to Roger?'

'She dumped him,' Doreen said.

'I had to,' Angie said. 'I've got Gene now.'

'Gene? Is that the fella with the Italian name?' Mrs Smith said. 'Works near Harry's place on New Street?'

'How do you know Gene?' Angie said.

'Your dad was having his hair cut in there one day and met him. He tried to sell him a shirt.'

'Oh God!' Doreen said.

'Gene never said anything,' Angie said.

'So, who's going out with him?' Mrs Smith said. 'I thought you were the one who liked him, Doreen. Your dad said you were all over him in the Fleece one night. He said he saw you across the bar.'

There was a silence. Mrs Smith reached over the table for the marmalade. Angie stared at Doreen.

A faint pink rose on Doreen's cheeks. 'For God's sake, I don't think so! You sure it wasn't Angie? You know what Dad's like.' She got up. *Why now?* She thought. *Why did you have to mention it now, Mum? Why couldn't you have said something when we were in on our own, watching* Armchair Theatre *or* Emergency Ward 10? 'Anyone want another cup of tea?' No one answered. 'He's Angie's bloke,' she said, with her back to them, filling the kettle. 'I've hardly ever spoken to the man. I haven't got time for small town shopkeepers!'

'I don't think Gene would do that,' Angie said, frowning. 'Go out with my sister.'

'If it was anyone, it was probably Janice,' Doreen said. 'He's more her type.' *Shut up,* she told herself. *Shut up! Shut up!*

'Janice?' Angie's eyes widened.

'No, of course not!' Doreen said. 'Dad needs glasses. It probably wasn't even Gene. It was probably Cliff Evans.'

'Who?' Angie said.

'Oh, for goodness' sake. I'm messing about. Why would I go out with Cliff Evans? I haven't been out with anyone.' *Shut up! Just shut up!*

'So now you're going out with this Italian fella,' Mum said.

'Yes,' said Angie. She looked at Doreen. 'I don't care what he does. After today he probably won't want me anyway.'

'Don't be stupid.' Doreen filled the teapot. 'He wanted you before you were rich, he wanted you when you were rich and now you might be poor again, he's still going to want you.' She put the teapot back on the table and sat down. 'Why wouldn't he?' Doreen took another cigarette from the packet and lit it with the one she had laid in the ash-tray. She inhaled, stubbing out the old cigarette. *What am I doing?* she thought, *Gene's the most unreliable person in the world. After Dad of course.* Yes, today was a bad enough day, without Angie having to worry about Gene. With the fresh rush of nicotine she felt calmer. 'The big question is – what about Dad?'

'I'm going to ring all the aunties,' Mum said, 'to see if they've heard anything.'

'Better do it quick, before they cut the phone off,' Doreen said.

'Oh Doreen. Well, I'll ring up his friend Barney who he drinks with in the Ship. And Dennis in the Dolphin. See if they know anything.'

'They'd better not,' Doreen said, 'or they're definitely off my Christmas card list.'

'You never send Christmas cards,' Angie said.

'Well, they're not getting one if I ever do,' Doreen said.

Mum pushed back her chair and stood up.

'Before you start ringing half the world,' Doreen said, 'I'd better tell Bolingbroke's I'm not coming in. I'll tell them there's been a family tragedy. For once it's true.'

Angie stood up. 'I'm going to have a bath. Before the electric gets cut off and we haven't got any hot water.'

Mum sank back into her chair. 'Oh, no. The bill's going to be enormous. I've been keeping the rooms so warm and the immersion heater's been on non-stop since he won.'

'You won, you mean,' Doreen said. 'They were your choices. He never even filled it in.'

'He put the x in the box,' Mum said sadly.

Doreen and Angie walked into the hall.

Mum called out, 'Switch off the immersion heater.'

Angie ran up the stairs, saying, 'I can't believe it, I can't believe it.'

'Believe it.' Doreen said. She sat down and looked in the phone directory for the Bolingbroke's phone number. The phone rang and made her jump. 'If that's for me,' Angie called from the bathroom, 'I'm not in.' She slammed the bathroom door.

Doreen picked up the receiver. 'Chelmsford 5135.'

'Is that Doreen?'

'Yes.'

'I'm glad I caught you.'

'Who is this?' she said, but she knew who it was.

'It's my birthday today,' Gene said.

'Really?'

'How about a date?'

'Aren't you going out with Angie?' Doreen whispered. Why was she whispering? Why wasn't she just telling him he'd got the wrong person? Why wasn't she calling Angie downstairs to talk to this . . . this two-timer? Was he really asking her out on a date? Was she really contemplating going? This was terrible. But what was more terrible was that her dad had just left home and taken all the money. All the money. He'd left them, abandoned them, her dad. She wanted to wail at the sky. They were all going to drown in debt. Did debtors' prisons still exist? She remembered learning about it in school.

'No, she's going to see some terrible group at the Corn Exchange that no one's ever heard of. I'll be all on my own in Chelmsford on my birthday. That's not right, is it?' His voice was deep and rich, with that romantic edge of a London accent.

'Well . . .' Doreen murmured.

'So, how about a slap-up birthday meal?'

Birthday Meal? Date? She couldn't take the words in. It was as if he was speaking another language. In the kitchen her mum was crying, and upstairs Angie didn't know what had hit her . . . God, what was Angie going to do? She'd have to give up her wonderful new job. If her suspicions were correct and Dad really had taken all the money, they were going to lose everything. All the dreams she had had of what the money could bring; a small flat of her own, some really modern furniture, a deep rug to walk on with bare feet, they'd all gone. Her dad had taken them away, packed in his suitcase with his flamingo covered shirt. They'd all been spending like mad, she'd encouraged them. How would they pay off their debts? At this rate, they'll end up homeless, and she'd be the one who had to sort it all out. Mum was in no fit state and Angie was too young. It wasn't fair. Her shoulders sagged. Suddenly she needed to get out, go anywhere, get away from her life.

'Still there?' Gene's voice purred in her ear.

'Oh! Yes,' she murmured.

'So what do you say? A nice, expensive meal, with a gorgeous girl by my side. I couldn't think of a better birthday present.'

'Yes!' she said with a firmness that shocked her. It was a bad idea. She knew it was a bad idea, but she didn't care.

She heard the bathroom door open, and the sound of taps running. 'Who is it?' Angie called.

Doreen put her hand over the mouthpiece. 'No one! Have your bath before the water gets cold. You may never be clean again.'

The door slammed once more.

'Where?' Doreen spoke softly into the receiver.

'I was thinking of upstairs at the Golden Fleece.'

'We can't go there. People we know go there,' Doreen said. She saw herself as her dad must have seen her, laughing with Gene, clinking glasses, sitting close, letting her skirt ride up.

'But there's nothing to see, is there?'

'You know what people will think.'

'All right, how about the County Hotel?'

'You like that place, don't you?'

'It's not bad. For Chelmsford. And you know, it's a hotel.'

'We're just going out for a meal,' she said firmly.

'Yes, ma'am. For a meal.'

'One night only.'

'I'll see you in the Railway Tavern.'

As she put the receiver down, Doreen looked up the stairs towards the closed bathroom door. She wondered what Gene would have said if Angie had answered the phone.

'Right!' she called. 'We're all going out for the day. We'll . . . we'll catch the bus up to Galleywood Common and pick blackberries or have a picnic or something. Or just go into the pub there and get drunk. We're not going to think about this anymore today. We've got fifteen minutes before the bus goes!' And tonight she would see Gene and forget about everything.

Gene was already in the Railway Tavern, standing at the bar, in his sheepskin. There was so much of him, with that big coat and then his beautiful face, that strong nose, those dark eyebrows, his thick brown hair. She shouldn't have come. She should have left well alone, left him to Angie. But she had to get away from the mess that was her real life and . . . she had wanted to see him. She wanted to talk to him. She fancied him. She felt it in the pit of her stomach as she looked at him. What was it about him? She just wished she didn't feel so guilty. But she was guilty. She was doing the dirty on Angie. And so was he.

And there he stood – Gene, Gerry, whatever his bloody name was. Perhaps, she thought, as she crossed the room, calling him Gerry was a good thing, as if he was someone else, someone different, nothing to do with Angie and her swooning over Gene. Tonight she, Doreen, would be with Gerry, another person. She wouldn't actually be hurting Angie.

He looked up as she approached. He smiled at her, his big warm generous smile. He was pleased to see her. *It's just dinner*, she told herself. *We're not doing anything wrong. I didn't tell Angie so as not to upset her. But I could have done, because it's just dinner.* It was all perfectly innocent. Oh God, but they'd done it. They'd done it in the back room of the shop, on the bloody camp bed, with a half empty bottle of champagne on the floor, and boxes full of Fred Perry shirts in the corner. And she'd enjoyed it.

Now he put his arm round her and kissed her cheek. 'Hello, gorgeous.' She could smell alcohol on his breath.

She shook her head as he called the barman. 'Get the lady whatever she wants.'

'I'll have a gin and tonic.'

'And I'll have another one of these.' Gene pointed to a small glass of something that looked like whisky. 'Do you want to sit down?' he said.

She thought of sitting down with him, how he would be so close, sliding his arm along the back of the seat, pulling her to him. 'No,' she said, 'I'm all right here.'

He began to make light easy small talk; the man who'd come into the shop for a belt and gone out with a jacket and slacks, a box of shampoo meant for Harry that he'd hung on to for a month thinking it was a box of shirts, the barman in the Saracen's Head who'd got a special bottle of whisky out because he said Gene was a special customer but then took a nip himself. She began to relax, to enjoy herself. Yes, this is where she should be tonight. She needed to be here. Gene glanced at his watch, a chunky expensive silver thing. 'Shall we go?' he said.

Outside the pub he moved to the outside of the pavement and took her elbow. 'I'm looking forward to this, a nice birthday meal with my best girl.'

'One of your best girls,' she corrected him.

'How can you say that? After what we've ... shared?' he said.

'Just one of your best girls,' she repeated.

'As you like,' he said. 'I'm still looking forward to a nice meal.'

In the large, dimly-lit room the tables still had the white tablecloths and big heavy cutlery she remembered from the evening when she'd seen Gene in here with his wife. A powdery looking man in a tired black suit took her coat and showed them to their table. She thought she recognised him. They passed other couples, older couples, women who had had their hair set for the occasion, and lightly perspiring men in shirts and ties, with hand-knitted

V-neck jumpers under their suit jackets. She pitied them. They were so old and so past it. She watched them watch her, the line of her sweater outlining the curves of her body, down to the tight pink trousers. And her red hair, tonight caught back in a French pleat. She knew that every man in the place wished they could be Gene. And she knew that Gene . . . Gerry was proud to be with her. It felt good to be noticed.

Gerry murmured something to the waiter and they were seated at a discreet table behind a large plant. She was rather sorry. She would have liked to be a visible presence, to be a beautiful visible presence, to cause a bit of a stir because surely there was no danger that anyone here was going to inform on her to Angie, they were all too old.

'This all right?' he said. 'Nice and inconspicuous. No risk of anyone seeing us here.'

'I didn't think you were worried about that,' she retorted. 'As you said, we're not doing anything wrong.'

'Really?' he said. 'With you in that sweater?'

She stared at him. 'Don't get your hopes up,' she said.

'I can dream, can't I?' He laughed. 'So, what will you have?'

She picked up the leather-bound book that was the menu. 'I don't know. What are you having?'

'Prawn cocktail and a well-done steak,' he said.

'Then I'll have grapefruit and lamb chops,' she said.

He laughed again. 'This is why I like you, Doreen. You're always ready to have a go. What do you want to drink? Shall we get a nice claret?'

'Do you mean red wine?'

'Yes, to go with the steak. And your lamb.'

'Why do people make such a fuss about the colour?' she said. The wine arrived and Gene filled her glass.

As they ate he told her another story. 'I had a customer in this afternoon. Came in with his wife. She was so insistent her husband was six feet tall and needed longer trousers. He was standing there! He was five foot eight at most.' They both laughed.

'Well, last week I had a customer who wanted a dress with a veil attached and a head-dress with another veil and a cape with a veil. We put them all together and she looked like a meringue. She changed her mind when she saw herself in the mirror.' They laughed again.

There was a pause and they looked at each other. He raised his glass, 'Cheers.' They clinked glasses.

This was nice. Conversation flowing freely and being the absolute centre of Gene's attention. When she was with him she could believe she really was his one and only.

'Now what are you smiling at?' he said.

'Nothing, nothing.' She didn't want him to get the wrong idea.

After the meal Gene examined the bill, balancing his cigarette on the side of the ash-tray.

'Unfortunately, I can't pay a penny towards this meal,' Doreen said.

'And I wouldn't expect you to! Why do you even say that?'

'You don't want to know.'

'Don't I?'

'Our dad's run off and taken all the money.'

'Oh, Reen, I'm so sorry. Where's he gone?'

Doreen shrugged. 'I don't know and I don't care. I never liked him anyway.' She gave a small laugh. 'It's left all of us in deep shit.'

Gene took a thick roll of notes from his back pocket and peeled off a sheaf of pound notes. 'Want some?'

'No!' she said, although part of her wanted to say, 'Yes, yes please.'

'Sure?'

'Yes. And I hope you didn't get those out of your till!'

'My shop, my money,' he said.

'Has it gone through the books yet?'

'Give over,' he said.

They walked back into town, past the Pavilion cinema and the bus station, to the railway station to get a taxi.

On the way he pulled her into the doorway of the Cumf tea bar, closed at this time of night, and kissed her. 'God, I've wanted to kiss you all evening,' he said.

'Look Gene, Gerry, I like you and everything, but there are other people in your life. You're going out with my sister and you're married. Basically, you're taken.'

'I thought we'd resolved that one. No one says anything, no one gets hurt.' He lifted her chin with his finger. 'Don't tell me you didn't like what happened. You did, I could tell.'

'Yes, I did,' she said and her stomach flipped. There was certainly something between them, even now.

'So, when am I going to see you again?' He leaned into her and he kissed her once more. She kissed him back, pressing her body against his. Here, in this moment, she could forget everything that was wrong in her world. It was the first time she'd felt anything as normal and as good as this all day. She didn't want to let go of the feeling.

How could he do this to her? She was trying so hard to be fair to Angie. Angie was her sister and she was really suffering now. Angie needed Gene, even if he was the most unreliable person she'd ever known. But his arms were still round her, holding her close, keeping her safe. She knew it was madness.

'All right,' she said, breathless. 'We might go out again. But no more hanky-panky.' She had to think of Angie. 'Definitely, no more hanky-panky.'

'If you're sure.'

They walked past the bus station, under the railway bridge. A car hooted. A scooter beeped. 'Anyone you know?' Gene said, putting his arm round her protectively.

'I hope not,' Doreen said. She shivered against him.

They walked round to the taxi rank beside the station. Gene was looking at his watch. When a taxi came, he opened the door and pressed a pound note into her hand. 'I'll see you soon. I've enjoyed tonight. Best birthday for years.' He blew her a kiss and walked away.

'Oh well, goodbye,' she murmured. She slid into the taxi. She had a strange raw feeling inside. She felt cheated. She had wanted more. She had wanted him to climb into the back seat of the taxi with her, because he couldn't help himself. She had wanted him to crawl on top of her, his need for her too great to stop. She had wanted . . . oh, everything.

CHAPTER 25

THE NEXT DAY, ANGIE WOKE UP from a dream about the College, tutors were smiling at her, telling her how talented she was, looking at exotic dresses she had made. As her eyes opened she was smiling, then with a jolt, she remembered. Her dad had run off and taken all the money. And that meant her job, her lovely new job, would have to end. Her life was in tatters. She lay in bed staring up at the ceiling. She could afford to go to work for one more week she had calculated. And then that was it. She almost couldn't bear it. This had been her dream job. Even Miss Darling knew that. In fact, Miss Darling had almost set it up. Miss Darling knew she had it in her, to go on to something bigger, to make something of herself.

But now everything was ruined.

Of course, they hadn't absolutely confirmed that Dad had gone for good. There was a chance, an outside chance, but a chance that it was all a mistake and he'd come back. Or at the very least that he'd left the money, or some of the money behind, so that they wouldn't be left poor and destitute. Doreen would ring the pools people and the bank in the morning.

Oh, but she was bound to find out it was true. And then, all the bills would pile in. Her own debts, her mum's and Doreen's. All the new things they'd bought, the money they'd spent. It was all debt.

It was true. Dad had gone. On Monday morning, in her coffee break Doreen rang the pools people introducing herself as Mrs Smith. The pools people said that yes, a bank account had been opened at Barclays in Chelmsford, for Mr Smith's winnings. Then still posing as 'Mrs Smith' Doreen rang the bank and they agreed that the account had been opened a few weeks before but emptied on Friday. And, the helpful assistant manager had added, Mr Smith had changed the money into American dollar Travellers cheques.

'Of course,' Doreen said, as calmly as she could. 'Just like he said.' She put down the phone.

All that money, she thought, all that money. Gone with her dad. She couldn't quite believe it, her dad, taking that dramatic step. All the planning he must have done, buying the new clothes Angie had seen in that suitcase, deciding when to go, taking the money out of the bank. She couldn't believe he'd done it.

But done it he had, and left his family behind, up to their necks in debt.

The phone rang. It was Angie, ringing from London, as they had arranged. 'It's true,' Doreen told her. 'He's gone. And so has the money.' She repeated what the bank had said. 'Travellers cheques!' she seethed. 'What an idiot! All that money in Travellers cheques. He'll probably lose them.'

'Oh Reen,' Angie snuffled down the phone.

'Don't worry,' Doreen said. 'We'll think of something. For the moment, we'll just carry on as usual. We'll go to work and we'll sort things out and he won't beat us.'

'Oh Reen,' Angie said again.

They were going to have to do something.

CHAPTER 26

As she drove into town Doreen reflected on the current state of affairs. Dad had disappeared into thin air, and so had the money. Mum was now spending hours on the phone, ringing anyone she could think of, asking if they knew anything about Dad, and each time she put down the phone she sobbed quietly for at least five minutes. And Angie was just a weeping wreck, thinking about losing her beloved job. And then there was the debt, the enormous pile of debt that could destroy them all.

She was having to get rid of everything. She had returned three new dresses, an expensive necklace and four pairs of beautiful shoes already, and cancelled all the new furniture, which left her missing the old three-piece suite and the curtains and rugs they had so cheerfully thrown out. Thank God the sinks and the toilets were fixtures or they'd have gone too. The house was almost as empty as the day they'd moved in. And now she was losing the car. She thought back to the time before the money arrived and wondered if they'd ever again be as close and as happy as they had been then. It hadn't been the greatest life, but at least everyone wasn't crying all the time.

Doreen parked the car outside the showroom, opened the door, put her high heel shoes on the pavement and stood up. At least she looked good, she thought. She shut the door gently. Oh, she loved this car, she was so sorry to see it go.

But now there was business to be done.

She straightened her shoulders and sauntered in to the showroom as casually as possible. She glanced at one or two of the cars, as if she was considering making another purchase. She had worked out her strategy. She wanted to look successful, relaxed, but smiling, as if she was doing them a favour. Which, of course, she was – she was giving them the gift of a lovely car, one careful lady owner, who'd had the car for a mere five minutes. There was hardly any mileage on the clock. The mileage was so low, it was just as if one or two customers had taken the car out for a test drive.

It wasn't Saturday. The boy was nowhere to be seen. The man she had finally dealt with when she bought the car came out of his office, looking smart and cheerful.

'Hello.' She smiled as prettily as she could. 'Remember me?' She turned and indicated the Triumph at the kerb.

'Of course. How's it going? Is the car getting you everywhere you want to go?'

'Oh yes. Well, I mean, I've hardly been out in it. It's been parked outside the house for most of the time. The

time it's not been in the garage. All I've done is wash it!'
She smiled again.

'The car will appreciate that. And so will you. They give
back as much as they're given!'

She couldn't believe the nonsense people talked. 'And
I've given it a lot.'

'I'm sure you have.'

'But now I need to get rid of it.'

'Ohhh.' His voice draped over the word in surprise.

She had spoken too soon, been too blunt. She smiled
again. 'I can't keep it.'

'Perhaps it's got a bit too much horsepower for someone . . . like yourself.'

'No!' *Keep calm*, she told herself. *Keep smiling.*

'I know some ladies do find the convertible aspect a
little difficult. Especially when it rains! With your hair
and everything.'

'What's my hair—' She stopped herself. She mustn't let
him annoy her. She mustn't get mouthy. If he felt challenged
or threatened in any way he would run and phone his bosses
in Coventry or somewhere and they would tell him to say
no dice, no chance, go to hell. Take it back? The very idea!

But he was still talking, giving her his showroom patter.
'I mean, we've got some lovely new little cars that you'd
look smashing in. We've got a new Mini that a lot of the
ladies are going for – so their husbands tell me anyway!'
He smiled knowingly. She still wanted to smack him.

She took a breath. 'The Triumph is a lovely car,' she said. 'I love it. I love every inch of it. You were right to suggest this car.' She smiled at him, with her eyes, and a little pout of her mouth. He stepped back a pace.

Wrong angle, she thought. *I've frightened him, coming over all Brigitte Bardot. He'll think I want to snog him. Or he'll wonder what's been going on, on those lovely leather seats.* She put a concerned expression on her face. 'What car do *you* drive?'

'Me, ah well, I've got what you might call a good reliable family car. I've got a Vauxhall Viva.' His tone had changed.

'Of course. That's what you need when you have children. Sorry, what's your name?'

'Charles.'

I bet that's your middle name, she thought. *I bet your first name's Fred.* 'How many?'

'How many?'

'Children.'

'Just the two, thank goodness.'

'Oh lovely! How old?'

'Five and seven. Boy and a girl.'

'Gorgeous. I bet they're a handful.'

'Like you wouldn't believe!' He grinned.

'I bet they are!' She chuckled.

'Do you have children yourself?' he asked.

So this was his thing. Family. 'Soon, I hope!' she said. 'Just waiting for Mr Right!'

'I'm sure he'll be here before too long.'

'Fingers crossed.'

'Then a Triumph Spitfire won't be any good to you at all.'

'No.' She nodded sadly. 'Not when you've got kids. There's no room for kids in this gorgeous car. And you can't take the risk, can you? All that speed.' She looked into his eyes. What was he seeing? A desperate woman? A smug bitch? Or was he wishing a Triumph Spitfire was his, for once, for a moment, that he was free and could drive anywhere, anytime, maybe even with an attractive woman by his side? Keeping her voice as neutral as possible, she said, 'Have you ever driven a sporty car?'

'Oh, that was a long time ago. Once. I did once.'

'Well, before this goes back, do you want to have a quick spin? Up to the Miami Grill, say, and back. Go on!'

The corners of his mouth twitched. He struggled to contain a smile. She had touched the spot.

'I'm not sure,' he said.

'And you'll be able to inspect the car, make sure I haven't broken anything. Which I haven't,' she added quickly. 'I have really taken care of it.' *I even washed out the ash-tray*, she didn't say. 'It's not even run-in properly.'

'Well . . .' He pushed back the white cuff of his crisp, pale blue shirt and looked at his watch. 'Perhaps a short run would be useful.'

'If you think so,' Doreen said, with a pretty frown. She handed him the keys.

She watched his posture change. His back straightened, his head went up, he was young again. If she'd asked him, but of course she couldn't because it would break the spell, but if she did ask him how he was feeling, she knew he would stress that he loved his wife and his children, more than life itself, but if he could turn back the clock for just ten minutes, he would, just ten minutes. He rattled the keys in his hand. 'Let's go,' he said.

He walked round to the passenger side of the car and opened the door. She smiled and got in. She put a scarf over her hair while he sat in the driver's seat and groped for a moment for the ignition. The car revved into life and they drove down Market Street, through the town, into Moulsham Street and up to the Miami Grill.

'Runs very smoothly,' he shouted. 'Shall we just go along the bypass for a moment? Give the engine a bit of an outing.'

'Lovely idea!' she shouted. Whatever made him happy.

Back at the showroom he slid out of the car. He glanced quickly at the floor and then at the pale leather driver's seat, and when he'd opened her door and she'd climbed out, cast another glance at her seat. 'I'll just check the roof,' he said.

'Of course!' she said, hoping a bird hadn't flown in in the night.

He strained to pull up the roof but she knew she couldn't offer to show him the trick. When he'd got it in place, she smiled a congratulatory smile. She wanted to weep. It was such a lovely car, so neat and smooth, everything in its place. But it had to go back.

They walked into the showroom and she took off her headscarf, and shook her head in a straightforward way, not a coquettish way, to straighten her hair. As they passed the shiny new cars, she looked at them as if she might be in the market for a new vehicle very soon.

She waited for him to start the conversation.

'So, you say you want to return the car.' His salesman persona was creeping back up, his voice was taking on its original nasal tone.

'I do. I must. It's . . . well, it's my mother. Well, my grandmother really.' *Nan*, she said silently to her long departed grandmother, *forgive me for what I am about to do. I always loved you.* 'She lives in . . . Australia.'

'Really?' he said.

'She was married to one of those convicts.'

He frowned. She was going too far.

'No, sorry, that was always her joke. She's got a great sense of humour. Oh, I love my nan, I miss her. She's not at all well, and my mum needs to go out to see her. You know what it's like these days. A boat takes forever. So I said I'd see if you'd take the car back, so that I can pay for her to fly out there.'

'Well. That's a sad story.' He looked at her and sighed. 'Quite frankly I don't believe a word of it,' he said, 'but I think I can do something for you.'

She looked at him and laughed. At last, she was dealing with the real man.

'You paid how much?'

'£550.'

'How about I give you £450 back?'

'Don't you remember, I paid cash.'

'Yes, you did. So?'

'How about £500?'

'It's a deal.'

They shook hands. She'd lost £50 but it could have been worse. As she left the showroom, she looked back at him. 'I really loved it though.'

'I'm not surprised.'

She'd taken the morning off work and there was an hour before she had to be back. But there was more business to be done. Business with Gene. She'd spent a lot of time thinking about Gene – Gene and Angie and Gene and herself. It was absurd, it was wrong in so many ways and it couldn't go on. She wasn't going to do that to herself. Yes, being with Gene was one of the most exciting things that had ever happened to her, the chemistry crackled between them, but when he was given a choice he hadn't chosen her, he'd opted to carry on with both of them, her and Angie. And it wasn't good enough. She couldn't stop Angie from seeing him – that would only cause her more heartache, and goodness knew she had enough heartache to be going on with at the moment. She couldn't end it for Angie, but she could end it for herself.

She decided to go into work, there'd be no one in the staffroom at this time. She would ring him up from there. She would tell him it was all done and over. It shouldn't have started in the first place and now it was finished.

She rang the boutique and before he could say anything warm or funny she blurted out, 'It's over. We're finished.' He said nothing. She realised she wanted to cry, just when she wanted to be strong.

'Oh,' he said. 'I see. You sure?'

'Yes.'

He paused. 'Well, we had a good time, didn't we?'

'Not good enough! How can I go out with the same man as my sister? It's no good. Not for me. Not to mention the fact that you are still married.'

'It didn't matter before.'

'It matters now.'

'Oh, come on, Ange, don't be mad at me. It was fun, wasn't it?'

'My name,' she said, as coldly as she could manage, 'is Doreen. I think you've made your point.' She slammed down the phone.

She went into the toilets and shut herself in a cubicle. She punched the wall and howled. As she came out a new junior from furniture came in and looked at her with wide eyes.

'I had a fishbone stuck in my throat,' Doreen said.

'Like the Queen Mother,' said the junior.

'Just like the Queen Mother,' Doreen said. She coughed, clearing her throat. 'Do you want a cup of tea?'

'No thanks.'

Doreen made herself a cup of coffee. If she examined her feelings now, she had to admit she felt better. She only wished he hadn't agreed to it quite so quickly. A bit of an argument might have made her feel he'd cared a little. If he'd moaned, 'Why, Doreen, why why?' If he'd pleaded with her to change her mind, she might have felt more heroic. But no, he'd been calm and reassuring. Well, good riddance to bad rubbish. She just hoped he cared more for Angie.

CHAPTER 27

ANGIE WALKED OUT OF THE TECH with Cath. She had intended that this would be her last class. Her hours at the job in London were too unpredictable, and anyway, there she had all the classes she needed. But the job in London was going to go, it had to go, she simply couldn't afford it. There would be no more exhausting, exhilarating classes in London, no more learning lovely new tricks and turns in stitching. It was all gone, with the money. So she would stay at her evening class in Chelmsford. It was the one good thing to come out of this horrible mess. Tonight in the Tech class she'd felt as if she was clinging on to a lifebelt after a shipwreck at sea, hanging on to her dreams in the middle of chaos.

It had been a lovely class, she had felt happy for the first time in days. As she and Cath left the building they laughed about the latest homework, to make an outfit for a child's teddy bear. Cath was going to make an evening suit with a waistcoat and a bow tie. Angie was wondering where she could get some offcuts of suede to make a coat for a mod bear. She would be back next week, and she was looking forward to it. Perhaps there was light at the end of the dark tunnel of Dad leaving and the money going.

On the road a scooter was parked. She gave a small gasp of surprise when she realised it was Roger.

'Ooh, who's that?' murmured Cath.

'He's my boyfriend – my old boyfriend,' Angie said. 'And I don't know what he's doing here.'

'Well, if you've finished with him, I'm happy to step in to mend his broken heart,' Cath said.

Angie didn't know if she was pleased to see him. She would have preferred to see Gene. But no, disappointingly he had a business meeting. She still had his birthday present. She had bought him a tie-pin, with a small diamond in the centre. She'd bought it before Dad ran off and had kept it in her pocket ever since she walked out of the shop. She liked carrying it around with her. It made her feel close to him. Now it was another item on the pile of money she owed.

'Hello Angie,' Roger said, with a bashful smile.

She was pleased to see him, she realised. He was so solid and familiar.

'I thought I'd give you a lift home, or, if you like, we could go for a drink.'

'Oh Roger. We said we wouldn't see each other for a month.'

'I know, I'm sorry. I just—' He shrugged. 'I just wanted to see you.'

'I suppose you've heard.'

'What?'

'Our dad's run off with all that money.'

'Oh my god, Angie. That's terrible. Are you all right?'

So he hadn't heard, he hadn't come to laugh or sneer or say 'It serves you right.' He'd come because he wanted to see her. He really was a lovely man.

'Come on,' he said, 'let's go and have a drink. You can tell me all about it. I'll buy you a brandy.'

'Make it a large one.' Almost without thinking, she climbed on to the back of the scooter.

'Where do you want to go?'

'I don't mind. Oh, let's go mad. Let's go to the Fleece,' she said.

They drove along Broomfield Road. Angie put her arms round Roger's waist. It felt warm and comforting.

They turned into Duke Street, past the bus station, under the bridge and down to the Fleece. As they were getting off the scooter, Roger unwinding his scarf and Angie straightening her coat, he turned to her. 'I saw your sister in town the other day.'

'Oh really? She was probably off to drown her sorrows.' Angie smoothed her hair. 'She owes more money than I do.'

'Well, she obviously found someone to drown them with.'

'Oh, not her friend Janice.'

Roger lifted the seat of his scooter and put his gloves and scarf inside. 'No. She was with that bloke from the boutique in New Road, near your cousin's. Perhaps he'll pay her debts for her.'

'What?'

'Perhaps he'll . . .'

'No, who? Who did you say?'

'That bloke from the boutique, with the Italian name. What is it? Vino? Geno?'

'Gene,' Angie said shortly. 'It can't have been him, she knows he's . . . he's my . . . he's married.'

'Oh, and how do you know, Miss Know-it-all?' He grinned at her. 'I'm pretty sure it was him. That sheepskin coat of his. And I know it was your sister, because I'd recognise her red hair anywhere.'

'Really?'

'Yeah. They were pretty lovey-dovey.'

Angie felt as if she had been picked up, turned upside down and shaken hard. 'I feel sick,' she said. 'Take me home.'

'Don't you want a drink? You look like you need one.'

'Take me home,' Angie said. 'I want to go home.'

As they pulled up outside the house Angie said, 'Don't bother turning off the engine. You're not stopping.'

'Are you all right, Ange? Was it something I said?'

She looked at his face. He was anxious, concerned. He'd been so happy when she said they'd go for a drink.

'It's nothing to do with you,' she said softly. 'I just don't feel very well. It's my time of the month, don't worry.'

'You should have said!'

'Well, I'm saying now,' she snapped. His face fell. 'Sorry, sorry, I didn't mean it like that. I'm just not . . . I don't . . . I've got to go in.'

'See you in a couple of weeks?' he said.

'If I haven't been locked up,' she said.

'Why? What have you done?' He risked a smile.

'It's what I'm about to do,' she said. 'You go now. It's cold.' She pecked him on the cheek.

'I love you, Angie,' he said quietly. 'Take care of yourself.'

'You too,' she said.

Mum was indoors watching the telly.

'Where's Doreen?'

'Somewhere.'

The kitchen door opened and Doreen walked in. She was humming the song 'Personality'.

'Been having a good time lately?' Angie said.

'Not particularly. Why?'

'Just asking.'

'Oh. How was your class? Was that Roger I saw just now, on his scooter? Is it all back on?'

'I suppose you'd like that, wouldn't you?'

'Girls!' Mum shouted from the living room. 'I can't hear myself listen to this programme. If you want to have a conversation go upstairs.'

Angie looked at Doreen. 'Well, come on then. Let's go upstairs.'

'Oh, I thought we'd finished. You asked me about my life and I asked you about your evening. All very nice, thank you.'

Doreen was being so cool. She was being so relaxed. Angie hoped it wasn't true. 'Come upstairs!' she hissed.

Doreen followed her into the hall. As they walked up the stairs Doreen stumbled, and grabbed the banister.

Angie turned. 'Careful you don't break your neck. Or someone might do it for you.'

'I don't know what you're talking about.'

'Or is it guilt making you trip over your own feet?'

Angie went into her bedroom.

Doreen walked in and closed the door behind her. 'What's this all about?'

'You! You and him!'

'Who? What?'

'Dad saw you. And now Roger saw you. You were with him. You were with Gene, all lovey-dovey.' A terrible thought came to her. 'And I saw you, didn't I? That night Roger came round and ruined your Sloppy Joe. I saw you in town with him, by the cathedral, and you lied about it to me. How could you? How could you? He's my boyfriend!'

Doreen felt faint. She had known this day would come. She had wanted it to come in a way. Angie needed to know the truth about the type of man Gene was. Doreen had wanted to tell her, but she hadn't had the nerve to turn and say, 'Oh, by the way, I've had sex with your boyfriend.' She needed to sit down but Angie was still standing.

She looked at Angie. She could see that even now, if she denied it vehemently enough Angie would believe her. Angie would probably end up apologising for having mistrusted her. But if she lied now, if she denied it again, it would never end. There would be more denials, more made-up stories, more suggestions that it was Angie's wild imagination. She couldn't do that to her. Angie was her sister. 'All right! All right. Yes, I was seeing him.'

Angie's face went white. She put her hand to her mouth and shook her head. Doreen wondered if it was Angie who was going to collapse. She moved towards her.

'Get away! Get away from me!' Angie stepped back. 'How could you? How could you?'

'Oh Angie. At first I didn't know about you and him. You mentioned him that once and then never again till the night we went out for the drink. And then I only saw him once more I swear. And then I – I ended it.'

'Oh, really? Just once more? Is that supposed to make it OK? You saw him, after you knew how much I really cared about him. And I don't believe you it was just once. When was this? When?'

'Angie!'

'Don't speak to me in that tone of voice. You knew what you were doing. He was my boyfriend.'

'I was just . . .'

'Just what?'

'I don't know. But it's over now.'

'Over? What do you mean? What was there to be over?'

'For a while I saw him, and now I don't.'

'How often did you *see* him?' Angie's voice cracked. 'How long for?'

'Angie, I didn't know. I swear . . .' Her voice trailed away.

'How could you?'

'Honestly, I didn't know you were seeing him. But look –' She spread her hands desperately. 'I didn't know, but we both know who did. He knew about you and he knew about me. We've both been had,' Doreen said.

'But I love him. And he loves me. And . . .' Angie turned away, full of sorrow, '. . . I bought him a tie-pin for his birthday and I haven't been able to give it to him.'

'Oh Angie.'

'Shut up! What am I going to do with it? I can't take it back to the shop, I've rubbed the corners off the box, I've been carrying it around for so long.' She lifted her tear-stained face.

'Angie—'

'I'll ask him!' she said. 'I'll ask him and see if his story is different from yours.'

'Go ahead,' Doreen said. 'He'll say the same thing. Unless of course he lies, which I think we both know he's capable of.'

'I hate you!' Angie said. 'I hate you both. I feel so stupid. All this time. And I got so upset about the stupid jumper Roger ruined that night. I'm upset about a stupid jumper and you're out stealing my boyfriend.'

'Oh Angie,' Doreen moved towards her. 'You're my sister and I am really, really sorry.' She put her arms round Angie and Angie began to cry into her jumper, big heaving sobs. 'If it's any consolation, you're doing a fairly good job of ruining this sweater,' she said.

'Good!' Angie's voice was muffled. 'I'm just going to blow my nose on it.'

Doreen sprang back. 'No, you're not. Have a hanky.' She pulled out a handkerchief from her sleeve.

Angie blew her nose.

'I'm sorry. I'm sorry. I was stupid. I should have told you.' *But not about the camp bed in the back of the shop.* 'And then you could have told me whether you were OK with it. I mean, if you were going out with Roger, isn't it fair that someone else could go out with Gene?'

Angie stepped away. 'So you *were* going out with him! You were having a relationship with him!'

'No, no.' *Oh God, why did I say that?* Doreen thought. 'I just meant, how did you feel having two people on the go? Roger and Gene. You didn't think you were hurting Roger, did you?'

'Oh, shut up. There's no comparison and you know it. You're my sister! And, oh God!' She twisted Doreen's handkerchief in her hands. 'I thought he might be seeing other women, but I didn't think he was seeing my sister! And I had to find out through other people. Through Dad, for God's sake, the world's worst human being, after you. And through Roger. How could you? How could you?'

Because his arms were strong and he was gentle and good and he made me feel like I was the only woman in the world.

'Dad said you were all over him, Roger said you were lovey-dovey.' Angie drew breath. 'You're never to see him, ever again.'

'I know. I'll try my best.'

'You won't see him.'

'I can't stop going into pubs. What if he's in there?'

'Walk out again.'

'All right, all right, I will.'

Doreen moved over to the door. 'Oh Angie. Why don't we all just go to Australia? Forget any of them ever existed? Dad, Gene, Roger . . .'

'Nice try,' Angie said. 'I'm not going to Australia, but you're welcome to.' She turned away and fiddled with a hairbrush on her dressing table.

'I'm going to bed now,' Doreen said, softly. 'I'm sorry.'

'Just go,' Angie said. 'I'm too tired to think of any more horrible things to say to you.'

'Tell me in the morning.' Doreen crept out on to the landing and allowed her tears to fall.

CHAPTER 28

'HELLO DARLING,' GENE SAID AS ANGIE walked into the boutique.

'I want to talk to you.'

'Well, that looks like a serious face. Can it wait? We've got a couple of customers.'

Angie looked round. 'One.'

'All right, but every customer is an important customer.'

Angie walked over to the man who was looking at shirts hanging on a rail, 'Excuse me, I don't think we have anything in your size.'

'You don't know what size I am.'

'I know, but all our sizes are wrong. Everyone says so.'

'I don't know what you're talking about.'

'What I mean is, could you leave? We need to shut the shop.'

'What?'

'For – for stocktaking. I'm sorry.'

Gene was frowning but he said nothing.

The man looked over at Gene. 'They're crap shirts anyway.'

'And a very good morning to you, sir,' Gene said.

The man left the shop and Angie locked it after him. She turned the open sign to closed.

'That serious, eh?' Gene said. He came from behind the small counter and leaned against it with folded arms.

'What's going on Gene?' Angie said.

'What do you mean?'

Angie threw up her arms. 'I don't know why I'm asking you. I know what's going on.'

He frowned.

'An innocent expression isn't going to do it this time. Nor will a bracelet. Or any smooth talk.'

'What are you talking about, babe?'

She opened her mouth, but nothing came out. She was so angry, so sad, so overwhelmed with shock. Finally she said, in a low voice, 'I know about you and my sister.'

'Oh,' he said.

'Is that all you can say?' She wanted him to rage, to deny it, to say it wasn't true, it was all a big misunderstanding. She wanted him to hold out his arms and promise to never let it happen again.

But he was silent.

Tears of frustration and sorrow sprang from her eyes. She stood in the middle of the shop, sobbing.

'Oh baby,' he said. He came to her and wrapped his arms round her. 'It was nothing. It was just a thing.'

'Doreen said it was just drinks,' she said, before he could say something different, something that would really break her heart.

'Yes, yes, that was all it was. But it was stupid and I shouldn't have let it happen. To be fair, I didn't know she was your sister.'

She jumped back. 'Oh, so if it hadn't been my sister it would have been all right! If it had been . . . been Janice, that would have been OK?'

'Who's Janice?'

'My sister's friend.'

'Oh. Oh no, that's not a name I know.' He shook his head. 'That name means nothing to me.'

'You mean if I found another name, the right name, that might mean something to you! Mary, Gillian, Susan! Any of those mean anything?'

'Oh, baby, no. Look – don't get all worked up – I was stupid. I'm always stupid.' He was still holding her tight. Gradually his arms relaxed and he was holding her in the secure, comforting, loving way she recognised and loved.

'And now my dad's run off with all the money he said he was going to share with us.'

'Oh, baby, that's terrible.' He didn't seem shocked. Perhaps in his world people did that all the time. Her heart sank. Perhaps Doreen had told him.

'And I shan't be able to keep my job at the College of Art because I shan't be able to afford the train fare.'

'Oh no! You love that job.'

'So I don't know when I'll be able to pay you back.' The tears returned and she sobbed into his sweater.

'Oh babe,' he crooned. He rocked her from side to side. 'Don't worry about that. We can deal with that later. Perhaps we can sort something out about the train fares.' His hand went to his pocket.

'I can't take any more money from you! I shall be in debt forever. This is the most terrible time of my life. First my dad, then you, and now my job.'

'Hey! Hey!' he said. 'Firstly, I haven't run off and secondly, don't worry about the debts.'

She raised her head to protest.

'Pay me when you can, even if it's ten years from now.'

'Ten years!' She groaned.

'Or ten months, or ten minutes. Whenever you get things sorted. Tell you what, seeing as the shop is temporarily closed, why don't we go along to the Saracen's – it's almost our place, isn't it? – and we can have a coffee.'

He was being so nice, she felt herself smiling. Then she remembered. 'You're not going to give me another bracelet, are you?' she asked.

'No, no, but I have got some news that I think will cheer you up.'

'What?' she asked in a flat tone. She was exhausted now, with the anger and the crying and the fear.

'Let's go and get that coffee, and I'll show you the letter.' He tilted her face up to his and kissed her on the nose. 'I'll get my coat.' He went into the back of the shop and came out sliding his arms into a raincoat.

'You look like Harold Wilson,' she said, dabbing her eyes. She blew her nose.

He unlocked the shop door and ushered her out. 'I just need a pipe and I could lead the country,' he said. 'And you could be my Barbara Castle and do all sorts of good things for the workers of the world.'

She knew he was being charming and soothing just to make her feel better, but it did make her feel better. She linked her arm in his and leaned into him as they walked towards the pub.

Sitting in the pub with their coffee in front of them Gene drew out a letter from inside his coat. He handed it to Angie.

'What is it?' she said.

'Open it.'

She looked at the envelope. It was addressed to Gerald Battle at a street in London she'd never heard of. She'd never known his London address. There was a name in the top left hand corner and she saw the words Commissioner of Oaths.

'Open it!' he repeated.

She drew out three or four folded sheets of paper. Slowly, she unfolded them, looking up at Gene from time to time.

'Oh, the top one's just the covering letter.' He pulled it from her hands. 'The next page is the one. There, look.'

She felt it was exciting and important, but it was just a jumble of words. She saw his name. 'What is it?'

'It's my decree nisi!'

She looked at him, amazed.

'I told you, I'm getting a divorce!'

Her hand was shaking. 'How?'

'On the grounds of adultery.'

Her heart almost stopped. 'With me?' She didn't like the thought of it. She felt afraid.

'No, silly.'

'Not Reen?'

'No, it was all done perfectly properly. I went to Brighton. I told you.'

'You said it was for business.'

'Well, it was. It was for the business of divorce. You know, they have to catch you with someone.'

'I thought that's only what . . . sleazy people did.'

'Oh, come on, babe. It's what you have to do.'

She put her head on one side and looked at him thoughtfully.

'Anyway.' He took the papers from her and folded them back into the envelope. 'Six weeks from now I'll be a free man.'

'Six weeks,' she said slowly.

'Yup! And now . . .' He stood up. 'I'd better get back to the shop. Are we OK?'

'I suppose so,' she said.

'What are you going to do now?'

'I'm going up to London, to enjoy the last few days of my job.'

'Well, here's a tenner,' he said, pulling out his roll of notes. 'Buy yourself a nice sandwich for dinner.'

Outside the Saracen's he kissed her on the top of the head and walked off towards the boutique. Slowly she walked past the Shire Hall and along Duke Street to the railway station. There was a lot to think about. She felt so tired. This had all been so emotional. She couldn't bear to think about him and Doreen. But he was almost divorced. He'd shown her the papers. This could be the start of something new. But could she ever trust him again? Should she?

CHAPTER 29

Doreen was lying on her bed, staring at the ceiling. She'd been lying here for an hour. She still had her coat and shoes on. Her lipstick had worn off. She knew she looked a wreck.

The house was empty which was something. *I should get up and start making the tea, not lying here like a wet weekend,* she thought. *I should pull myself together.*

Now, when she needed someone to talk to, she was alone. Usually, Angie was the first person she would tell. But she and Angie hadn't spoken for days. And she certainly couldn't tell Mum. She couldn't do it to her. Mum was on the edge of a nervous breakdown herself worrying about Dad and the debt they were all in. And she would go mad, shout at Doreen, tell her what a fool she'd been. Doreen couldn't bear that at the moment. She couldn't even tell Janice because she was the biggest gossip in the world. And this was such a huge, terrible secret. No, there was no one. She was going to have to deal with this on her own. She was so scared.

An unmarried mother, that's what she would be, forever known by that name, whatever else she achieved in her life. An unmarried mother, a slut, a sex-mad tart who couldn't keep her legs together. She'd got what she paid for. She could hear them now, people in the shop, people on the bus, looking at her and murmuring behind their hands. It would be awful. She saw herself, walking round the Crescent, smiling at people, saying hello and what would they be thinking? She could almost hear the curtains twitching as people looked out and turned back into their front room, saying, 'Well she got what she deserved. Showing her knees, driving that car, laughing so loud.' She couldn't bear it. She turned over and buried her head in the pillow. She had never felt so alone in all her life.

She had a bun in the oven, they would say. She was in the family way. The next thing they'd say is, she had to get married. Was that it? Was that what she could hope for? To get married to the father? Of course there wouldn't be a word said against the father. He might be expected to do the decent thing, to help her out, to walk her down the aisle to hide her shame. But otherwise, it was all on her shoulders. She was the one who had to sort it out.

Well, guess what! she shouted silently to her invisible critics, *the father's married already, so there!* A tear trickled onto the pillow. She turned onto her side and pulled her knees up to her stomach. How far gone was she? Two months, she reckoned, working backwards. Another seven months of this worry, guilt, shame, in the middle of this big ocean of debt that the family was drowning in. All the debts she had, mounting up, week by week. How could she hope to pay them off? Her job wasn't safe. She couldn't stay at Bolingbroke's much longer, selling wedding dresses in her condition. And she was sure they wouldn't let her have her job back afterwards. An unmarried mother selling wedding dresses to virgin brides! She was sobbing now. She loved her job at Bolingbroke's. She didn't want to leave it. But she'd been sick every day for a week. The first time it happened she'd hoped it was just something she'd eaten or a touch of flu. But no. She was pregnant. Just this morning she'd had to rush away from a client, dashing to get to the toilet, to throw up.

No job, no money. She couldn't bring up a kid on fresh air. And even if she got a job, if she was out working all day, how was she going to look after it? Being an unmarried mother might have been possible when they had money, but not now.

Well, there's only one thing for it, she thought. She would just have to get rid of it and then they could all get on with their lives, like it never happened. She'd been trying already. She'd drunk what felt like ten gallons of gin. She'd done a lot of jumping, and last night she rolled down the stairs when everyone was watching *Emergency Ward 10*. But of course, it didn't work. She was still pregnant.

She had to do something and do it soon. It wouldn't be long before Mum guessed. A bit thicker round the tummy, not able to fit into her tight skirts, not wanting to eat sardines on toast any more, her favourite thing for tea. Doreen heaved just thinking about sardines.

She shivered. She was cold. She pulled the eiderdown round her. She rocked from side to side. What was she going to do? Get an abortion? It was illegal, everyone knew that, and it was dangerous. She'd heard the stories. Sad women, going into someone's dirty basement where knitting needles and washing-up liquid sat in a dirty bowl. Women died, she knew that, bleeding to death on their own, or butchered inside so badly they could never have children. It was terrifying. She curled into a ball. Anyway, she hadn't a clue how to go about getting an abortion.

Of course, the one person who might know was the person she didn't want to talk to ever again.

Perhaps she should just go to Australia and be done with it, start a new life there, say she was a widow, buy a wedding ring from Woolworths, think up some tragic way her husband had died, be a new, different person, leave this horrible steaming mess behind. But was that what she wanted from her life?

She let out a deep sigh. What were her options? Should she tell him? Should she tell Gene that he was the father of her child? What would he say? And apart from the fact that he was already married, did she want to be tied to him with all his charming philandering ways for the rest of her life? And oh God, what would Angie say? It was bad enough now when Angie thought all they'd done was have a couple of drinks in the Fleece. It would destroy her. Just when she thought things couldn't get any worse – she'd lost her dad, lost all the money he'd promised and along with that she'd lost all her dreams, the lovely job she'd started.

She stared up at the ceiling again. A tear ran from the corner of her eye. What did she want? What did she really want? A baby? Her job? A husband? A life in Australia? An abortion? She didn't know. And there was no one to talk to.

It was all too much, Doreen thought. She needed to be outside, breathe in some fresh air. Take a walk, clear her head.

She walked down Sperry Drive and along the Main Road. As she passed the Parade, someone shouted, 'Cheer up! It may never happen.'

'It already has,' she called back, dully. She wondered if she should look for the nearest river. She wondered where it was. London Road? The High Street? It was all so public. The rec? She walked along Broomfield Road, occasionally shaking her head, kicking at stones, swearing to herself.

A car stopped on the other side of the road. It was black, shiny and smooth and looked foreign. The driver rolled down his window. 'Hallo, my darling.'

'Oh, it's Charlie Drake,' she said. It was the comedian's catchphrase. Of all people, it was Gene. Her stomach gave a small flip. Was this a sign? Should she tell him? Oh, Angie would never forgive her, but if Gene was about to be a father . . .

Carelessly she walked across the road and a passing car hooted. She stuck up two fingers. She went round to the passenger side and Gene leaned across the seat and opened the door. She slid into the car. It was comfortable and warm.

'What are you doing out on a fine evening like this?' he said.

'I could ask you the same question.'

'I'm giving the new motor a run. I just bought it. In Braintree. Welcome to my gin palace.'

'I could do with a gin. And then another one.'

'Let's go,' he said. He turned into Fourth Avenue, made a big show of reversing the car into a driveway, and drove back out onto the main road, in the direction of the estate.

'Where are we going? I'm not going home.'

'I found a nice little pub right out in the country recently,' he said, turning into Patching Hall Lane. He crashed a gear. 'Sorry, just getting used to the car.'

They sat in silence and Gene concentrated on driving. Doreen watched him, a half-smile on her face. She was better at driving than he was. She shook her head. She couldn't decide whether or not to tell him.

'You OK?' Gene glanced across at her. 'You look like death warmed up.'

'Thanks a lot. I've just had a bad day.'

'You should have come into the shop,' he said. 'I'd have cheered you up.'

'That's not what we do anymore, is it? Where are we going?'

'The Pig and Whistle.'

'Aren't you meant to be seeing Angie tonight?' Doreen asked.

'Yes, but not till later. We've got time for a drink.'

She settled into the seat. She felt easy with him. That and the warmth of the car made her feel comfortable, comforted. She stretched her legs and let her sandals fall from her feet. 'Actually, I don't care where we go. I'll just sit here and you can go where you like.'

'Promises promises,' he said.

Doreen sighed. 'Oh, don't start that again.' She closed her eyes. 'Wake me up when we get there. Mine's a triple gin.' The engine of the car purred smoothly. The shadow of the trees flickered on her eyelids. Her thoughts drifted. If she went to sleep here, perhaps she wouldn't need to wake up. She shook her head. Tears pricked her eyes. Her hands crept protectively of their own accord across her belly. She didn't know what to think. How could she get rid of it? Was that what she wanted? But how would she even go about it? You could hardly go into a shop and ask for an abortion. It was illegal. You couldn't even go to the doctor. But people knew people. She'd heard Mrs Evans knew people. But wouldn't it be dangerous? She was sure it would hurt. What if it went wrong and didn't work but something happened to the kid? Oh, let this journey go on and on. And what about Gene? What would he think, if she told him, what would he say?

There was a crunch of gravel and the engine stopped abruptly. 'Right we're here.' Gene was leaning over the seat, grabbing his jacket from the back of the car. 'Wake up, Sleeping Beauty.'

'Was I asleep?' But he was out of the car, looking at the tyres. *As if he knows what he's looking for,* she thought. She slipped her feet back into her sandals and swivelled out of the car. She rubbed her finger under her eyes to wipe away any smudged mascara and blew her nose.

'All right?' he said.

'I'll live. Unfortunately.'

'God, we'd better get that gin down you.' He put his arm loosely round her shoulders and she felt a pang of something she thought had gone. He guided her towards a jumble of shed-like buildings with a low roof. He opened the latch on a small door and they stepped into a room filled with dark wooden furniture and peach coloured lights and the comforting sound of ordinary people having ordinary conversations.

He brought the drinks over to the table and sat down beside her. He looked at her. 'Go on then.'

She blinked. 'My dad's left home.'

'So you said.'

'With all the money we thought we were going to have.'

'Yes.'

'My mum still wants to go to Australia.'

'I think I'd heard that too.'

'Nothing's definite,' she said.

'Are you going?'

'I don't know. Angie doesn't want to go.'

'So I understand. It's funny because I've thought about going myself now and again.'

'Australia? You?'

'Yeah. You know – new start, new opportunities. I could take fashion to parts of the world that are starving for it.'

'Maybe.' She toyed with her glass.

'But, as awful as all this is, none of it's new. Why is everything so terrible today?'

She looked at his face. Remembered why she'd liked him, loved him even. He had made her whole body quiver with desire, he'd made her melt, he'd made her feel wonderful. She could feel tears in her eyes. 'Oh. I might as well tell you.' He raised his eyebrows. 'I'm pregnant.'

'Good God.'

His expression made her laugh and kept her from saying it was his. 'You've gone all white. Don't worry – it's not about you. You're not the problem.'

'But am I the father?' He took a mouthful of beer. 'I think I've aged ten years in the last ten seconds. What do you mean I'm not the problem?'

She took a breath and made a decision, 'It's nothing to do with you.'

He put his glass on the table. He smiled. 'That's a shame. Any child we made together would be brilliant and beautiful.'

And there was the smooth Gene she knew. Charming, urbane, back in control. 'D'you reckon?'

He sat back in his chair. 'So?'

'So, what? I'm just telling you. That's why today is a rubbish day. That and being sick all over the place.'

'Who is the father?'

'It's no one you know.'

'I should hope not. I'd have to kill him.'

She wanted to tell him, *Of course it's yours, what kind of tart do you take me for?* but she couldn't. He didn't belong to her. She couldn't do it to Angie – not that he belonged to Angie really, but she couldn't do it. This was her problem and hers alone. And she was alone. She looked at Gene.

'Oh Reen,' he said softly.

'Don't.' She scrabbled in her bag. 'Don't be nice. I'll just cry and . . . where's my bloody hanky?'

He pulled a handkerchief from his pocket. 'Here.'

She took it and dabbed at her eyes, but the tears wouldn't stop.

'Have you told your mum?'

'Not yet.' She hiccupped.

'What are you going to do?'

'Don't ask. I don't know, I don't know!'

'Have a drink.' He pushed her glass towards her.

'Gin hasn't helped so far.' She took a sip. 'I think I'm going to throw up.'

'Just take a breath. Calm down.'

'Don't tell me to calm down!' she hissed. She twisted the handkerchief in her hands.

'OK, OK.' He held his hands up.

'I'm sorry,' she said. 'I'm a bit on edge. Look, can you help me?'

'What do you mean?'

He moved closer and put his arm round her, and it was just easy to put her head on his shoulder, and reach up and hold the lapel of his jacket.

He looked down and kissed the top of her head. 'So what do you want me to do?'

She couldn't speak, there was a lump the size of the iceberg that sank the Titanic in her throat. Maybe she should tell him.

'Do you want me to marry you?' he said.

'Oh, Gene.'

'Don't make up your mind, straightaway. Think about it. Now, I've just got to make a phone call.'

Doreen watched him as he walked up to the bar to ask where there was a payphone. She watched him walk back out to the small vestibule. She thought about what he'd said. It wasn't the most elegant of marriage proposals, but it would certainly be one way out of the problem. Get married. Give the kid Gene's name. Be a family. Start a new life. They could go to Australia together. They'd certainly have to go somewhere to get away from the wrath and grief of Angie. Angie would probably never speak to her again. Could she live with that? And marriage, that was a bit final. The next fifty years, living with Gene, forsaking all others. Well, Gene certainly wouldn't do much forsaking, she knew enough about him to know that. Take tonight, he was meant to be with Angie. She'd be wondering where he was. Now he was on the phone, making up excuses. That could be her, in five, ten years' time. She didn't want that. She'd rather have Angie, she realised, than Gene.

Angie was getting ready to go out. She had decided to wear her green dress. It was the most complicated dress she had made and she liked it. And so did Gene. And now she had black shoes to go with it. She was clipping on the charm bracelet when the phone rang.

She threw a glance at her reflection. She smoothed her dress and smiled. She was pleased at what she saw. She ran downstairs and picked up the phone.

It was Gene. 'Hallo, babe,' he said.

'Hallo? Why are you ringing? I'm going to see you in a few minutes.'

'Well that's the problem, sweet pea. I'm a bit held up.'

She heard the sound of laughing and clinking glasses. 'Why? Where are you?' Suddenly the sound stopped.

'I – I'm in the pub.'

'What pub? Where? I can come and meet you, can't I?'

'It's business, honey.'

'Well it can't go on all night, can it?'

There was the sound of laughter again, as if a door had opened in the pub.

'No, but I'm out in the country. You couldn't get here.'

'Out of the country? Where are you?' She had a sick feeling in her stomach.

'In the country. Just the country, Chignal way, I think.'

'What are you doing there?'

'I told you. It's . . . it's business.'

'Business,' she said. 'It's not more divorce business, is it?'

'No no, nothing like that, it's . . . it's about the shop. You know. Maybe expanding. Maybe moving.'

'Really? You've never said that before. You're making it up!'

He laughed. 'I'm thinking about it.'

'Who with?'

'Just some of the guys.'

'Guys? Are you with Cynthia?'

'No! Not Cynthia. Not anyone. Just, just the guys.'

She tried not to let her fear sound through her voice. 'So, so when am I going to see you?'

'Oh honey, you sound so sad.'

'Well – well I, I'm all ready to go out.'

'I'm sorry, honey bunny. I'll make it up to you, I promise. We'll go somewhere fabulous.'

She was silent.

'Are you still there, babe?' he said.

'This is going to cost you more than a piece of cheesecake in an Italian cafe, I can tell you.'

'I was thinking of somewhere French actually. In Paris! How about that?' She could tell he was smiling, relieved, thinking the crisis had passed.

Suddenly she felt very tired, she had an overwhelming urge to cry and she wanted to talk to someone. Is this what it would always be like? Her sitting at home, worrying, wondering where he was; him making a late phone call, making excuses in his softest voice, promising to do better, maybe buying her a trinket, another bracelet. Would it be worth it? She took a deep breath. 'Actually, Gene, you know what? Let's just say goodbye, shall we? You go your

way, and I'll go mine. That's it. We're finished. OK? Bye.'
She put the phone down before he could say anything.

As Gene walked back into the bar, he looked serious,
almost sad. He sat down silently.

'Well,' Doreen said, 'I've thought about it. It's a very nice
offer, but no thanks.'

'Sorry? What?'

'You did just ask, in a roundabout way, to marry me.'

'Did I? Oh God, yes, of course.'

'Yes, and I'm saying thanks for asking, but no, I won't
marry you.' She could almost smell the relief in him. 'And
of course, bigamy's a crime and you are still married.'

'Not for much longer.' He patted his chest and she heard
the crackle of paper. 'Soon I'll be free to marry whoever
I want!'

'Well, darling, I don't think it's going to be me.' She picked
up her bag. Stubbing out her cigarette, she said, 'I think you'd
better take me home.'

He dropped her at the top of Sperry Drive. She hurried into the house. Angie was sitting at the kitchen table.
They hadn't spoken since their big argument. Doreen hovered in the doorway, scanning Angie's face, not sure if she
should enter or leave.

'You'll be pleased to know,' Angie said without looking
up, 'that he's in the country somewhere, doing business.

So I've finished with him. Forever. And I feel awful.' She burst into tears.

'Oh no, oh no,' Doreen knelt down beside Angie. 'Are you sure he wasn't doing something perfectly legitimate, something generous, something honourable? You know he can be all of those things.'

'Yes, maybe he was tonight. He said he was talking about expanding, about moving the business.'

'Oh, was he?' Doreen said.

'But he could just as easily have been with someone he'd picked up off the street, or in the pub. I'd never know. I'd always worry. He's gone, it's over. I've done too much crying over him.'

'Oh Angie,' Doreen said. 'I'm so sorry.'

Angie pulled a hanky from her sleeve. The charms on the bracelet jangled as she wiped her eyes.

Doreen looked at it and shook her head. How many secrets could she keep? She squeezed her eyes shut tight. 'Look Angie. I've got to tell you something. It was me he was with in that pub tonight.'

Angie's head reared up.

'It was completely by chance. Honestly. Nothing was arranged at all. I was walking along the road. I was really upset and then he came by in a swanky car.'

'Oh, he's bought it, has he?' Angie said mechanically.

'He has.'

'And you were upset?'

'Yes.'

'Why?'

'I'm pregnant.

'Pregnant?' Angie's head shot up. A flood of emotions crossed her face. 'Oh my God, Doreen, you're . . . Oh no, oh no, it's not, it can't be . . . Is it?' She raised her face, her eyes were huge with brimming tears.

Doreen knelt beside her. 'I am so sorry, kid. It is. It's his.'

'What did he say?' Angie sounded fearful.

'I didn't tell him it was his. I couldn't. He said if he met the bloke who did it, he'd knock his block off.'

'Yes, that's the sort of thing he says.' Angie drew a shuddering tear-filled breath.

'I'm sorry, lovely. I'm sorry about tonight. He rang you, didn't he? He was a sad man after that.'

'So he should be. So what did you do in his swanky car?' she asked suspiciously.

'He bought me a large gin and then . . .' *he asked me to marry him,* '. . . and then he brought me home. He dropped me off on the corner.'

'Are you going to see him again?' Angie asked.

'Oh, lovely, of course not. No. In fact I can't think of anything worse. Do you think you might see him again?'

'No. Never. It's too exhausting.'

'And anyway, you're my sister and I love you and I'm sorry, and it should never have happened.'

'Oh, Reen. What are we going to do?'

'I don't know. For now,' Doreen stood up, 'I'm going to make us a cup of tea and a slice of toast, even if it's just the crusts.'

'Oh big whoop!'

'I know. We are the last of the big spenders.'

'In every way.' Angie stood up. They hugged. Angie loved her sister. She wanted to trust her. Doreen had told her about tonight. She'd shared the awful truth that she was pregnant. She could tell that Doreen wouldn't see Gene again. They would go through this together. Things felt clearer now. She wouldn't have to worry about Gene anymore. She felt better.

CHAPTER 30

TEN DAYS LATER, ANGIE'S JOB AT the college had ended, although Alison Fairfield had said anytime she wanted to come back she should be sure to get in contact. 'Unless I come into some money, that's not likely,' Angie had said. 'And that's not going to happen.'

There was no prospect of going back to English Electric, her mum had told her sadly. Mandy had taken her old job and the management job had been taken. She was jobless.

So this morning she'd been in to Bonds. She'd gone up to personnel and, reviewing their records, and seeing how well she'd done in haberdashery they'd said yes, there was a job, in the Beds Department if she would like that. She could start tomorrow. In fact, if she wanted, they'd be very happy if she'd like to spend this very afternoon learning the ropes and watching what was required. And so she had.

By the end of the day she was exhausted. The Beds Department was really not at all interesting, but it meant money and that was all she would allow herself to think about. As she entered the house she heard a strange sound. It was her mum. She was singing.

'Mum?' She called. 'What are you doing?'

Her mum was standing in the living room, sorting piles of clothes. 'If your dad's not coming back, we've got to make plans.'

'Ye-e-es?'

'We're going to Australia! We're going up to London tomorrow to finally sort things out, get a date, organise the voyage. In the meantime, I'm packing, and I think you've got one of my cardigans.'

'Mum!' Angie took a pile of nightdresses from her. 'Are you really going? Now? What shall I do without you? Who's going to pay off all our debts?'

'We're not going straight away,' Mum said. 'In the meantime, I have upped my hours at English Electric.'

'I know you have.'

'And those couple of nights a week behind the bar in the Clock House are helping, and Mrs Evans has put me in the way of a little cleaning job, in the school round the lane.'

'Oh Mum, you're doing too much.'

'So we'll be paying off what we can, as quickly as we can. And Doreen has said she'll do some cleaning. She can't get any more hours at Bolingbroke's. We'll pay off the electric and the gas, though that's not so much. And we'll be able to make the payment on Doreen's overdraft this month.

The furniture in the front room has been returned. And I'm going to sell off anything that's not going to Australia with us. The fur coat's gone back already. I shan't need that in Australia.'

'God, Mum, how much did you spend?'

'Too much. But I didn't know. I'm doing what I can,' she whispered.

'I know,' Angie said.

'And I do keep asking about a job for you at English Electric.'

'Thank you. But I got a job this morning at Bonds, so I can help out too. It's in the Beds Department, but Cath reckons there might even be a job in haberdashery soon, which would be lovely.'

'Oh Angie, love, that's great news. But look, are you sure you won't come to Australia with us? We could leave all this behind,' her mum said.

'No, Mum, really. I'm not going to give up now, just because of Dad.'

'You've got to be careful.' It was the old Mum talking, disapproving of Angie working in fashion. 'You'll have to find a new place to live. You won't be able to stay here.'

'Yes, I will!' Angie protested.

'You'll need something smaller and cheaper. You just won't be earning enough. I'll send you anything I can, and I'm sure Doreen will too, but it's not likely to be much, if anything. I want you to be happy.' She stretched out her arm and stroked Angie's hair. 'We've all done stupid things, but we'll find a way out of this.'

'Oh Mum.'

'You know.' Her mum smiled. 'I can't wait to get to Australia. I just spoke to Ivy on the phone.' She stopped. 'She rang me this time, but I think the phone bill's going to be another big one. Oh dear, oh dear.'

'We'll sort it out,' Angie said.

'I hope so.'

'What did Ivy say?'

Mum's face lit up. 'She's thrilled we're coming, and even more thrilled we're coming without Dad. She never liked him.'

'That's great for you and Doreen!'

'Oh, I can't wait!' Mum said. 'All that sun, and parties in the garden and on the beach! Ivy says they have them all the time. Are you sure you won't come?'

'I'm sure.'

'If you're sure.'

'I am.'

'But do you think you could run me up some shorts?'

'Mum, you're wild!' Angie laughed. 'Of course, I could. How about something in green to go with your eyes?'

'On that basis they should be red,' Mum said.

'Actually Mum, you look better than you've looked for years,' Angie said.

'Yes, this perm's lasted well, hasn't it?'

'Well, it's not just that, but yes, the perm's not bad.'

'Talking about hairdressers,' her mum said, 'when I rang Harry again yesterday, to see if he'd heard anything, he said we weren't the only people to lose someone. I said, "What do you mean?" He said his assistant, that flowery girl, what's her name?'

'Rose,' Angie said.

'Yeah, well, she's gone off somewhere too. Just one morning, she didn't come in to work. And that was it. There must be something in the air.'

'Yes,' Angie said slowly. 'There must be.'

'Anyway, have you got that cardigan? The blue one with the collar.'

'No, I haven't seen it. Mum, you don't think . . . ?'

'What? Don't think what?'

'Nothing.'

'Well, if you haven't got it, Doreen must have it in one of her drawers.' Cheerfully Mrs Smith went upstairs, and Angie heard her ask Doreen about the cardigan.

Angie looked at the piles of clothes in the living room. Mum was certainly feeling better and that was great. But really, this idea of them all working their socks off to clear the debts was going nowhere. It just wasn't going to be enough. And they'd returned everything they could. Except the sewing machine. Perhaps it was time to return that too. This was all such a mess. She could hear Doreen coming downstairs. Doreen's position was the worst of all, and one that Mum had no idea about. She went into the kitchen. She and Doreen were going to have to come up with some ideas.

Angie sat down at the kitchen table. 'I think we should talk,' she said.

Doreen looked at her warily.

'Not that,' Angie said. 'We've got to think of ways to get some more money.'

'Well, selling my body is out, I'm afraid,' Doreen said. 'Do you think we should start a pop group? We could call ourselves the Swinging Smith Sisters.'

'I don't think so.'

'What was that we used to do when we were kids? We used to make lemonade and little necklaces and bracelets out of daisies and sell them,' Doreen said.

'Be serious. Anyway, we never made much money, if I remember. No, we've got to think of something sensible.'

'Like what?' Doreen said. 'I mean, I've said I'll do some cleaning, but that's not going to last long.'

'Something that will bring in lots of money.'

'We could rob a bank.'

'Something that's legal.'

'Perhaps you could be a teacher, you know all that stuff about sewing.'

'I think you need qualifications for that. Perhaps you could teach people how to be a good salesman.'

Doreen pointed at her stomach. 'I think they might say I'm not setting a good example.'

Angie laughed. She leaned against Doreen.

Doreen put an arm round her and hugged her. 'I'm sorry,' she said. 'I'm sorry for everything.'

'I know,' Angie said. 'I'm just trying to forget it all. Are you and Mum really going to Australia?'

'It's her dream. We've got our skills.'

'Why do they want glassblowers in Australia?'

'From what I hear, they drink out of glasses over there.'

'So, are you going for this ten pound passage thing?'

'And all we can eat thrown in. Sounds good to me. We can't afford anything else.'

'What about the baby?'

'I . . . I don't know. But what I do know,' Doreen said, 'is that we should be getting organised. It's all a bit piecemeal. Mum's extra jobs here, your Bonds wages there. Mum's started packing, that's good. We're going to London to get the passage sorted out. I should be packing. If I've got a case to pack.' She looked up at the new matching set of suitcases, piled up on top of her wardrobe. 'They haven't been paid for yet. They'll have to go back.'

'Oh,' Angie sighed. 'It's all just so – so huge.'

'What we should do is sit down and work out what's got to be done, who we've got to pay and when, and how we're going to make any money. Going to Australia isn't going to fix everything. It's going to be pretty hopeless. God knows how many glassblowers they need. There ain't going to be much money.'

'Oh Reen,' Angie whispered. 'What are we going to do?'

'We're going to have our tea and then sit round the table and sort it out properly. All right?'

'Yes, ma'am!' Angie said and made a salute.

The beans and the toast were cleared away and Doreen pulled out a pencil and an old exercise book from a drawer in the sideboard. She opened it and drew vertical lines on an empty page.

'All right,' she said, holding the pencil over the paper. 'What do we need to do?'

'Pay back our debts.'

She wrote a heading on one of the columns. 'OK, and how are we going to do that? Mum's working like a mad thing.' She scribbled some notes. 'I'm going to do some cleaning with Mum. And I'm going to get a few evenings in the Saracen's if I can.'

'It's a bit of a race against time, with you going off to Australia soon. Well, I obviously can't keep the sewing machine now, or my new table,' Angie said sadly. 'I'll have to take them back.'

Doreen looked at her, frowning.

Mrs Smith came into the room, putting on her coat ready for her shift in the Clock House. She looked at the paper in front of Doreen. 'What's going on?'

'We're having a pow-wow,' Doreen said. 'We're making plans.' She wrote another heading.

'Am I not included?'

'Of course you are,' Doreen said. 'We're just getting started. We're trying to think of a way round our money problems and that means we've got to think of things to do.'

'How far have you got?'

'Not very far. Angie wants to give up her sewing machine.'

'I don't *want* to,' Angie began.

'I should think not,' Mum said.

'What do you mean?'

'Because there's your answer right there, surely.'

'Where? What?' Angie asked.

'She's right,' Doreen said. 'Stand up.'

'Why?'

'Stand up.'

Angie stood up.

'There. Look.'

'What am I looking at?' Angie said.

'Your dress. You made it.'

'Yeah, so?' Angie looked down at her dress. 'I made it,' she said slowly. 'But . . . come on. One dress.'

'No,' said Doreen. 'There's your green one, and the one you wore to the interview, and the ones you made for me. And all your skirts. You make clothes.'

'So?'

'Well!' Doreen leaned over the exercise book. 'How long did it take you to make this dress?'

'Oh well, this one was really straightforward. The strip at the bottom was fiddly, so that took a bit of time.'

'All right, all right. But how long? Roughly.'

'A day? Less probably. You've got the cutting out and the pinning and sewing and putting in the zip.'

'So, if you started in the morning, and say I did some of the sewing, the straight bits, the seams, how many could you make in a day?'

'I don't know. I'd need material. Well I still have all the material I bought. You can't return it once it's been cut off the roll.'

'OK, so we've got the material.'

'I've got to run,' Mum said. 'Keep going. You might be the saviour of us yet, Angie.' She walked into the hall to fetch her coat.

'OK,' Doreen said. 'We've got the material. And let's just say we've got the zips and the cotton and everything. How many could you make in a day?'

'I don't know. Four or five.'

'Well, there you are! We've got a fashion range. Now you just need a name.'

'Hang on, what are we talking about?'

Doreen laughed. 'We're talking about you – Angela Smith fashion designer, and her range of designs. That must be the way out of this. It won't happen overnight, but if we all get stuck in and help out with the sewing, this could be the start of something big.'

'I think Doreen's right,' Mrs Smith said, buttoning her coat. 'I think it sounds like a wonderful idea.' She walked to the back door. 'I wish I wasn't going out now. But I think this could be it.' She grinned widely at her daughters. 'I'm a lucky woman,' she said. She picked up her handbag.

'OK, let's say, for the sake of argument, that I could make a few dresses, where would I sell them?'

'Anywhere,' Doreen said. 'Put an advert in the paper.'

'And say what? I'm selling dresses in the garden of 34 The Crescent?'

'Well, of course you do know someone who's got a clothes shop,' Doreen said.

'Who, Dorothy Perkins?'

'Idiot! You know someone who sells clothes.'

'What? Gene? You're joking.' Angie looked at Doreen with a frown. 'Anyway it's a men's boutique.'

'Isn't there a little corner that could be girls' clothes?' Doreen asked. 'That part where he's got the record player. He could put a rail in there, no trouble. Your dresses would look a treat.'

'How come you know so much about it?'

'I've looked inside. It's my job!' Doreen said quickly. 'That's what I do. Seeing what modern shops are doing, how they're selling. It must be a good idea.'

'I don't know if I could bear it.'

'Really? Don't tell me you miss him.'

'No, not really, but, working with him . . . ?'

'Angie, he owes you this. And you and Carol are forever complaining there's not a boutique for girls in the town.'

'Are we?'

'It would be great. And I really could do some sewing – I did it at school. And if you want to do a bit of contrast, put different colours on, I could do that. Or beads, if you want to jazz things up. Mum could even do stuff. At night, when she gets in.'

'You're going to Australia.'

'Not straight away. We can even put if off for a while, just while we get started.'

'Who's "we"?'

'Us. You, me and Mum.'

'And you're saying I could keep my sewing machine?'

'And your new table! How else are you going to maintain your production line?' Doreen said. 'And since Gene will be getting some of the benefit, he can't complain if it takes a bit of time to pay back the money you owe him. Can you speak to him?'

'I don't know. I'll try.'

'Will you be OK working with him?'

'Will you?'

'A girl's got to do what a girl's got to do,' Doreen said.

'That's true.'

'Well, there's a lot in it for him. He'll see you're serious about paying him back, and there'll be a whole load of new customers. And shopkeepers always want new customers. He'd be mad not to agree. But of course, there's not just his shop. What about markets? Markets sell clothes, don't they?'

'Chelmsford market?'

'Maybe,' said Doreen. 'I was really thinking of all those markets in London. Portabella something. And Petticoat Lane. And there must be others.'

'Portobello Road, you mean. Yes, they're all selling fashion clothes these days.'

'This is exciting!' Doreen said.

'For you, maybe,' Angie said. 'I'll be on my own soon.'

'Oh, come on Angie,' Doreen said. 'Chin up! Look, if we both have an early dinner hour tomorrow, we can meet in Bonds about half past eleven and buy the bits and pieces you still need – oh, you'll probably get a discount because you work there – and by Friday you'll have half a dress shop. Imagine. How much will you charge?'

'Depends on the material, doesn't it? But hang on, we've got to talk to Gene first. There's no point in buying loads of stuff, running up even more debts, if I haven't got anywhere to sell these dresses.'

'We'll talk to him first.' Doreen looked up at the clock. 'Come on. He sometimes does stock-taking on a Tuesday evening.'

'Does he?' Angie frowned.

'Sometimes. Let's go and see!'

The boutique was open and empty except for Gene. 'Hello Angie! How lovely to—' Gene said, looking up as the bell on the door announced their arrival. 'And Doreen! Well, hello.' He looked from one to the other. 'This is a surprise.'

'A nice one, I hope,' Doreen said.

Gene was putting a record onto the record player. The unexpected sound of Dusty Springfield filled the room.

'It's great to see you, girls,' Gene said, smoothly. 'Have you come to buy something for that Roger of yours, Angie?'

'I told you,' Angie said, '"that Roger" is history.'

'Oh yes.' Gene smacked his forehead. 'How could I forget!'

Dusty Springfield sang, 'You Don't Have to Say You Love Me.'

Doreen looked at Angie and mouthed, 'OK?'

Angie nodded. She looked around the shop. 'Gene?'

'Yes?' he said, copying her inflection.

'Do you need to have your record-player just there? Couldn't you hear the music just as well if you put it in the back room? There's enough space. You don't really need that bed in there, do you?'

'Don't I?' he said. His eyes flicked quickly to Doreen. She looked at the ground. 'What are you talking about?'

'I need to make some money to pay you back, obviously.'

'There's no rush, I've told you. Take your time.'

'Yeah, well, things are a bit different now, aren't they? I want to pay it back as soon as possible.'

'And so?'

'I want to make some dresses, like this one.' She indicated the shift she was wearing. 'And I want to sell them here, hang them up on a rail that will be standing under that spotlight, where the record player is now.'

'But this is a men's boutique.'

'Where does it say that? It just says Battini's.'

'I only sell men's clothes.'

'Not necessarily.'

'Girls won't come.'

'Girls *don't* come,' Angie said.

'But they do come,' Doreen said. 'They come with their boyfriends.'

'And it only takes one or two to start talking about it and all the mod girls from Chelmsford will come,' Angie said. 'And from Braintree and Great Waltham and Little Waltham.'

Gene held up his hands. 'I get the point. But what am I selling? Two exclusive handmade dresses or a range that's going to keep coming? I mean how many have you got to sell?'

'Well . . .' Angie began.

'How many do you need?' Doreen said quickly.

'I dunno. If it's going to be a range, ten? Fifteen? With a promise of more to follow.'

'That's exactly what we've got!' Doreen said. 'We thought you'd need sizes ten and twelve.'

'Oh, did you? Well, I suppose so, if they're all as skinny as Angie.'

'And maybe a few fourteens,' Doreen said.

'And a sixteen or two,' Angie said.

'Hold on! This would be a bit of a gamble, you know. It's all new to me. Tell you what. Why don't you bring in a few dresses next week? Tell your mates they'll be in here. We'll see how they go. And for the first couple of weeks, I won't take any commission or charge you any rent. All right, sugar plum?' He smiled at Angie.

Angie whispered triumphantly to Doreen. 'Yes!' Then, turning to Gene she said, 'Just to be clear, I'm not your sugar plum. This is a business arrangement.'

'You're right,' he said. 'Of course.'

'Now excuse us,' Doreen said. 'We've got to go and get you those dresses.'

As they left the shop a boy in a parka was looking in the window, with a young woman in a suede coat.

'Come back next week and you'll be able to buy mod dresses here,' Doreen said.

'Really?' the girl said.

As they walked up to the bus station, Doreen said, 'Well that was easy. I didn't think he'd agree so fast. You haven't gone back him, have you?'

'No!' Angie said. 'I think he feels guilty about the way he treated me – and you. And this way he's not going to lose anything. He loves making money. He loves that roll of tenners he carries round with him.'

'And we are just about to make it bigger.'

'Are you really sure you're OK with working with Gene?' Angie said.

'I can do it if you can,' Doreen said.

'But how are we going to do this?' Angie asked. 'When are we actually going to make these dresses?'

'Tonight, every night. For some reason, neither of us has a social life. We'll get up early, do a couple of hours in the morning before we catch the bus.'

'If you say so,' Angie said.

CHAPTER 31

WHEN DOREEN WENT INTO JOHNSON'S, THE newsagents, on the parade of shops on Greenway Road, Mrs Evans was in there buying a birthday card.

'Oh Doreen,' she said, 'what do you think of this one?'

Doreen looked over her shoulder as she paid for her cigarettes. 'Very nice.'

'Good, that's the one I'll have. Wait for me, we can walk over to the Crescent together.'

They walked out of the shop together and crossed the road to the Crescent. Doreen was silent.

'Everything all right, dear?' Mrs Evans said.

'Yes.'

Mrs Evans looked her up and down. 'Is everything really all right?'

Doreen frowned.

'You can tell me to shut up, dear,' she said, 'but you look like you've got a bit of a problem.'

'What do you ...?' Doreen felt a blush colour her cheeks. 'I don't know what you're talking about.' She began to walk faster.

'Slow down, lovey. You're in no fit state to be running anywhere, are you?' Mrs Evans said.

Doreen slowed her pace.

'Don't worry, your mum didn't tell me.'

'She doesn't know,' Doreen said, then wished she hadn't. She'd given herself away. This was awful.

'Your secret's safe with me,' Mrs Evans said.

'How did you know?'

'The way you walk, maybe. The look in your eye. Your ankles. They're still lovely, but they're a bit swollen, aren't they?'

Doreen looked down at her feet.

'Now from your reaction,' Mrs Evans said, 'I would imagine this is not the sort of situation you're happy to be in.'

'I don't—'

'So I'll just say this once, that there are people around who help girls like yourself.'

'You?' Doreen asked.

'No, no, not me, but you know. People know people, don't they?' They had reached Mrs Evans' front gate. 'Think about it, dear,' she said. 'If you need any help, or just someone to talk to, you know where I am. Now I've got to get in and get their tea. Look after yourself, lovey. And remember I'm here.'

The kindness of Mrs Evans words were like balm to Doreen. She had been feeling so alone. She was determined not to burden Angie any further, and Gene couldn't help her. And now somehow there was someone who was sharing the load. Tears ran down her face as she walked to the house.

A week later Doreen walked up the road. She was afraid. Very, very afraid. She felt weak. No one at home knew what she had decided to do. At the last minute she had thought of telling Angie, Angie might even have come with her, but she'd thought it best not to tell anyone. This was something she needed to do on her own. Timidly she tapped on the door of the Evans's house. She hoped to God that Cliff wouldn't be in.

There was a long wait and then the door opened. Mrs Evans smiled with a warm, enveloping smile. 'Come in, duck,' she said. She glanced up at the large clock in the hall. 'You're right on time. My friend is expecting us. You've got the necessary?'

Miserably, Doreen nodded. The envelope with the notes was at the bottom of her bag. She had managed to persuade the bank manager to extend her overdraft, with a smile and a cheerful tilt of the head.

'The kids have gone to my sister's for the day,' Mrs Evans said, buttoning her coat.

Doreen said nothing.

Mrs Evans looked at her pale, drawn face. 'Are you sure about this?' she said gently.

Doreen nodded, afraid to speak for fear she would burst into tears.

Together they walked up to the shops, through the narrow passage at the side, past the field where the polling booths were erected at election time, down and round into the road of white cement houses that was part of a new estate at the back of the Greenway.

They stopped in front of a house with a neat garden and a small silver birch tree. Mrs Evans looked at Doreen. 'All right?'

Doreen nodded. She cleared her throat. 'Yes,' she said.

They walked up the path and Mrs Evans knocked on the door. As they waited on the doorstep Mrs Evans rubbed her hands together. 'Chilly day today, isn't it?' she said.

'Yes.' Doreen forced herself to speak. 'But I don't mind it, when it's cold.'

'Ah, you're young,' Mrs Evans said. 'Cliff's the same. Never wears enough clothes.'

Hearing Cliff's name made Doreen start. Tears filled her eyes as she thought of a time when she would have responded to Mrs Evans's comment with a saucy reply about the number of clothes that Cliff might wear. Cliff. Things might all have been different if she'd gone down that path. But she hadn't. She was here. She put her hand on her stomach. She was about to allow someone she didn't know to do unspeakable, intimate things to her. She stroked the warm curve of her stomach.

'Don't worry.' Mrs Evans patted her hand. 'It'll be all right. I'll stay with you if you like.'

'Oh no! Oh no, no. You don't have to do that,' Doreen said.

The door opened. Mrs Evans's friend looked at them and frowned. She was wearing a faded cotton overall, that tied at the waist, and she was wiping her hands on a towel that had stains on it that Doreen didn't want to think about. 'I thought we said tomorrow,' she said.

Doreen turned desperately to Mrs Evans. 'I'm at work tomorrow.'

'Oh, I'm sorry, Bet,' Mrs Evans said. 'I was sure we'd said today.'

'Well, don't stand there on the doorstep. You'd better come in.'

Squashed in the narrow hall, Mrs Evans said, 'This is Doreen, Betty. Doreen, this is Mrs Clokes.'

Doreen and Mrs Clokes nodded at each other.

'The thing is,' Mrs Clokes addressed Mrs Evans, 'I'm busy today.' She looked over her shoulder, along the hall. There were three doors. They were all closed.

'Oh, please, please,' Doreen said. 'I can't come tomorrow.'

Mrs Clokes shook her head. 'I don't know. I don't like to be rushed.'

'Take your time,' Mrs Evans said. 'We've got all afternoon. Why don't I make a cup of tea?'

'All right, you know where everything is, Nora.'

Doreen sat on the sofa, in the dark living room, a weak cup of tea on her lap, her knees tight together. *Should have thought of that before*, she told herself grimly. The curtains were drawn and the only light came from a standard lamp with an unexpectedly complicated lampshade of pink tassels and red ribbons. *I'm in a brothel*, Doreen thought. She hiccupped, almost laughed, at the irony, and the cup rattled on the saucer. *I'm hysterical*, she thought.

Then she heard a scream of pain and a loud wail. Someone in another room was crying. She sat up sharply. 'What's that noise?'

'Nothing, nothing,' Mrs Evans murmured. 'Sometimes it takes girls like that. It's the shock of it all. Don't worry, it doesn't mean anything.'

How could she say that it didn't mean anything? People didn't wail like that for nothing. What was she thinking, sitting here in this, this bordello, waiting for someone to probe so deeply into her that she would howl the house down? Carefully Doreen put the cup and saucer down on the grubby rag rug. She felt sick. She looked at Mrs Evans.

Mrs Evans looked back at her, with a small, questioning smile.

Doreen put her arms tight across her stomach. She rocked forward slightly.

'Are you cold?' Mrs Evans asked. 'I'll put on another bar of the fire if you like. She won't mind.'

'No, no, I'm fine.' There was too much saliva in her mouth. She was sweating. The shabby, dark room seemed to be closing in on her. What did she think she was doing? 'I – I don't think – I can't – no, no, not this. Not here.' She stood up.

Mrs Evans stood up with her. 'Are you sure? She's never lost one yet, you know. It sounds worse than it is.'

'I can't. I just can't.' Again she put her hand protectively on her stomach.

Mrs Evans looked down at Doreen's waist. 'You don't have much time, duck. If it's not today, I think you'll be too late.'

'Oh, you know everything, do you?' Doreen shouted.

Mrs Evans made the face of an adult dealing with a small demanding child. 'I know a thing or two.'

Doreen began to cry. Mrs Evans put her arms round her. 'What do you want to do?' she said quietly.

'I don't want to stay here.' Doreen's mind was racing. She thought of the next twenty-one years looking after a child. That was a long time. But what else was there for her in life? This way, she'd have a baby. Perhaps she would go to Australia. Her mum would be there to help out.

Perhaps she could persuade Angie to come too. They'd find a story that would explain everything. They'd say she'd adopted the child, say it was the child of a close relative, no one would know any different.

'I'm not sure she'll be able to fit you in another day,' Mrs Evans said.

'I'll take the consequences.'

'Are you sure?'

'Yes,' she said. 'I'm sure.'

They walked to the front door.

'Should we tell Mrs Clokes?' Doreen said.

'She'll know what's happened. She's used to it. But are you really sure?'

'I'm not sure about anything,' Doreen said, 'except I have to get out of here. Now.'

They stepped into the cool fresh air. The sky was getting dark and a street lamp opposite the house was already glowing. Doreen took a deep breath. She had made a decision. One decision.

She'd saved fifty pounds. That was something.

'Well, between you and me,' Mrs Evans spoke in a comforting tone, 'I think she'd have said you were too far gone for her to do it safely. She's very strict about that. She has to be, of course. Now, how about we go and buy a nice cake at Sally's and go back to mine and have a real cup of tea? I saw this morning she'd got some fresh vanilla slices. Do you like a vanilla slice?'

Doreen murmured that would be very nice. She wasn't ready to go home. Mrs Evans kept talking about her favourite cakes. Doreen's head was full of thoughts about what she had done, what she hadn't done, and what she might do in the future, tomorrow, next week, next year . . .

In the baker's she chose a chocolate éclair, although she couldn't imagine herself eating it.

Mrs Evans sat with Doreen in the neat sitting room. Doreen had eaten the chocolate éclair and most of a vanilla slice, when she heard a key in the lock. She knew who it would be. Only an adult would have a key, and the only adult who lived in this house apart from Mrs Evans was Cliff. What would he say? What would he think? She looked wildly round the room – if there was an open window, she could quite happily jump out of it now. There was nowhere to go. Too bad. She ran a finger under her eyes to catch any smeared mascara, and touched her hair.

She heard Cliff go into the kitchen, she heard his voice in conversation with Mrs Evans. He said something and Mrs Evans laughed. His voice got louder as he left the kitchen and she held her breath but she heard him go upstairs. He wasn't going to come into the sitting room.

She went into the hall and Mrs Evans came out. 'Feeling better?' she said.

'Yes, thanks,' Doreen said. 'I'd better get going.'

They both glanced up the stairs.

'Yes.' Mrs Evans lowered her voice. 'You know, I think you made the right choice. For some girls Mrs Clokes is the best way and I like to see them happier. But for you . . .'

'Yes, well.' Doreen tightened the belt on her mac. She couldn't tighten it as much today as she had last week. 'Thank you for everything. Thank you for taking the time.'

'Of course, Doreen. It was no trouble. And as I say, anytime you want a chat, just let me know.'

'Thank you,' Doreen said. She opened the door and stepped into the street. She walked along the road wondering how her life was going to change. How all their lives were going to change. Was she mad? A child? How would she afford it? How would she look after it? How would she play with it?

She was at the gate when a voice said, 'Weren't you even going to say hello?'

It was Cliff.

Without turning she said, 'Obviously not.'

'Or apologise?'

She turned. 'Apologise? What for?' He looked so cool in his black jeans and grey shirt.

'You ate the vanilla slice that I was going to have!'

She laughed. That was something, he'd made her laugh, even today. 'Did I? Sorry. It was very nice.'

'Glad you liked it! So, you're a friend of my old woman now, are you?'

'We've got things in common,' she said.

'Want a cigarette?' He took out a packet of Benson and Hedges.

'I'm glad someone's in the money.' She took one from the packet.

He struck a match and held it to her cigarette, holding his hand round hers to protect the flame. Then he lit his own. They stood in silence. 'I hope my mum's helped you out,' he said.

So he knew! She looked at him, he was examining his cigarette.

'She's a very kind woman,' Doreen said. Tears pricked her eyes. 'She did what she could.'

'And you're all right?'

'I'm all right. Thanks for the cig.' She opened the gate. 'See you.'

'Yeah,' he said. 'See you.' He flicked his cigarette into the air and they both watched the red glow as it soared and then fell to the ground.

CHAPTER 32

It was seven in the morning. Doreen walked into the front room where Angie was cutting mint-green material into dress pieces. Three piles of material, mint-green, pink and royal blue, sat on the sofa. Over the back of the sofa were three completed dresses. On the new table by the window sat the expensive sewing machine, threaded up with mint-green cotton.

Angie looked up from the floor. 'Where are you going all poshed up? We've got two dresses to make before we go to work.'

'Ah, well, I can't help you right now,' Doreen said.

'Oh, thanks a lot. This was your big idea, and now you're running out on me.'

'Mum and I are going to Australia House, to sort out our passage. You don't need me,' Doreen said. 'You know that. You're the creative one, you do all the designing. I can do a bit of sewing, but anyone can do that. Most of the time you hate me, anyway.'

'I know,' Angie sighed. 'But I'd have given Gene up at some point. You were right. He played both of us.' She sat back on her heels. 'And you don't just do a bit of sewing. You're the one who found a way to sell the dresses, the one with the exercise book, the one who's drawn lines in the pages and written it all down, what we've spent, where we spent it and you put the heading on that big wide column, "Money In" ready for the money we're going to make.'

'I know,' Doreen said mournfully.

'Well, out of my way. I've got to cut out another two dresses before I go to work.' She waved her scissors at Doreen.

Doreen laughed. 'Look at you!' she said. 'I haven't seen you this enthusiastic since you staggered up the stairs with that bloody sewing machine.'

'That's because this is the most exciting thing I've ever done. It's what I've always wanted to do. And you did that, Reen. You made it happen. I'd never have thought of asking Gene. I'll probably never have the nerve to ask anyone about getting a market stall.' She put down the scissors. 'Reen, instead of you asking me to go to Australia all this time, why don't you stay here with me, and we can really make this work.'

'Oh.' Doreen lifted the pile of royal blue material and sat down. She was silent.

'What do you think?'

'That would mean Mum going on her own.'

'She's got Ivy out there and all those barbecues she's going to. She's going to be taking a new pair of shorts as well!'

'Mum in shorts!' They both laughed. 'It would mean me having the baby in this country.'

'Are you going to keep it? You could put it up for adoption.'

'Mum would be the one who'd want me to do that and she won't be here. No, I think I will keep it. But I'd have to think of how to explain it. If I stay here, no one's going to believe my widow story or any of the other ways people get children.'

'Do you really care what people think?' Angie said. 'I don't care and we'd all be living together.'

Doreen looked at her with big eyes.

'People will get over it.'

'Will they?'

'Do you care?'

'I suppose not,' Doreen said. 'I'll be a scarlet woman and proud of it! But if I stay, I'd have to get a job. Bolingbroke's won't even want me in the back room.'

'You'd need one of those in Australia too. And you'll need time off when the baby comes, and by then, if you stay, we'll have started making millions, according to you.'

'We might.'

'But do you want to?

Doreen jumped up. 'Of course I want to! Of course I bloody want to. I can't think of anything more exciting and thrilling and fantastic.' She stopped. 'But I'm scared, Angie. It's not going to be easy, me with the baby and you with your business.'

'I know, Reen. But we can do this, we can do it together. All you have to do is take a chance.' Angie stood up. She walked over to Doreen and hugged her. 'I love you Reen,' she said.

'I love you too, kiddo,' Doreen said. 'All right, big decision. I'll stay. I can't believe I'm doing this. Now let me go before my mascara runs. I've still got to face my public and take Mum up to London. And I've got to tell her I'm not coming with her. As for you, you've got half an hour to run up a couple of seams before you go to work.'

'You aren't going to get all bossy on me now, are you?'

'No, but look. If we're going to do this properly we are probably going to have to start thinking about some serious financial backing. And before you say anything, I don't think Gene is the right person to ask. For all sorts of reasons. So while I'm on the train, and you're at work, think about it. We're going to do this, and we're going to do it well.' They grinned at each other.

'Mum!' Doreen shouted. 'We've got to go. And I've got something to tell you.'

A week later Angie rang the boutique and said she was coming in with ten dresses.

'Really?' Gene sounded pleased. 'Just a minute.' She heard him say to someone in the shop. 'You're in luck, I've got my supplier on the phone. If you'd like to come back in an hour, I think you'll find what you're looking for. But don't hang about, because I've got four chicks on my waiting list already.' He spoke into the receiver. 'So I'll see you in thirty minutes, Miss Smith.'

'Have you really got a waiting list?' Angie asked.

'Well, if you can manage to get me a few more for the Kings Road shop, that would be great. I know they're going to go like hot cakes here too.'

'There's no Kings Road shop.'

'That's right,' he said.

'I'll come up as soon as I can,' Angie said.

She and Doreen walked into the boutique carrying the dresses. They had wrapped them in covers bought from the haberdashery department of Bonds. 'We must make sure we bring them back,' Doreen said. 'And, whatever you do, don't fall in love with him again.'

'Who do you think I am? No, this is too important,' Angie said.

In the boutique Gene was chatting to two mod boys in long suede coats. They were looking at Ben Sherman shirts. When he saw Angie and Doreen, Gene said to the boys, 'And while you're at it, tell your girlfriends that from today we're selling original dresses for mod girls, so they should come and get them quick, because I've already got a lot of people waiting for them.'

He walked over to them. 'The rack's in the back, waiting. Have you got hangers? Good. Then when you're ready we'll wheel it out and put it in that corner. I've put a new bulb in over there, so it'll be good and bright.'

The camp bed was gone. In its place was a chair with the record player on it. Angie unzipped the covers and Doreen carefully hung the dresses on the rail. They looked perfect, hanging in a row, the colours glowing in the dark back room. They were all the same simple design, a shift with short sleeves and a contrasting stripe at the neck and the hem. A label at the neck of each one read 'Regina', embroidered in maroon, on small squares of black satin and sewn into the neckline. They had decided on the name together, Regina was a mix of Reen and Angie. And they had made price tags, pinned to the sleeve, that resembled Gene's price tags.

Angie stuck her head into the shop. 'Ready to rock and roll.'

Gene smiled. 'Let's have a look.' He walked into the back room. 'Wow, they look fantastic.' He picked up the hem of one of the dresses. 'Very nicely finished. That's great. Now just tell all your friends to come and buy them. You know what? I might ring the *Essex Chronicle*, a chap I know, Brian, I'll get him to come and do an article. Take a photo. That should get them in.'

He wheeled the rack of dresses into the shop and placed it under the spotlight in the corner where the record player had stood. He stepped back and looked at them. 'They look fantastic, my darlings,' he said.

'Here's the invoice,' Doreen said, and handed him the document that she had prepared.

'Very professional. I like to see that.' He signed it and handed it back.

'And here's one for you,' Doreen said. 'Now we've got to go back to work.'

'Look after them, won't you?' Angie said. 'Don't let people run their dirty hands all over them.'

'I'll do what I can.' He laughed. 'But get your friend Carol to come in here and all your other mates.' As Doreen pulled open the door to leave, he said, 'Great job, girls. Oh girls, you may have broken my heart.'

'Shame,' Doreen said. 'And once more, for those in the back row, this arrangement is strictly business.' She took Angie's arm.

Angie looked back across at the dresses, crisp and new and waiting to be sold. 'Good luck,' she whispered to them.

As they walked back along the high street, Doreen said, 'I think that went very well.'

Angie laughed. They had done it. He had asked for dresses, they had supplied dresses. They were on sale in a shop, her dresses, with their label. *This is where it all begins,* she thought.

Doreen crossed the high street to Bolingbroke's and Angie turned into Bonds.

'And why are you looking so very happy?' It was Miss Darling, coming out of the shop, looking as always, out of place in the street and not in a classroom, dressed in a sharp-cut grey crêpe suit, with a tumble of embroidery on one lapel.

'Oh Miss Darling!' Angie stopped. Miss Darling had helped her get the job in London and she had thrown it all away. 'I'm sorry.'

'What for?'

'You got me that job at the College and I had to leave.'

'Yes, I understand there were some difficulties. That is why it's such a pleasure to see you smiling. Do you have another job?'

'I do! I'm working in Bonds.'

'Oh, Angela. Is that satisfying?'

'It's not bad. The people are nice. But . . .' She felt herself swell with pride.

'Yes?'

'Today my sister and I delivered ten of my dresses – dresses I'd designed and made – to a boutique just down the road. They're hanging up there, on sale. My dresses.'

'Angela! That's magnificent news. Well done. Is this a one-off or is it a business you're starting up?'

'This is the start. We're going to see how this goes.'

'So you're not doing it all yourself?'

'It's a business with my sister. If it goes well, I don't know.'

'Let's go and have a cup of coffee and you can tell me all about it.'

'Aren't you supposed to be at school?'

'Didn't you hear, dear? I've retired.'

'I didn't know! Oh but I can't have a cup of coffee. This is my dinner hour and I'm almost late. Another day.'

'Off you go,' Miss Darling said, patting her arm. 'I wish you all the very best. Perhaps I'll pop into Bonds one day and we can talk then.'

'That would be nice,' Angie said. 'Why don't you go into the boutique and look at the dresses?'

'I definitely will. See if you've remembered all I said about finishing a hem.'

CHAPTER 33

IT WAS SIX O'CLOCK ON SUNDAY morning. Doreen couldn't sleep. She had been awake since four. It was wonderful how many dresses they'd made and how Angie was so happy and applying herself to making their Regina business work. But lists of figures were running through her head, people she owed money to, how she was going to repay them, ideally before the baby came. Regina would take time. They needed a benefactor. She really hoped they wouldn't have to ask Gene.

She got up and quickly dressed. She needed cigarettes. She walked round the Crescent and crossed Greenway Road to the shops. In the newsagent Mr Johnson, the manager, looked up from the Sunday newspapers laid out on the counter at the far end of the shop.

'Oh Doreen, I'm so pleased to see you. I have to nip home for about fifteen minutes. Could you keep an eye on the shop? There's a packet of Bensons in it for you.'

'Of course, no trouble. Shall I come through now?'

'If you could, love, that would be very helpful.' Mr Johnson knew that Doreen worked in Bolingbroke's and knew she could handle the shop.

She lifted the flap in the counter and walked round to the display of the children's sweets, the penny chews, the threepenny bars of chocolate.

'Right. I'll be back soon. I've got to make breakfast for Mrs Johnson. She's not been too well. Twenty minutes at most. If the paperboys come back, tell them they can wait or I'll pay them in the week. And if anyone rings to complain about the wrong paper, say I'll be back soon.'

'Yes, of course.' She put on her Bolingbroke's voice.

Mr Johnson lifted the counter flap, and shrugging into his coat, pulled open the door and disappeared.

It was quiet in the shop and she walked round to the newspapers to read the headlines of the newspapers upside down, *News of the World*, *The People*, *The Sunday Times*, *The Sunday Citizen*. When the bell over the door tinkled, she expected to see Mr Johnson back, sooner than expected. But it wasn't Mr Johnson. It was Cliff Evans.

He was wearing a beige windcheater, tight blue jeans and rusty-coloured cowboy boots. His dark hair was brushed back off his face. He looked like a handsome villain, someone who knew about life.

'I didn't know you worked in here,' he said.

'I don't. I'm helping out.'

'Sorting out the newspapers, I see. Do you deliver them as well?'

'No. Oh, you're not here to make a complaint, are you?'

'No. I'm here for ten Embassy. Where's old man Johnson?'

'His wife's not well. He'll be back in a few minutes.' She walked round to the cabinet where the cigarettes were kept. 'Did you say ten?'

She stretched up to the Embassy shelf. She could feel his eyes watching her. She handed him the packet. 'That'll be two and three.' As he put his hand in his back pocket, pulling out money, she said, 'You know people on the market, don't you?'

'Yeah?'

'If my sister wanted to sell something, who should she talk to?'

'Chelmsford or Petticoat Lane?'

'Petticoat Lane,' she said quickly.

'I know a bloke up there. I could have a word. What's she selling?'

'Dresses. Mod dresses.'

'Interesting.' He held out a ten shilling note, across the cabinet with the expensive sweets, the tired boxes of chocolates. She took hold of it, but he didn't let it go.

She tugged it. He held on to it.

'Unless you're thinking of running out of the shop without paying for those cigs, you're going to have to give it to me,' she said.

'Can I ask you something?' he said. 'What does the father think of all this?' He nodded his head towards her belly.

'Well, you can ask me something, but I'm not sure you can ask me that.'

The doorbell jangled and Mr Johnson walked into the shop. Cliff let the ten shilling note slip from his fingers. Doreen fell back a pace, then walked to the till as Mr Johnson lifted the counter flap and walked round to the newspapers. Her hands were trembling as she put the note under the clip in the till, the fact he'd asked her that question . . .

'Morning,' Mr Johnson said to Cliff. He looked across at Doreen. 'Everything all right?'

Doreen rang up two shillings and threepence and scooped out three half crowns and a threepenny bit change. As she handed them to Cliff, he squeezed her hand. 'You going to be here for a bit?' he murmured.

She frowned.

'I might have a phone number for that bloke.'

Mr Collins from up the road came in, closely followed by Mrs Weston. Doreen looked across at Mr Johnson. 'I can wait if you like,' she said.

Mr Johnson was ringing up Mrs Weston's paper bill and Doreen was wrapping an old copy of the *Essex Weekly News* round a block of Neapolitan ice cream for Mrs

Piper, when Cliff came back. A stillness filled the room. Cliff looked at the customers and then over at Doreen. He raised an eyebrow. He looked cool and out of place in the small shop.

Mrs Piper carefully tucked the ice cream into her string bag. Smiling at Doreen and nodding to Cliff she left the shop, but Mrs Weston lingered. 'It's all getting so expensive,' she said as Mr Johnson gave her her change. She looked at the money in her palm and shook her head.

'Well, unfortunately, prices will never go down,' Mr Johnson said.

Doreen looked at Mrs Weston. She was wearing her slippers. *She shouldn't even be out*, Doreen thought.

Mrs Weston looked round at Cliff and laughed nervously. 'Sorry to take so long.' He shook his head and said, 'You're all right.'

Mr Johnson looked at Doreen and nodded towards Cliff meaning she should serve him.

'It's OK, I'm just making up my mind,' said Cliff.

Finally Mrs Weston turned and left, softly in her slippers.

Again the room was still. 'Time for tea, I think,' Mr Johnson said. 'Let me make you a cup for being so helpful, Doreen.'

'Thanks,' she said.

Scarcely glancing at Cliff, he murmured, 'Keep your eye on the shop, Doreen,' and went into the back room.

Doreen and Cliff stood silently looking at each other until there was the sound of water rushing into the kettle. Then, still without speaking, Cliff lifted a large white and gold bag over the counter and handed it to her.

'What? What's this?' Doreen whispered furiously. The bag was full, white tissue paper peeped over the top, but it was almost weightless.

'It's the phone number of my mate.'

'In a bag this size?'

'Oh and something else. Something you need.'

She looked at the white tissue paper. 'What do I need? Oh God, it's not baby clothes is it?' She didn't dare look beneath the tissue.

'No,' he said.

She stared at him. 'Where did it come from?'

'Look at the bag.'

She read the gold lettering. De Soutta.

'De Soutta!' she said. '*The* De Soutta?'

'It's only an up-market Dorothy Perkins.'

'In Chelsea. Yes, that's likely.'

'At last, a smile!' he said. 'All right, an exclusive Dorothy Perkins that you don't leave without spending fifty quid.'

'Fifty pounds! You didn't.'

'No, not fifty pounds.' He laughed.

'So . . . how much do I owe you?'

'You don't owe me anything! It's a present.' He smiled at her. 'Don't worry,'

'You didn't nick it, did you?'

'They wouldn't have put it in a bag with all that tissue paper nonsense, would they, if it was nicked?' He paused. 'Well, you don't have to say anything.'

'Thank you,' she whispered. She lifted a piece of tissue paper. She was looking at soft, expensive black mohair. Her finger brushed against it, it was soft, warm, almost alive. She shook her head. 'Oh my god,' she breathed. 'How did you . . . ?' She laughed. 'I'd forgotten I told you all about my ruined sweater.'

She could hear Mr Johnson opening a biscuit tin and rummaging through the biscuits. She looked up at Cliff who was drumming his fingers on the wooden edge of the counter.

She held up the black Sloppy Joe, letting it drape over her arms. 'This is gorgeous. It must have cost a fortune. It's . . . it's fantastic. How on earth . . . ?' Quickly wiping her hands on a handkerchief, she looked over her shoulder to the back room and slipped the sweater over her head. It slid down over her shoulders, almost to her knees. 'How do I look?'

'Not bad,' he said.

'Is that all?' she said.

'Very nice.' He shrugged. 'I knew it would look nice.'

'It's lovely,' she said. She gazed down at the sweater. 'Really lovely – but why?'

He smiled. He looked almost nervous. 'I— I wanted to give you something.'

'You could have given me a box of chocolates. But this!'

'Something I knew you'd like. Something special. Something . . . something that would make you think of me.'

'Thank you.' She couldn't really believe it. That he'd remembered what she'd said about the sweater, that he'd thought about it. That he'd found the most perfect thing for her.

'It's a kind of going away present,' he said.

She stopped smiling. 'What do you mean? Who's going away?'

'Me. I've got a new job. Merchant navy.'

'What? Why?'

'Well there's not much future in death is there?'

'If you put it like that, I suppose not.'

'I got into a bit of trouble. A rowdy mourner and I had a falling out. They asked me to leave.'

'And so you're joining the navy. But, but when will you be back?'

'Oh, I don't know. It depends where we go, doesn't it? I've signed up for the long journeys. South America, that kind of thing.'

'Will you be going to Australia?'

'I don't think so.'

'That's a shame. You could have said hello to our mum.'
Reluctantly she took off the sweater. She folded it tenderly
and put it back in the carrier bag. As she bent she was conscious of the curve of her belly. 'I'll be sad to see you go,'

'Will you? You know, if things had gone another way,
I might be giving you my itinerary and asking you to write
to me.'

'Well, I don't mind receiving letters, though I think I've
got my hands full in terms of writing back.' She pointed
to her stomach.

'Oh Reen.' He looked up at the ceiling. 'Don't worry
about that. But I don't want to step on anyone's toes.
Perhaps you've got other fish to fry? Sorting things out
with the daddy, for example?'

'The daddy has his own fish – and chips – to fry,' she said.

'What does that mean?'

'He's no part of this.' She looked at him, suddenly anxious to make him understand. 'He was never anything.
Not really.'

'Well, Reen, just remember, if things get rough, there's
someone on a ship, on the other side of the world, thinking
about you.'

She put her head on one side. 'Even with a baby?'

'Why not? I like kids. I like you.' He lowered his voice,
so she could hardly hear him. 'It could just as easily have
been mine,' he said. 'If that evening had gone the way
I wanted.'

She smiled. 'That's a nice thing to say.' She took a breath. 'Are you really going?'

'Yes. Next week.'

'Well, you never know your luck. I might write you a letter or two.'

'I'll look out for them. It's going to be a long trip to Argentina.'

Unexpectedly, tears sprang to her eyes. 'You'll really be that far away?'

'That's what I've signed up for.'

She wanted to say, don't go, but she knew she couldn't.

'For God's sake, don't cry,' he said. 'Do you like it?' He nodded his head towards the bag.

'I love it. Oh, come here,' she said. She leaned across the newspapers; *The People*, *The News of the World*, *The Sunday Mirror*. She put her hand on his neck and pulled him to her. She kissed him. He kissed her back, but his arms didn't move. She stood up. 'Oh Cliff. We've always met at the wrong time, haven't we?'

CHAPTER 34

THAT EVENING GENE RANG THE HOUSE. Angie answered.

'How many dresses have you got?' Gene said.

'What do you mean?'

'I mean, I need some more dresses.'

'Really? How have they gone? We were going to ring you tomorrow.'

'Well,' he said, 'let me see. I've got . . . one left. But someone's paid a deposit on that.'

'What?'

'They went like hot cakes. Saturday, it was mad. So, if you've got another twenty or so, that would be perfect. All the different sizes, like before, and maybe some different colours. I mean as many as you can. There's a reporter coming in to talk to me tomorrow, a mate of mine who's going to do some pictures for Friday's paper. So, first thing in the morning would be great. Regina rules the waves! I might suggest that to Brian as a headline.'

'OK, right,' Angie said. 'I've got to put the phone down now and get sewing. We'll be up all night.' As she spoke she could hear the sewing machine whirring in the front room. Gene had seemed so pleased with his first batch of dresses they hadn't stopped sewing since. Doreen was just now finishing a pile of dresses they were planning to take up to Petticoat Lane. She had spoken to Cliff's friend who had stalls in three markets in London, and he seemed very enthusiastic. They hadn't finalised a delivery date with him so these dresses could go to the boutique tomorrow, and they'd get a new batch ready for Petticoat Lane.

'Ten dresses tomorrow would be fine, bring the rest in on Tuesday or Wednesday.'

Angie replaced the receiver. 'Mum! Reen!' she called. 'We've got to get moving.'

The next day she took ten more dresses into the shop. Gene was standing with a tall man in a brown iridescent mac. He had a pad of paper and a pen, and he was making notes as Gene spoke.

'Brian, this is Angie! She made all the dresses.'

'Impressive,' he said, nodding.

Angie was unzipping the covers. 'I've made some with long sleeves,' she said, hanging them on the rail.

'Is that one of your designs?' Brian said.

'They're all my designs.'

'No, the one you're wearing.'

'Yes.' It was the green dress. She knew Gene liked it. She still wanted to impress him, she knew that. But that was all, no more than that.

'Well, then why don't we do a picture of you and Gene, standing by the rail of dresses? The photographer's on his way.'

'He'd better be quick, I've got to go to work.'

'If these dresses keep selling at this rate, you're going to have to give up work,' Gene said.

'I think my girlfriend might like one of these,' Brian said.

'There you are,' Gene said. 'I've had the boys looking at them too. They want their birds to look cool and special.'

Brian was still making notes as the photographer walked in. Awkward but smiling, Angie stood next to the rail of clothes with Gene, and the photographer did his job.

She'd been back at work for an hour, still thinking about the dresses and how they'd looked when the photographer asked her to hold them out in a proper display. Maddy from bed linen came across saying there was someone to see her. 'There she is, over there.'

She pointed to Miss Darling, who was looking at eider-downs. Angie walked over to her.

'Miss Darling. How nice to see you.'

'Angela. Still that lovely smile on your face. Are things going well?'

'You have no idea. I've just had my photo taken for the paper.'

'Excellent! Do you have time for a coffee?'

'I could have an early lunch, now.' She turned to Annette her colleague who nodded with a rueful smile. Angie grinned at Miss Darling. 'I've got so much to tell you.'

'It sounds like it. Let's go and have a sandwich in Wainwrights.'

The egg sandwiches had been eaten, and the tea drunk, and Angie had told Miss Darling everything – her dad's sudden disappearance and her mum's imminent departure to Australia, how wonderful her time had been at the college in London and the exciting last ten days, including Doreen's involvement and the recent re-order of twenty dresses that Gene had asked for.

Miss Darling pushed away her cup. 'I'm so pleased to hear that things are going so well,' she said. 'I went in to look at the dresses and I was very impressed. They were perfectly cut, beautifully finished, and the sleeves could not have been set any better.'

Angie laughed.

'The man in the boutique was very fulsome in his praise. And very grateful. You say you're going to keep on producing clothes?'

'If people want to buy them,' Angie said.

'How will you manage?'

'Well, I work full time in Bonds, so I'm cutting and sewing in the evening and at weekends. My sister is helping me. She's also doing the book-keeping. She is pregnant though, which is good and bad. She'll leave her job which means less money, but she'll have more time to help with Regina clothes.'

'I do like that name!' Miss Darling said.

'Thank you. But she'll have the baby, so that will probably take up more of her time. My mum is helping out but she's off to Australia. At the end of the week, in fact.'

'A baby! Australia!' said Miss Darling. 'Things are certainly happening. And who is backing you in all this?'

'Well, Gene, I suppose. It's his boutique.'

'You mean he's supporting you by selling the dresses.'

'Yes.'

'He hasn't put any money in.'

'No.'

'Well.' Miss Darling sat back in her chair. 'I love hearing about your work. Fashion has been my life you know. Now I've got a proposition for you, but first I think I should tell you who you're dealing with. I think you know I started off at Hornsey myself, that's where I was trained, and then I went to Paris and worked in some of the best fashion houses there. I married a rather rich man. Of course, the war got in the way. He died. I came back, I worked in London, I designed for one or two of the big houses and for once in the fashion industry I was paid rather well. But I was beginning to suffer from arthritis in my hands, and I wanted a quieter life so I came to Essex and began teaching. I didn't need to, but I loved it, being around you girls with all your energy and ideas, and still being in the thick of fashion, especially now when it's all happening with you young people. And now I have retired, I find I miss it. I miss the excitement of working with my students, I miss their passion. I think what I need is a new venture. So my proposition is this. I would like to invest some money in you so that you can perhaps cut down your hours in Bonds, and maybe if things go very well, rent a space to use as a workshop. Big enough – and pleasant enough – for more people to work there as the business expands. I could be on hand to give you advice on who to contact, how the fashion industry works. Sort of a consultant if you like. In return, we could agree that once the business is profitable you could pay me back.'

Angie stared at her. 'Really?'

'I have enough money and more to live on. I have money piling up in the bank. I have no one to leave it to, and no use for it myself. I have always admired you, Angie. You have spunk and determination. I'd like to help you develop that.'

'Even though I didn't stay at the college?'

'I understand there is a place open for you there, should you ever wish to take it up again. I wouldn't be surprised if you were soon working there as a tutor rather than a technician.'

Angie's mind was racing. 'My sister works just across the road. Will you stay here and I'll go and get her? She's the money person. She'll be thrilled, and you can explain everything to her and what we need to do.'

'That's a good idea' Miss Darling said. 'But before you go, can I ask you one thing? I think it's time you called me Barbara.'

'I'm not sure if I can. But you can call me Angie!'

EPILOGUE

Three years later

DOREEN WAS ALONE IN THE SHOP. She had the sales book in front of her. Quickly she added up a list of figures. Things were going well. She had just got off the phone from the London store. She looked down at the numbers in the book. They were very satisfying. Sometimes she really could hardly believe how far they had come from that very first day when they had delivered those first few dresses to the boutique. Now they had two boutiques of their own, and even employed staff. Doreen still spent most of her time in Chelmsford, but Angie had fulfilled her dream and she not only ran the London shop but had a flat in Chelsea. They met up at least once a week to discuss the business and Angie enjoyed these times, staying with her sister and playing with her niece.

Angie came into the shop now with two special order dresses. 'They're going mad in the workroom. Maureen says the new pop-art design is doing her head in.'

'And was Cath able to do that embroidery?' Doreen asked.

'Look. It's fantastic!' Angie pushed back the cellophane cover and showed Doreen some intricate needlework on the collar of the short white wedding dress. She laid the dresses carefully on the counter and took a blue airmail letter from her bag. 'You have got to read this!' she said to Doreen.

'Is Mum still having a ball?' Doreen asked.

'Yes, but read it.'

Doreen unfolded the letter and looked at her mother's neat handwriting. She scanned the page. 'I can't believe she keeps having all these barbecues.'

'Well, she and Joe like company.'

Doreen looked up. 'Don't you think it's amazing that a woman who never went out into our garden is now throwing all these parties at the home where she lives with a man she's not married to.'

'That's what happens when you wear Regina shorts.'

'She loved those shorts.'

'And she sold four pairs to her new mates.'

'And now she's happier than she's ever been in her life.'

'Yes, but carry on reading.'

Doreen turned back to the letter. 'Oh she's still on about the baby. Why didn't I tell her? Why did we wait till she was half way round the world before the news got out?'

'You know why she says that.' Angie shook the two dresses.

'I know. *We're waiting for you two and little Alexandra to come and visit!*' Doreen read aloud. '*I understand the business is doing well. There was a picture of one of your dresses in our local paper. Some article about Carnaby Street. You should sell them here, you know. Joe is all set to start a campaign, and there's a lovely little shop in town that I can see myself running.*' Doreen looked up. 'Bloody hell, Angie, we're in Australia! *Give my love to Cath and Maureen, you were very lucky to find such talented girls to help you with the business. And when Miss Darling pops in for her cup of tea, tell her that she's done my girls proud.*'

'She has,' said Angie. 'This shop, Carnaby Street, Petticoat Lane and Portobello. We couldn't have done it without that money.'

'And paid off all our debts. And we've paid her back too, with interest.'

'It's who supports you at the beginning that counts,' Angie said. 'If Gene hadn't decided to close his boutique, we'd never have had this shop, and the goodwill that went with it.'

'Yes, Gene was very good at goodwill.'

For a moment they looked at each other in silence. Angie shook her head.

'And we mustn't forget Cliff Evans,' Angie said. 'He got us that first stall.'

'Yes, hooray for Cliff!' Doreen said.

'Where was the last postcard from?' Angie said.

'Somewhere in . . . Argentina, I think,' Doreen said.

'Oh, you say that, sounding so uninterested!' Angie laughed. 'I know you keep all the postcards. And the letters.'

'Well, funnily enough, he writes very nice letters.'

'Which is, of course, why you write back.'

'It would be rude not to.'

'And why you have a letter in your bag right now with a South American stamp.'

Doreen looked down at her bag, on the floor beside her. There were three letters in there from Cliff. She liked to carry them with her. She liked to read them when there was a quiet moment in the shop. When the pressure of being stared at in the street had got too much, with the bump of her pregnancy and then the pram in the garden, his letters had been a sort of balm. At the beginning, just after Alexandra was born, some people on the estate had been quite unkind, seeing her only as an unmarried mother, someone who'd broken the rules. They cut her dead, crossing the road, turned their heads. Once or twice she'd even wondered whether she'd made the right decision – for her, for Alex – when she failed to get on the ship to Australia. But Cliff knew all about her and still he cared for her. 'I like the paper he writes on,' she said. 'And he's got nice handwriting.'

'Yeah, yeah,' said Angie. 'I'll just hang these dresses up in the back.' She went into the store room.

Doreen raised her voice. 'Mrs Pippin and her daughter are coming in for them at dinner-time. They've paid a twenty pound deposit, and they've got the rest to settle. And now I've got to go and pick up Alex before Miss Darling starts giving her her dinner. We're going to Galleywood Common on the bus this afternoon. She's very excited. And so am I.'

'Don't you want a drink?'

'No thanks. I'll pop into Roberts's on the way home, pick up something for tea. Are you in?'

Angie came back into the shop.

'No, I'm treating Roger and I to a beer in the Golden Fleece.'

'You and Roger! Don't tell me . . .'

'There's nothing to tell. But he was so good, doing that delivery down to Brighton, last week. Roger is just a good friend.'

'He'd have to be. All that transporting he did at the beginning – London, Bristol, Manchester.'

'God, yes, remember those days. And you with the baby. Sometimes I thought we'd never make it.'

'And yet here we are! But don't you wish sometimes it had worked with Roger?' Doreen began rolling notes from the till into elastic bands.

Angie thought for a moment. 'No, I don't. I really don't. Anyway, I think he's got a little thing for Cath.'

'As long as he doesn't carry her off and marry her, that sounds good.'

Angie was in the stock room waiting for the kettle to boil and Doreen was making some final notes in her ledger. The doorbell tinkled

'Can I . . . ? Doreen began. She looked up. 'Well, well.' In spite of herself, she felt her cheeks warm. He was wearing jeans and a very white shirt. His hair was a little longer, curling at the neck. She began to smile. 'Home is the hunter.'

'I don't know about that,' Cliff said. 'I'm back from the sea.'

'I didn't know you were due back so soon. I only got your letter this morning.'

'I beat it home, obviously.'

'How long are you here for?'

'That depends . . .'

He looked around him, at the rails of dresses, skirts, coats. 'This is impressive.'

'We think so.' There was a pause. 'Have you come to buy something?'

He laughed. 'No. I came to see you.'

'That's nice.'

'Do you mean that?'

She looked at him. 'Yes, yes I do.'

'You got my letters?'

'Yes, I did. And I hope you got mine.'

'I did. It was the best part of the voyage, going into port and seeing if there was any mail, and recognising your handwriting on an envelope.'

She laughed. 'It was the least I could do after you gave me that expensive sweater.'

'Well, I've got a sheepskin rug for you in the car.'

'That sounds nice but does it mean I've got to write more letters?'

'Not necessarily.'

Her eyes widened. 'What do you mean?'

'The ship leaves again on Thursday. I've got to decide if I'm going to be on it.'

Her heart quickened. 'Well, today's Monday. You've got three days to make up your mind.'

He smiled. 'Yes, I have. I'd like to spend some of them with you.'

She smiled back at him, gazing into his eyes. Then she started. 'Oh, but Cliff, I'm sorry.' She was picking up her bag, shrugging into her coat. 'This is a bad time. If I'd known you were coming . . . I'm just going to pick up Alexandra. We're going to have a picnic at Galleywood. Ham sandwiches and marshmallows.' She didn't know why she was giving him so much detail.

'That's OK,' Cliff said. 'I like ham sandwiches. I'll take you in the car.'

'Oh, but we've got to go on the bus. I promised.'

'I'll come on the bus then.'

She smiled. 'OK.' She turned and called to Angie. 'We're going now.' Cliff pulled open the door and as the bell tinkled above them, together they stepped out of the shop and into the street.

Angie walked out of the stock room, holding her mug of tea. She watched Doreen and Cliff standing by his car, laughing and chatting. Doreen was so happy. Angie looked round the shop, at the glowing colours of the clothes on the rails, her dresses, her skirts, her designs. Doreen was happy and so was she.

Acknowledgements

I'D LIKE TO THANK CHRIS WILKINSON, Gill Butler, Maureen Hanscomb and Roy Kelly, for keeping the faith and offering coffee and support when it was needed; Yvonne Peecock for giving me another room of my own in deepest Essex where I could write in the prettiest of surroundings; Kit Habianic, James Young, Iris Ansell, wonderful writers, who gave me critical support and ideas; Amanda Manley and Chris Jacobs, my old school pals, who provided me with a real feel of what art schools were like in the '60s; Brian Southall for being a tall journalist; Wayne from Buckhurst Hill, an original modernist, who supported the idea of telling the story of mods from outside London; Graham Staples who went to Clacton on his scooter and had a horrible time but shared his story with me; and all the people in Chelmsford who have talked to me about their experience of the '60s, face to face but also on Facebook and Twitter.

Huge thanks to Tara Loder and the team at Zaffre who have guided this book through to completion, and to my agent Annette Green for her support and encouragement.

And thank you to Chris Wallace, who went through the '60s with me, and of course, a never ending thank you to Caroline Spry, without whom none of this would ever have been put down on paper.

Welcome to the world of *Elizabeth Woodcraft*!

Keep reading for more from Elizabeth Woodcraft, to discover a recipe that features in this novel and to find out more about Elizabeth Woodcraft's inspiration for the book . . .

We'd also like to introduce you to MEMORY LANE, our special community for the very best of saga writing from authors you know and love, and new ones we simply can't wait for you to meet. Read on and join our club!

Dear Reader,

I hope you've enjoyed this new book about Chelmsford in the '60s, where sisters Angie and Doreen follow their dreams. My last book, *The Saturday Girls*, was about life as a mod girl, a life that I had lived, and for *The Girls from Greenway* once again I dived into my diaries to give me inspiration for the book.

It's hard to remember what life was like in those days. No mobile phones – a lot of people didn't even have a phone in the house. Women's education was still not always seen as important, since it was assumed that girls would get married as soon as they could after leaving school, and as for having an illegitimate baby – well! That was almost the worst thing a girl could do.

Morals and mores were quite strictly adhered to, so when young people in the '60s tried to break out, to have their own fashions, their own music or their own style, the establishment didn't really know how to handle it. I became a mod, my friends were mods – we were all fairly quiet, we drank frothy coffee in our coffee bar and danced to the music of Tamla Motown on Saturday evenings. But the newspapers wanted to talk about hooligans and fights at Clacton and Brighton, which as far as the girls in Chelmsford were concerned, passed us by.

But other things were beginning to change, and on television there were exciting new programmes, not just *Emergency Ward 10* and *Coronation Street*, but *Armchair Theatre* and *The Wednesday Play*, where every week a new play would appear on the screen, dealing with the issues of the day, showing a different side of life.

I've tried to capture some of those feelings of uncertainty, of hope, of excitement, in this book. Angie's parents want her to have a sensible job in the local factory, and earn a decent regular wage. But Angie wants something more, and she's going to get it!

While I was writing the book, I listened to a lot of the hits from those days, because they always take me back to the coffee bars and the dance halls of the time, and what we were doing and wearing at the time.

Then a friend in Essex asked me if I'd like to come and stay in her little nineteenth century cottage where I could have a room to write in. It was the most wonderful room on the first floor – a little bed, a small table and chair, and a French door that opened on to a tiny balcony from where I could look at her garden, with its tangle of fruit bushes and scented flowers and fish ponds. It was like a dream. I sat and contemplated my computer with just the buzzing of bees and the tweeting of birds outside the window as an accompaniment. The words poured out. It was a strange mixture of nineteenth, twentieth and twenty-first century life – because of course I had the Internet so I could check some of the facts of the day.

I do hope you enjoyed the book as much as I enjoyed writing it, and I hope it brings back some memories of your own. If you did, please do share your thoughts on the Memory Lane Facebook page 🅵 MemoryLaneClub.

Best wishes,
Elizabeth Woodcraft

Pineapple Upside-Down Cake

A real classic of the 1960s and one that was regularly on the menu for our school dinners! Doreen chooses this rich indulgent dessert in chapter seven while out for dinner with Angie and their mum. Sweet, delicious and beautiful, it is a perfect summer treat.

You will need:
For the topping:
50g unsalted butter
50g light muscovado sugar
7 slices tinned pineapples in juice
14 glacé cherries

For the cake
100g unsalted butter
100g caster sugar
2 medium eggs
100g self-raising flour
1 tsp baking powder
1 tsp vanilla extract
Pineapple juice (from the pineapples used for the topping)

Custard, cream or ice cream to serve.

Method:

1. Pre-heat oven to 180°C/160°C fan/gas 4.
2. For the topping, cream together the butter and light muscovado sugar in a bowl.
3. Spread this mixture across the base and a little up the sides of a 20cm round cake tin. Place the pineapple slices on top, keeping back the juice for later. Place the glacé cherries in the centres of the rings, and use the remainder to fill in any gaps.
4. For the cake, mix the butter and caster sugar together in a bowl until smooth, then add the eggs, one at a time, mixing thoroughly. Sieve in the flour, baking powder, then add the vanilla extract and leftover pineapple juice. Stir until smooth.
5. Pour the cake mixture into the tin over the pineapple, then smooth until flat on top.
6. Bake for 30–40 mins. If the top starts to burn, cover with tinfoil and return to the oven.
7. Remove from the oven, then leave to stand for 15 minutes before turning out onto a plate upside-down.
8. Serve warm with custard, cream or ice cream.
9. Enjoy!